Blue Lunar And the Apex Grail

R.L.Baxter

R.L.Baxter

Contents

$\mathscr{P}$rologue

Within the depths of a sleeping and derelict volcano, on a cold night, a prisoner stays forever bound. Kept company by the ashen and gloomy walls of the inner mountain, the prisoner displays a look of hopelessness. At times the moon above would peek its presence - casting down its light like a sympathetic visitor. On this occasion, the moon is not so giving, dwelling beyond the clouds with a family of stars.

"For love..." the prisoner whispers, looking down at the tools of their constriction. Binding the captive, a series of chains stay fastened - emanating a pulsating light that never ceases. Each flicker sickens the prisoner further, as a reminder that the chains are not fashioned by standard means but imbued with powerful magic. "The gods... the gods abandoned us, long ago."

Eyes closed, the bound individual inhales the familiar smog from the smokey walls and escapes to the world of memories and regrets - their only respite from an eternal sentence. "My friends... hold on."

At that moment, the sound of a steel sword chiming into the volcano intrudes upon the ears of the prisoner. The walls tremble as the sound echoes from surface to surface - piercing the captive's daydream like a rude awakening. The noise of the blade feels refreshing for the captive, who hasn't heard the sound of a weapon for over one hundred years. And as the eyes of the detainee open, they gaze upon an angel.

Covered with white armour that exudes a dazzlingly bright light, the angel stands with a blade in hand - bearing two magnificent wings.

Eyes locked to the other in complete silence, a mutual desire is shared between the pair, one that needs no words - despite never having met before.

A thirst is seen within their eyes, one that can only be satiated by the help of the other. And as the pair stand as though prisoners of their fate, a joint smile overcomes them. Being the keys to the other's prison, one offers the other what they have been yearning for the most: Freedom.

A story where the brightest light,

casts the darkest shadow.

Blue Lunar & The Apex Grail

R.L.Baxter

Chapter 1: Bloody Beginnings

I n an age of magic and miracles, the inhabitants of the world live in relative contentment. The expansive continent of Sol is a vast land that consists of two friendly and neighbouring countries, watched from above by a single blue moon. To the north, taking up the greater portion of Sol lies Superbia, a mighty country known for its famous army of soldiers and spectacular warriors. South of Sol lies Veritas. Being far smaller, it relies much on the ever-powerful Superbia above it for resources. Within the southern country, a small seaside town by the name of Heline can be found. Within it, on a bright and sunny day, the locals enjoy the warmth as families and friends play together - mainly by the shore. Smiling faces can be seen in almost every person... except one individual.

∞∞∞

Standing upon a small sandy hill, looking over the buzzing shore of cheerful people, one boy stands apprehensive. Dressed in bright blue shorts, sporting short black hair, he stares at a small party of girls and boys his age, playing volleyball. Taking a deep breath, he whispers "come on Luke... you can do this." A battle rages on within him, one that he has been fighting alone. His mind tells him to leave the pleasant shore, while his heart stands firm, like a coach on the sidelines of a fighting ring.

Clenching his fists before entering a bright smile, he strolls toward the group. His heart pounds as sweat falls from his forehead. Every cell in his body is screaming for him to turn in the other direction - yet he refuses and fights his fears. An opposing gust of wind brushes against him as if the whisper of nature were warning him to retreat, to which he also refuses.

Stopping only inches away from the group, he clears his throat and says "hey guys... can I play with you?" His voice is drowned out by their chatter and laughter together - failing to hear his voice at all. Not to be deterred, he takes a single step forward and addresses them with a louder tone.

"Excuse me! If it's not too much trouble, will you let me play with you?"

The party freeze instantly - turning around to face the optimistic looking boy. Within seconds they burst into laughter - rolling around on the sandy ground as Luke stands embarrassed. Their laughs continue for many moments before one decides to approach the boy. Coldly and bluntly, the child replies "you could never play with us, not in a million years because you are an orphan!" The voice echoes through the air - carried by the wind into the distance for all to hear. At that moment, every single gaze is locked onto the boy, like a spectacle for their amusement.

Further laughter ensues, as the child's insult pierces Luke's soul. His once brave smile turns into a frown, before becoming a complete look of sadness. Hanging his head low, he looks to the ground - too embarrassed to move an inch.

"But... I am still a human being."

∞ ∞ ∞

Later that evening, as the sun fully sets, the boy returns to his place of stay: The orphanage of Heline. Situated atop a great hill that overlooks the whole town, the orphanage is a tattered and worn-out structure. Compared to the colourful seaside houses of Heline, it makes for a distasteful sight.

Within a small and cramped bedroom, filled with baskets of unwashed clothes, Luke lays upon a single mattress. The familiar musty and recycled air that fills his nostrils, offers mild comfort, like a soldier who has returned to their garrison after an earlier battle. A battle for the boy, whose heart was pieced from words of spite. Looking out the only window before staring at the clouds and twinkling stars, he recollects his earlier moment of embarrassment as tears fall from his eyes.

"It happened again. Nobody has ever wanted to get to know me, because I am an orphan."

The room is silent, like all the other rooms in the orphanage. In the place of chatter and rampant children, creaking floorboards and ticking clocks sound off quietly. No other child lives in the building, for they all have either been fostered or fled of their own volition.

Sitting upward before slamming his fists against the wall, he shouts "I want to be like everybody else. I want to fit in and not be different!" Sound echoing through the hollow walls.

At that second, Jill the orphan minder swings open the bedroom door and shouts "what's all that racket? You ok?"

As the only minder of the orphanage, Jill takes care of the day to day running of the building - although the many unorganised items and clothes throughout show that she is overwhelmed. Constantly behind on errands and tasks, she usually keeps her interactions with Luke to a minimum. Body as large and wide as her personality, Jill bears all the hallmarks of a typical aunt: close enough to share one's concerns but not close enough to solve them. Nevertheless, Jill is the nearest thing to family for the boy.

"Oh, I am sorry Jill. I didn't mean to disturb you. I kinda lost my temper."

"Hmm, now why would such a kind-hearted boy like you lose your temper?"

Looking away, the boy lowers his head as she enters the room to sit beside him. Looking upon his deflated posture, she stays quiet for many moments before asking "did you have trouble with some of the other kids again?"

"Yeah... they were laughing at me."

"Oh don't take it to heart. You just gotta try harder" she responds, in a kind yet unhelpful manner. "Did you try to dress like them? Did you wear the blue shorts I bought you?" She asks, further troubling the boy. For although her intentions are genuine, Jill's suggestions are empty and without depth. Although the two are sitting close, they are worlds apart - as though a whole universe were between them. This fact they know well, which pains them both.

"Yes, I wore the blue shorts and tried to be like everybody else. However, it didn't matter at all. To them, I am just different."

Unable to respond to him, the lady produces an awkward exhale - mixed with vague words that die out within milliseconds. With nothing left to add, she quickly stands up and responds "Well, it will sort itself out... just you wait. I am sure that any day now, a foster family will come on by and take you into their arms. Once that happens, I'll most likely shut this shoddy building down. Then you and I will both be happy, haha."

Her attempt at lightening the mood falls flat, as Luke produces a half-hearted grin that is easily discerned. She strokes his forehead, which causes him to forget his woes for but a moment. Her fingers are rough - worn over years of managing and cleaning the orphanage. However, her touch is warm.

Standing to her feet, she turns around and leaves the bedroom. As the door closes on her way out, the sad boy turns his gaze to the starry sky through the window - left once again with the moaning floorboards to communicate with. To his surprise, he finds that the blue moon is shining bright tonight. With a heartfelt plea, he glares at the blue wonder and makes a wish. "Goddess of the moon, if you can hear me, please give me a normal life like everybody else."

Slanting backwards before laying flat on the mattress, Luke closes his eyes and eventually falls asleep.

Hours pass as the rest of the townsfolk of Heline retire for the night. The town is quiet and peaceful, with only the distant sound of the crashing waves to be heard under the moonlit night.

Suddenly, the inhabitants are woken by a harsh and screeching laughter. The sound is piercing and loud, causing the people to cover their ears with fright. Equally startled - Luke jumps and almost instantly turns to the window to see the source of the frightening cackle. "What is that laugh?"

To his surprise, the boy spots a single individual - levitating in mid-air as if by magic. As the townsfolk also spot the bizarre character, they can be heard gasping and screaming with fear.

As the cackling stops, Luke squints his eyes to get a clearer look at the being. The mysterious figure looks to be a man, covered from neck to toe by a purple cloak. His face is painted with unreadable symbols of black and white, and upon his head, he wears a thorny wooden crown.

"Is... is that a wizard or something?" Whispers Luke, trembling at the sight of the floating stranger in the sky. With a sinister grin, the mysterious man addresses the people of Heline.

"Greetings, allied dogs of Superbia. I am Phantom: The Wizard King of Despair. I hope that I have caught your attention because tonight marks a very special night." Like a helper of the dark figure, the wind carries his voice through the town for all to hear. His voice is dry and raspy, as though his tone were plucked from the deepest depths of the earth. A collective fear grips the town, one that keeps them still and unable to flee.

Unravelling his cloak, the sorcerer reveals a golden sceptre, complete with a gemstone at the top that sparkles like the brightest jewel. Raising the staff above his head, the wizard shouts "Veritas and Superbia shall fall! Kwehehehehe!"

At that moment, a great and large portal of darkness materialises above the town. The portal is gigantic, large enough to swallow the helpless town whole. To their horror, the townsfolk watch as hundreds of monsters emerges from the portal - descending towards the helpless town.

"Oh my..." Luke shrieks, coming away from the window before panicking in the bedroom. "This isn't happening, this isn't happening!" He says repeatedly, as the loud and screeching cackle of Phantom the Wizard King of Despair can be heard in the distance.

The beings that fall into the town vary in size and shape, bearing ghastly features. Some possess large snouts and numerous claws, while others resemble men but with the skin of beasts. Like droplets of water, they rain down over the town. A loud crash is heard, followed by many more as the creatures land upon the ground and houses - causing the earth to shudder with terror. Within seconds, blood and limbs fly through the air as the monsters begin to devour the inhabitants. Screams and desperate cries fill the night, as the laughing wizard delights in the bloodshed - dancing through the air with exquisite joy. "Kwekekeeeee. Die, die, dieeeeeee!"

Within the orphanage, Luke sprints out from his bedroom and calls for the orphanage minder "Jill help! We're in trouble!"

"Luke!" The lady shouts - racing to him from nearby. Holding onto his arm, she puts on a brave face and orders "stay close to me and don't leave my sight!"

"Ok."

They leave the orphanage - stepping outside with sweaty and trembling fingers glued to the hand of the other. The boy rattles with fear, just as much as she does. However, trying her best to stay in control, she holds a firm expression like a bold mother, attempting to stay calm and collected. Her efforts are easily seen through, for as the sounds of surrounding screams fill her ears, pools of sweat leap from her face.

To their shock and horror, they find that the monsters are marching towards them - mouths and razor claws hungry for more blood. Standing in front like a protector, the lady mumbles "damn, this whole place is covered."

"Jill I am scared."

"I know... we all are."

Fallen bodies litter the grounds as more and more fierce beings emerge from out of the portal. The town is now overrun, and as each person attempts to flee, they are mercilessly cut down before being eaten half alive. Overwhelmed by the nightmarish scene before him, Luke stands petrified - telling his heart that this must all be a horrible dream. "This isn't real... this isn't happening," he says, expecting his mind to pull him out of the nightmare at any moment. He waits and waits, but the scene doesn't end.

Without thinking, the lady pushes the boy away and shouts "go, escape through the forest. Make your way to the capital city of Spiritus and warn the King about what is happening!"

"What? The capital city? How do I even find it?"

"Stop asking questions and just go!"

Shom - at that second, a claw is pierced through the heart of the orphanage minder - causing her to scream in agony. As her blood showers the ground, the boy's voice is the first to escape - becoming a terrified scream that flees into the air. Finding an escape of his own, Luke sprints in the opposite direction towards a vast and thick forest.

"Oh god, why is this happening? I don't want to be next. I don't want to die!"

Running as fast as he can, Luke darts into the forest while being pursued by the vast amounts of enemies behind. As though his feet have of their own, they lead the way - aimlessly dragging the boy along without ceasing. Deliberately sprinting along uneven terrain and streams, he attempts to outrun the foes behind him. Not knowing whether his tactic is working or not, he dares not glance back for even a second. "I need to tell someone, anybody about what is happening. We are all in danger!"

Overcome with panic, the boy trips over a vine before tumbling down a steep slope. He hits the muddy ground before rolling to his knees - looking backwards for any sign of the creatures. To his relief, he finds not a single enemy behind him. Proceeding to take many deep breaths, Luke slowly stands to his feet - looking for any sign of the foes. The moment is quiet, as the rain starts to pour - hitting the leaves of the dense forest.

Sighing with a feeling of victory, the boy closes his eyes and whispers to himself under the rain. "I did it... I lost them" he whispers, hearing the soothing sounds of raindrops hitting the many leaves. The smell of fresh soil invades his nostrils - cleaning out the putrid smell of blood. "Thank the gods..."

Shom - at that split second, a sceptre is stabbed through his back. Instantly, Luke coughs forth blood as a familiar and unsettling voice speaks into his ear.

"Kwekekekeee. Foolish boy. Do you still think that the gods care about us? The gods abandoned us, long ago."

With the sceptre still lodged within him, Luke turns his head and finds the attacker to be the wizard: Phantom. Mustering the only strength he has left, the boy can only plead "why, why are you doing this?"

With a stone-cold stare, the wizard responds, "for love!" pulling the staff out from the boy. Falling to the ground, the helpless orphan closes his eyes and dies.

Chapter 2: Chosen by Blue

"How long are you gonna stay asleep? I don't have all day, Mr hero" comes an unfamiliar and firm voice that speaks to the boy. Opening his eyes, Luke finds himself within pure darkness.

"Where... where am I"? He asks, finding himself floating within a mysteriously dark space. Glancing up, he sees a ball of blue and white light - shining immensely. From within it, the same voice replies "you have fallen. You were killed by that old wizard and now your soul is drifting, somewhere in the afterlife."

"That is right, the last memory I have was of being struck by that horrible wizard. He attacked Heline and so many people lost their lives. I thought that I was so close to escaping."

The ball of light drifts closer to the boy, before responding "well, all is not lost, Mr hero. For I have come to answer your earlier prayer. Behold..."

Before the boy's eyes, the ball of light changes form to

become that of a grown woman. Dressed in thin robes, her face is covered by a veil before she introduces herself. "I am Diana, divine goddess of the blue moon. I have heard your prayer and wish to address it."

Astounded by the sight before him, the boy stays speechless - looking upon the image of a real goddess. Her aura is humbling - causing the boy to perform a half-hearted bow, as though his very soul were submitting to her presence alone. As he digests her words, Luke remembers the earlier plea he made to the blue moon.

"So... have you come to offer me a new life? A life akin to everybody else?"

"Yes... and no. I will grant you the life you seek: to live like a normal boy with a loving family. Before that, however, you must first become even more different than before and fulfil a task for me. I want you to kill the wizard that has threatened your land."

Her proposition astounds and confuses the boy, who is unable to tell whether she is being serious or mocking him. As her face stays hidden behind the veil, he wonders what the deity looks like. Could it be a beautiful being or a she-devil that has come to trick him? He assumes the latter, for surely it would be impossible to stand against a wizard alone.

As if reading his thoughts of warring conclusions, the Goddess utters "I will give you power, the mightiest power known to any mortal. All you need to do is accept. Agree to my offer and return to the world of the living, before killing the wizard. In turn, you will be rewarded with family, friends and belonging. Refuse my offer and remain in the darkness where your soul will drift upon the shores of the afterlife. The choice is yours."

The boy gasps at her offer and chance to live again. If he accepts, he will indeed reclaim his life but will need to defeat the wizard to truly have a normal life. If he rejects her offer, he will remain in the afterlife.

Within the dark and quiet space, he ponders her words

- weighing his options. "So terrifying... I am so scared" he whispers to his heart. Gripping the soul of his chest, overcome with fear by the mere thought of the dark sorcerer. As the fiend's dreaded cackle stays etched in his mind, the boy closes his eyes. "Perhaps staying within this darkness where it's safe isn't so bad? After all, I wouldn't want to go through any more pain."

Words of refusal begin to form within his mouth, as his heart stays satisfied with the decision. However, as though in complete disagreement, Luke's mind intrudes before presenting glimpses of what his reward would look like. At that moment, the boy is no longer within the dark space but instead within a field of flowers. A refreshing wind blows over him, followed by a school of petals that stroke his cheeks. Behind him, a cottage resides, where a family of his own dwells inside. He feels at peace, and although it is just a brief daydream, the experience feels as real as they come. The vision is enough to sway his doubts and fears.

"I accept your offer. I don't know how I can succeed, but if I could get help from the nation's capital, then maybe the wizard can be stopped!"

Taken back by his resolve, the goddess flinches with delight before uncovering her veil. She is stunning, bearing diamond eyes of blue sapphire. Her hair is long and pale white, and upon her forehead lies a small chakra bead.

With a grin, she says "good answer, Mr hero. From this day forth, you shall be my one and only herald: Blue Lunar. Go now. You have the power and support of my moon to fulfil your heart's desire. And only when you have completed this task will you have the life you have always wanted."

A great and blinding light emerges from her chakra bead, which fills the darkness. Covering his eyes, the boy is engulfed - feeling a divine warmth as he is transported back to the world of the living.

∞ ∞ ∞

The first thing he hears is the sound of fireflies, followed by the hooting of a nearby owl. Opening his eyes, Luke finds himself in the familiar thick forest, in the same spot the wizard left him. It is still night - although how long time has passed since his period in the afterlife is not clear. Noticing that the rain has ceased, the boy assumes it might have been a few hours. The familiar smell of fresh soil is noticed, like a pleasant affirmation that he has truly returned to the land of the living.

"I am in the forest. It looks like I am back, just like that goddess said. Wait... so if I am alive again, what about me has changed? I don't feel particularly different."

Sitting upward, the boy scans his body and upon doing so, he gasps "what the hell is this?" To his shock and surprise, he finds that his upper body is covered by blue steel body armour. Each shoulder is protected by bulky shoulder pads, and by his arms, he wears a pair of shining steel gauntlets.

"I am a... I am a knight?" He stutters - jumping to his feet to inspect his body further. His thighs and knees are also protected by the mysterious blue armour, and his feet are polished with stunning greaves. Extending down from his collar, he sports a white cape that almost touches the ground. "This was what she meant by being more different than before. I didn't expect to be like this."

Feeling his face, the excited boy realises that he possesses a helmet on his head. A small trace of light hits his eyes from nearby. Turning to the side, he finds it to be a mere reflection of the glowing moon upon the surface of a small pond. Using its waters as a mirror, he finds that his helmet has covered his entire face - save for his eyes and mouth. "No way, this is unreal. All this is fighting gear. Does that make me some kind of hero now?"

An intrusive flashback of his minder's death enters his

thoughts once more - saddening his heart. Sitting opposite the pond for many short moments of silence, he whispers "who am I kidding? Somebody like me could never be a hero. This fancy armour is most likely all for show. Nevertheless, I need to do what I can to let everybody know of what is coming. Jill said that I should head to the capital city of Spiritus. The quicker I let the King of Spiritus know, the quicker they can prepare and hopefully defend themselves against that wizard."

Suddenly - a desperate cry is heard, coming from just up ahead. "Stay away! Leave me alone... somebody, help!"

Jumping to his feet, Luke faces the direction of the cry and gasps "somebody is in trouble!"

∞∞∞

Thinking fast, he runs through the forest, towards the sound of the desperate voice. Before long, he emerges out to find himself within a flower field. Under the starry and windy night, he spots the person who called for help. Screaming with fear, a single girl can be seen, sporting a formal and modest grey dress, surrounded by three monsters. Bodies similar to men, their skin is scaly and green. The creatures hiss like snakes as they bear sharp claws that are as long as spears.

"Why are you doing this? Why do you want to hurt everybody?"

The foes ignore her pleas - snarling as they tread closer to her. Trembling at the prospect of death, all she can do is stand helplessly - hoping for a miracle.

To her surprise, the boy runs to her aid and stands protectively in front. She gasps - not believing her eyes at the sight of the mysterious stranger before her. "What in the... are you a knight from the capital?"

"No, I've just come to help that's all."

As bold as his actions were, the boy finds himself at a loss at what to do next, for he too is terrified. Petrified at the sight of the inhuman beasts, he trembles while trying to keep his composure. "What do I do now? I am scared…"

"Look out!" Screams the girl, watching as one of the fiends lunges forward to swipe at the boy. Reacting almost instantly, Luke raises his arms defensively while closing his eyes with fright. The sound of the enemy claws can be heard colliding against his armour, followed by a second sound of something shattering.

"What the…"

Opening his eyes, the boy is stunned to find that the enemy's claws have broken into pieces against his armour - fragments now on the ground. The three monsters step backwards, frightened of Luke. Shocked also, the girl says "oh wow. Its hand was completely smashed against your armour. Are you one of the capital's elite guards or something?"

Marvelling at the strength of his mysterious attire, a wave of confidence begins to stir from within Luke. Throwing caution to the wind, he steps forward and performs a straight punch on the first enemy. A mighty thud reverberates through the field as his fist connects with the creature - emitting a shockwave that plucks the many flowers from their roots. The first foe is sent spiralling miles into the distance.

"Did I just do that?" Luke gasps with disbelief - eyes wide with adrenaline and excitement.

As though confirming his strength, the girl smiles and shouts "by the gods… you're amazing!"

"Am I? Thank you!" Luke responds - gaining even more confidence in the face of the two remaining enemies. Lunging forth, the boy grabs hold of the second monster's arm before spinning it around like a whirlwind. The enemy is tossed continuously, like a rag doll before being slammed furiously to the ground. The impact and force of its collision are so great, that the earth trembles as debris flies through the air. Its body crumbles to pieces, as the blue saviour stands victorious.

"I did it. I beat another one!" He cheers, as his long white cape blows through the wind, like a hero from a fairy tale. As he stands astonished by his strength, he mumbles "this suit... with it, I can stop the monsters."

Breaking his thoughts, the girl shouts "it's getting away. The third creature is escaping!"

To his surprise, Luke finds the third monster has turned around and fled - disappearing into the distance. Standing in awe at himself and the suit given to him, the boy whispers "it ran away... because of me? I am more different now, so much so that I can fight off those monsters. And if I can stop that wizard, I will finally have the life I've been waiting for..."

From the corner of his eye, the first rays of a rising sun catch his vision as the night slowly disappears, giving way to the morning. A mild breeze rushes over the field, as Luke stands calm and confident, reminded of a familiar moment. "Deja Vu? Where have I seen this before?" He asks his thoughts - hoping for an answer. It is at that instant he is reminded of the earlier daydream, where his mind revealed a future possibility of having his long sought after wish granted. The sun, field of flowers and touch of the wind are almost the same as his brief vision. And as the girl takes a small step by his side, he gasps "this is just like what I saw in my mind." Happiness overcomes the boy, upon experiencing an almost identical scenario to his earlier daydream. However, his joy is quickly drowned out as the realisation of his situation hits him. The girl is simply a stranger. Moreover, he would have to first defeat the wizard before claiming his reward for a normal life.

As the sun continues to rise, she steps forward and with a grateful smile says "thank you for saving me, I am truly within your debt. My name is Rose Mead and it is a pleasure to meet you."

She bows her head, and with a reciprocating nod, the boy responds "my name is Blue Lunar. But please call me Luke."

Chapter 3: One of a Kind

The southern country of Veritas has been invaded by a powerful wizard named Phantom. Along with his army of monsters, he has set out to take over Veritas, starting with the town of Heline. After being killed by the mysterious wizard, Luke was offered a second chance at living again, on the one condition that if he can defeat the wizard, the promise of a family and acceptance will be granted by Diana: Goddess of the Blue Moon.

He accepted the offer and was given the title of Blue Lunar: Herald of the blue moon. Shortly after returning to the land of the living, it wasn't long before he discovered just how different he had become. With no choice but to protect a girl named Rose, Luke discovered that his armour wasn't just for show. Upon beating and fending off a trio of fiends, Luke realises that he just may have the strength to challenge the monsters, created by the mysterious wizard king of despair.

∞ ∞ ∞

An hour has passed since their meeting, and Luke is seen following behind the girl he saved. Keen to ensure her safety, he stays close, making sure she gets back to her home in one piece. Upon a sun-filled morning complete with blue skies, they trek along a grassy path, next to a small stream.

"Did you say your home isn't too far from here?" Asks Luke, glancing around with caution.

"Yeah, that's right. I am from a small village named Armley. I sure hope the others are ok."

"How did you end up so far away from your village in the first place?"

"Well, It all started after a heated argument with my mother. It was about my future and what I should do with it. You see, I dream of relocating to the great allied country of Superbia, to study as a doctor. Compared to here in Veritas, Superbia has the best schools and opportunities. However, when I told my mother of my plans, she hit the roof and got angry. She accused me of being selfish and leaving her all alone - however, that isn't true at all. Once I have become a fully-fledged doctor, I hope to return and help our people here."

Stopping, she looks downward as though lost in thought before continuing "so, after a few back and forth insults, I ran away, just to clear my head. I was gonna return - however before I knew it, I was being chased by loads of those monsters. It seemed like they came out of nowhere."

"Yes. I was there when it all started. I come from Heline the seaside town. Last night, a wizard appeared and summoned those things. For some reason, he wants to wipe out everything here. Everybody was killed by those horrible creatures, so now I am trying to find my way to the capital city of Spiritus to warn the King. Although I have no idea how to get there."

Turning to the boy before holding her chest with worry, Rose asks "wait… did you just say that everybody from Heline has been killed? So, even your family are no more?"

With an apprehensive expression, the blue-suited boy replies "well I've never really known my family. I… I am an orphan from birth."

Looking away with embarrassment, Luke prepares to receive the same response he has always received when others had discovered how different he was. Expecting the girl to back away from him, he takes a deep sigh amidst the quiet yet tense moment. He counts from three to zero, anticipating the sound of her footsteps to fade into the distance, much like the rest. To his surprise, her footsteps grow closer, which causes him to blink with dismay. She leans forward before gently taking hold of his hands. They are warm, which calms his worried body. He gasps, wide-eyed by her action, as she proceeds to respond.

"I am so sorry, Luke."

"Huh… why are you apologising? You didn't do anything wrong. It's not your fault that I am different."

"It doesn't matter. You are still a person… a human being, right?"

Her words touch his heart. For the first time in his life, Luke feels acknowledged and respected, rather than shunned. Pureness is felt by Rose, which fills Luke with happiness. Looking at her face, he replies "yes, you're right. Thanks, Rose."

"Haha, I should be the one thanking you. After all, you were the one who saved my life. I can't wait to tell my mother and the others. Come on, let's keep going… we're almost there."

Turning around, she skips onwards cheerily, as the boy stands on the spot - marvelling at her kindness while watching her back. Still stunned by her response, Luke dwells on her uniquely warm nature.

"This girl… she is so kind."

Upon journeying a little further, the two finally reach Rose's home village of Armley. Dwelling within a grassy plain, each house is a wooden cottage, with a farmyard attached. Chickens and pigs can be seen scurrying around, as the pair stroll further within. However, an overwhelming sense of emptiness can be felt all around.

A cautious look can be seen on the girl's face, and as Luke notices her expression, he asks "what is it? Is there something wrong?"

Stopping, Rose glances left and right - holding her silence as though something was off. A lonely wind creeps into the village before she replies "something doesn't seem right. Do you not feel it?"

"Hmm, well I can't say I feel anything out of the ordinary... other than the fact that it's a little quiet."

"Precisely" she responds - taking a deep breath before shouting "is anybody there?" Her voice echoes through the air, and the only response she receives is the oinking of the nearby pigs. As she begins to panic, the girl runs onwards and cries "they are gone. Everybody is gone!"

"Wait up!"

Following behind her, the blue knight watches as she continues to call out for the other villagers. Her worries heighten with each minute - fearing the worst. "Nobody is here. Oh god... what if something terrible happened to them?"

Heading for her home, the girl wastes no time barging through the front door before screaming "mother, where are you?"

Covering each room within her cottage, the girl searches hysterically - yanking cupboards from their place and turning over mattresses. Giving up in one of the bedrooms, she breathes with exhaustion and heartache - clutching her chest. "Could it be? Were they all killed by those horrible creatures? Am I the only one left? Oh, mother... I shouldn't have left you alone!"

She weeps as tears begin to stream down her face. Crying uncontrollably, she recollects the argument she had with her mother. Feeling nothing but guilt, she says "I can't believe that I said such horrible things before I left. I wish I could take it all back. Now… now I will never have the chance to…"

To her surprise, the warm tone of the boy companion interrupts and says "I don't think they are dead, not in this case."

Confused, the girl turns around and stares at Luke who can be seen standing in the doorway. His thoughts provide an ounce of hope for the girl, although yet to understand his reasoning. Nevertheless, his words help to ease her worries, like a temporary elixir cure. With a gentle and fragile tone, she responds "how do you know that?"

"There is no sign of any blood or massacre, not like how my town ended up. Compared to Heline, this place doesn't have a shred of death in the air. Although their disappearance is strange, I don't think the monsters got them" he replies like an experienced soldier of war.

As the girl gasps at his opinion, she stays speechless as he approaches her before holding her hands. "Rose, think carefully. Is there any other place nearby where the others may have escaped to?"

Staring into space, the girl thinks hard about any possible chance that they may still be alive. She digs deep into her mind - persuading her thoughts to deliver something that she may have overlooked. Upon a slightly relieved sigh, she replies "there's one place that is not too far off. However, we have all been forbidden from going there."

Like a lightbulb switching on, Rose smiles before strolling out from the bedroom and saying "give me a few moments to get my head together. I think I may know what has happened to them."

"Sure thing."

With a small head nod, the girl leaves the blue knight within the room before closing the door. With the door firmly shut, the boy takes a deep breath and falls backwards onto a comfy bed. Absorbing the peaceful moment, hearing the faint squeal of the rambling pigs outside, he whispers "wow, it looks like things are becoming even more out of the ordinary. I sure hope the villagers are not in any danger, wherever they are? Jeez, all this worrying is giving me a headache, and this big old helmet is not helping either."

Attempting to ease his stress, Luke tries to take off his blue helmet. However, to his dismay, he finds that he cannot free himself from it. "What is with this helmet and why can't it come off? Is this some kind of joke?"

Try as he might, the helmet seems to be cemented onto his head. Breathing with exhaustion yet not to be defeated, the boy sits upward and attempts to loosen his left greave. Again like magic, his footwear refuses to come off. "This is ridiculous. Did that goddess lady infuse this armour with some kind of hyper glue? How am I supposed to wash or eat?"

Standing up, he approaches a small mirror upon the wall and inspects his armour. "Hmm, it doesn't look like there are any traces of cement or glue anywhere. Was that lady truly a goddess or some kind of she-devil?"

"Excuse me, Mr hero? I have you know, I am far from a wretched devil!" Says a familiar voice. Turning around, Luke shrieks with fright at the sight of the goddess Diana, sitting elegantly upon the bed.

"Woah it's you! What are you doing here?"

"What am I doing here? Well, I am a goddess after all. I can go anywhere I please, and today I have decided to check up on my brave little herald."

She smiles with a playful yet mischievous expression. Her eyes are as blue as they were in the dark, which captures Luke's gaze once more. And like an amateur knight in the presence of their queen, he stands to attention. "So, how's the suit I gave you?"

"This suit? It's incredible. I was able to fight off some monsters and protect somebody. However, there is a slight problem. Am I stuck with this amour all the time? I can't seem to get it off."

Casually, she responds "oh, didn't I tell you before? You are bound to that suit, forever!"

Lost for words, the boy stands speechless as the woman holds a serious glare. His heart drops, knowing that he will never look the same again. As his mind races with panic, a grin creeps up on Diana, before she bursts into laughter.

"Just kidding! Hahaha... I would never do that to you. If you wish to temporarily free yourself from the armour - place your index finger on your forehead. Whenever you need to equip your armour, just do the same thing."

"Touch my forehead with my..."

Following her instructions, Luke proceeds to touch his forehead with his index finger. Miraculously, his blue suit disappears like magic - revealing his standard attire.

"Oh, that's such a relief!"

"You are most welcome, Mr hero."

Catching his eye, the boy notices the letter D engraved onto his forehead while looking in the mirror. Attempting to rub it off he asks "why is this letter printed on my head? It's like a permanent tattoo or something."

"Yes, that is my mark. It stands for Diana, of course. It is proof that you are my one and only noble herald" she says proudly - giving off a divine aura that fills the boy with a sense of gratitude and privilege. To be the one and only herald to a goddess is quite an achievement for the boy. Hotness can be felt upon his cheeks, which he quickly realises is a result of him blushing, which causes the goddess to chuckle.

At that moment, a gentle tap is heard on the door from the other side. "Luke, is it ok to come in? I think I know where everybody went" says Rose.

Wondering how a normal girl would react to the sight of a real-life goddess within the room, Luke turns to Diana and asks "hey, do you mind leaving for now? I think my friend might be a little scared by your sudden appearance."

With a smirk, the goddess winks before replying "aww, you are quite the thoughtful one. However, you needn't worry. Normal human beings cannot see me. Just pretend I am not here."

"Oh... ok then," the boy says, as the bedroom door opens. Rose steps inside and gasps at the sight of Luke without his armour.

"Oh wow. So this is what you look like. Where did you store your fighting attire? I don't see it."

As the girl awaits the boy's reply, the goddess laughs. "Hmm... I wonder what you will say, Mr hero" looking upon Luke's nervous face.

Without thinking, the boy replies "it's magic. It is a long story, but the armour I carry is unlike anything else. That is all I can say."

"Well I'll be... you are so fascinating, Luke! Or should I say: Blue Lunar? Haha!"

As the girl chuckles away, the goddess keeps a curiously amused gaze on her, before expressing "she is pretty. It's a good thing I am not a jealous goddess, otherwise I would have stolen her beauty and made her live the rest of her life as a toothless pygmy."

Trying his best to ignore Diana's words, Luke continues to converse with the girl. "So, have you managed to think of where everybody could have gone?"

"Yes, as a matter of fact, I did. However, we're gonna need a few weapons!"

To Luke's surprise, Rose pulls out a bag of onions, a crucifix and a large saucepan. With a strong and focused glare, the girl declares "the village has been kidnapped by a vampire. Please, help me to rescue them!"

"A what?"

Bursting out into laughter, the goddess expresses, "this sounds like it's going to be a lot of fun. Good luck, Mr hero!"

Shortly after - Luke and Rose depart the village of Armley and can be seen walking along a single path, surrounded by wide and tall trees. Progressing side by side, the girl holds onto the boy's arm nervously, holding a single crucifix and a bag of onions. Using the saucepan as a helmet, it sits upon her head - swaying to and fro. The trees shiver from a menacing wind, which would typically frighten Luke. However, the creative sight of Rose's items serves to lighten his otherwise worried mind.

"Rose, so where are we going exactly and why do you believe that a vampire took the villagers?"

"Well... in my village, there have always been rumours about a manor, not too far from here. Nobody has dared to set foot there because apparently, a vampire dwells within it. Some say that on nights of a full moon, the vampire sometimes visits Armley to steal innocent children."

His heart stops for a second, as his soul briefly escapes his body out of fear. He had only ever heard of vampires within storybooks or at best in legends of old. In both instances, vampires are seldom spoken of positively. "Maybe we shouldn't go any further?" He wishes to say to the girl. However, doing so would most likely disappoint but not stop her. Judging by her determination, it is clear that she would continue alone regardless.

"Have you ever known someone who was taken by the vampire?" Luke asks.

"Well... no. However, there must be some truth to the rumours. We were always told to stay away from the manor, to not arouse any attention to what was inside. My theory is, the vampire must have grown confident since the appearance of all those horrible monsters around, and decided to abduct my mother and the villagers."

"I guess that could make sense..."

"It makes perfect sense!" She shouts like a stern sergeant - sensing a drop of doubt within his tone. Her eyes are like fire, as Luke covers his mouth to suppress the urge to laugh. A nearby crow cackles in the distance, as though expressing what he is thinking, while the girl continues her rant. "The vampire probably hasn't counted on me and the fact that I am armed with its weakness. He won't know what hit him!"

An amused smile opens up on Luke's face as Rose displays an expression as though ready for war. Holding her tools tight, she states "it is well known that vampires are afraid of onions and crucifixes. I read it once in a book!"

"Me too! However, does that truly work against vampires?"

Shrugging her shoulders as they continue, the girl replies "beats me. However, it's the best idea I could think of. Besides, if it doesn't work, I can always count on you, right Luke?"

Stopping abruptly, the girl produces a slightly ashamed face before saying "sorry, that came out wrong. What I meant to say was: If my way doesn't work, could you perhaps give me a hand?"

"Of course Rose, you don't even have to ask. I want to rid Veritas of those monsters as much as you do."

"Thanks, Luke."

As midday approaches, with the sun and blue sky still present, the path finally leads the pair to the entrance of a large mansion. The building looks wealthy - possessing a classical style of fine colourful brickwork. Contrary to his assumptions, Luke finds the mansion to be bright and welcoming.

"Is this supposed to be the home of the vampire? I am quite surprised."

"Don't let your guard down. The fiend most likely built it to lure its prey."

Taking a step forward, the girl bravely shouts forth to the mansion "Mr vampire, I know that you have taken my mother and the villagers. Come on out, otherwise, you'll be sorry!"

Surprised by her threat, Luke stands on guard - keeping his index finger ready to call upon his miraculous armour. The pair stay tense, preparing for the worst to happen at any moment.

After moments of silence - the window above swings open. As the pair brace themselves, they watch as a single boy peeps out from inside. His face is unnaturally pale, bearing curly black hair. Sporting a black tuxedo, fitted with an oversized collar and black cape, he bears a tired and grumpy face while addressing the pair.

"What's with all the racket? Can't a vampire sleep in peace!"

Shocked by his statement, Luke and Rose gasp at the same time - unsure whether to scream with excitement or fear. With a strong gaze, the girl points to the being up by the window and shouts "so the rumours were true after all. A vampire does live here!

"Is that why you woke me up, to tell me that? Get off my property, this instant!"

Chuckling at the human-like behaviour of the apparent creature of darkness, Luke stands intrigued by the owner of the mansion. An unthreatening aura is felt by the vampire and as such, Luke chimes in and speaks calmly - watched from above by a cheerful sun.

"Listen, we didn't come here for trouble. We only wish to find the villagers of Armley. If you have them, please let them go."

"Eh? How did you know about that? No matter. In any case, I refuse to give up my humans to you!" He shouts aggressively. However, the tone of the vampire is without malice, like an outburst from a grumpy neighbour.

"So it's true, you did kidnap the villagers. Give them back to us!"

Rolling his eyes, the vampire responds "why should I hand my humans to a girl who is armed with vegetables, sticks and a saucepan? Your partner also looks ridiculous with that menacing tattoo upon his forehead. You're nothing but a pair of hoodlums, not even worthy to drink blood from. Hell, I'd probably die from food poisoning!"

Slamming the window shut, the boy disappears back into the mansion - leaving the pair flabbergasted.

"The nerve of that creep. How dare he insult us like that?"

Unable to contain his amusement, Luke laughs for many seconds before responding "I am sorry, but he's quite a character. I know this sounds crazy, but I don't think he's doing this for any malicious reasons.

"Hmm, maybe. Be that as it may, he still has the villagers, and that is not ok. I refuse to leave without them!"

"Well then, let's pay our friendly host a visit," says Luke

before touching his forehead with his index finger. At that instant, a burst of light is released from the boy - lighting up the area with such force, that the girl covers her eyes from the brightness. As the light disappears, the boy can be seen equipped with his mighty blue armour once more. Holding a glare of wonder, the girl stands ever impressed.

Turning his attention to the front door of the mansion, the boy gently pushes against it with but an ounce of his strength. Against the power of the divine armour, the door is propelled off its hinges and crashes to the ground. A mist of smoke and debris fill the front entrance - causing the girl to cough profusely.

"Stay close to me" Luke advises, as the two stroll inside.

Once in the mansion, they marvel at the pristine decor. A chandelier hangs above their heads as they stroll upon a spotlessly clean carpet and rug. The scent of fresh polish fills their noses. Up ahead, a large staircase can be seen - fitted with expensive-looking bulbs that brighten the foyer area.

"Woah, this place is incredible. This must be a very wealthy vampire."

Footsteps can be heard, stomping towards the pair from beyond the upper staircase. Before their eyes, Luke and Rose watch as the vampire races down the steps- carrying over a dozen tomatoes. With an enraged expression, he shouts "can't you take a hint? Nobody wants you here, so clear off. Furthermore, I am gonna need you to pay for my front door you just broke!"

Within seconds the once spotless foyer is painted red. However, not the red of blood that the young Luke experienced only a night ago, but a fresh and fruitful red, from the splattered remains of flung tomatoes. Thinking fast, Luke and Rose crouch underneath a nearby table. As food flies and crashes against almost every surface of the foyer, the two cannot help but laugh at the humorous scene.

"Is he serious? What will a bunch of tomatoes do, besides getting us a little dirty?"

"This is the most bizarre monster I have ever come across!"

Hearing their banter, the vampire grows even more enraged before shouting "I can hear you! If you must know, these tomatoes were plucked from the gardens of hades and ripened with the souls of the damned. By the way, do not compare me to a mindless monster, I am nothing like them. I am Umbra the vampire!"

Ignoring his rants, Luke whispers to the girl "use your onions. He should be vulnerable to them, right?"

"Ah yes, good thinking" she replies before pouncing out from under the table, ready to retaliate against Umbra the comical host of the mansion. "Try this for size!" She says before throwing a single vegetable that hits his forehead. As the onion falls to the ground, the vampire stops and displays a boastful expression.

"Was that the best you had? It's gonna take more than one rotten vegetable to harm me."

"Wait... aren't you supposed to be afraid of onions? Everybody knows that vampires are repelled by those things!" Rose rants, watching as the vampire drops his last tomato to the ground with panic.

Adding to her suspicions, Luke addresses the vampire also. "Yeah, and vampires are not supposed to be out during the day. Sunlight is supposed to be your weakness!"

Producing a clear gasp and blink as though being found out, Umbra stutters while responding "oh really? Well... I knew that... of course, I knew that. I am a vampire after all."

Holding his face in a melodramatic fashion, the house host cries "you've defeated me, using the power of the holy onions and rays of the sun! Leave me now and let me die with dignity... ugh." Like an actor in a stage show, the vampire falls to the ground and plays dead.

The pair stands quietly - baffled by the bizarre actions of the humorous vampire. Eyes as confused as the other, they hold their breath - expecting another antic from the frenzied host, while the sounds of dripping tomatoes can be heard from the walls and ceiling.

Suddenly, many footsteps can be heard coming from the top of the staircase. Looking up, the two gasp with shock and relief at the sight of the villagers, safe and sound.

"Oh my goodness…" Rose cries, blinking twice. "You are all here. You are all alive!"

The people of Armley sigh with relief as they see Rose, standing beside the blue knight. A joyous and collective gasp dances from their mouths, as more and more villagers pour into the foyer area, all seemingly unharmed.

From out of the crowd, a single lady rushes into the open and calls out "Rose? Is that you?"

"Mother? Mother!"

Mother and daughter run into each other's arms, crying tears of joy. Dressed in a similar grey dress as Rose, the mother looks almost a spitting image of her daughter, with only a few added wrinkles of wisdom.

"Oh, thank heavens you're safe, my precious Rose. When you disappeared, I feared the worst."

"Mother, I am so sorry for making you worry. When I left, the monsters came and hunted me down. Fortunately, I came across this warrior named Blue Lunar. He can beat the monsters!"

The mother looks at the armoured knight - pausing as she stares at his attire. With a grateful smile, she bows and says "thank you so much. Thank you for protecting my baby. She is all I have left."

"You are welcome. I was just doing what anybody would have done. Did that vampire harm you?"

With a smile, the woman replies "no, not at all. Umbra helped us. When we started to see the monsters from afar, Umbra brought us here for safekeeping. Unlike our cottages, this mansion offers greater protection. We were fed and kept safe. He is a little weird but, he's on our side."

Looking over at the boy who still can be seen playing dead on the ground, Luke wonders "so… is he a vampire or just a human, like me? He behaves like a regular kid but, something seems different about him."

"Umbra, get up, will you! This here is my daughter Rose and her new friend" shouts Rose's mother.

Opening his eyes before sitting upward, the mansion host smiles and responds "Eh? So they weren't just a pair of hoodlums? Could have fooled me. However, I guess this changes everything."

Jumping to his feet, he strolls cheerfully to the pair and claps his hands. "Welcome to my humble mansion. I am Umbra the vampire. It's a pleasure to meet you."

"It's a pleasure to meet you too. I am Luke. Are you truly a vampire?"

"Yes, of course I am. Granted, I am not the most conventional vampire in the world. What about you? Most normal folks wouldn't be able to knock a door down, not to mention the fact that you can wear such heavy-looking armour with ease?"

"Oh… That is quite a long story" Luke says nervously, before glancing over at Rose's mother and the rest of the villagers. A sense of comfort overcomes him, knowing that other people managed to stay safe from the merciless monsters who have taken over the land. His relief is followed by guilt, however, as the screams from his fallen hometown echo into his ears like an ever haunting nightmare. Even the smell of death is whiffed up, bringing his mind back to that horrible night. "If only… if only the people of my town were able to find safety."

Breaking out from his daydream - a roar is heard from afar, which sends shockwaves throughout the building. Luke and the others flinch with fear, instantly discerning the sound to not be of anything natural. The intensity of the roar seems to fit a large beast. Seconds later, they hear mighty footsteps that begin to grow nearer. With each stomp, the ground rumbles and cries, so great that segments of the mansion begin to give way. The hanging chandelier above falls before smashing to pieces, causing Rose and the villagers to grow terrified even more.

"It's another monster!" Shrieks Rose, looking to Luke for comfort. He too is frightened, knowing that whatever is outside is headed directly for them.

Upon a deep and courageous exhale, he states to the villagers "everything will be ok... I am Blue Lunar the herald of the goddess Diana!" His words take initiative before his mind can even stop to ponder.

Legs leading the way, the boy runs out of the mansion to face the monster outside. However, as he steps into the open, Luke looks upon the foe and is paralysed with inexplicable fear.

"No way... we are all dead!"

Chapter 4: The Will To Live

U nder the blue sky, the young Luke stands just outside of the mansion that has kept the people of Armley safe. That safety is about to be compromised, due to the appearance of one of the wizard's monsters.

Its size is great, being easily taller than the mansion itself. Body consisting of green skin, it towers over the boy, staring down at him with one single eye. Upon another roar, it bears dozens of fangs, as it wields a hefty club in its right hand. It produces a foul breath that is so putrid, that the fowls that are resting on the many trees instantly fall to their deaths.

Watched by the blue moon, Luke struggles to hold his composure - sporting his divine armour. Afraid and with nowhere to turn, he simply stands on the spot, wishing it were all a dream.

"A cyclops" He whispers to himself, watching as the monster blinks with curiosity.

As rose and the others stay within the mansion, the need for help overcomes Luke, like a child being fed to the wolves. However, as helpless as he feels, the blue knight knows that no amount of support from the villagers would help. After all, he is supposed to be the hero, blessed by an eternal goddess.

$$\infty\infty\infty$$

"I have to do something. I am gonna need to divert its attention". Running away from the mansion, the boy calls out to the beast "come on, follow me you bulkhead!" Attempting to draw its focus away from the building that contains the villagers.

Just as planned, the monster follows the boy as he sprints into a deep forest. As the fiend gives chase, trampling along the ground, Luke notices a change in his speed. He is fast, faster than ever before, and with each step his speed increases.

"Woah, have I always been able to run this fast? No, of course not. It's because of this suit, I am sure of it!"

Countless trees zip past, and Luke's speed has increased so drastically, that he now resembles a speeding bullet that shoots through the forest. The boy is so fast, that he is unable to control himself as he panics "what the hell... I can't stop!"

His speed heightens further, causing a blue aura to surround him as he breaks the sound barrier. The force is so great, that the very forest itself is dragged behind, like a mighty tornado. "Somebody help!"

Emerging out from the forest, he races uncontrollably into a canyon area before slamming against a gigantic rock slab. The earth trembles from the impact - causing a loud thud that reverberates out for many miles. Falling backward to the ground, the young hero breathes slowly, covered with rock and grain debris.

"Wow, this suit is truly something. It's gonna take a little getting used to."

Not far behind, the monster emerges from the forest. As Luke sees the humungous beast, he slowly picks himself up and holds a defensive stance. "I guess there's nowhere to run now. I need to fight this thing. However, how am I supposed to get close with just these fists?"

The Cyclops produces another extreme roar, and the boy is forced to cover his ears from the intensity. However, as he does, the monster lunges forward and strikes him with the large wooden club with such force the weapon shatters to pieces - sending Luke skyrocketing. Crashing through the canyon, the boy hits multiple surfaces before landing in the middle of a shallow stream, by a waterfall. He is dazed and disoriented. However, to his surprise, he is not hurt. The godly suit has once again protected him.

Slowly sitting upward, he watches as the monster charges towards him yet again - not allowing a single moment to recover. "Here it comes..."

Clenching its gigantic fists, the monster slams into the boy - pounding him with a series of devastating blows. Its strength is so great, that the earth shakes with every punch - causing smoke and debris to scatter about. Helpless, the boy can do nothing but take every punch. However, as before, not an ounce of pain is felt.

"I don't feel anything. None of this... none of this hurts" Luke gasps with amazement. As he continues to receive blow after blow, the boy grows confident before extending his hands to grab hold of the monster's fists. Startled, the creature gasps as the blue knight proceeds to shout with anger. "Get the hell off me!" He declares before lifting the beast high above his head. A gasp escapes the boy's lips - astounded by the feat. As gigantic as the monster is, within Luke's hands it feels as light as a feather. With a great toss, the monster is sent tumbling yards away before crashing into the waterfall - leaving a scene of devastation.

"That will teach you..." holding an adrenaline-filled smile -

overcome with a feeling that he can't quite put into words. To be able to go toe to toe against such a deadly and strong beast validates a certain strength for the boy.

With much life still left within it, the monster slowly gets back up before glaring at the blue hero who holds an equally intimidating glare. "I am not gonna let you monsters have your way anymore. I am gonna wipe you all out, and when I am finished, I'll beat your wizard master to a pulp too!"

The monster screams with rage - emitting an earsplitting shockwave that is so unbearable, that the boy falls to his knees. "Uhhh... the sound... it's so loud, I can't stand at all" he mumbles to himself, as the beast treads closer to him.

As the monster continues its deafening roar, it raises its right foot high - ready to crush the struggling knight as he kneels helplessly.

"This doesn't look good. I don't know if I can withstand being stepped on."

Like a guillotine, the monster brings its heavy foot down to finish the boy. However, inches before being crushed, a mysterious figure swoops in and scoops the blue knight away from danger. As a result, the gigantic fiend slams its foot into the ground, causing a devastating scene of debris and boulders that scatter in every direction - leaving a crater in its wake.

"Huh?" Luke gasps, finding himself in the arms of the friendly vampire: Umbra. Surprised to see him, he stutters "you... what are you doing here?"

Gliding through the sky before landing to safety, Umbra responds as he settles Luke to the ground.

"That was a close one, wouldn't you agree? You were doing so well, for the most part. However, you wasted time and allowed the cyclops to gain the upper hand. Fear not young hoodlum... Umbra the greatest of vampires will take over from here!"

With a daring grin, the vampire takes a single step forward to challenge the beast as Luke stands shocked beyond disbelief. "Wait... this isn't some kind of game. Your tomatoes are not gonna do the trick!" Luke rants, as the smiling boy glances to him.

"Yes, I agree. I wouldn't want to waste my tomatoes on that cyclops anyway. However, I am pretty sure that it would make a mighty fine cuisine" he replies, before reaching into his cape to pull out a small black briefcase. Reaching into it, he takes out a pair of carving knives and laughs "I've always wondered what a cyclops stew would taste like. Finally, I'll be able to get the chance!"

"Stop! Don't do it!"

Ignoring Luke's words, the vampire runs towards the monster, holding a cheerful smile as though having no sense of danger.

"Mr cyclops - it's time to die now. You have been a pain in the neck for my friends and I. You'd be a lot better as a juicy meal in our stomachs instead!" Umbra laughs before throwing his pair of knives, which strike directly into the single eye of the monster.

The foe screams as black blood spews from its eye. However, the unwavering vampire only delights in its cries, as he arms himself with more knives. "You can moan all you like. Your deafening shockwaves may harm the humans but against me, your screams fall flat!"

The great monster swipes at the vampire - however, moving like the wind itself he dances around its attacks effortlessly, laughing as he throws dozens of knives in quick succession. The cyclops grows even angrier, yet try as he might, the beast is unable to lay a finger on the boy of wonder.

Watching the battle between the vampire and cyclops, Luke stands astounded. "Woah... he is incredible. How does he move like that?"

Pouncing up its body before leaping onto its head, the vampire finishes the foe by stabbing the cyclops with a mighty butcher's knife. Letting out one last cry, the monster stands still before slowly falling backwards, slamming against the ground. As the victor, Umbra stands with his ever-present smile, as though the fight were just a simple game.

"A piece of cake" he chuckles before opening his black briefcase once more. Like magic, the many knives that were thrown through the canyon grounds begin to zip through the air, before returning to the case. "I am glad that's over."

∞∞∞

Grey clouds begin to loom as rain begins to fall. Looking up at the sky, the pleasant vampire's smile falls for just a moment, before he whispers "it would seem that someone is planning something quite troublesome. The question is: What for?"

Running to his side, the blue hero calls to him and says "Umbra, thank you for helping me. I had no idea you were so strong."

Resuming his smile, the black-dressed boy replies "oh it was nothing. Besides, it was you who did most of the work. You weakened it enough for me to finish it off. I must say, I am quite intrigued by you, as well as what's been occurring recently with all these troublesome monsters around. Allow me to accompany you on your journey if you don't mind? Together we can stop this monstrous takeover of our land."

Luke pauses, digesting the friendly vampire's request to join him. He thinks back to the many difficult times of his life when he would beg for others to give him the time of day. He feels honoured and acknowledged that someone would offer to share their company with him.

"You could never play with us, not in a million years because you are an orphan!" The brutal and cold words of those who shunned him whisper into his ears, like a dark dream. Expelling the memory from his thoughts, Luke gives a refreshing sigh - leaving the wind to carry the painful memory away.

"Yes, I would like that. Let's both stop those monsters and alert the capital as soon as possible. The quicker we get there, the quicker we can save lives!"

"Oh, so you wish to head to Spiritus the capital city of this country. I know the way..."

Suddenly - breaking their communication, the pair hear many roars, much like that of the fallen cyclops. Before they have any time to process the situation, the pair gasp with shock at the sight of four additional cyclops who slowly surround them.

"No way. Where did those four come from?" Asks Luke, standing back to back with the vampire.

"I guess that those four heard the cries of their fallen brother, which is why they have come for us. This is so exciting... I wonder how we'll get out of this one? Teehee!"

"This isn't funny. We're gonna need to think of a plan..."

Suddenly, before he can finish speaking - the vampire pushes Luke out of harm's way, just as a gigantic heel comes crashing down. "Look out..."

In his place, Umbra is crushed by the feet of the monster - while Luke tumbles out to safety. The rest of the fiends jump in and proceed to stomp on the vampire continuously - causing a scene of devastation.

Under the pouring rain, the blue knight stands helplessly - reminded of a similar scene that occurred not too long ago.

"This... this is the same as that night... with Jill..." A feeling of failure overcomes him, as he thinks to himself "it's not supposed to be this way. I am supposed to be different now, stronger than before. So why... why has another person lost their life protecting me? I shouldn't need protection anymore. I am supposed to be stronger!"

Shouting with frustration, the boy's cry echoes through the air, under the grey clouds. Suddenly, a great thunderclap is heard - so loud that it surprises the four cyclops.

The blue moon above reveals itself, like a merciful king -

shining bright as though wanting to catch Luke's attention. As he glances upward to the sky, the boy watches as a shooting star falls from the moon before descending to his position.

"What the..."

The star hits the ground, mere inches in front of the boy. However, upon closer inspection, he finds the wonder to be a large claymore sword - emanating a clear blue aura. As it stays lodged in the ground, Luke stands enticed as though it were beckoning for him to wield it. "A sword? Did it just come from the...?"

"You said you wanted to be stronger, right? Here's your chance!" Comes a familiar voice. Glancing back, he sees the goddess Diana, sitting upon a nearby rock slab, bearing a stern glare. "Show me how strong you truly are then. Wield your sword and send those monsters to the afterlife!"

With a brave nod, Luke reaches forth towards the blade, as the fiends stand terrified of the sword's emanating energy. Upon taking hold of the hilt - holding the claymore weapon in both hands, Luke is filled with a rush of energy that surges through his body. "This power... it's incredible."

Within his hands, the energy from the blade increases - exuding a force that is so great, that the four cyclops find themselves being slowly pushed back. The many stones and rubble of the canyon are blown into the distance, as the knight proceeds to lift the glowing sword upward to the sky instinctively. Facing the direction of the foes, Luke hears the goddess shout to him once more.

"All of that pent up frustration, helplessness and pain... channel it into that sword. Those feelings you had, growing up with only fleeting friendships and no family... release it all into the weapon and strike those foes down. You are Blue Lunar, the mightiest warrior in the world. Let no other man, demon or god tell you any different!"

"I am Blue Lunar!"

With a great downward swing, Luke releases the power of the mysterious sword - unleashing a great wave of light that obliterates the four cyclops in an instant. The entire canyon is destroyed in the process, as the wave of light tears through the land - destroying everything in its wake. As a wonder of the world, the light is seen by many - marvelling upon it as though it were a divine act of the gods.

∞∞∞

The divine blast of light that was released from the radiant sword slowly fades - allowing for the astonished Luke to view what remains of the foes and the canyon, which seems to be completely wiped out. The only things that linger are pillars of steam, as though the earth had been scorched by fire. Finding the four cyclops to be no more, he stands lost for words at the power he wielded - still holding the sword in both hands. To his surprise, the blade begins to disappear into pieces of stardust that disperse into the sky. Similarly, his mighty armour also fades - revealing his standard attire.

Before he can begin to question the reason for his armour's temporary disperse, the boy is overcome with achievement. Turning around to thank the goddess who spurred him on, he says "Diana, did you see that? I got rid of those..."

To his surprise, he finds the blue moon goddess has disappeared from the slab where she was only a moment ago. With a common sigh, he whispers "jeez, she could have said goodbye at least."

Not forgetting about the vampire who risked his life for him, Luke looks over at his remains. Under the pouring rain, he stands with a sorrow-filled heart. "Umbra..."

Walking over to him, the boy looks down at the motionless body of the friendly vampire. His eyes are closed and at peace - however, the young hero cannot shake the burden of guilt. Kneeling by his side, Luke places his hands upon Umbra's chest softly.

"Thank you, for protecting me, my friend. Rest well."

Tears begin to well within his eyes before Luke cries - head held low with shame and sadness. The weeping continues for many moments, under the quiet rain. Suddenly - the vampire perks open his eyes before displaying a beaming smile.

"Wow, that was amazing Luke! Or should I call you: Blue Lunar? Haha!"

"What... what is going on? You're alive?"

Slowly standing to his feet while dusting himself off, the vampire marvels at the aftermath of Luke's power - paying no mind to his shock and confusion.

"Well I'll be... you managed to destroy this whole canyon in the process. God knows how far that destructive beam of light has travelled."

As the vampire turns his back to Luke, attempting to depart the area, the baffled hero stands on the spot before shouting "hey, how the hell did you survive? I saw those four crush you to death!"

Standing paces apart, with his back still facing Luke - the black-suited friend holds his silence as the young hero awaits his response. Umbra turns around and with a cheerful gaze, he replies "oh, did I not tell you? I can't die. I am immortal."

"You... you are immortal?"

The new friend winks before skipping onwards - followed by the even more confused Luke. "An immortal vampire, who fights for us humans?"

The afternoon carries on and the rain finally ceases - welcoming a bright sunset. Back within the mansion, Luke and Umbra are ready to begin their journey to the country's capital: Spiritus. However, before they do so, they say their goodbyes to Rose and the villagers.

"You should all be safe here in this mansion. Please, hold

on until I find a way to stop what has happened to this land. I promise that I will do my best" Luke says while looking at the girl who seems to hold an expression of sadness. Without her needing to put it into words, the boy senses her feelings - looking away with unease.

To his surprise, she steps forward and takes hold of his hands. Her touch is warm yet firm. And as the boy looks at her, Rose produces a teary smile. "Luke - earlier on, you told me that you never had a family. Well, now you do. As from this moment forth, you will be my brother and I will be your sister."

"Huh? You would like to be my sister?"

"Yes - so make sure to come back in one piece. Once this is all over, you can live here with mother and I. We will share stories and have picnics and feasts. What do you say?"

Luke's heart is moved beyond comprehension, and almost instantly he bursts into tears - trying to cover his eyes from embarrassment. As the tears stream down his face, he replies "I now have a sister... a family. Thank you."

Breaking their emotional farewell - Umbra sighs before expressing "oh for goodness sake. It's only been one day and you've already managed to cry twice now. Honestly, with that amount of tears, you could put out all the fires of hell!"

Leading the way - the vampire strolls towards the exit door, followed by the weeping hero behind. Watching as the pair disappear into the orange sunset outside - his new sister wipes a small tear from her eyes.

"Do your best. I will be waiting for you... my new brother."

Chapter 5: Defiers of the Darkness

T he sun begins to set over the land, replacing it with bright stars. The clouds are vast in number, and within them, the goddess of the blue moon watches her young hero and his newest ally as they trek through the night.

Holding a pleased smile like a proud mother, the goddess drifts high through the sky - under the quiet and peaceful night.

Grabbing her attention, a polite and deep voice calls to her - catching the goddess with mild surprise. "So, that boy is your newest herald I see? He is quite impressive."

Appearing out from thin air, a second deity is revealed. Bearing the form of a man, he is dressed in pure white robes like royalty, and upon his head, he wears a dazzlingly white crown. Holding his hands behind his back like a wise teacher, a single white dove can be seen perched on his shoulder. Looking at the god with a pleasant stare, Diana greets him.

"Long time no see, Obatala. What brings a fellow god like you here? It isn't like you to visit without good reason."

"Good evening, Diana. You are correct, I usually don't visit without good reason... which is exactly why I am here."

"Oh, so I guess you'd like to know how I managed to make the mortal my herald, right?"

Displaying a troubled gaze, the god responds "just how did you manage to make that boy your herald? That should not be possible, thanks to the Apex Grail."

"How could I forget about such a thing. The existence of the Apex Grail negates direct influence between deities and mortal men. However, I exploited a loophole of sorts. You see, that boy had died momentarily, during which he was technically no longer mortal. He was but an immortal soul in the afterlife. It was there that I had reached out to him before granting the boy life once more - as my latest herald."

Obatala glances down at the boy as he responds to Diana in a worried tone. "I must commend your intelligence. Not many gods would have thought of your strategy, Diana. However, why would you do that? Every last god and goddess accepted the decision to remain separate from the affairs of mortals."

"Have you not seen what has been transpiring? Phantom the wizard king of despair has been released from his eternal prison."

"I am well aware. However, what does he have to do with your meddling? Again, Phantom may be an unsightly mortal, but he is still a mortal nonetheless. We should leave the humans to fight their own battles."

With a strong and angry glare, the goddess of the moon shouts "no, there's something else going on that is bigger than Phantom. That detestable wizard should not have been able to escape his prison. It would have taken a god to break the chains that once bound him."

"So, are you assuming that another god or goddess is behind Phantom's release? That would be impossible... even you should know this. The Apex Grail would not make such an action feasible."

"I know... I know what you're saying. However, something is going on that concerns me about the timing of it all. For now, I will guide my young herald to get to the bottom of this."

With an exhausted sigh, Obatala turns his back to the goddess and responds "do as you will, I will not stop you. However, I hope you understand that you are playing a very dangerous game, Diana. That boy who you made into your latest herald; is he fully aware of what your pact with him entails?"

The woman does not reply - holding a slightly nervous expression as the fellow god looks at her with eyes of disappointment. Her refusal to answer speaks volumes, and upon discerning her feelings, the fellow god says "I thought as much. You have no intention of telling him the truth, do you? If I remember correctly, you did the same thing with your previous herald of old, back in the days of the Divine War. Hmph... you and that wizard are not so different, wouldn't you agree?"

"How dare you? I am nothing like that detestable wizard! Leave me now. Your company is no longer needed!"

Disappearing into the clouds, Obatala leaves the goddess of the moon alone within the dark sky. Taking a deep breath, she shrugs away her emotions before resuming her gaze to the land below.

"Boy - If you wish to hate me once this is all over... I will not blame you."

The night eventually comes to an end.

As early dawn breaks, Luke and Umbra wake after spending the night within a makeshift tent. Being the first to emerge, the young hero looks up at the bright and sunny sky - yawning aloud as he stretches.

Standing opposite a small stream, he says to himself "is it morning already? It feels like I only rested my head for a few hours. Well, in any case, I need to keep moving. Heaven knows how far the monsters have spread."

Following also from under the tent - Umbra yawns "why are we up so early? You'd think the world were to end today or something."

"Umbra, have you already forgotten? There are monsters wreaking havoc as we speak right now. We need to get to the capital city of Spiritus as fast as we can."

"You worry too much, you know that? Has it not dawned on you that other warriors throughout this land are most likely resisting the countless fiends? It's going to take some time for the monsters to completely overrun this country, especially the capital."

The confident look in his eyes pricks Luke's interest, who turns to him and says "it seems strange to hear you talk in support of us humans. I figured as a vampire, you would be on the side of the monsters."

Letting out an offended gasp, the vampire steps back and responds "what are you implying? Vampires have nothing in common with those mindless simpletons known as monsters. Do you know nothing about our world?"

"Well... I just assumed that you were of the same species?"

"No! Listen up, mortal. There are many species in this world and you would do well to know the main ones. First, there are the gods. The gods are typically the most powerful and revered. Some are said to have good intentions, while others do not. Next are the humans: amusing and pitiful beings who seem to fascinate the gods.

Skipping around the astonished friend, Umbra continues

"then there are the demons and creatures of the night. I fall into this category. Highly calculating and menacing, my kind are known for sowing discord and suffering. Last but not least are the monsters. Profoundly stupid and predictable, they make up for their lack of intelligence with their strength."

Digesting the knowledgeable ally's words, Luke crosses his arms and stays lost in thought. Snapping him out of his daydream, Umbra pokes his forehead and asks "the biggest question I have however is: what are you?" Inspecting the goddess' mark upon Luke's forehead. Slow to respond, the young hero averts his gaze.

"Um... well I am human. However, as you saw earlier, I can call upon a type of armour, thanks to the goddess Diana."

"That's incredible! So you are a herald? Such a rarity. I wonder what you did to impress her. It is said that the goddess of the blue moon is cold and apathetic to the lives of mortals."

His words create a pinch of concern for Luke, who blinks with surprise. "Really? Well, she doesn't seem very cold to me. She saved my life and gave me a second chance. I don't believe that for a second" the young hero says - holding his chest before producing a grateful smile.

Glancing at Luke from the corners of his eyes, the chirpy vampire shows a look of pity. It is only for a fragment of a second, too quick to notice by the untrained eye. As though raising a false smile, he continues "well, onto more important matters... food! I am sure I brought along a few sandwiches for our journey. Have you ever tried ogre eyeball panini? I won't be a moment..."

Scuttling back into the tent - the vampire can be heard singing to himself while digging around for food within his trusty and mysterious briefcase. Remaining outside, Luke looks up to the sky and grand white clouds - taking in a deep breath of fresh air. Eyes closed, he hears the soothing movement of the trees and small stream.

Interrupting his peace, the blue moon goddess appears next to him and says "good morning Mr hero. Sleep well?"

"Yikes Diana! Why must you always scare me to death like that? I've already died once!"

Bursting out into laughter, the deity claps her hands with amusement as the boy sighs with annoyance. "Haha, I am sorry my young herald. It's just so easy to spook you. Well, I just wanted to congratulate you on defeating those monsters yesterday. I knew you could do it."

"Oh yeah, that's right... yesterday. Well, it was thanks to you for helping me out. Were you the one who sent that sword for me to use? Why did it disappear afterwards?"

Sitting gracefully on the ground, the goddess looks out at the glistening water that reflects the sun's rays. She is quiet, holding a pleasant grin as the boy sits next to her - looking upon the water also, as the singing vampire continues to rummage within the tent.

"Yes, I was the one who sent down the moon sword for you to wield. You remember how you used it, right? Channel all of your emotions into it and let the blade do the rest. That is the invincible power of the blue moon and why you as my herald are the strongest warrior in the world. The armour and its weapon are powered by your will.

"Woah... so that's how the armour works? I just need to believe and focus my emotions on it. I think I can get the hang of that."

With a receptive head nod, Diana adds "in future, to call upon the weapon, simply shout for it and it will be by your side."

Scratching his forehead, the young hero responds "that's a lot to remember. Do you not have a book or scroll I could refer to?"

"Excuse me? I am not some second rate goddess. I am Diana, one of the strongest deities in the universe. As my herald, you will remember my teachings and commit them to memory, without the need for a shameful guidebook. Hurry up and get to the capital city of Spiritus before the monsters do, foolish child!"

Displaying a frustrated and cold glare the woman stands

BLUE LUNAR & THE APEX GRAIL

over the boy. An aura of intimidation overcomes Luke, who for the first time feels slightly frightened by her. Could Umbra's words about the goddess being cold hold true? Luke wonders - stricken with fear by the intensity of her beaming eyes that looks as though they could snuff out his soul in an instant. He gasps before looking to the ground, like a scolded child.

"Oh… ok."

Noticing his fear, the goddess steps back before glancing away with guilt. Upon a small sigh, she says "sorry, I shouldn't have spoken to you like that. I am just afraid we won't be able to stop the wizard. I can't say now but, I believe he is after something powerful. I… I just want to…"

Standing before putting on a brave and bold smile, the boy surprises the goddess and holds her hands gently. "It's ok, I understand the seriousness of it all. There are those I wish to protect too, so I will do my best as Blue Lunar."

Eyes perked wide, the goddess freezes with shock at the caring action of the boy. A distant memory comes to her mind - one that she had long forgotten, and as she gazes upon his smile, Diana is reminded of someone from long ago.

"Solomon…"

At that moment, the cheerful vampire finally re-emerges from the tent, holding a dozen rotten looking sandwiches in his arms. Gasping towards Luke, he drops the food and shouts.

"Hey! Why didn't you tell me we were having guests Luke? Is she a friend of yours?"

Both Luke and she stand with fright - puzzled as to how the black-suited boy can see the goddess.

"Impossible. How can you see me? No other human apart from my herald should be able to gaze upon my presence!"

"Oh really? Sorry about that then. I will just pretend you're not here" Umbra says, as he covers his eyes. "See… now I can't see anything! Haha!"

The deity stomps toward the vampire, each furious step causing a distant earthquake. For a moment the sun hides its face behind the clouds, as though terrified of the goddess's temper that has reached the heavens. For an individual to surprise even a goddess is an achievement, and the look upon her confused eyes is confirmation.

Grasping his chin like a strict teacher, she asks "who are you?"

"Who am I? I am Umbra the vampire."

The vampire's simple response vexes the woman, who squeezes his chin further. "Don't insult my intelligence. Not even vampires can detect my presence, so cut the crap! I am going to ask you one last time: Who... are... you!"

The moment is tense, as Luke watches the furious goddess converse with the vampire who seems to find her threat amusing. With a somewhat sinister gaze, he replies to her.

"Oh my... you have quite a temper. You must be Diana of the Blue moon I presume? Your reputation precedes you."

Taken back by the vampire's bold taunts, the goddess gasps - looking into his eyes for many moments of silence. Eventually, she steps backwards and sighs "fine then, keep your secrets. Just make sure not to make my herald's journey harder than it already is."

Looking at Luke, she adds "boy, I will take my leave now. I suggest you resume your journey. Time is of the essence."

"Right..."

Upon a small wave, the lady disappears into thin air, leaving the two boys by the stream. Excited by the encounter, Umbra laughs "teehee... did you see how angry she was? For a moment there, I thought she was gonna rip my heart out!"

"That wasn't funny Umbra. I don't think it's a good idea to anger a goddess. I am pretty sure she could harm you or worse" Luke says worryingly.

"Oh relax my dear friend. I am immortal after all. Killing me would be futile".

Breaking the conversation, the pair hear a mighty explosion in the distance. The ground cries while the air screams, as a great plume of fire erupts into the sky. Followed by a trail of smoke behind the fire, seen about a mile beyond a small forest, the pair grow alert.

"Umbra, what was that just now? Could it be the work of the monsters?"

"Perhaps. Let's go and investigate!"

Wasting no time, the pair sprint towards the direction of the smoke, as an unsettling feeling overcomes them. As they run, the blue sky is interrupted by grey clouds, like a bad omen of something unpleasant. Whispering to himself, Luke says "please, don't let it be another massacre", while his trusty ally skips beside him.

Eventually, they come across a small town that looks to have been set on fire, as seen by the lingering cinders. A heavy heat overcomes them, as though they were at the entrance of an intense pit of flames - causing pools of sweat to constantly fall. It is hard to breathe as if the air itself were snuffed out. Treading inside carefully, the pair notice houses and structures, which look to have been partly burned away - yet no sign of monsters. To their shock, they find dead remains of human beings that are now nothing but ash.

Rain begins to fall, which the pair welcome against their heated bodies - cooling their skin. However, the rain is unable to cool their troubled minds as they continue to inspect the grounds of the nameless town.

"Everybody in this place looks to have perished but, it wasn't because of the monsters. It looks as though a fire had spread. Might it be an accident? What do you think, Umbra?"

Displaying a focused gaze, the vampire strolls in front and glances from left to right. With his arms folded like a detective, Umbra responds "no, this was no accident. Also - the fire of this magnitude couldn't possibly be caused by natural means."

"Well then, what could have caused it?"

A flash of lightning brightens up the sky, and the sound

of thunder cackling can be heard, just as the vampire turns around to reply in a troubled manner.

"Magic. This town was destroyed by magic."

Lost for words, Luke gasps as he hears his friend's assumption. At first, he is unable to make sense of such a theory. However, within seconds, he thinks of only one person responsible.

"The wizard. He must have been the one!"

"A wizard you say? Tell me more."

"Oh, I must have forgotten to mention earlier. You see, before all the monsters appeared, a wizard showed up. He had a long golden staff in his hands and he wore a crown made of thorns."

Stepping backwards while covering his mouth with surprise, the vampire pauses for a short moment and says "wait... you don't mean, Phantom the Wizard of Despair, do you?"

Eyes perked wide, the young hero replies "yes, that was his name! Do you know of him? What are his motives?"

Turning away with a concerned expression, Umbra says "I guess I do know what his motives are. However, what I am most concerned about is how he broke free from his imprisonment. If he is free, then we are in more trouble than I had imagined."

Breaking their conversation, the sound of a single horse can be heard galloping to their position. The pair stand close, on alert and ready for anything. From behind a semi-destroyed structure, a pure white steed comes into view. By its forehead, a single horn protrudes outward, and by each shoulder, a large wing can be seen.

"Is that a unicorn?" Luke asks - astounded by the beauty of the wondrous creature.

Riding upon its back, a single woman can be seen sporting a pure white coat. Her hair is long and golden - covering most of her face. Amidst the grey sky and constant rain, the unicorn and her look like angelic beings, as the two boys stand transfixed by their presence.

The horse and rider stop mere paces away from the duo

before the mysterious woman disembarks from her steed. Upon setting her feet on the muddy ground, she flicks her mesmerising hair to one side - allowing a clearer sight of her face. Displaying pure red lipstick amongst her olive skin, she sports a black left eyepatch. Bearing a monotone and cold expression, she stands still - observing the two boys who become slightly nervous. An air of hostility exudes from her, which causes Luke and Umbra to hold onto one another for comfort.

"What happened here?" She asks, with a soft yet authoritative tone. Refusing to be the one to answer, Umbra pushes Luke forward to respond.

"Well... um... my friend and I believe that this was the work of a wizard."

Crouching, the woman proceeds to slowly run her fingertips along the dirt. After a few tense seconds of silence, she stands before whispering "the warmth of the ground is unnatural. The only explanation is magic. Damn, I was too late." Turning her gaze to the pair once again, she raises her voice and says "the people of this town have all been destroyed. Why is it that you two are the only survivors?" Her tone is assuming, as though inferring that the two had something to do with the scene before them. Not just her tone, but her very demeanour shifts to a somewhat readied stance - like a lion ready to pounce at any moment.

"We have only just arrived ourselves. After seeing the explosion, we came here and found the town like this."

Upon a light chuckle, the woman reaches by her waist - revealing a straight sword within a gold and white scabbard. Before Luke and Umbra's eyes, she slowly unsheathes the blade, causing a firm and resonating chime that reverberates through the empty town. Pointing the weapon in front, she says "you don't expect me to believe that, do you? So you're just a pair of innocent children, who have wandered into this unfortunate town? Give me a break!"

Stepping forward, the vampire responds "look at us. We're

not wizards."

"Hmph… evil comes in many forms, even those who look most innocent. Furthermore, you smell like a demon. You and your polite looking friend are not fooling anybody. You had better tell me what I want to hear, or I will draw your blood!"

As the woman keeps her sword held outward, sweat begins to fall from Luke as he witnesses a confrontation about to take place. The moment is tense, as a further sound of thunder intrudes amongst the downpour of rain. Glancing at Luke, Umbra displays a confident smile.

"Well my friend, it looks like she won't let us go without a fight. Let's give her what she wants" Umbra says - pulling out the trusty briefcase from his cape.

"Are you crazy? Nobody needs to get hurt. We just need to explain what we're doing and why!" Luke rants - bemused with the reasoning of his tuxedo sporting friend.

Taking a mild step toward the female opponent, Umbra replies "we could talk this out. However, it wouldn't be any fun now would it?"

Reaching into his briefcase, the vampire takes out four cutting knives, which he holds between each finger. Eyes wide with adrenaline, the boy displays a thrilled grin as the lady holds a firm and cold gaze. The opponents stay still - hearing nothing but pouring rain against the ground, a prelude to a duel. A frozen glare can be seen upon both Umbra and the mysterious woman, not blinking for even a second.

Running towards one another, the two begin to battle. Taking the offensive, Umbra acts first and throws his knives at the opponent. The sharp cutlery flies through the air towards the unnamed warrior - cutting through the wind and raindrops. Before the vampire's eyes, the woman performs a quick motion of her straight sword - swatting the four knives to the distance with astounding precision.

"Magnificent…" the vampire gasps as the lady leaps in close.

"It would take more than kitchen knives to harm me," she says before performing a clean leg sweep. The vampire falls flat on the ground and as he lays helpless, the woman holds her sword high, ready to inflict a killing stab. "Say goodnight, demon. When you return to hell, tell your master who sent you: Aurora the invincible!"

As she readies to finish off the vampire, Luke shouts forth "stop fighting!" Placing his index finger against his forehead - transforming into the blue knight. As a great light exudes from him, the woman known as Aurora stands transfixed and surprised.

"What in the world is that?"

As the light of his transformation disappears, Luke produces a bold and courageous stance before addressing the warrior.

"Listen. My friend and I are not your enemies. I come from the town of Heline. Recently it was destroyed by a wizard named Phantom, who unleashed all the monsters we've been seeing around. My friend here is a vampire, but he is not evil I can assure you. However, if you insist on coming at us, then I will have no choice but to fight you!"

The woman pauses before letting out a light chuckle. Upon rolling her eyes, she proceeds to walk towards the blue knight - holding her sword tight. As she strolls closer, under the rain and muddy ground, Luke grows nervous - unable to anticipate what she will do next.

Stopping only meters apart, she looks into his eyes for many seconds before responding "so you too are different, just like me."

"Excuse me? What does that mean?" Asks Luke - baffled by her words. Following a small sigh, the woman turns her back and sheathes her blade.

"Forget I said anything. I will take my leave now and track down the wizard. You two are free to go. Stay out of trouble and don't get in my way."

Stepping forward, the boy asks "wait... why don't we go together? It's dangerous for you to wander around alone."

Glancing back at the blue armoured boy, the woman blinks with surprise at his caring suggestion. Upon another mild laugh, she replies "thanks but no thanks. I have no interest in travelling around with a pair of weakling kids. You will only get in my way. If you had any sense, you would find a safe place to hide."

Nearby, the vampire stands before dusting off his cape and attire. "Oh my... could you be any ruder? My crybaby friend and I are not just a pair of children I have you know!"

With a surprisingly gentle head nod, the woman smiles before strolling away from the pair. "My apologies then. May the gods be with you."

As she brushes past the vampire, he responds with a smirk "you too, Aurora the invincible. Or should I say... Stigma Child?"

She freezes with shock - exuding a mild aura of anger while glaring at Umbra who displays a taunting grin. The look in his eyes communicates a sense of grand wisdom of the woman, which unsettles her. Climbing onto her unicorn, she prepares to depart - however not before saying one last farewell.

"That tongue of yours will get you into trouble someday."

Upon her steed, she flies into the sky - disappearing beyond the clouds, leaving the two boys within the empty town. With a mysteriously pleased smile, Umbra continues to look upward as Luke addresses him.

"You shouldn't go around picking fights when a simple explanation would have cleared things up. Also - what is it with you and that mouth of yours? That was the second female today who you angered by your words."

Twirling around playfully - the black-suited friend responds "oh give me a break, Luke. I am a menacing vampire after all. What did you expect? Besides, I only told the truth."

"Oh yeah? And what truth did you say exactly?"

Looking up at the sky once more, the vampire responds "she is a Stigma Child, forever cursed to be exceptional and excluded." His voice flows into the air, exuding a deep empathy for the stars to witness, as the puzzled Luke remains wanting answers.

"A Stigma Child…"

The day carries on as the pair depart the empty town. The rain finally ceases and while the sun begins to slowly set over the land, the two friends walk along a quiet field of grass. As the orange rays of the sun come down over them, Luke trails behind Umbra, bothered by the encounter with the mysterious woman named Aurora.

"Umbra - just who was that lady we met earlier? You seem to know a lot about her."

"Oh, Aurora? Why yes, as a matter of fact, I do. Everybody knows about Aurora the invincible. She is the strongest swordsman on the continent. She hails from the upper country of Superbia and used to serve as the highest-ranking soldier of the capital: Ergo. I am not quite sure why she is in Veritas mind you. Perhaps she caught wind of the monsters around? In any event, having her around will greatly help against the fight against the monsters."

"Woah, she is the strongest swordsman? What makes her so strong exactly? I can't put my finger on it, but I sensed something powerful from within her."

Waving his hands around like a master storyteller, the vampire responds "yes, what you felt was what almost everybody feels when coming into contact with a Stigma Child."

"Why do you keep calling her that?"

"Well, that is what she is. I assume you have no idea what I am talking about, correct? You see, in this world there exist certain humans who are unlike the rest. Girls who possess golden coloured hair and boys who possess silver hair are born with supernatural traits, along with a peculiar mark upon their left eye. These small percentage of humans are incredibly perceptive and possess much higher strength, speed and intellect when compared to average humans. As such, these gifted individuals are often envied and shunned by society, as well as penned with the name: Stigma Children. Approximately one out of a hundred humans are born a

Stigma Child. It is often seen as a bad omen. However, whenever danger has approached, it has always been up to a Stigma Child to save the day - never being truly acknowledged or appreciated."

Head held low, the blue knight whispers "that is so sad. How could people be so cruel?"

"Beats me. You humans are full of contradictions. One can only imagine what someone like Aurora must be going through. On one hand, you are shunned by those around you, and on the other hand, you are called upon for the very thing others fear about you."

"I know all too well how it feels to be treated differently. I wonder why she is putting her neck on the line to fight the monsters when she most likely won't get the appreciation she deserves?"

"Well... maybe she's just a nice person? There doesn't need to be much more to it than that."

Taking his mind back to their encounter with the woman, Luke cannot seem to shake a certain loneliness that he saw within her eyes.

"She reminded me... of myself."

Chapter 6: Deep Desires

D eep underground, within a vast catacomb of long and winding tunnels, a dark lair can be found. The air is thick and foul - enough to poison the average man. Along the haunting walls, slithering insects scuttle up and down each surface, as the sound of chilling howls can be heard from various corners.

Within the centre, seated on a large black chair, an old and frail man can be seen. Body wrapped in dirtied wool, he holds a weak and desperate look - sporting long, tattered white hair that covers his forehead and eyes. Nails long and full of dirt, the man stays almost motionless, with only his blinking eyes to show any signs of life. Each breath he takes is painful, and to move but an inch would be the equivalent of moving a mountain. An ocean of regret and resentment drowns him - yet as he curses his existence, the man's will refuses to give in.

A dark portal appears in front of the seated man. Before his lonely eyes, a single wizard appears from within - bearing a golden staff, along with a crown made of thorns. Holding a sinister grin for many quiet seconds, the wizard kneels before the man and greets him.

"My lord... I have returned. I, Phantom the Wizard King of Despair have come to report on my progress."

The weak man's eyes widen by only an inch, as though intrigued to hear of the wizard's work.

"The country of Veritas will almost soon be enveloped by my monsters. It will only take a few more days for the capital to fall. I shall personally watch Spiritus crumble. Once Veritas is gone, I shall head to the upper country of Superbia, where our true goal resides. Are you not pleased, my lord?"

The old man takes a deep breath, and with a strained voice replies "how long... how long until you find the Apex Grail?"

"It is not simply a question of finding the Grail. After all, we know that it is being housed in the powerful city of Ergo, the capital of Superbia. Breaking their defences has always been the main problem. However, this time we will not fail... not this time."

Tilting his head before gazing up at the moist ceiling, the seated man speaks in a vengeful tone that betrays his soft gaze.

"How I await the beautiful night... when I shall lay my hands on the cursed Apex Grail. Words can not express how long I have waited to seek my revenge and to kill that wretched woman!"

The next morning arrives in the form of a hot and humid day. Emerging out from a small cave for the night, Luke greets the sun and bright sky. Already wiping a trail of sweat from his forehead from the heat, the boy glances back to find his friend who is still fast asleep.

"Jeez... Umbra is quite the deep sleeper. If I don't wake him, he'll probably stay sleeping for hours. I guess I'll give him a few more moments until then."

Glancing in front, Luke lays his eyes on a small pond. The sight fills him with relief at the prospect of sampling but a sip of cool dew to counter the unbearable heat. With haste, he approaches and kneels. With delight, he plunges his head into the pond. As he does, the boy instantly pulls his head upholding a look of disappointment.

"This water... it's warm."

As he lets out a deflated sigh, the voice of a familiar woman intrudes "haha, you should be grateful to have come across a pond, to begin with. If the goddess who nurtures this area heard your moans, she would be most upset."

Turning to his right-hand side, Luke gasps at the sight of Diana the blue moon goddess once more. Although he has become accustomed to her visits, the beauty and majesty she exudes never fails to overwhelm the boy. Sitting beside him, she takes a deep breath while looking at the pond with him. Side by side, they admire the pond and the busy insects that occupy it. A spirit of peace flows between the goddess and herald, like a mother and son under a blessed morning.

"So... how are things?"

"Well... not much has changed since yesterday. Well actually, Umbra and I did come across an interesting lady. She was strong and beautiful. However, something about her seemed familiar."

"Hmm... it sounds like you have a crush."

Blushing - the boy turns away and responds "no that's not it. It's nothing like that..."

"I am just playing. I am sure you can find many similarities with others, Luke. You have an empathy about you that is unlike most other humans in this world. Oh, before I get sidetracked... there was something I wanted to tell you."

Holding his breath, awaiting whatever the goddess hopes to reveal, Luke watches in anticipation as Diana smiles.

"Your sister has been eagerly awaiting your return. Every day so far she has been glued to the window, hoping to see you again."

"Sister? I don't have a…"

Stopping himself, the boy glares with surprise - reminded of his new sibling. Smiling with joy, he leans forward and asks "Rose is waiting for me? Wait, how do you know that?"

"I know because I went to check up on her. She spends almost every day and night looking out the window, talking to herself as though she were talking to you. The girl cares deeply for you."

Slumping backwards while taking a deep breath, Luke's heart grows warm with a feeling of comfort. To hear the words said by the goddess eases his soul, to the point where he could almost cry.

"My new sister… she is thinking of me."

"She sure is. So, if you want don't want to make her sad, hurry up and get rid of that troublesome wizard and his minions. The sooner you do that, the sooner you can get what you want… a family."

Wasting no time, the boy springs to his feet - filled with a renewed sense of drive and purpose. Looking up at the bright sun, he holds a firm smile while the goddess continues to sit - marvelling at his ambitious eyes.

"I won't fail. I will stop that wizard and then return to Rose, to live like everybody else. However, there was something I have been meaning to ask you. Why is the wizard doing this and what for?"

Caught off guard by his enquiry, the goddess flinches with surprise - staring wide-eyed at the boy for many short but noticeably awkward moments. Before she attempts to respond, the voice of the troublesome vampire breaks their interaction.

"Good morning boys and girls! God, it's mighty hot today!"

Watching as Umbra emerges from the cave, the goddess rolls her eyes and says to Luke "you should try asking your new friend. Now run along. Although the advancement of the monsters shows no signs of stopping, you have almost reached the capital city of Spiritus. The sooner you can assist them, the better."

"Right, we'll leave now then" states Luke, before saying to the vampire "come on umbra. Let's make haste!"

"What? But I've only just woken up. Could you not give me a few hours or so to at least eat breakfast?"

"We don't have the luxury of a few hours. We'll eat along the way!"

The two bicker as they stroll into the distance - leaving the blue moon goddess by the peaceful pond - kept company by the butterflies that dance above it.

At that moment, a violent wind blows through the area, and the pond begins to sway as a figure emerges from the water, before Diana's eyes. Lower body wrapped in fine cloth, holding a gourd under her right arm, the emerged figure is a female goddess bearing long flowing hair. Standing upon the water itself, she holds a bothered and stone-faced expression.

An air of hostility exudes from the deity of the pond, as she proceeds to ask "Diana… why are you lying to the young mortal?" Her voice is grand and numerous - akin to multiple tides of a fierce and raging sea. However, as mighty as her tone is portrayed, the moon goddess stands unthreatened, like a cocky adolescent in the presence of an elder.

With a confrontational rebuttal, Diana responds "good morning to you, Coventina. A simple greeting would have been nice."

"You don't deserve any pleasantries. You know as well as I do, that the boy will never be able to live a normal life. You are leading him on with false promises, all for the sake of your desires. Do you wish to be hated by yet another mortal, the same way Solomon ended up detesting you?"

Standing to her feet, Diana grows angry and rants "silence Coventina! Some sacrifices are necessary, and the boy will be no exception. At least I am doing something to prevent another Divine War from occurring. What are you doing? What have you ever done besides watch from the sidelines in the luxury of your useless pond!"

The blue gaze of the moon goddess is sharp and unwavering - causing the water goddess to step back with intimidation. Like two fighters in an arena, they are watched by the flowers and fluttering butterflies around them.

Taking a deep breath - surrendering to the goddess of the moon, Coventina begins to descend back into the pond, leaving a final farewell.

"Diana, you have learned nothing."

Disappearing into the water - Diana is left alone. Her facade of strength falls as she glances to the ground, now overcome with an air of shame.

"That may be true... but I am doing this for the greater good."

Travelling through the plains of Veritas, the duo continue their journey under the intense heat. With a grumpy Vampire leading the way, Luke follows behind.

"Umbra, you're not still annoyed with me are you?"

"Of course I am. I haven't even had a chance to tuck into one of my delicious goblin sandwiches or stews. You are becoming quite the slave driver!"

"No, it's just that I don't want to waste any time at all. Besides, don't you ever grow tired of those sandwiches? You have given yourself food poisoning, more times than I can count."

Stopping before spinning around to face the young hero, Umbra leans forward and replies "well it's my immortal life, not yours. It is not my fault that you humans only have one life to worry about. At this rate, I'll probably die of starvation... thanks to you!"

Carrying onwards, the vampire stomps his feet as Luke tries his best to hold in his laughter. Whether happy, sad, angered or insulted, the expressive vampire always seems to put a smile on the young boy's face.

∞∞∞

A further hour or so passes, and the intensity of the heat begins to wane as a refreshing breeze overcomes the land. As they continue, Luke's mind is taken to the mysterious wizard and his motives.

"Hey Umbra, can I ask you something?"

"No, leave me alone."

"Oh come on. It is just one question. What do you know of the wizard and his motives? I figured someone as smart as you must know something."

Slowing his pace, the vampire produces a somewhat concerned sigh before looking up at the clouds.

"So, you wish to know of Phantom: Wizard King of Despair. Ok, I will tell you everything I know and what I think he is after. About one hundred years ago, that god awful wizard appeared. He wielded powerful magic that crippled kingdoms and he led an army of monsters that he would summon over the lands. Not only was he known for causing destruction, but he was also said to be utterly detestable. Part of his magic allows him to peer into the hearts and souls of his foes - reading their thoughts, fears and deepest desires. Once read, it is said that he would kill loved ones belonging to his adversaries, for mere sport."

Flinching with surprise, Luke is overwhelmed by what he hears of the detestable wizard King. He struggles to understand why such a person would want to cause such pain and suffering. Umbra continues - watched by the setting sun.

"You see, Phantom was on a rampage. He was trying to obtain... The Apex Grail."

"The what?"

As unfamiliar as the name sounds, the young boy cannot help but feel a sense of weight and grandness, based on the tone of Umbra's words. Luke stops in his tracks, signalling for his friend to explain further. As a small howl of the wind sings, the vampire crosses his arms and feeds his curiosity.

"The Apex Grail is the most powerful relic in existence. It was the last thing the gods left to mankind before they departed."

"I don't get it. Why did they create it in the first place and what is so special about it?"

"Your guess is as good as mine. Whatever power is stored within the Grail, Phantom had set his sights upon it. Fortunately, he was defeated, by the combined might of Veritas and Superbia before being imprisoned within a sleeping volcano, where he was said to remain for eternity. Now that he is free, it is only logical that he would seek revenge and resume his scheme once more. I am afraid that is all I can tell you. The wizard is a dangerous mystery."

Questions race through Luke's mind as a wave of fear overcomes him. Just who is the wizard and why does he seek the Apex Grail? Why does he delight in suffering so much? What power is contained within the Apex Grail and why did the gods create it?

"Umbra, do you know where the Apex Grail is?"

"Yes, I do. It resides in the country of Superbia, within the capital city of Ergo, protected by its invincible knights. My guess is, once the wizard is done here in Veritas, he will attack Superbia."

"Damn that awful wizard... all for the sake of one stupid item. The next time I get the chance to face him, I am gonna look him right in the eyes and..."

Stopping his words, Umbra steps forward and covers Luke's mouth with a single fingertip and says "don't do that. Have you not been listening? The worst thing you could do is look him directly in the eyes. If you do that, he will know everything about you."

"I don't care. I already died once by his hand, so it's not like he could do any worse. There is nothing he could know about me that would cause me harm" Luke responds - swatting away the hand of his friend. A sad look overcomes the vampire - one that the young hero does not quite understand.

Stepping past the black-suited boy, Luke leads in front, holding a dedicated gaze ahead while the vampire stands still - watching the back of his friend. As the blue moon emerges from behind the clouds, Umbra whispers to himself - pitying his friend in the distance. "Now I know why that cruel goddess chose someone as naive as you to become her latest herald. You are kind but, you are the most foolish human I have ever met. Words can not express the amount of pain that will soon befall you... my friend."

∞ ∞ ∞

With the sun fully set, a dark and chilly night arrives. Having made much progress, the pair arrive at the start of a thick and large forest.

"Oh wow - it looks like our only way forward is through this treacherous looking forest, right Luke? I must say, it isn't the best time to venture into it, especially with the threat of monsters around. Who knows what could be in there."

"If it's the fastest way to get to Spiritus, then we must go through it - regardless of what dangers may lurk within."

"How did I know that you would say something like that. Very well. Don't come crying to me later when things take a wrong turn, haha."

Catching his gaze, Luke notices traces of white feathers on the dark ground in front - trailing deep into the forest. Kneeling to inspect it, the boy cannot shake the feeling that he has seen the feathers once before. Closing his eyes, he allows his mind to suggest a theory and significance of the peculiar sight. Like a light bulb switching on, he stands and shouts.

"That's it! These feathers are from the unicorn that we encountered with that warrior: Aurora. I am sure of it."

"You must be joking, right? Do you mean to tell me that the Stigma bully is somewhere in the forest too? Oh, I do hope she has been gobbled up by some monstrous gargoyle or something."

Breaking their conversation, a mighty roar rips through the air - disrupting the trees and shaking the very earth. A flock of birds can be seen escaping the forest - soaring madly into the night sky for safety. The sound seems to come from within the forest itself - filling the pair with a jolt of fear that almost causes their hearts to leap out of their chests.

Forcing himself to breathe, Luke glares at his friend for answers while the hairs on the back of their necks stay upright. "What in the world was that just now?"

"It sounds like a monster, a very powerful one at that. I guess that the woman has attempted to slay a beast."

A debate takes place within the boy - one that has constantly stopped and started for many years of his life. The debate of his heart and mind quarrels once more, this time as to whether he should enter the forest or retreat. The many pools of sweat that trail down his every pore begs him to flee. After all, the roar from the beast is greater than anything he has ever heard. By the sound of it, the monster could easily be much larger than the cyclops he had encountered before. Not to be intimidated, his gut becomes heavy, like an unmovable statue that refuses to allow him to run away. After all, he possesses the power of the blue moon, a legendary force bestowed upon by the goddess. Thoughts of victory are clouded by fears of defeat, and as his bodily tussle rages on - a gentle hand is placed upon his shoulder.

"Come on, let's assist the warrior together" utters Umbra, in a tone that is enough to ease Luke's worries. "You don't need to struggle alone. I will be with you" he adds - displaying a smile that is enough to brighten the very night. An aura of companionship washes over the young hero, so much that it is almost overwhelming - quieting his inner conflicts.

"Thank you. Ok... let's go..."

Upon a burst of light, Luke summons his invincible armour. And as the light disappears into the sky, the blue knight takes a mighty step forward and races bravely into the forest - ready to aid the lone warrior.

Chapter 7: Higher than Hope

D eep within the dark forest, where the trees are tall and ominous, the very light of the blue moon is blotted out. The leaves tremble and flutter, due to more than just the wind. A deadly presence has made the forest an abode, causing the fowls of the air to soar away desperately. Upon the ground, the squirrels and rabbits flee with terror, as the insects follow suit like a mass exodus.

Despite the unknowing threat, a single woman runs fearlessly towards the centre of the disturbance - riding upon her trusty steed. Sporting a dazzling white fur coat, she tears through the wind as her long golden hair flows behind. Her unicorn steed possesses a natural glow, like a wondrous firefly in the night that gallops bravely.

Sporting her left eyepatch, the woman bears a determined gaze - overcome with panic.

"We must make it in time!" she proclaims - growing even

more worried by the second. The cause for her concern is due to recent news. The local villagers reported a kidnapping by a ferocious monster. A pair of adults had been snatched away by a beast that has been said to delight in torturing its victims slowly. Naturally, the woman's sense of morale refuses to allow an innocent person to suffer. However recently, her sense of justice has begun to wane.

As a Stigma Child, her existence is both envied and feared. For far too long she has gotten used to the same result, regardless of a civilian's safety. In the end, they have always found a reason to detest her. She knows this story far too well, and yet there is something inside her that wants to believe that this time will be different.

"Pick up the pace, Starlight..." she pleads to her steed - breaking a sweat upon feeling many eyes upon her. "Damn... we are being followed."

Her instinctive guess is correct, for within the trees she spots dozens of shadowy figures, swinging from tree to tree - gazing at her with deep and deformed eyes. The figures resemble that of apes. However, they bear six ghastly arms that help them pounce from tree to tree. As they stay hot on the trail of the woman, the monsters let out cackles and hungry moans.

Drawing her straight sword - Aurora holds her weapon high, just as a glimmer of moonlight pierces through the trees causing the blade to shine amidst the dark woods. Showing not an ounce of fear, she shouts to the beasts "accursed creatures. None of you shall stop me!"

At that moment, the enemies leap into the open to attack. Some come from above while others from below. Sword held tightly, the warrior swings her sword in a zigzag motion - faster than the naked eye. Within seconds the monstrous apes fall to many pieces, as their limbs are cut down - resulting in a shower of blood to tarnish the surroundings. Remarkably, as their blood showers the ground, leaves and trees, not a single droplet touches the woman and her steed - a testament to her unrivalled swordsmanship.

"Weaklings. Your cries will have better luck reaching me than your claws ever will!"

She carries on, sensing the unsettling presence coming closer. "Get ready Starlight. Our target is just up ahead!"

Leaping over one last bush, the woman and steed find themselves in a large open meadow, flourishing with white roses. With no trees to obstruct it, the blue moon above shines bright and bold - illuminating the meadow with its light. The sweet and fresh scent from the roses is pleasant. However, the domain belies a sense of thick dread in the air.

Before her eyes, Aurora finds the two kidnapped men, huddled together in the centre - afraid but very much alive. A sigh of relief is produced from the woman, who whispers "thank the gods and heavens..."

Suddenly - before she can rest easy, a great stomp is heard which causes the ground to shake and flowers to dance skyward. Another stomp arrives as the sound grows nearer. Coming off from her steed, the warrior holds her sword in both hands - watching as hundreds of monstrous apes step into the opening, as though leading a ceremony. The loud thud halts and an air of suspense covers the area.

At that moment, a humongous ape much larger than the rest steps into the meadow. Like its minions it possesses six gigantic arms and hands as it peers down at the helpless men, licking its lips like a hungry child whose dinner has finally arrived. The tall ape bears red skin in contrast to the darker underlings, who kneel before it like it were a king.

Aurora stands cautiously and whispers "god damn these fiends. They seem to come in almost all shapes and sizes. It looks like I will need to use my full power to beat the red one."

Reaching to her face, the woman prepares to untie her left eyepatch. The covering itself is more than just for show, for behind it lies the true power of a Stigma Child. For all Stigma individuals, an exposed left eye unleashes a temporary boost in power. It is what those around them have always feared. Even now in such a crucial moment, Aurora hesitates as all her previous experiences of being shunned and hated come flooding into her mind. What if after saving the men, they turn around and ridicule her? It wouldn't be the first time something like that would happen. Opting for a safer approach, she decides to keep her eyepatch fastened before turning to her trusty steed.

"Starlight - blind our foes!"

By her command, the unicorn lets out a great shout - standing on its hind legs. Like magic, its single horn flashes before emitting an intense light that is so great, that the apes including their leader cover their eyes.

"Now is my chance!" she blurts out - racing towards the terrified men while the sounds of the screaming monsters fill the forest. Rather than fight the gigantic foe with a taboo power that would bring judgment from the innocent pair, she instead plans to simply flee with the men. Approaching the kidnapped males, she holds her hand outward.

"I have come to get you out from this place. Quickly, while the creatures are disoriented, come with me and we shall ride out of here!"

The two look at the woman as though she were an angel - basked in the moonlight with her striking gold hair. Their eyes light up with relief as one of them proceeds to ask "is this for real? Have you come to save us?"

"Yes, so quit stalling with your mouths wide open and come with me!"

"Ok..."

The first man attempts to reciprocate her help by reaching out to hold her arm. However, the second man stops him and says "wait, don't do it. I have seen many like this before. Golden hair and an eye covering? She must be a Stigma Child... a monster... a freak!"

Her heart stops - eyes wide with pain upon being struck by the volley of words that have always haunted her. Even while choosing the safest plan, she has still received insults and rejection. Refusing to back down, she shouts to the pair with frustration.

"Now is not the time to embrace your stupid preconceived ideas. The real monsters will soon regain their vision again, and once they do they will be angrier than ever. Come on!"

"Get away from us!" Swatting her helping hand away, the pair attempt to escape from both her and the monsters who are already beginning to see again. As the men run desperately, tripping over themselves in a pitiful break for freedom, the woman stands on the spot - taken back by their foolish choice.

"Even when offered help, they still push me away. I am damned if I do and damned if I don't. Why... why me?"

Head held low, she stares into space as the sounds of monsters increase around her. They are angry and more violent than ever.

"Am I really what they say I am? Am I no different from a monster?"

Suddenly, the sound of shattered bones and torn flesh fills her ears, signalling for the warrior to lift her head. Gazing in front, she sees the corpses of the two villagers on the bloody ground next to the largest ape, who now bears eyes of fury. As expected, their fate was sealed the moment they tried to escape without her help. Holding a defenceless stance, she slips further into doubt.

"They would rather die than accept my help. Perhaps I have been deluding myself all this time. I thought that I could prove to everybody that I was more than just a freak of nature, by being a defender of justice. However, what's the point if nobody even wants me to save them? What am I fighting for?"

Dropping her weapon, Aurora loses the will to fight as the gigantic ape reaches forth to grab hold of her. She moves not an inch, and surrounded by the cheering minions the woman is scooped up and held tightly to the sky, like a prized possession.

Amidst the frenzy of roaring apes, she pleads to the monster that has caught her in its grasp, "go on, kill me. I have nothing left to live for anyway."

Increasing its hold, the red ape slams her to the ground,

destroying the meadow of flowers. The underling monsters clap and cheer as the woman lets out a painful scream - blood oozing from her face. Held in the clutches of the monster, Aurora spots her unicorn steed - standing a short pace away. Wondering why it hasn't fled, she calls out to it.

"Why are you still here? Go on Starlight... fly away. I am no longer your rider. I don't want to live anymore."

Refusing to obey her order, the unicorn stands fast, keeping its eyes locked on her as she is lifted high into the sky once again. As the beast holds her above, ready to give her one final crush, Aurora looks to the blue moon and bids farewell to someone special.

"I am sorry Yohan. I wasn't able to find peace."

Suddenly when all seems lost, the sound of a blade can be heard chiming into the meadow. The woman feels the grip around her loosen, as she falls to the ground, not knowing why. Before she has any time to react, Aurora is caught in mid-air by a pair of small and warm hands. Upon landing on the ground, she opens her eyes - finding her rescuer to be the black-caped vampire, Umbra.

"Well, that was a close call, teehee!"

"Who are you? Wait... you're that annoying demon from yesterday. What are you doing here?"

"My kind-hearted friend and I spotted the trail from your unicorn and came to investigate. Little did we know that this forest would be subject to such large numbers of cretins."

Looking directly in front, the woman finds the blue knight, standing back turned while holding his bright and glowing claymore sword. By his feet lies the gigantic arm of the red ape - proof that he was the one who broke the tight hold it had on the warrior. As his white cape blows through the wind, Blue

Lunar glances back to address the woman, while the monster apes stay shocked by the duo.

"Are you ok? I hope you're not hurt? I came as quickly as I could."

Baffled by his words, the woman stares with confusion - wondering why the boy would so much as think about her wellbeing. Breaking the silence, the gigantic ape produces a harsh roar - signalling for its minions to attack the trio and like a stampede, they charge from all sides. Surrounded, the blue hero holds his sword tight as his partner in crime stands cheerfully with his briefcase of cutlery, watched by the woman who continues to lay injured on the ground.

"Haha...the odds look very much stacked against us, wouldn't you agree Luke?"

"Yes, it does. Even so... we are not gonna lose any more lives this night. We will all make it out alive!"

Together the duo take on the horde of six armed apes, watched by the leader who stands afar, roaring profusely. With his mighty sword, Blue Lunar cuts each foe with a single swipe - standing protectively in front of the helpless warrior. Covering their backs, the chuckling vampire throws dozens of knives that pierce the skulls of the beasts. As they fight for their lives amidst the chaotic meadow, Aurora screams to the helpers.

"What are you idiots doing? Leave me alone and let me die. I have nothing left to live for. The world doesn't want me. The world doesn't need a freak like me!"

Dancing through the night, Umbra continues to take down numerous monsters while responding to the woman "have I heard you correctly? Why would such a formidable person like yourself wish to lose the only life she has, let alone care about what the world thinks of her?"

"You wouldn't understand. No matter how much I try... nobody ever wants to get close to me. They would rather risk death than accept my help!"

Overwhelmed yet not willing to give up, the blue hero stabs

and cuts through the many enemies - hearing the lady's woes while also responding to her. "I know exactly how you feel. Nobody ever wanted to get close to me either, for being an orphan. I didn't think anybody would accept me until I met people like Rose and Umbra. As much as some may dislike you, others in this world will... so don't give up on yourself!"

"What the hell do you know, boy? Just because you might have been lucky, doesn't mean that I will. Not a single person has liked me for being a Stigma Child!"

Cutting down the last of the lesser apes, Umbra and the blue knight prevail against the horde - leaving only the monster who stands astounded with fear.

Facing the direction of the final ape, Blue Lunar responds to the woman and says "well, I guess I'll be the first person to tell you that I think you're amazing. The goddess of the blue moon has promised me a normal life, once I defeat the wizard. You can stay with us, once this is all over!"

Channelling his emotions into his sword, the blue hero takes a deep breath before slowly raising his weapon to the heavens. An immense build-up of energy and light swirls around the blade - causing the flowers and nearby leaves to scatter into the distance. Surrounded by the light, Blue Lunar intends to finish off the petrified monster, the same way he did to the four cyclops previously.

Behind the knight, Umbra stands with an excited gaze - squinting his eyes from the intensity. "Magnificent..." he whispers.

Eyes wide with wonder and shock - Aurora can not take her eyes off the sight that is before her. The boy who she passed off as a mere nuisance is now the centre of her fascination and intrigue. The meadow continues to grow brighter like the sun, as the boy channels every last emotion he can think of into his sword.

"We will succeed!" He shouts before swinging his glowing sword downward - releasing all its power. Like a tsunami of energy, a mighty burst of blue light is fired directly at the last remaining foe. The monster's screams can barely be heard as it is instantly engulfed by the light and obliterated in an instant. An explosion of stardust erupts as a result, while the released ray of energy continues tearing through the rest of the forest, mowing down countless trees in its wake. Like a wondrous rod of the gods, the invincible projectile trails off into the night sky, where it resembles a fleeing star.

∞∞∞

Completely gobsmacked by the power displayed, the three stand speechless - frozen under the now quiet night. They stand silent for many moments - in awe at the aftermath of the weapon.

Looking down at his sword, the boy marvels as the blade continues to pulsate with energy. Held loosely within his hands, he absorbs the aura that flows from it - coming to a startling discovery.

"These are... these are my feelings."

∞∞∞

Within moments, Luke's suit and sword disappear into particles of light. Breathing a sigh of relief, the young hero looks up at the moon - hearing the already returning sounds of pleasant wildlife. Like a song of victory, the tweeting birds fill his ears alongside the accompanying melody of crickets.

Upon a single step forward, the vampire proclaims "spectacular my friend. I have never seen such a wonderful display of heroism!"

"Thank you umbra. However, I couldn't have succeeded without your help. For a moment there, I didn't think we'd make it."

Interrupting the duo - the lone warrior Aurora strolls to her rescuers. Eyes focused only on Luke, she holds her silence as he does the same - bracing himself for whatever is ready to leave her lips. To his surprise, the lady emits a warm and appreciative smile.

"Thank you, boy. Not in a million years would I have imagined that a kid would give me a reason for living. Thanks to you, I have the strength to go on. Please, allow me to be your sword and fight by your side."

Pausing with astonishment, the young lad's eyes light up with joy. Upon a short chuckle, he bows his head in an embarrassed and overwhelmed fashion, before responding "it would be my pleasure to have you with us. My name is Luke, and this here is my friend Umbra."

"Nice to meet you both. I am Aurora, and that steed over there is..."

Turning to the direction of her four-legged companion, Aurora readies to introduce her trusty unicorn to the pair. However, before she can do anything, she notices the steed expanding its wings, ready to take flight.

"Starlight? Starlight... what are you doing?"

A sad feeling overcomes her, as she watches the horse depart the forest and ascend into the night sky - leaving the woman behind.

"Starlight no, don't go. Come back..." she cries as tears emerge from her eyes. However, her companion does not halt and continues soaring through the stars.

"Why is she going away?" Luke asks, standing beside the woman. Taking a short moment to compose herself, Aurora slowly dries her eyes and replies softly.

Unlike all other steeds, a unicorn is never chosen by an owner. It is the unicorn who chooses its master. To maintain their trust, one must show unwavering resolve at all times. When I briefly lost the will to fight, I broke her trust and thus lost the right to be her rider."

Chiming in, the grinning vampire adds "the bond of a unicorn is said to be the strongest and yet most delicate. Such an alluring creature indeed."

Accepting her fault, Aurora lifts her head high and says "it's ok... I can handle it. It was an honour to be her master while it lasted. Goodbye Starlight. Thank you for blessing me with your companionship. May your travels be safe and prosperous.

∞∞∞

Later that night, resting under the sheets of her room, the sister of the blue hero can be seen looking at the starry night through the window. Safe within the mansion of Armley, she embraces the peaceful and quiet night - watching a shooting star fly by her line of sight. The fleeting wonder of the night fills her with unexplainable feelings of hope and comfort.

"A shooting star? So beautiful... I have never seen one quite like that before. Oh, am I not supposed to make a wish right now?"

Climbing out of bed, she tiptoes to the window - careful not to wake the others who are fast asleep in the other rooms of the mansion. Leaning against the window, feeling the coldness of the glass against her warm hands, she peers up at the sky - hoping to catch the tail end of the shooting star.

Upon a deflated sigh she whispers "I missed it", losing the once in a lifetime chance to wish upon a star. Not to be deterred, she holds a smile and says "it doesn't matter. I don't need a star to make my wish come true."

Holding her hands together, Rose closes her eyes and makes a prayer. With nothing but the singing crickets and hooting owl in the background, she remains still and calm - offering the words of her soul to every last god and goddess she can think of.

Reopening her eyes, she takes a deep breath and says "there... I did it. Stay safe, my dear brother."

Chapter 8: Companions

M iles across the land, the young hero and his two companions can be found sitting around a campfire. Small snowflakes begin to fall from the night sky - warning of a change in season. The night is cold, much colder than any other night as of late, causing the three to routinely hover their hands over the fire to keep warm. As the satisfying sound of snapping sticks under the flames fills their ears, Luke and Umbra explain their current situation to Aurora.

Understanding their predicament, she expresses "that is quite a series of events. You are the herald of the goddess Diana and are tasked with stopping the wizard Phantom. I suspected that a magic-user of some kind was behind the recent events, but I never would have imagined it would be him. What I'd like to know is, who released him in the first place and how? The chains that had bound him were enchanted with the strongest magic there is. It would have taken a god to release him."

"Well, perhaps the enchantment ran out of juice? We all know how pathetic humans are at using magic!" Umbra taunts - frustrating the golden-haired warrior.

"Don't speak such nonsense, silly demon. Honestly, the type of things that come out from your mouth is so infuriating."

"Well, at least I've bothered to think of something. You could learn a thing or two from my way of thinking, silly succubus."

"What did you just call me? Say that again and I'll make mincemeat out of you!"

Interrupting the pair, Luke says "wait... Perhaps both of you have a point? What if the chains were indeed broken by a god? I mean, gods do you exist after all?"

Immediately shaking her head as though his suggestion were more absurd than Umbra's, the lady replies "no... what the hell is wrong you numbskulls? That would be impossible, for the Apex Grail doesn't allow it. Did you not learn that in school?"

Blinking with surprise and revelation, Luke leans forward and asks "why is it impossible and what does it have to do with the Apex Grail?"

"The Apex Grail is a negator. Because of it, we mortals are unable to see the gods and goddesses, let alone interact with them. As long as the Apex Grail exists, the gods cannot tamper with the affairs of our world. That goes for breaking enchanted chains."

Biting his fingernail with frustration, the young hero remains at a loss as Aurora rolls her eyes, exhausted with the conversation. Whispering to himself, Luke says "perhaps I should ask Diana the next time I see her."

Tossing a nearby stick into the fire, the cheerful vampire smiles at the woman and asks "hmmm... I've been meaning to ask you something. You are supposed to be the lead knight of Superbia, the country just above Veritas, correct?"

"Yeah, so what?"

"Well, what are you doing down south? The country of Superbia is quite far from here you know."

"You ask far too many questions, demon."

Ignoring his enquiry, the woman stares into the flames of the fire - becoming lost in its hypnotic and soothing flow. Realising that Luke too is awaiting a response from her, she takes a deep breath and replies.

"Very well. I indeed used to fight as a knight of Ergo, Superbia. My brother and I grew up there. A couple of years ago, a large division of soldiers decided to stage a coup to overthrow our king. There had been much resentment within the ranks of our knights who had blamed certain past famines and poverty on the ruling class. The majority of knights supported the coup - coming to a number of around seventy per cent. I wasn't part of the majority and was against the plan."

Eyes widened with interest, both boys sit with mouths opened wide like kids being told a bedtime story. With each word said, Umbra and Luke lean forward more and more.

"So... what happened then?" Asks the young hero, heart ready to leap from his chest.

With a look of sorrow and soullessness, Aurora replies "I stopped them. To maintain order within the capital city of Ergo and Superbia as a whole, I killed my former comrades... all of them."

Crossing his arms, the black-suited companion looks upward as though remembering something.

"So that explains it. About two years ago I had heard some rumours about the strongest swordsman in the land, who slaughtered a bunch of soldiers that were planning a revolt. It was said that you unleashed the full power of your Stigma... untying that eye patch of yours before sweeping through your former comrades. You were said to have looked like a fiery Phoenix who singlehandedly..."

"That's enough!" Barks the woman - causing the pair to freeze with sudden fright. Standing up before stretching her arms, she continues "after the failed coup, things got a little too stressful for me, so I left my line duty and decided to travel around the land. Once I had heard about the monsters, I set out to find the root cause and here I am now."

Clapping like a toddler, Umbra cheers "Bravo! That was an amazing story. Now tell us another one!"

"Not a chance, demon. I am going to bed. See you all in the morning!"

Strolling away from the campfire, she leaves the pair. Sitting quietly as the snow begins to increase, Luke says to his friend "we sure have met an interesting person. She is a little intimidating, but I think she is nice underneath."

"Hmph, speak for yourself. I have never met anybody as grumpy as her!"

"That is rather rich, coming from you. Have you forgotten what you're like in the mornings?"

Jumping to his feet, the vampire gasps and responds "how dare you? I am nothing like that vile succubus. Anyways... I fancy a little midnight stroll. See you in the morning..."

At that moment, something about Luke's appearance catches the vampire by surprise. Blinking twice, Umbra pauses and asks "Luke, have you aged?"

Humoured by the friend's question, the hero replies "what kind of question is that?" Yet the look on the vampire's face holds a serious form. Amidst the now low flame of the campfire, Umbra strolls to Luke and points to his head.

"Your hair has turned grey. Some of the front."

"What? You gotta be kidding!"

Touching his front hair before pulling it to eye level, Luke indeed finds a handful of hair has become completely grey. "Why would only the front change?"

Portraying a carefree smile, the vampire shrugs his shoulders and says "who knows. This world is full of mysteries. I must say, it rather suits you, my friend. Goodnight for now."

Luke sleeps by the small fire while Umbra wanders through the night. He walks for some time, taking in the soothing solace of the quiet night. Eventually, he stops by the bank of a small and shallow stream - looking up at the sky. Like most of the inhabitants, the moon and stars have also retired for the night, making the vampire feel like the only one awake in the land. The moment is accurate to how he feels inside; a being who is woke to the truth of the world, yet surrounded by those who are still asleep.

"So... it looks like the countdown has already started. I wonder if the poor chap will ever figure things out...?"

Suddenly, a dark presence can be felt from behind Umbra, which makes the hairs on the back of his neck stand up. The presence is hostile and malevolent, which would bring most ordinary people to their knees.

Remaining still, back turned - the boy closes his eyes and says "oh, it would seem that I have company."

Behind him, a hooded figure appears. Facial features hidden by the shadows, the mysterious being bears glowing red eyes and a long tongue like a snake. Standing menacingly, the uninvited guest continues to allow its devilish aura to saturate the area. Not before long, it takes a single step forward and greets the lone vampire.

"Are you the one named Umbra?"

The boy glances at the being from the corner of his eye and replies "that all depends on what you came here for. It is not every day that I am met by a fellow demon. What is your business with me?"

"My master has sent me to get rid of a little pest. Your existence is a threat to his kingdom."

Letting out a small chuckle, the relaxed child closes his eyes once again and responds "my existence threatens his kingdom? Now why would anybody feel the need to get rid of a little old vampire like me?"

"Vampire? Don't insult me. You most certainly are not a

vampire!"

"Is that so? Well in that case, what am I?"

The foe does not answer. However, its lack of response is not deliberate. It stutters to provide an answer as though lost for words. Delighting in its struggles, Umbra presses on in a carefree manner.

"No answer? That is a shame. Perhaps you can answer something else then. Just who is your master?"

"Silence! You are not in a position to be requesting information from me. In case you haven't noticed, your comrades are far and fast asleep. Nobody can save you."

Shrugging his shoulders, the boy responds "I guess you do have a point there. Not only have the succubus and crybaby retired for the night, but I am also without my briefcase. It really isn't my night tonight..."

Within seconds, the shadowy demon shoots forth a single claw from under its garment and like a torpedo it tears through Umbra's chest at lightning speed.

Blood bursts into the air like a fountain before showering the ground, as the demon's claw stays lodged halfway into the boy. Upon letting out a fatal gasp, the vampire falls to the ground as the demon retracts its arm like an elastic band. As the fiend watches the motionless boy tumble into the shallow stream, he gloats while looking up at the night.

"It is done. Lord Megethos will be most pleased. Farewell... fool."

Turning his back to the bloody scene before him, the mysterious demon disappears into the night - carrying its malevolent aura along with it.

Left for dead in the stream of bloodied water, Umbra's corpse remains still, murdered by the unknown demon. Many short moments pass and upon opening his eyes, the black-suited boy springs back to life - being the immortal that he is. With nothing but the sound of flowing water amidst the cool night, he sits upward and produces a cunning smile.

"Hmph, it is you who is the fool. Death is not something that is in my vocabulary" Umbra whispers, in response to the insult left behind by the already departed adversary. Sitting upward before coming to his feet, the boy stands alone and assumes a troubled gaze at the clouds - focused on a name that the enemy unknowingly let slip.

"Megethos. I thought as much. So, it seems that the demon prince of the underworld has finally awoken from his slumber. The Wizard is not our only problem in that case. We are up against an alliance of powerful forces at work."

The night soon comes to an end, bringing forth a dull morning. Due to the constant snow during the night, the land is now covered with thick snow. Having woken up early once again, the three have already begun trekking towards their destination. However - although Luke seems to be in high spirits, his two comrades are the complete opposite. Walking side by side along a tall hill, the young hero senses a mild resentment from his companions.

"Is something the matter, you two?" He says, to which the vampire ally turns to him and responds.

"Oh don't act clueless, Luke. You already know why I am in a foul mood this morning. It is far too early to be walking around now, especially in such cold weather!"

"Jeez, is that why you're upset with me? I already told you that we don't have much time. How about you Aurora? Are you annoyed at me too?"

Glancing at the boy with an even moodier look, the woman replies "yes I am. However, I am not angry because we have gotten up early, I wanted to wake up much earlier. In other words, we got up too late!"

Slapping his forehead with grief, Luke cannot help but

chuckle to himself and respond "so one of you is a night owl and the other is an early bird? I just can't win with you two, can I?"

Like a strict mother, the woman orders "just make sure tomorrow morning we get up much earlier. Time is of the essence!"

Butting in like an opposing father, the vampire points to the warrior and rants "hold it right there, miss bossyboots. There is no way in the seventh hell that I'd wake up any earlier than we did today!"

"Fine then, suit yourself. We will just have to leave you behind" taunts the female warrior.

"Leave me behind? Luke would never abandon me to go draping off with a vile succubus like you!"

Within seconds the two bicker - marching onwards while pointing fingers and hands into each other's faces. Their antics are a pleasant sight for Luke, amongst the grey and cold morning. Deliberately trailing behind, he observes them from the distance while playing with a single grey hair upon his head.

At that moment, the all too familiar presence of the blue moon goddess descends over the boy, causing him to expect her appearance anytime soon. Right on queue, she appears by his left side with a warm smile.

"Good morning my little hero. It is quite a cold day today, isn't it?"

"Good morning Diana. Yes, I have never seen so much snow."

In an effort to read her face, the boy wonders why she has appeared. From past interactions, their meetings have almost always involved a new revelation of some kind. Taking a deep breath, he prepares himself for her words - however, to his surprise she kindly asks "how are your new friends?"

Mildly caught off guard by her simple question, he pauses before thinking of his answer.

"Umbra and Aurora... they are great thanks. I don't think they are too fond of each other though, however it shouldn't be anything to worry about."

"That is good. Your journey stands an even better chance of success with the addition of the golden-haired warrior. You are also much closer to Spiritus than you think. Well done."

Her praise settles Luke's slightly anxious mind, warming his heart in the process. Such a comment makes the boy forget the severity of their predicament. However, it isn't long before the reality of the situation brings him down from the clouds - presenting to him many questions for the goddess.

"Diana, I have been meaning to ask you something. What do you know of the Apex Grail?"

Her smile drops, becoming a frown that suits the grey sky. As though holding back a strong reaction, she responds "how do you know about that?" In a tone that contains mild aggression. Sensing her discomfort, the boy replies as sincere as humanly possible.

"Well Umbra told me a little about it and Aurora explained what it does, although it was kinda hard to understand. We think the wizard is most likely after it, for what reason we don't know. Is it true that the grail prevents gods and humans from interacting?"

The woman pauses - mind drifting away as though warring with herself as to how to answer. Before the innocent hero, she juggles with potential replies, as the wind whistles patiently.

"Yes, that is correct. It is an item of tremendous power that we deities had created. The detestable wizard is willing to kill whoever he pleases just to obtain it. The Grail was made to sever the link between mortals and immortal beings as we believed this would ensure world peace. I don't know what he plans to do with it - however, I am certain that it will be for nothing noble."

Her words fill the boy with even more questions. If a goddess is unable to understand the reasons why the Apex Grail is so sought after, then what comfort and surety does that bring him?

Assuming a courageously forced smile, the boy says "in that

case, I'll just have to stop him and foil whatever plans he has. With Umbra and Aurora by my side I can't lose, right?"

Like a mother pretending to be overly interested in their child's hopes, the blue-eyed goddess responds "you got that right, my most powerful herald. Do you have any further questions?" She asks with a surprisingly patient grin. Her tone is inviting and warm, which encourages the boy to converse with her further.

As he plays with his hair, the young hero finds it the perfect time to ask "well, I noticed that my hair has changed. It is only a little but the front has turned grey. Would you know anything about that?" Turning to glance at the goddess, the young hero is stunned to find that she has disappeared in an instant, without so much as saying goodbye, let alone answering his question. An air of aversion and dishonesty overcomes him, which disturbs the boy. "There she goes again" he whispers.

"Come on slowpoke. We have reached Spiritus the capital city!" Shouts the golden-haired ally, causing the boy's eyes to light up. Running as though his feet had a mind of their own, he sprints through the snow to join his friends - heart racing with anticipation. Approaching the two as they hold a collective look of relief, Luke looks over the vast scenery and spots a great city not too far away.

Consisting of protective brick walls that are large and wide, numerous houses dwell inside. Situated in the centre, a large castle stands proud - beautifully white and glossy, like a beacon of hope.

"This is Spiritus. The monsters don't seem to have reached it yet. Thank heavens."

Overcome with emotion, the boy feels close to tears. He is overwhelmed - not knowing how to act or behave upon gazing upon his destination.

At that moment, the sound of chiming blades can be heard from behind the three. Instantly becoming on edge, the trio tense up as the voice of a soldier says "that is far enough. You are now under arrest!"

Chapter 9: A Sip of Despair

After a difficult journey, Luke and his two companions had finally reached their destination: The Capital City of Spiritus. However, their moment of relief was brief, for before they knew it, they found themselves under arrest by the imperial soldiers of Spiritus.

The soldiers gave no reason for their actions and quickly subdued the trio. As powerful as Luke and his friends are, they found it wise to not resist and instead comply with the men. It has now been many hours since their arrest, and upon being taken to a single prison cell within the castle walls, the three remain helpless and at a loss.

The walls of the prison are surprisingly clean and well kept -

a stark contrast to the images Luke had of a cell for criminals. Many candles hang on the corridor walls, which brighten the room they are in. Sitting on a small wooden bench, the young hero looks down with a troubled gaze, while Aurora lays on the cold ground, portraying a bothered body language. Leaning against the steel bars, Umbra cries with grief and has been doing so ever since being brought in.

"This is an outrage! Why are we being locked up like a bunch of ruffians? I demand to speak with a representative right now!" The vampire cries, amongst the echoed walls of the cell. Regardless of his protests, not a single soldier comes to their aid.

"Be quiet, pip-squeak. The soldiers are not gonna get here any faster with all that noise you're making. Just sit tight and be patient. I am sure they have a reason for their actions" the lady says - letting out a frustrated sigh.

Reluctantly the vampire listens to her words and folds his arms like a grumpy child. The walls are quiet for many moments as the three keep their thoughts to themselves, lest they make their situation any worse.

Unable to contain his worries, the young hero expresses "I wonder why they locked us down here? Do you think we did something wrong?"

Tutting as though having reached the limit of her frustration, the golden-haired ally sits upward and responds "we did nothing wrong. However, they don't know that and are cautious. They probably don't want to take any chances, seeing as the land has been overrun by monsters. It is nothing personal, even if their actions seem rather senseless."

"Oh, well in that case I guess I can sympathise with them a little. I am sure somebody will come and clear up this misunderstanding."

At that moment, a pair of footsteps can be heard coming from the distance. The trio instinctively face the steel bars - awaiting to see who has come to meet with them. As the steps grow nearer, they hear casual whistling coming from the oncoming individual, like a prison officer who is all too familiar with their duties.

Strolling into vision, the three find a single male soldier. He looks much older, perhaps in his late forties or fifties. Sporting fighting gear of brown leather armour, he possesses short blonde hair that looks to have been groomed for many hours. A cocky smile stays proudly on his face as he leans in to greet the prisoners.

"Sorry for making you wait kiddos. Things have gotten rather hairy lately. So, before I can consider setting you free, I am gonna need to hear you out."

Slamming her hand against the wall before stomping towards the steel bars, Aurora reaches through its gap and grabs hold of the man's collar. His smile remains, as though entertained by her actions, and as the two look into each other's eyes, Luke senses that the man and woman may have already been aquatinted.

"Don't act like such a cool hotshot, Gillberg. Hurry up and get us out of here! We don't have time to waste. Clearly you have heard about the monsters that have swarmed the land!"

"Of course I know, sunshine. I am the lead commander of the Spiritus knights, remember? You all were arrested because of what's been going on..." the man replies before brushing her firm grip from his collar. Pointing to the trio, one by one, he continues "after all, you are of the Stigma. It also doesn't help that you were found with a demon and rather innocent-looking chap with a strange marking on his forehead. You can't blame us for being cautious. We don't know what caused the sudden appearance of the monsters."

"Idiot - isn't it obvious who summoned the monsters? Phantom the wizard king of despair has been released and has come to bring down Veritus, possibly Superbia afterwards!"

Stepping back with sudden surprise, Gillberg pauses with silence upon hearing the woman's words. Watching their back and forth verbal tussle, Luke and Umbra observe quietly, wondering how the soldier will respond. Hoping that her revelation is enough to free them from the cell, Aurora breathes heavily with bated breath - oozing a subtle sigh.

"Hahahahaaaa!" laughs the man, slapping his stomach as though lost in a frenzy of humour. "You sure are funny, Sunshine. Have you gone mad? Everybody knows that the chains that bind Phantom are enchanted with the strongest magic there is - held within mount Bemba. Now I am definitely not gonna let you out, not until I get a proper story out of you. Nice try though."

"Wait... I am telling you the truth. Phantom is free and as long as he is released, we are all in danger!"

Turning his back to the heroes, the man prepares to depart and says "I expected better from the legendary knight of Superbia. How the mighty have fallen." Letting out a jolly whistle, the blond-haired knight strolls away and exits the prison area, leaving the three lost for words.

The reality of their situation begins to sink in even further - becoming one of the worst possible situations they could end up in. For Luke, the idea of being locked away in the prison of the county's capital city was not what he expected, let alone not being listened to. Looking to his lady companion for answers, he displays a worried look which only angers her even more.

"Stop looking like a pitiful puppy and get it together. It is not like we're about to be executed."

"I know but, what if we never get out of here?"

"Nonsense. We will get out of here eventually. Either through that idiot soldier or by force. In many ways, at least it's warmer down here than outside in the cold" Aurora says while coming away from the prison bars to lay down once again on the ground. Holding a wise gaze, the vampire chimes in.

"Hmmm, you and that man seem to know of one another. Might I say that you and he were once comrades?"

With a humoured chuckle, the woman responds "hardly. Gillberg was just an acquaintance who I had the misfortune of bumping into, on my travels. He is a cocky character who believes far too highly of himself. He has been jealous of my title as the strongest swordsman, which explains why he delights in keeping me locked down here right now."

Pondering her words, Umbra sighs "humans are a baffling bunch. Even though the land is on the brink of destruction, you still find time for jealously."

The trio remain within the cell, abiding their time while staring at the four walls in hopes that their situation changes.

∞ ∞ ∞

High above the city of Spiritus, amidst the snowy sky, a single individual materialises forth. Body covered from neck to toe by a purple cloak, a cackling man is seen levitating in mid-air. Upon his head, he wears a crown of thorns and within his hands, he holds a golden sceptre.

Within the city below, the inhabitants go about their daily routines, unaware of the uninvited guest that hangs within the sky. Their relaxed complacency fills the cloaked figure with unbridled excitement, and as the wizard of despair proceeds to hold his sceptre up high, he produces a bloodthirsty grin while cackling to the wind.

"We meet again… wretched Spiritus. One hundred years ago, you allied yourself with Superbia to imprison me. Now I am free, I will not allow the same unity to foil my long-awaited ambition. I will crush you before the gods can hear your prayers… Kwekekekeeee!"

By his command, Phantom summons forth a great and wide portal which envelops the city like a dome. The portal is dark and almost colourless, blotting out all light, akin to a dark eclipse.

It only takes a few seconds for the city folk to notice the dark magic that has encased them, resulting in a torrent of screams and panic that fill the city. Running in every direction possible, thousands of people can be seen racing to and fro - unable to understand the phenomenon around them, yet sensing something sinister at work. Above, the wizard's eyes widen with amusement, watching their actions as though they were mere insects.

"Kwekeke... it is too soon to be panicking just yet. The real fun is just beginning. Come forth my monsters!" He calls out, at which point an army of creatures emerge from the dark portal before descending into the snowy city. Their numbers are almost innumerable, falling from the sky like raindrops of terror before crashing onto streets, homes and structures.

The fiends waste no time hunting the city folk - killing and devouring the inhabitants. The once peaceful streets have now become a horrific bloodbath and mayhem, while its orchestrator remains above the carnage, proclaiming to the heavens "for love... for love... for love!"

Within the prison cell, the three companions grow alert as they hear the commotion outside.

"Do you all hear that? Something is going on!" Luke shouts - looking at his friends with panic.

Shrugging his shoulders as though not the least bit surprised, the vampire responds "well it is to be expected. The monsters were going to turn up sooner or later I suppose. The only problem is, we are locked down here."

"Not for long," says the already inconvenienced Aurora - approaching the steel bars before drawing her sword - blade singing upon its release. With an aggressively mighty tone, she says "I am through complying. We are gonna do this our way!" Cutting the bars with a clean horizontal swipe. The barriers collapse instantly - falling perfectly to the ground in unison. Pausing with astonishment, Luke and Umbra stand with mouths wide as she steps out of the cell. "Well... are you coming or not? We need to protect as many innocent lives as possible!"

Without stopping to wait for their response, the golden-haired ally races through the corridor, leaving the pair even more stunned. As the sound of destruction heightens in the background, Luke and Umbra stand with feelings of both excitement and dread.

"Well, you heard the succubus. It is time to join the fight" The vampire chuckles, also departing the prison cell before skipping into the distance.

Left alone, the young hero stands with a worried heart - overcome with a familiar kind of fear. The more he hears, the more he is reminded of his home town. "This feeling... it is just like back in Heline. It is the same as back then" he stutters, holding his hands together to keep them from trembling. Taking a deep breath, he struggles to compose himself and says "relax Luke... you are different now. You are stronger. I won't allow this city to fall like Heline because I am Blue Lunar!"

Striking his forehead with a burst of courage, the boy transforms into his knightly appearance. With his arm extended outward, he completes his arsenal by calling out "sword!" Summoning the blue claymore to his side. As he feels his body surging with strength, the hero's nerves disappear.

"I am ready for you... Phantom!" He says before hurrying to join his friends.

∞∞∞

The civilians continue to be massacred along with the many soldiers who have come to their aid. The knights fight desperately to protect their people from the monstrous creatures, however, their efforts fall short for they too are easily done away with. Blood flies from every direction like a nightmarish jubilee, where the cries of agony are music to the ears of a single wizard. Waltzing along a wide-open path, the menacing man makes his way towards the great white castle of Spiritus, which sits just over a dozen meters away. Cloak blowing elegantly behind with each footstep, his presence is like that of a dark messiah, stepping over dismembered bodies as his monsters run rampant. Eyes focused on the great castle doors that are locked tight, he reminisces of a time long gone.

"The house of Spiritus... oh how I have longed for this day. You brought this all upon yourself when you chose to interfere in matters that did not concern you. All I ever wanted was the one item that is housed in the land of Superbia. Yet, because of your meddling one hundred years ago, I was unable to claim it. By wiping out all trace of this city I can redeem myself, before heading to my ultimate destination... Kwekekekeee."

Upon reaching the footsteps of the castle, the wizard blinks with surprise at the sight of the brown knight Gillberg, wielding a long spear. As the man holds a fighting stance, standing protectively in front of the castle doors, he locks eyes with the grinning intruder who stands with a lofty posture. Both holding their silence for many seconds amidst the surrounding scenes of carnage, the man addresses the wizard with a nervous tone.

"You... how did you get here? You're not supposed to be free!"

With a calm and haughty demeanour, Phantom replies "if I were to tell you, would that make any difference to your own life? Even more so, would that save your people from destruction?"

His question carries an undertone of murderous intent, which sends shivers down the knight's spine. Even looking upon the sight of such a terrifying individual causes Gillberg to doubt his sanity. For some time, he had believed the wizard of despair was nothing more than a silly wives tale, told to frighten the young.

As the guest stands before him, he stutters "what is it you want from Spiritus? Is it the Apex Grail? The holy relic is housed within Ergo capital of Superbia, not here!"

"I am fully aware of that. I am merely here to kill you all for being such a nuisance one hundred years ago. Now, step aside and allow me to eliminate your King" says the cloaked wizard, before holding his sceptre in front.

Without explanation, Gilberg finds himself flung into the air by an invisible force. As quickly as he is brought up he is slammed down to the ground by the feet of the grinning wizard, as the force of the collision leaves a crater within the earth. Blood splatters forth due to the impact - leaving the blond-haired knight barely breathing.

Stepping over his broken and bloodied body, Phantom proceeds to waltz up the stairs of the castle entrance before stopping in front of its closed golden doors. Catching his attention one last time, the heavily injured Gillberg can be heard pleading to the wizard of despair.

"Please... spare this city. Don't destroy Spiritus... I beg of you..."

In response to his cries, Phantom lets out a wide yawn and stares into space as though lost in thought. From the outside, one may assume the wizard is perhaps reconsidering his actions, seeing as the sight of suffering and destruction would bring almost any human to repentance.

Ending his brief daydream, Phantom glances at the fallen knight and says "I think I've had a change of heart. I was going to let you suffer and watch as your city falls. Instead, I think I will feed you to my pets right now. Farewell."

Within seconds, a pack of monsters swarm over the knight and ravage him to pieces, filling the chaotic city with even more bloodshed. Limbs fly from left to right, while the wizard turns his attention to the gold plated doors of the white castle - feeling a sense of fulfilment.

"Open," he says to the doors, commanding yet again an invisible force to tear the front doors apart. With the castle open for entry, he steps forth elegantly like a guest star of a royal gala, along with his entourage seen behind.

∞∞∞

Within the castle walls, hundreds of Spiritus soldiers race back and forth through the vast quarters and corridors. As panic fills the air, three individuals are seen running together to challenge the monster threat outside.

Leading in front, the golden-haired Aurora displays a mighty and fearless gaze - blade in hand. Inches behind, the vampire and blue knight run alongside one another. With his trusty briefcase held underarm, Umbra portrays a curious face like an ever learning child - observing the unorganised formation of the soldiers as the sound of destruction carries on outside.

Maintaining a focused aura, Blue Lunar holds his divine sword in both hands. "These walls keep going on forever. Where is the exit?" Utters Luke.

"How should I know? This isn't my castle, genius!" Shouts Aurora, stopping abruptly to place her hand against a nearby wall. "Looks like we'll have to create our exit."

The boys glance at one another, preparing themselves for their newest companion's ideas which seem to become riskier than the next. In only such a short space of time, Luke has come to understand her habits. Unlike him, Aurora has no problem making her own rules. He admires such a trait, while at the same time is wary of it.

"What are you gonna do?" He asks.

Turning to him, the woman replies "well isn't it obvious? I am going to smash this wall down so we can get out of this annoying castle!"

"Good idea..." adds the vampire before chuckling "... although I must admit, your actions are not very ladylike. First, you cut open our prison and now you wish to break down a wall. Whatever next?"

"I could always smash your face in if you keep annoying me?

Step aside you two!"

Wasting no time, she begins kicking the wall continuously and within seconds, small cracks begin to show. Upon a final strike the solid wall caves in, creating a large hole that leads to the outside.

The cold air and snow are the first to rush into the castle, followed by the unfiltered sounds of roaring beasts and the cries of their victims. The smell of blood and death fills the trio's noses as they look out at the city that is now overrun with monsters. Cyclops, gargoyles, serpents and hundreds of indescribable creatures litter the once noble city of Spiritus.

"You fiends... I will make you all pay!" Shouts Aurora, as she leaps into the bed of danger itself before taking on scores of monsters.

Taking a deep breath, the tuxedo sporting comrade rants "hey, wait for me. I can't have you stealing all the fun, damn succubus!" Leaping outside to the city also.

As Luke prepares to follow suit, standing at the edge of the exit, he holds his chest softly - attempting to calm his growing nerves. He has seen this sight once before, back in his home town of Heline. The images and sounds before him bring back nightmarish memories that cripple his body. It is as though he is right back within that unfortunate night.

"I can do this... I can do this..." He chants to himself, beginning with a small step forward. As familiar as the scene may be, he reminds himself that he now is different. Long gone is the helpless boy. Now, he is Blue Lunar the herald of a goddess. "I am strong now... I am..."

Suddenly, before he takes his full step out into the city, the young hero hears a menacing and familiar cackle "... Kwekekekeeee!"

The boy's heart stops as he hears the familiar laugh. As the sound echoes from within the castle, he makes no mistake as to who it belongs to. "He... he is here" Luke stutters, mind racing back to the image of his first encounter with his murderer: The Wizard King of Despair.

Conflicted about whether to follow the laughter or join his friends outside, the boy holds his head worryingly. Weighing his choice, the blue hero pep talks himself and whispers "this is all his fault. If I can stop him now, then all of this will be over!"

Turning his back to the mayhem outside, the boy holds his head high and runs through the castle quarters - led by the ongoing laugh from Phantom. As the sinister voice grows nearer upon every turn, the boy finds the presence of castle soldiers growing smaller. "I am getting closer... I can feel it."

His path soon leads to a wide hallway of a red carpet and vast royal portraits that hang on each side of the walls. The boy's fears tell him to turn in the other direction - however, regardless of the many protests his body makes, something else within spurs the young knight forward. Is it bravery, stupidity or something else he wonders?

He keeps his guard up before finally reaching the end of the hallway, which leads to a single gold-plated door that is shut tight.

A dark and foreboding feeling overcomes him, which seems to emanate from the other side of the door. The constant cackling is heard once again, causing him to step backwards with fright. His heart screams for him to retreat and his knees shudder back and forth, again protesting for the boy to leave. He stands his ground - reminding his heart that it is encased in an impenetrable armour designed by a powerful deity. Looking to his trembling knees, he tells them that the only running they will do is towards their foe. The bodily objections hold their peace, allowing for the blue hero to step forward and enter the room.

He shoves the door open and takes a small leap inside, before holding a strong fighting stance - ready to challenge the one responsible for the land's suffering.

Taken back by his surroundings, Blue Lunar finds himself in a great throne room that is both large and wide. The ceiling stretches high above where numerous chiming chandeliers hang. White pillars of stone populate the room, and by the walls, a row of large windows adorn each surface. The marbled floor reflects every trace of light - making the room seem more like a stage.

Shifting his eyes directly in front, the young hero finds the Wizard of despair, standing over the bloodied corpse of a single noble. Judging by the attire, Luke sums up the fallen individual to be the King of Spiritus.

"Damn it..." He says to himself - voice echoing through the quiet room before it reaches the ears of the wizard who stands with an absent expression.

Slowly tilting his head to the position of the boy, Phantom's eyes beam with surprise as he lets out a great gasp. As still as a statue the foe stands petrified, even dropping his golden staff at the sight of the young hero. His mouth begins to tremble, attempting to piece a phrase or word together, before stepping forward to call out to the blue knight.

"Solomon... is it truly you? What are you doing here and how did you..."

Analysing the wizard's shock and questions, Luke stands confused - holding his sword and silence before him.

After a short moment, the cloaked man collects his staff from the ground and says "what am I saying? You are not Solomon. In that case, if you are not him, then who the hell are you and why are you wearing his legendary armour!"

"What?"

The boy stands beyond speechless, unable to understand the man's words. The indication that the wizard of despair seems to possess knowledge of the goddess bestowed suit, troubles the young hero. Whispering to himself, Luke wonders "what made him act so bizarrely by my presence? Who is Solomon and did he say my armour once belonged to somebody else? Where is Diana when I need her?"

Striking his staff to the ground, grabbing the boy's attention, Phantom shouts "I asked you a question, imposter. Who are you?" Proceeding to stomp toward the blue knight.

"Here he comes..." Luke says, throwing caution to the wind

before running head-on towards the wizard. Trusting in his strength, the boy leaps forth, blade in hand - preparing to attack the menace with a downward strike. "I am not afraid of you!"

Suddenly - being only inches apart, the boy is stopped in mid-air by the wizard's invisible magic force. Try as he might, Luke cannot seem to break free from the mysterious hold and finds himself suspended like a puppet. "What is this? I can't move!"

"Hmph - not only are you an impostor, but you are also unable to effectively use the suit!"

By his command, he propels the boy across the room before crashing him into a stone wall. As smoke and debris scatter outward, Luke finds himself lodged halfway into the wall, pinned against it by the invisible magic from the wizard.

As he stays helpless and unable to break free, the dark wizard appears inches in front and says "if you will not disclose your identity, I will just have to pull it out myself" reaching to the boy's neck - forcing their eyes to lock. "Allow me to share a well-hidden truth. The eyes are windows to the soul, and with these eyes of mine I shall know everything about you!"

At that moment, the man's eyes change colour rapidly - illuminating a series of hypnotic patterns as he glares into the boy's eyes. A feeling of violation overcomes Luke, as though the deepest parts of his being were intruded upon. Again he attempts to break free, however, the invisible hold continues to overpower him.

Stumbling backwards with surprise, the wizard displays a menacing grin upon having peered into the hero's core. "You... you are the boy I had killed back in Heline. The goddess Diana brought you back to life and charged you with stopping me, after giving you the Blue Lunar suit. Kwekekeke... that wicked woman just can't help herself."

"Impossible... how are you able to read my memories?"

"I haven't just read your memories, little boy. I have read your entire soul. I now know everything there is to know about you.

I am going to make your life a living hell, and when you finally know the truth, it will be too late!"

The invisible force throws Luke again - this time to the opposite side of the throne room. As he slams against another surface, the wizard continues "you poor pathetic boy. You should have stayed dead and passed away an insignificant orphan. After all, none of this has anything to do with you, and it's not as though you ever had anything worth protecting in the first place."

"You are wrong!"

To the wizard's astonishment, the blue knight begins to resist the magic hold - slowly standing to his feet. The magic force feels heavy - however, the boy maintains his focus and holds a mighty posture with his blade held tight. "Yes I am an orphan who never had a family, but that doesn't mean I had never valued the people in this world. Furthermore, I now have people in my life who I want to protect, which is even more reason to stop you!"

Channelling his emotions into his sword, Luke prepares to finish off the dark wizard with one single attack. A surge of light and energy flows around the blue moon sword - powering it up like a bulb. As the blue aura lights the room, Phantom stands with an unthreatened yet amused demeanour.

"Hmm... it makes sense as to why Diana chose you. Only a naive fool who hopes to find a place in this hopeless world would take up her offer. Give it your best shot... imposter!"

"I am not an imposter, I am Luke: Blue Lunar of the goddess Diana!" The boy shouts, releasing a mighty beam of light that races towards the stationary opponent.

To his disbelief, the beam collides against the wizard's forcefield, which protects the magic-user. The walls shake, the grounds tremble and even the chandeliers above fall from their hinges due to the collision of energies.

At that instant, the projectile is deflected upward - tearing and smashing through the ceiling of the castle itself before ascending to the sky above.

"Oh no... I didn't get him?" Luke gasps. However, his troubles will prove far more detrimental than he can imagine. Like a bomb of atomic magnitude, Luke's deflected energy blast explodes, obliterating almost everything beneath it. The numerous houses of Spiritus are torn to pieces, along with the many historic structures. The soldiers and innocent civilians fall victim to the blast, as the devastation of Luke's attack fills the city with a blinding light that vaporises all life under it.

"What... what have I done!" He screams as the pillars of the castle give way, causing countless boulders of debris to fall all around him. Buried under the great tons of stone, the boy lays helpless while the menacing laugh from the wizard can be heard ominously.

"Kwekekeke... thanks for finishing off this city for me, I couldn't have done it better myself. I could have killed you again, but that would have been too easy. No, I am going to destroy you from the inside out... make you feel what I have felt. I am going to crush that foolish and naive sense of morale you currently possess, and by the end of your suffering, you will be just like me. Until we meet again, Luke. Don't take too long, for I am sure that grey hair of yours is already spreading!"

Disappearing into the clouds, the wizard leaves the destroyed city, having accomplished what he had set out to do. The rampaging monsters disappear, along with the wide portal that had covered the sky, like a nightmare that has retreated.

unsettling quietness overcomes the fallen city, as the whispering of a sad wind howl rushes by. The roars of the monsters are no more - however, there are also no victory cheers or even moans of sadness from the people of Spiritus. Not a single soul is heard amongst the vast rubble and ruins of what was once a great and proud city.

Many hours pass and stumbling through the rubble, only two individuals can be seen. The first is a boy who sports a black cape. Holding his trusty briefcase he scans the scene of the disaster, showing a rare expression of concern. He and the other have been looking for their third ally but to no success. "Where could he possibly be? You don't suppose that the wizard…"

"No, don't say that!" Shouts the second individual - body covered with vast scars and bruises. Her pure fur coat is tattered and torn, as she hobbles behind the vampire. "Keep looking. Everybody else in this city may have died but Luke is not one of them!"

"Ok sheesh!" Umbra responds before glancing to the ground in front, only to blink with disbelief at what he finds. A hand can be found, half-buried under a pile of rubble. Wasting no time, he grabs hold of the hand and pulls it forth. To his delight, he finds the young hero, unconscious. "It is a miracle. We have found him!"

"Oh thank heavens. Give him to me!" Aurora says, kneeling to the boy like an overprotected mother. "I knew he would be ok. Everything is going to be ok. Once he wakes up, we can plan our next phase of action."

Taking a deep and burdensome breath, the vampire pauses before saying "however, once Luke does awaken, how will we explain to him that the one responsible for wiping out Spiritus, was none other than himself?

Chapter 10: A Hero's Bloodied Hands

M iles underneath the ground, within the vast catacombs of darkness, the mysterious and frail old man stays within his black chair - staring into space. He is tired, tired of looking at the same dank surfaces for what seems like an eternity. A pair of flies buzz over him before landing on his matted grey hair, which he finds comforting to his lonely existence. Adding to the brief moment of pleasure, the squealing sounds of rats can be heard, squabbling with one another as they dart by his malnourished feet that bear long and dirtied nails.

At that point, a dark portal materialises in front, to which the thorn-crowned wizard appears. His appearance frightens the pair of flies and scuttling rodents, who flee into the dark corners for safety. Upon a respectful and humbled bow,

Phantom greets the seated man.

"I have returned, bringing both pleasant and unpleasant news."

With a small nod of his head, the mysterious man signals for the wizard to continue.

"The first task has been completed successfully. The city of Spiritus has fallen, along with its King and people. With that, the allied country of Veritus will almost certainly slip into disorder, making it unfit to support the grand country of Superbia. Now, our chances of obtaining the Apex Grail will be much easier. We do however have one problem..."

Joining their interaction, a third individual strolls into the open from beyond the shadows. Dressed in a pure red tuxedo suit, along with a long red cape, a being appears before the pair. Face as pale as the clouds with blackened lips, two dark horns protrude from his forehead. Hands inserted into his pockets wisely, the red sporting man asks "a problem you say? What could pose a problem to the world's most powerful wizard?"

Glancing at the horned man, Phantom smiles and says "greetings my friend. For the great demon prince to find interest in our conversation is truly a blessing, Kwekekeh."

"Well, let's just say that I have a hunch as to what your little problem could be. It is about the blue moon, isn't it? I have felt it too."

With a confused gaze as though being left out, the seated man leans forward and grunts "the blue moon? Tell me!"

Upon a deflated sigh, the wizard replies "the goddess Diana... she has selected a new herald to be the next Blue Lunar. His mission is to stop us."

Eyes wide with disbelief, the old man looks as though his soul were snatched from his chest upon hearing the revelation. Holding his head low, he begins to weep as tears fall from his eyes.

"No... no... no..." He says repeatedly, slamming his hands upon the chair with frustration. "I hate her, I hate her... how dare she? Phantom... Megethos... do not let her have her way again. Please... for love!"

"For love" the wizard repeats, slowly turning before disappearing into his portal - leaving the weeping man with the third comrade.

With a firm nod, the horned individual also turns his back and departs into a dark tunnel, leaving the man once again alone. Before long, the rodents slowly come back, lifting his heart once again. Closing his eyes he enjoys their presence, before whispering among the darkness "how utterly beautiful."

∞ ∞ ∞

A week has passed since the fall of Spiritus, and the three heroes have been continuing their journey. Upon assessing the actions of the dark wizard, the three have concluded that his next target is Ergo, the capital city of the land Superbia, which houses the ancient relic known as the Apex Grail.

Eventually arriving in the land of Superbia, the friends stop within a vibrant forest on a warm day. Schools of chirping birds adorn the blue sky - bringing a sense of life and prospect to all those under the shining sun. However, with all the hopefulness the day brings, there is one boy whose heart remains shrouded with guilt. According to his two comrades, the city of Spiritus and all within it were destroyed by the energy blast of his all-powerful sword. He too remembers it well, as he tussled and struggled against the wizard of despair. Since then, the young hero has kept to himself - rarely communicating with anybody.

Choosing to be alone he finds a quiet spot within the forest to think and reflect. Sitting upon a large rock he hangs his head in silence and shame - his mind recollecting the scenes of his failure. Almost half of his hair has turned completely grey, reminding him of the frighteningly cryptic words of the magic-wielding nemesis.

"He was too strong for me. Even with all this new strength of mine, I still lost" he says to himself while gripping his forehead with mental anguish. "I... I killed all those people. I destroyed the whole city. It is all my fault!"

His stomach turns with disgust at the realisation of his actions, along with his heart that cries with regret. "What in the world was I thinking? Somebody like me could never hope to save anything. I don't want this anymore. I don't want to risk harming anybody else."

"Giving up so soon?" Comes the voice of the blue moon goddess, appearing short meters behind the weeping adolescent. Whereas before he would jump with surprise or simply greet her with a smile, now her presence is almost unwanted as he keeps his back facing the deity.

"What do you want, Diana?" He asks in a cold and disconnected manner, surprising the divine woman. "It is not as though you have come to make things easier for me."

"Oh wow, what's with all the attitude? Is that the thanks I get for bestowing you with the powers of the blue moon? I think you'll find that I have done more than enough for a mere human like you."

Gritting his teeth before clenching his fists with anger, the boy turns around and shouts "these powers of mine couldn't so much as touch that awful wizard. The only thing it did was destroy the very city I wanted to protect!"

"I never said that being a hero would be easy, Luke."

"Well, you never said anything that truly mattered, and yet the very enemy you wanted me to kill was able to reveal more information than you ever did. For example, who the heck is Solomon and how did the wizard know so much about my armour? Was it true that it first belonged to that other person?"

Pausing with shock, the woman gasps before turning her gaze away from the boy. With a far from convincing manner, she replies "Solomon is nobody... nobody at all."

"You liar! How do you expect me to trust you if you won't even tell me the truth?"

Resisting the urge to disappear from his sight, the woman exhales with a grieved sigh - taking pity on the distressed boy.

"Ok, fine, I will tell you this much. Solomon was the first Blue Lunar, the original wearer of the suit you now have. Regarding the wizard, I honestly don't know who he is - however he seems to know much, about me and Solomon it seems. I know you are probably tired of me barking orders but, that wizard cannot get his hands on the Apex Grail. Please, you must do everything within your power to stop him!"

Semi satisfied by her reply, the boy turns his back to her and they both stay in silence - tensions still running high. "Diana, leave me alone now and please don't return unless I need you. My friends and I will figure the rest out on our own."

A feeling of guilt overcomes the woman as she looks downward, hugging her shoulders. "I respect your decision. If I may, allow me to leave you with a final piece of advice. The suit you carry... it has memories."

Vanishing into thin air, she leaves the hero to ponder her last words. "My suit has memories? What does that even mean?"

Breaking his brief solace, a small rustling can be heard from behind. Upon turning around he finds his two comrades: Umbra and Aurora, both holding a cheery expression. In contrast to their warm smiles, he holds a low gaze of burden.

"Let us keep moving. We have much to do" states the golden-haired warrior.

Continuing onwards, the trio carry on - emerging from out of the forest before walking along a long brick road, surrounded by fields of blossoming flowers. The air is fresh and the atmosphere is peaceful, with not a single monster in sight. Since setting foot in the large country, not a single fiend has been seen, which makes a change. The absence of danger pleases the vampire and swordsman, who show a happy demeanour. However, for the young Luke, his heavy heart is all too noticeable to the pair.

"Are you gonna stop feeling sorry for yourself, crybaby? You're not still thinking about that city are you?" Asks Umbra, before slapping his hand against the boy's back.

"That city was called Spiritus, capital of Veritus. How can you be so carefree and nice to me, especially after what I did? I killed all those people. I could have killed you both too!"

"However, you didn't kill us so quit being such a victim already!" Says Aurora, in a stern yet supportive manner.

Crossing his arms, Umbra rants to the woman "speak for yourself, succubus. Although you didn't die during the devastation, I was completely obliterated while protecting you from Luke's misfired explosion!"

"Yeah well… nobody asked you to protect me, moron."

Expressing his shame further, Luke raises his voice to the pair and says "don't you get it? I killed innocent people!"

Shrugging her shoulders, Aurora remains unmoved by his guilt and responds "welcome to the club. What you are experiencing is what every warrior feels at one point or another. It is nothing new. If I had a gold bar for how many times I let innocent people die, I would be insanely rich."

"I second that!" Says the tuxedo sporting vampire, raising his hands to the sky. "I once mistakenly poisoned a whole city, when I decided to open a cafe within it. How was I supposed to know that humans could not eat rotten bat soup? Teehee!"

Speechless at their nonchalant admission of past failures, the boy scratches his head and wonders "so, are you saying that even heroes sometimes make fatal mistakes?"

"That is exactly what we're saying. Did you truly think that real warriors can save lives every single time? Perhaps in old fables and tales. No, in this world nobody is blameless. The most we can ever hope for, is to learn from our mistakes and try not to make them again. At least when you encounter the wizard next time, you'll think of a different approach. We will also be by your side next time, so don't worry."

A renewed sense of what it means to be a hero fills the young Luke, who stays with his mouth open wide. The words are truthful and yet refreshing for the boy, who although is not at full sprits, he is now able enough to carry on. His heart now lighter, the boy produces a small smile, which the pair see and mirror.

"Thank you... my friends."

Chapter 11: The mystery of Fiory

S tanding upon a tall mountaintop, high above the clouds, the goddess of the blue moon observes the land beneath her. To the casual observer, she seems calm and collected, hands crossed together neatly amidst the sunset. However, in truth, her feelings couldn't be more opposite.

Laying on the ground beside her, a fellow god keeps the lady company. The deity is a boy, dressed in fine white robes that cover his lower body. Within his hands, he plays with a small branch, and upon his head, two petit wings can be found - one on each side of a brow. With a drowsy look, he yawns continuously, as though struggling to stay awake.

"Ok, so let me get this straight, Diana. You want me to help you figure out the identity and motive of that troublesome wizard, correct? Are you out of your mind? Besides, how on earth do you expect me to do that?"

Glancing at him with an expression of irritation, the goddess tuts under her breath and replies "you know exactly how to do it. After all, you are Hypnos: God of sleep. You practically own half of mortal life, seeing as they enter your domain every night. Peering into the dream of Phantom should be a piece of cake for you. You are one of the only gods whose powers are not negated by the Apex Grail."

Under the retiring sun, the childlike god huffs before planting his face in the ground, like a teen refusing to obey an elder.

"Jeez... how did I know that you'd ask me to do something like that? Can't you ever give me an easy request?"

"This is an easy request. Hypnos, stop being so difficult!"

Upon a bothered sigh, he slaps his forehead, shrugs his shoulders and responds "such a pain... I didn't want to have to tell you this, but here goes. I have been trying to look into the dreams of the wizard, for longer than you know. You wanna know what I found?"

Lost for words, the goddess flinches and panics - glaring at the small god with her beaming blue eyes. "Are you serious? Well, what did you find about him?"

"Nothing, nothing at all. To be more precise, I wasn't able to observe his dreams. The wizard has used powerful magic to block my interference."

"That is not possible. No wizard in the world has that kind of power. He would first need to understand the powers of us gods to even attempt such a thing!"

A confused and somewhat scared look appears on the face of the woman, as Hypnos continues to shrug his shoulders. Between the pair, a feeling of great mystery is sensed regarding the infamous wizard of despair. As the dark clouds cover an already setting sun, more questions begin to pop up inside Diana's head.

Looking at the woman with a hint of hesitancy, the boy deity displays a reluctance to speak his mind. Having already noticed his apprehension, the stern woman says "out with it. What are you thinking?"

"Well, now that I think about it... there was one wizard who potentially could understand the powers of us gods. I am sure you remember him very well, don't you?"

A cold aura exudes from the goddess, offended by the words of the winged boy. Turning away she stares at the clouds and maintains a worrying silence, a silence that speaks a thousand words. Seeing this as his time to leave, Hypnos stands up before slowly strolling away. However, before he departs completely he stops, turns around and asks "Diana... if the wizard gets his hands on the Apex Grail, there won't be another Divine War, will there?"

To his surprise, the troubled goddess disappears - leaving him upon the mountain, surrounded by the quiet night. Looking upward he displays a struggling smile and whispers "how predictable... running away as usual when the truth comes to light. How long will you pretend to be asleep?"

The light gives way to the night, and an all too keen moon wastes no time showing her bold appearance to the world - sending down a warm wind over the land.

After trekking for some time, the trio arrive at the entrance of a small town. Standing by the foot of its wide-open gates, they analyse the destination before them.

"This looks like a nice place. Perhaps we should stay for the night and continue in the morning?" Lukes suggests, awaiting his approval from the two comrades.

"Good idea. I believe this place is called Fiory, a hospitable town where travellers tend to pass through. We should find a guest house to stay overnight" replies Aurora, who shifts her gaze to the vampire who seems to display a perplexed expression. "Is that ok with you, mr vampire?"

The black-suited boy is slow to reply - scanning the entrance as though lost in thought. "Hmmm... I can't quite put my finger on it, but there is something about this town that disturbs me. In any event, let's find out shall we?"

As soon as he finishes his words, the three start to hear loud singing and celebrations, coming from within the town.

"Is there a festival going on? Come on you two!" Says Luke - running chest first into the town with his comrades close behind. Following the sound of music, while exploring Fiory, the trio encounter the townsfolk who seem to be in good cheer and high spirits. Every eye contact they make is followed by a pleasant greeting, making the visitors feel at home almost instantly.

Hundreds of people are out under what seems to be a night of celebration. Many walk the streets while others sit upon balconies of colourfully fashioned homes.

Not an ounce of hostility or worry is felt, despite the precarious situation that has gripped the lands. As the three travellers continue, walking along classical cobbled streets and bright street lamps, they converse.

"Whoa... Kids, adults and families are all out tonight. I wonder what it's all about?" Asks the young hero.

"I am sure we will find out soon enough, for it looks like everybody is heading in the same direction. I am a little surprised that there wasn't a single guard by the entrance though. Considering the threat of the wizard, most cities and towns would be expected to stay vigilant" Aurora adds, displaying a mild look of suspicion. Amongst the ongoing cheers, laughs and music that consists of violins and wind instruments, the warrior can't help but glance at the vampire who holds an uncomfortable presence.

Biting his thumb like a troubled detective, he says "I agree, it is not just surprising, it is downright spooky. Word of the wizard and his monsters must have travelled to all in Superbia, so unless they have lost their minds, they shouldn't be this exposed."

Before long they are led to a wide-open square, where even more people can be found. In the centre, a large and wide water fountain catches their eyes. Made from a type of steel, its design is mesmerising - consisting of exquisite patterns and unreadable symbols on its exterior. Filled with perhaps the clearest water ever seen, it is as though the fountain were designed with the love and care of a god.

As the root of the celebrations becomes clearer, the three watch as the townsfolk dance and sing around the icon of wonder.

"Are they celebrating a water fountain?" Luke expresses, showing a gaze of disappointment. "What is so special about that?"

Upon hearing his question, a nearby inhabitant takes it upon herself to enlighten the three. "That there is the blessed water fountain that appeared about a week ago. One morning, we all woke up to find the mysterious wonder in the centre of town. Even more miraculous, was the fact that ever since it came here not a single monster or beast threatened Fiory. Somehow the fountain repels evil influence."

"You have got to be joking right?" Asks the golden-haired warrior - far from entertained by the story.

"No, it is true. Even our guards realised this and have retired, seeing as there was no reason to defend this town anymore. The blessed fountain protects us now, and to ensure it never goes away we celebrate it, every night. Its water is also revitalising, and never seems to run dry, no matter how many times we drink from it."

Slapping her forehead before letting out a blatant sigh, Aurora expresses "that's it, I am done for the night. There's only so much crazy I can take for one day. Come on you two. Let's find a guest house to stay in tonight. I am already looking forward to seeing the back of this ridiculous place."

Brushing her hair to one side, she begins to stroll away, followed by the young Luke who moans "oh don't be like that Aurora. Fine, let's turn in for the night. However, I wanna buy a souvenir before we leave this town tomorrow..."

To the boy's surprise, he finds the black-suited friend is

not following behind. Instead, the vampire stands unmovable, continuing to hold a disturbing stare on the fountain. "Umbra... what's wrong?" Luke Asks, sensing a troubled aura coming from the comrade. It is unlike the prankster to behave in such a serious manner, which confuses Luke even more.

Turning to face the warrior and herald of the blue moon, the vampire assumes a false smile and replies "sorry you two, I am going to stay here for a little while longer. There is something that I need to figure out. I will find you once I am done."

Luke pauses with an unsettled heart, wondering what matters the vampire would need to solve alone. With no choice but to respect his decision, Luke nods his head and leaves the area with Aurora.

The festivities carry on hours into the night, as acts, performances and dozens of musicians take part in the nightly celebration of the special fountain. Men, women and children of all ages each take their turns approaching its mysterious waters to drink from.

Eventually, midnight arrives, bringing the town-wide festival to an end. The people of Fiory retire - going back into their warm and cosy homes upon another night of joy and togetherness. The sounds of music and chatter die down, as a calm quietness overcomes the town, save for the small moaning of street cats in one of the many alleyways.

As the townsfolk lay their head to sleep, secure and at peace under the protection of the mysterious water fountain that had appeared only days ago, one individual remains far from content. Being the only one left in the town square, the tuxedo sporting vampire stands opposite the wonder. He hasn't moved an inch for the past few hours - his thumb now sore from the constant biting, owing to frustration.

"Magic symbols... incantations... a spell..." he whispers to himself while inspecting the unfamiliar words inscribed upon the fountain's exterior. "Now where have I seen those before and what could they possibly mean?"

To the untrained eyes of mere mortals, the mysterious

fountain seems divine - a gift from the gods. However, to an experienced veteran such as Umbra, the fountain is anything but. Like an item summoned from the depths of darkness, its presence baffles and bothers him by the second. And yet, the boy is unable to confirm why.

He attempts to jog a distant memory. However - try as he might, nothing of significance comes to mind, which annoys him even further. "How troublesome. I guess this leaves me with no other choice" he mumbles, reaching into his dark cloak to locate a particular item. He pulls out an old and tattered book, the type of book that might be found within an antique store. Pages barely held together, the item emanates a dark aura, giving a sense that it should not be handled by mortals.

Blowing the dust away from the front cover, Umbra states its title "The Grimoire of Obscurum. With this, I shall surely find out what you truly are." Sitting upon a nearby bench, he proceeds to read the contents, page by page - kept company by the moon above and the light it gives.

By the farthest section of the town, within a small guest house, another individual also stays awake. Overlooking the house balcony, Luke can be seen staring afar into the distance. Mind taken back to the fall of Spiritus, he replays the event in his mind - imagining a different outcome and what he could have done to achieve it. "If only I hadn't been so reckless. If only that horrible wizard had never arrived in the first place. Why is he doing all this?"

To his surprise the balcony door slowly opens wide, revealing Aurora who stands with a considerate and warm smile. "Having trouble sleeping?" She asks - joining him amidst the quiet night. Standing next to each other, they look out to the distance and hold their silence for many moments. As though reading the thoughts of the other, a shared concern is felt, explaining their reluctance to sleep.

"Aurora, tell me something. Why do you think the wizard is after the Apex Grail?"

"Have you not already asked me that once before? Well, I have been trying to figure that out for some time. Interestingly enough, I think I may partly know the reason. As you know, the wizard first officially appeared about one hundred years ago, attempting to do the same thing as he is doing now. However, there was another event in history, which in turn gave birth to the Apex Grail."

Intrigued, the boy turns to her and says "another event in history? What exactly was it?"

Looking at Luke with a firm gaze, the woman replies "it was called the Divine War. You see, before the creation of the Apex Grail, gods and mortals lived together. We were able to see, speak and interact with the gods as we do with each other. However, something caused a great conflict, which pitted various gods against one another. The war was so horrible that lands and even stars above crumbled. It is said that after the destruction, the gods regretted their actions and in shame created the Apex Grail, to never again involve mortals in their matters."

"Whoa... I've never heard about this before. So, are you suggesting that the wizard is hoping to use the Apex Grail to start another war somehow?"

Shrugging her shoulders, the comrade replies "who knows? It is certainly a possibility though. Although the ancient records do not speak of the dark wizard's existence within the Divine War, we can't rule anything out."

As intriguing as her revelation is, the boy is once again left with more questions and few answers. It is though the very nature and motives of Phantom are a mystery in itself. Gripping the sidebars of the balcony, the young hero again feels powerless, inadequate and one step behind.

"I wish we knew what is going on? I wish we knew what had caused The Divine War all those years ago and how it relates to the wizard?"

"Me too. Perhaps you should ask that goddess of yours: Diana was it? I am sure she should know something?" Aurora suggests to the boy.

Like a light bulb switching on, Luke remembers something the blue moon goddess mentioned earlier that day. "The suit has memories," He says - repeating the words she had left him before departing. "That's it... I need to look within" he states, proceeding to touch the D symbol upon his forehead, transforming into the blue knight.

Watched by the golden-haired ally who stands patiently observing his actions, Luke looks down at his shining gauntlets and speaks to the armour. "Diana tells me that you have memories. In that case, please help me. What do you know that can help us stop the wizard?"

To see someone talk to their armour is a bizarre site for Aurora, who covers her mouth to hide the laughter. However - as humorous as his actions seem, the blue hero is anything but. Although this would be the first time attempting something so unorthodox, the boy feels confident - trusting in the advice the goddess gave him.

For many seconds nothing seems to occur. Not a tingling sensation, grand voice or spectacular lights show. Suddenly, before their very eyes, a ball of stardust begins to materialise in between his hands. Astounded, the lady jumps back and holds the hilt of her blade - a natural reaction to anything unexplainable as the young hero gazes at the energy before him.

At that second the ball of wonder shoots into the distance, like a bullet being fired forth. Its speed is so fast, that the pair have trouble tracking its trajectory. Barely catching sight of it, the two watch as it zips towards a distant mountain before exploding into a magnificent firework - lighting up the sky. To their surprise, the light illuminates a ruin of some kind, on the very tip of the faraway mountain.

"Whoa! That thing just up and flew away. Did I do something wrong?" Asks Luke - baffled as to why the energy disappeared into the distance.

Pushing him out the way before leaning over the balcony edge, Aurora replies "no, you did nothing wrong. Look carefully at where it landed. The exploding ball of yours wants to lead us to that mountain. What could be over there but an old ruin or temple?"

A smile opens on the boy's face, feeling a sense of excitement and progress. Upon a deep and relieved exhale, he faces the woman and says "well, at least we know where to head next. I am sure that whatever is on that mountain, involves the wizard. My suit... it's trying to tell us something!"

Sunrise comes, bringing with it an alluring purple sky, accompanied by thin clouds that drift over the land. The early songs of nature's birds can be heard in attendance, as though serenading the new day. The morning noise of a single rooster sounds off like a pleasant alarm, to which the inhabitants slowly begin their day.

It isn't long before the streets are filled with busy townsfolk who go about their lives. The leftover atmosphere from yesterday's festivities still lingers through Fiory - as seen on the many content and happy faces. However, amidst the growing hustle and bustle, there is one who displays the complete opposite.

"Damn it... this is bad... this is really bad!" Rants the black-suited vampire, who can be seen darting through the main street, panicking immensely. With a black book held underarm, he runs desperately, attempting to find his two comrades who he had briefly serrated from last night. The locals look on with confusion at his distress - watching as he trips and stumbles, as though genuinely terrified.

"Luke! Aurora! Where are you?" he shouts with all his might, falling to his knees with exhaustion. Head held low with grief, he whispers "we should have never come here in the first place. This city, it was doomed from the very moment that cursed thing arrived here!"

"What are you doing on the ground, Umbra?" Comes the friendly voice of his friend. Looking up, the vampire gasps at the sight of Luke and Aurora who slowly approaches him, each with a baffled look. An air of relief overcomes him upon being reunited with his friends. However, his relief is quickly erased due to the information he has discovered about the mysterious water fountain.

As though having lost his mind, Umbra stands before taking hold of Luke's collar with surprising aggression and shouts "we are all in danger. You, me and everybody within this town. No, everybody in this town is already done for. We need to escape as fast as we can!"

"What? I don't understand what you're saying?" responds Luke - puzzled yet concerned by his friend's hysterics. Unlike many times before, where the dramatic vampire would embellish situations, this time feels different somehow.

Chiming in, the warrior comrade says to Umbra "start making sense, dumb vampire! What do we need to escape from?"

"The water fountain is not what we thought. Its true name is Sitis Monstrum: an evil magic weapon that corrupts all who drink it, which means everybody in this town has been corrupted!"

The sky begins to dim, as though something supernatural and sinister was observing the trio. Dark clouds begin to overshadow the town as rain begins to fall, followed by a frightening thunderclap. Before Luke and Aurora have any time to process the words of their comrade, the inhabitants of Fiory begin to act bizarrely. Upon stopping all at once, the townsfolk begin to shake violently while screaming inhuman sounds as though possessed.

"It has already begun. Damn, this place was nothing more than one big trap to lure us!" Umbra Panics - watching as the inhabitants slowly gaze at the trio with pitch-black eyes.

"Are they transforming? We gotta help them!" Says Luke - unable to believe his eyes at what is happening to all the people of Fiory. The sight looks like one big nightmare, as the features of the townsfolk morph even more - now bearing fangs and sharp claws. For a second the young hero questions his sanity. Surely a sight like this should not happen. "Perhaps I am dreaming?" He wonders. Unfortunately, his constant pinching does nothing to take him away from the sight before him.

"Save your questions for now. We need to find a safe place to figure all this out!" Orders Aurora, gesturing for them to flee. Running together under the rain, they search for a building to enter, all the while hearing countless screams and horrific roars from what was once the people of Fiory. Giving chase they sprint on their hands and feet - like animals pursuing their prey.

With luck, the trio comes across a large white cathedral, like a beacon of hope within the darkness. Wasting no time they open its wide and wooden double doors before racing inside. Fastening the doors shut before reinforcing them with a pile of chairs and tables, Luke and his friends attempt to rationalise their predicament.

"So let me get this straight. The people of Fiory all drank from the water fountain, which has turned them into mindless monsters?" Aurora asks, pacing around the inside of the holy building, glancing up at the stained glass windows of angels and sages."

Strolling the opposite direction, unable to keep still, the vampire responds "it is not just any fountain. I told you before that it is the Sitis Monstrum. Once a mortal being drinks from its cursed waters, they become its servant and have no choice but to do its bidding."

"Hmph, you sure do choose your moments, dumb vampire. Why didn't you tell us this before?"

"I had no idea yesterday. I spent the whole night trying to figure out what the wretched fountain was. I only found the truth this morning!"

As Umbra and Aurora argue, Luke stands frozen with shock, mind racing with disbelief as the sounds of the corrupted people outside can be heard growing nearer. "Guys, none of that matters right now. How are we going to turn them back to normal? What do we need to do?"

Stopping, Umbra looks at Luke with a worried gaze as though considering the effect his reply will have on the sensitive soul. Upon a deep breath, the tuxedo sporting comrade responds "there is no way... no way to turn them back to their original selves. Believe me, I have tried all night to figure out a solution."

A loud thud shakes the cathedral, as the townsfolk can be heard pounding against the front doors, causing the three to jump with fright. Tutting aloud, Aurora moans "damn... looks like the doors won't hold for very long. Umbra, are you sure that there is no way to save them?"

"Trust me, not even the greatest spell can undo a curse like this."

"Umbra, how can you say that so confidently? There has to be a solution!" Shouts the young hero, holding a desperate stare.

Stunning both Luke and Aurora, Umbra loses his temper and screams "how many times do I have to repeat myself to you two simpletons? I am telling you that there is no cure!" Pulling out the mysterious black book, he violently throws it to Luke to catch. An aura of ancient and dark magic oozes from the item. And as the boy looks upon its tattered front cover, he feels as though his soul were being sucked into its very pages.

"That is called the Grimoire of Obscurum. It is the greatest encyclopaedia and spellbook on all the dark arts in the world, along with how to undo all afflictions. In the case of the Sitis

Monstrum, no magic exists to reverse the damage it does."

As the pounding and screams continue all around the cathedral outside, the golden-haired warrior sweats under pressure and stutters "is that the famous dark Grimoire? One of the three supreme Grimoires? You should not have that, for it is said that it belongs to Megethos the sleeping demon prince!"

"It belongs to me now... that is all I can tell you. More importantly, we need to figure out a way of escaping this town. There is nothing left for us to do here."

Feeling helpless, a wave of disappointment overcomes the young hero, a feeling that he has become all too familiar with. First Heline, then Spiritus and now Fiory are added to the list of misfortune. "Very well, let's escape this place. Although, this all just feels so... wrong."

Lifting her head high, the warrior looks at a statue of the cathedral's goddess by the pulpit, lost in thought for many moments. As though having received a revelation from the heavens, Aurora produces a deep sigh before stating to the pair "no, I will not leave the people of Fiory to suffer as corrupted servants of that cursed fountain. If I leave now, they will run amok and cause many more casualties across Superbia."

"What? Have you not been listening, succubus? You cannot save them!"

"Yes, I can... my way!" She responds, unsheathing her pure white blade from its golden scabbard. Turning her back to the pair before strolling towards the doors, Luke and Umbra slowly but surely figure out her intentions.

"Wait... is she about to do what I am thinking she will do? The mad succubus intends to slaughter the whole lot of them!"

"No Aurora... what are you thinking? They are human beings!"

Their pleading falls on deaf ears, as the swordsman stops inches apart from the door. A strong resolve is felt from her - one that will not be swayed. By now the constant banging is so loud that it is almost unbearable. Nevertheless, the woman holds a bittersweet smile and whispers "it looks like I am about to be the bad guy once again..." before untying her left eyepatch. As the covering falls to the ground, she opens her closed left eye, revealing a glowing letter V that is imprinted within her pupil. Great energy begins to flow from out of the comrade, in the form of golden streams that disburse throughout the cathedral.

"She is going to do it. She is going to release the power of the Stigma!"

Within seconds the entrance explodes, causing a pile of smoke and debris to sweep outside. Along a wide street, the ghastly and possessed people of Fiory stand under the pouring rain, watching the settling dust from the exposed cathedral entrance. By now, the whole town has surrounded the building in their droves, commanded by the dark fountain to target the three heroes. With only the sound of soft raindrops amongst a tense silence, a single warrior steps into the open.

Body exuding a golden light, the female swordsman stands before the entire army of foes, holding a strong and mighty stance. Her hair and attire moves hypnotically, emanating a divine aura. To top off her mystifying transformation, a pair of golden wings sit upon each shoulder - expanding outward like an angel. As though favoured by nature itself, the dark clouds and rain halt, as sun rays pierce the skies to shine down upon her. Her countenance is humbling, as the servants of the dark fountain shudder with fear.

Gazing around with a glowing left eye, she declares to her enemies "I Aurora of the heavens have come to free you all from your pain. I promise you, I will make this as painless as possible!"

The foes charge at her, hissing and bearing their claws along with blackened eyes. Whatever trace of humanity the people of Fiory had is now gone, for they are nothing more but slaves to the Sitis Monstrum. The ground trembles under the stampede of once human foes, as an atmosphere of bloodlust and murderous intent fills the town, a far cry from only yesterday.

Unlike the warm reception they provided the trio, now the only gift the town can offer is death.

Engaging their numbers, the winged wonder takes flight into the sky before releasing golden rays of light that obliterate hundreds of foes in an instant. Explosions erupt across the town and houses crumble, due to her deadly beams of light that rain down on the targets. As she sweeps through the carnage like an angelic messenger, her comrades stand in awe.

"I hope you're not blinking my friend. This is the taboo power that your kind fear from those like Aurora" the vampire says - struggling to catch a clear sight of the golden warrior who zips from one end of the town to the other.

Unable to comprehend the massacre before him, the young hero covers his mouth with both amazement and horror. As the people of Fiory are slaughtered at the hands of Aurora, Luke responds "no, I can't believe she is truly doing this. We are supposed to be protecting innocent lives, not killing them!"

"I told you before... they are no longer human and they are far from innocent," says Umbra, attempting to rationalise the sight around them. "Nevertheless, Aurora must feel heartbroken by the decision she is making. Who knows how many times she has had to make such a difficult choice? If there's one person in the whole world I don't envy, it is her."

The vampire couldn't be more correct, for although the woman ascends through the air like a feather, her heart is heavy enough to hit the depths of the deepest ocean. Drifting to the ground she holds her sword tightly, preparing to fight the oncoming foes in close combat. "I am sorry. This is the only way I can save you" She utters - voice trembling with heartache as the fiends blindly race towards the invincible glowing knight.

A pack of foes leap forward to attack - however, with a swift swipe of her bright blade they are sliced into perfect halves. Before their blood can even touch the ground, Aurora has already darted to the next group, making quick work of the townsfolk like a holy maiden of the battlefield. Not a single foe can touch the winged fighter, for she is a master of the sword, especially in her true state. Nevertheless, with each blood she spills, a gallon of guilt deposits in her already burdened heart.

"I am sorry... I am so sorry..." She says over and over. Her ears are almost deafened by the death cries of her victims, while her nose stays overwhelmed by the smell of blood. Each slaughtered servant was once an innocent person, and as the image of their once smiling faces clouds her thoughts, Aurora curses both her misfortune and theirs. "I don't want to do this, I don't... but it's the only way. I don't have a choice, I can't leave you all as you are now!"

Releasing a final blast of light from her wings, she obliterates every last attacker - wiping out the people of Fiory completely. A multitude of explosions erupts in the wake of her light, causing buildings to collapse and crumble to the ground. Covering their eyes from the catastrophe, Luke and Umbra hold onto one another for support as the aftermath of smoke blows over them.

The dust settles, and the pair reopen their eyes and gasp at the sight of the town. Not a single building is left standing, as the city resembles that of a broken toy box that has been stepped on by a giant. An even clearer resemblance comes to mind by Luke who stands speechless at a sight he hoped he would not ever see again.

"This is just like Heline and Spiritus" he whispers, while a small wind howl blows over the town. Much like the unfortunate capital of Veritas, an unpleasant silence hangs in the air. Gone are the sounds of chattering townsfolk, music and celebration. Equally, the screams due to their twisted minds are now absent. Now, the once populated town is reduced to mere memories and ghosts of the past.

"Look over there. The succubus hasn't finished yet."

"Huh? What is she doing?"

Looking to the distance at the bulb of light that is Aurora, the pair find her standing in the central square - opposite the Sitis Monstrum: the very thing responsible for corrupting the minds of the townsfolk. Being the only structure still standing, its waters continue to flow as though unashamed of its doing. With her left eye pulsating with anger, the winged warrior stands quietly - glaring at the cursed fountain for many moments. Taking a small step forward she addresses the mysterious creation.

"Well, are you not going to say anything at all? This is all your fault... all of it. Tell me, who created you and what was their motive? Answer me!"

Voice echoing throughout the tarnished town, carried by the wind, her cry reaches the ears of the young comrades who stand afar in suspense. To their shock and surprise, a gruesome and otherworldly voice is heard from the evil fountain.

"Hawww... my creator? My master is the one who shall obtain the Apex Grail, and there is nothing you can do to stop him!"

"The Apex Grail? So you must be referring to Phantom the wizard king. Why does your master want the Apex Grail so badly? Is all this suffering and bloodshed truly worth it?"

"The suffering you mortals experience today is but a speck of dust compared to the horrors of the great Divine War. I was merely placed here to apprehend you, nothing more, nothing less. Now, do you realise? You will always be one step behind my master. Worry, not foolish warrior, for everything my master does is for love... love... love..."

The fountain repeats its words - its voice growing louder and louder. The notion of love confuses and angers Aurora, who shouts "what does that even mean? How could this possibly be for love? Explain yourself!"

"Love... love... love..."

"Shut up!" Screams the warrior - taking flight into the sky and clouds above, watched by her two comrades who stand transfixed as she prepares to finish off the cursed structure. Wings beautifully stretched wide for the rest of nature to adorn, she gazes down at the wicked creation like an angel of judgement.

Before their very eyes, she descends towards the fountain, blade in hand and surrounded by a magnificent aura that is almost blinding. As she gets closer, the energy around her takes shape, forming that of a golden phoenix that carries a divine melody.

"So beautiful..." Utters Luke, eyes glued to the descending wonder. Staring upon the falling phoenix in all its beauty, its sight and sound touch his spirit - transporting him to a brief nirvana where nothing matters at all.

Breaking his trance like state, the tuxedo sporting vampire yanks his arms and says "quit daydreaming, will you? We need to run to safety!"

At that moment, Aurora collides with the Sitis Monstrum with the full might of her power - resulting in a gigantic explosion of light that engulfs the entire town. The force is so great that buildings, roads and all in between are blown skyward. Not an inch of the town is left untouched - causing Luke and Umbra to spiral into the distance also. Seen from the clouds, the sight resembles that of a divine pillar of light that stretches high into the celestial realms for all the gods to marvel upon.

Eventually, the light disappears, revealing what is left of the town. Upon covering his eyes during the duration of the explosion, Luke is the first to scan the aftermath while laying grounded next to Umbra. A gasp is produced, for what he sees trumps the sight of Spiritus and Heline put together. Not a trace of what was Fiory exists. Gone are the buildings, stalls, benches and lampposts. All that remains is a wasteland of what once was, and a single woman in its centre.

Her invincible form subsided, she kneels with her head low,

as traces of her feathers fall all around, like a tribute to the doomed town.

"I am sorry... I never meant for this to happen. I never meant to harm any of you, but it was the only way to save you all" she cries - weeping like a child, hugging her stomach with unbridled grief.

Watched by her allies, they share her sorrow - holding their heads with shame and regret.

"Fate can truly be cruel at times. Even though her actions have most likely saved the lives of others, it still meant that this town had to pay the price with their lives. This is by no means is a proud victory" says Umbra, as Luke nods in agreement.

Holding his head high, the young hero walks towards the female comrade - past all the destruction, pain and loss of life. As he approaches her sobbing frame he gently places his left hand on her shoulder, causing Aurora to flinch. Slowly looking upward she gazes at the boy who displays an unwarranted smile. Nevertheless, the smile saves her from her guilt, giving her the strength to carry on.

"Come on Aurora. Let us go to that mountain we saw and find out what the wizard is hiding... once and for all.

Chapter 12: Bonds and Blood

F lying through the air, a single raven soars over the land. Unbeknownst to the three heroes, their actions had been carefully observed by the bird. Like a nosey telltale it hurries back to where it came from - amidst the clear blue sky.

"I must quicken my speed. I must tell my lord about all that I saw!" It says to itself, dodging a flock of oncoming birds within its path. "Get out of my way, annoying fowls. I have work to do!" It rants - speaking the language of men like a human being. Flapping its wings tirelessly, the creature zips across mountains, fields and oceans, before arriving on a small island. By the shore, a single deity sits upon a large rock, overlooking the calm and clear waters of the sea, bearing only one eye. The other eye had been given up, in exchange for cosmic wisdom that would make him one of the most esteemed gods in existence.

"Lord Odin!" The raven chirps, excited to return to its master.

It descends and lands upon the man's shoulder, its favourite spot as the old deity smiles.

"Welcome back, Huginn my child. What news have you found today?"

"You will not believe what I have just witnessed. Shortly after sunrise, the town of Fiory met a tragic end. The townsfolk became corrupted by Phantom's Sitis Monstrum - however, that is not all. Fiory was completely wiped out by what the mortals call a Stigma child. Her power resembled that of the Valkyrie but even greater!"

Upon a distinct gasp, the deity carries the raven in his hands and holds it in front. "Child - what did the mortal look like?"

"She sported a long white coat and possessed a glowing left eye. Her hair was gloriously golden, like the sun I would say. She was so beautiful my lord. I have never seen something so beautiful, since the legendary Brynhild!"

"Was the mortal seen with anybody else? Did you manage to discover what their motives are?"

"Yes my lord. She was seen with two younger-looking companions. The first was a demon of some sort. The second was a mortal who possessed the mark of Diana the moon goddess. They seek to stop Phantom the Wizard King of Despair. They plan to reach the capital city of Ergo, most likely to defend the Apex Grail. However, they will first take a detour and explore the temple of Venus it seems."

A troubled look overcomes the god upon hearing the words of the loose-lipped raven. Were it not for the soothing waves that crash against the shore, an even more distressing expression would have been seen upon Odin's face.

Successfully composing himself, he sighs and says "good work Huginn. Please continue to follow them and report back to me with any new revelations. While you're at it, please find Muninn for me. You know how much I worry about him."

"Yes, my lord!" Responds the loyal aid - taking flight into the sky. Left alone on the sandy shore of the small island, Odin takes a deep breath and closes his eye, sensing a worrying predicament that is yet to come.

At that moment he is joined by a goddess, appearing out of thin air. Strolling next to him before sitting side by side, the blue moon goddess Diana greets the man and says "good morning, old friend. It has been some time since we last met."

Glancing at the blue-eyed goddess with a look of mild deflation, he rolls his eye and responds "I believe the last time we met was at the end of the divine war, some one thousand years ago. If I were to be honest, it hasn't been long enough. Your name and appearance have always been associated with trouble, and I am sure today is no exception. I assume that the recent events have something to do with you?"

"No, you are mistaken. These events are to do with all of us - however, it seems that only I am the most concerned. My new herald and his companions are trying their best, but I don't have much faith in them. If Phantom gets his hands on the Apex Grail and decides to destroy it, the world of man and god will merge once again."

"Diana tell me something... is living side by side with the mortals such a bad thing?"

Taken back by the god's question, a hostile aura exudes from the goddess - dispersing the sand and causing the waves to change direction. "What are you saying? You know full well that we cannot live side by side with the mortals. The Divine War was proof of that!"

"Come now... you are being disingenuous Diana. The Divine War first began because you and I forbade the union of love between our kind and theirs. We were the ones who started it, remember? The creation of the Grail had nothing to do with protecting the mortals from our actions but everything to do with us being afraid... afraid of a new kind of love."

Standing up before strolling to the edge of the shore, the goddess does not respond. Instead, she looks to the distance, feeling the warm waters as they soak over her toes. Ready to depart, she says to the old god "perhaps you should have sacrificed both eyes for even greater wisdom? Losing one was clearly not enough."

∞∞∞

Continuing their journey, the trio make their way towards a particular mountain, upon guidance from Luke's suit. However - upon the recent events of the previous town, their spirits are far from confident. A collective concern is felt between them, as though the wizard were one step ahead. Walking along an open road, they see the mountain in question, far in the distance.

Attempting to shift the mood, the cheery vampire says "come on guys. Let us turn our frowns upside down. If we were to encounter the wizard now, he would mop the floor with us. We need to be in tip-top shape and fighting fit to beat the wizard."

"Nobody asked for your opinion, dumb vampire. I will change my attitude when I am good and ready" responds Aurora, paying no mind to Umbra's suggestion.

Feet dragging along the ground, they continue to walk in silence for many moments, before the young hero adds "well I think it's a great idea. Perhaps we can think of a topic that makes us happy? After that, we can each take turns saying something about it."

"That is a terrific idea, Luke! What do you think about that, Succubus?"

"I am not interested, so count me out!"

Ignoring the third comrade's outburst, Luke and Umbra converse amongst themselves, like a pair of yapping children. Spirits already half restored by their idea, the two jump up and down with excitement.

"Ok Umbra, how about we talk about family members? You never did tell me about your family and where you're from."

"Oh, I didn't? Well, it's nothing too special. I only have one family member. He and I used to be very close, long ago. However now, we barely even speak. His favourite colour is red and he has the worst dress sense."

"No way! Is he your brother or something?"

Scratching his forehead, the vampire laughs nervously and replies "no, he is much closer than a brother."

"Much closer than a brother? Is that even possible?" Luke Wonders, looking to the grown woman for answers.

Upon a mild scoff, Aurora responds "impossible. There is nobody closer than a sibling. The silly vampire is most likely lying. After all, he does belong to the family of demons."

"How dare you, succubus? I am telling you the truth. I do have a relative who is indeed much closer than a brother!"

"Oh yeah? What's his name?"

Stopping, the black-suited comrade shrugs his shoulders and blushes as though somewhat uncomfortable with the question. A feeling of dishonesty emanates from him as he lets out a rather unconvincing reply. "I have forgotten his name. Much time has passed since I last saw him, so it's only natural that I'd forget, teehee!"

Bursting into all-out laughter, the woman responds "you truly are something special, Umbra. So this relative of yours is closer to you than a brother and yet you do not remember his name? Haha. Well, if there is one thing you have achieved today, it's that you have brought a smile to my face. How about you Luke? Do you have any real siblings at least?"

As her gaze shifts to the grey-haired boy, he smiles instantly and readies to reply with a confidence that surprises even himself. "Yes, I have a sister. Her name is Rose!"

"Is that so? Tell me, what is she like?"

"Well, she is nice and friendly. Once we have defeated the wizard, I hope to see her again."

With a far from amused expression, the golden-haired comrade tuts under her breath and responds "you didn't exactly answer my question, kiddo. Tell me something interesting about your alleged sister. What is her favourite colour? Does she have a hobby?"

"Um... well she does have a plan to study in the capital city of Ergo, but I've completely forgotten what it was about. Sorry, she only became my sister a few days ago."

Slapping her forehead with grief, Aurora turns her back to the pair and sighs "a few days ago? That isn't possible. So are you saying that you and a stranger had decided to become siblings? It doesn't work like that!"

"It doesn't?" Asks the young hero - looking downward with doubt. The words of his older comrade are strong and stern, like a firm teacher whose word is golden. He begins to question whether he could indeed be a brother at all. "Maybe you're right. Siblings are usually born from the same parents after all. I guess Rose is not my..."

Coming to his defence, the vampire puffs his chest out before squaring up against the female ally. "Now listen here miss succubus. You above all people have no place to tell Luke what kind of relationship he has with his sister. A family goes far beyond just blood!"

"No it doesn't, idiot vampire!"

At that moment, the pair start to squabble and bicker - watched by Luke who assumes his usual position as an onlooker. Like a child caught among a parents' domestic, he tries to calm the pair down.

"Come on you two. We don't have time to be fighting one another."

"Stay out of this Luke!"

"Yeah. Don't interfere boy."

Amidst their arguing, a handful of nature's birds sweep upon a nearby tree - humoured by the antics of the pair. As though serenading a dual, the birds sing to the clouds as though encouraging the squabble.

Clenching her fists before entering a fighting stance like a boxer, Aurora states "I am through with words. I am going to clobber what little brain cells you have left!"

Mirroring her stance, the vampire also raises his fists and

responds "give it your best shot, damn succubus!"

"Cut it out you two!" Shouts the young hero. However, his words fall on deaf ears, and running head-on, the angry pair swing their fists to thrash at one another. In an almost comical sight, Aurora and Umbra slip over a patch of uneven ground. Before the eyes of Luke and the gang of nosey birds, they hit the ground hard - both losing consciousness. Slapping his forehead with grief, Luke looks up at the clear blue sky and sighs "good grief. What am I gonna do with you two!"

∞∞∞

Many hours pass and the day moves to sunset. A lazy afternoon feeling comes over the land as the orange sky hangs above. The sound of a distant crow adds to the relaxed time of day, as the setting sun glows wondrously.

Upon being unconscious for some time, Aurora opens her eyes to find herself by a small meadow.

"Where... where am I?" She asks herself, at which point a throbbing pain can be felt upon her head. Confused and exhausted, she simply breathes deeply - already having lost interest in how she ended up under a quiet sunset.

To her surprise, she hears the voice of her comrade Luke who says "I see you're finally awake. It sure took you long enough!"

Shifting her gaze to her right side, Aurora finds Luke and Umbra - each sitting upon a tree stump. The young hero displays a vexed expression, while the vampire shows a look of embarrassment. The sound of another distant crow sounds off in the distance, as the lady opens her mouth for answers. However, before she can say a word, the grey-haired boy stands and scolds her.

"I told you both not to fight, and yet you didn't listen. Thanks to your bickering, you knocked yourselves out and were unconscious for hours, wasting precious time for us all!"

As his voice echoes through the meadow, Aurora can only lay lost for words upon recollecting the failed tussle she had with her vampire ally. Glancing at Umbra's ashamed face, she can only assume that he too had received a telling off from the young hero. A feeling of disappointment overcomes her as she looks into Luke's eyes. Under the silent afternoon sunset, she apologises.

"I am sorry, boy. Thanks to my fooling around, I ended up injuring myself and wasting time. I promise that it won't happen again."

"Thank you..." responds Luke before proceeding to stroll away. "Let's all clear our heads for a few more hours or so. We can regroup and head to the mountain by nightfall."

He disappears beyond the trees, leaving the golden-haired warrior with the sinister suited vampire.

"Teehee... Luke sure was angry, wasn't he? I never knew he had it in him to lose his temper like that."

"It is not a laughing matter, idiot vampire. As unbearable as it is for us to work together, you and I shouldn't be making his life more difficult than it already is" Aurora replies.

Coming away from the tree stump, the vampire yawns casually and says "the poor chap's life has already been made difficult a hundredfold, ever since he chose to become the herald of that cruel goddess. If he had any idea of what it truly meant to become Blue Lunar, he would never have made such a decision. Nevertheless, I take your point."

Umbra's words leave Aurora with a sense of mystery and worry. An aura of unexplained wisdom and hidden knowledge can be picked up by his demeanour, causing the woman to sit upward with intrigue.

Looking beyond his pleasant smile she asks "hold it. What do you mean by that?"

"What do I mean by what?"

"Stop playing dumb, idiot vampire. You are a hell of a lot smarter than you are letting on. After all, not every demon happens to own the one and only: Grimoire of Obscurum. Out with it... you know something more about the boy and his pact with the goddess, don't you?"

Shrugging his shoulders, the vampire spins around and readies to depart. As he begins strolling away, cape swaying to and fro - the woman calls out desperately "can you at least tell me... is his life in danger?"

Stopping - the comrade pauses and remains back turned. A strong gust of wind blows through the meadow, causing the flowers to scatter about. Tilting his head to gaze at Aurora, he replies "Luke's life is in one of the worst predicaments a human being could ever be in. Be that as it may, I promise you that I will do everything in my power to protect him, for he is my friend."

As Umbra leaves the area, the woman remains perplexed - left to ponder the words of the vampire. Her worries continue to press upon her heart, as she thinks about the young boy whom she has grown to care deeply for.

The sun has finally fled from the sky - giving way to large clouds that cast strong winds over the land. Having walked far away from his comrades, the black-suited vampire finds himself within a dark forest, kept company by a single owl that rests on a tree branch. As though intentionally being as far away as possible, the vampire breathes a deep sigh - looking through the trees at the mountain that he and his comrades will soon traverse.

As he stares at it in silence, a feeling of nostalgia overcomes him. "It sure has been a mighty long time since I laid eyes on that mountain. It has been even longer since I entered the temple that sits upon it... the temple that was the cause of much heartache. It comes as no surprise why the boy's armour has guided him there. The suit must still remember... that tragic day."

Suddenly - a malevolent force enters the forest, causing the vampire to grow alert. The feeling is familiar and one that he has felt only recently. The single owl that sat above flees into the sky with fright as the murderous intent envelops the forest, and yet the vampire displays an amused smile.

"Well well... it looks like somebody has decided to pay me a second visit. I must be growing popular."

Turning around, the vampire finds the same hooded demon that he encountered many nights ago. Standing with its piercing red eyes and long tongue, the nameless demon displays an angry and frustrated gaze, as it addresses the grinning boy.

"You... why are you still alive? I killed you. I watched as your fallen body fell!"

"Indeed you had killed me, for a brief moment. You see, permanent death is not in my vocabulary and cannot be granted by the likes of you. However, you are welcome to try your luck again?"

At that second, the hooded demon launches its killer claw from under its attire and like a torpedo it fires toward the vampire. However, the boy evades the claw with a simple yet masterful sidestep before darting away from the enemy's line of sight. The evasion was so fast, that the hooded demon gasps as its claw retracts.

"Where did you go? Show yourself!"

To the foe's surprise, Umbra can be heard from behind the unsuspecting demon. Under the quiet night, he crosses his arms and sighs "oh dear, what a pitiful attempt. I barely leapt a few meters and you were unable to keep up with my speed. I even allowed you to kill me and yet you still failed miserably. Your grace period is over."

At that second, Umbra releases a malevolent aura of his own that far exceeds the one of the hooded demon. The aura is so intense, that the surrounding trees of the forest begin to wither and die within seconds. Terrified of the overwhelming force, the enemy demon stumbles backwards before falling to the ground in fear. Petrified, he sits helplessly - unable to move an inch as the vampire proceeds to enter a fighting stance.

"What in the world is going on?" Stutters the hooded demon.

"Bloody sword!" Umbra shouts - magically summoning a long blade composed of pure blood. As he holds the crimson blade in both hands, the blue moon pokes its head from out the clouds, casting down its moonlight upon the duel like a celestial spectator.

"It can't be possible. This power..." the demon trembles frantically, attempting to make sense of the sight before him. "... That power is the same as the prince. It is almost identical to Megathos: Demon prince of the underworld! Just who are you?"

"You wanna know who I am? I am everything that the demon lord fears!"

With a great swipe of the bloody sword, Umbra severs the demon in half with one strike, sending its torn body skyward.

With the enemy gone, Umbra breathes a sigh of relief and basks in the peaceful night once more. Looking up at the sky, he smiles while whispering to the wind.

"You had better prepare yourself. I have waited a thousand years to find you once again... Megathos."

Chapter 13: The Lost Ones

H aving regrouped, the trio resumed their journey under the moonlit night sky. Upon eventually approaching the foot of the mountain, they find what looks to be over one hundred stone steps that lead up to the mysterious temple. Standing close together they make their way up the old stairs that look to have survived centuries of use. Surrounded by countless trees that shiver from a mild wind, a feeling of apprehension overcomes the heroes.

"Does anybody know what exactly is at the top of this mountain?"Asks Luke, turning to his friends for an answer.

Shrugging her shoulders, the golden-haired swordsman replies "I have no idea. As far as I know, there's supposed to be an old temple but nobody has ever spoken about it."

As they continue ascending the steps, Luke and Aurora notice a peculiar gaze in Umbra's eyes. Looking as though he were in a daydream, the vampire answers boldly and knowledgeably.

"For your information, it is called the temple of Venus. Although you humans have forgotten its relevance, it is one of the most important temples in the world. You see, a tragic event was once centred there, which would change the course of this world forever. What occurred within the temple of Venus, triggered the Divine War of the gods, which in turn resulted in the creation of the Apex Grail" Umbra adds.

"Whoa, is that true? In that case, what was the tragic event that had caused the war" Luke asks, eagerly awaiting his comrade's reply.

With a warm and wise smile, Umbra replies "let us get to the temple first. After that, I promise to tell you everything I know."

They continue, pressing onwards up the stairs that seem to show no end. Upon a split-second glimpse behind, the young hero gasps with fright at how high they have traversed. The many towns and cities below now look like miniature modals from a toy box. As he marvels at the overwhelming scenery, he wonders why a temple would be made so dangerously high above. He guesses that perhaps the temple was most likely made for a deity alone, and not for the eyes of mortals.

To their relief, the long row of steps eventually ends. Finally reaching the top, they gaze upon a small white temple. Its shape is squared with no fancy symbols or statues to adorn its design. The simple architecture gives off a sweet and innocent character that is a pleasant surprise to look at. However, Luke cannot shake an added feeling of sadness upon its sight.

"So this is the temple of Venus? I was expecting something more" says Aurora - being the first to approach the building's entrance which is shut firmly by a simple wooden door. "Let us get this over and done with. I'll open the door. You two, cover my back for any surprises."

Attempting to enter, the woman proceeds to barge her way in. However, as she makes contact with the door, a mysterious force pushes her backwards.

"What in the world was that? I can't seem to open let alone touch the entrance."

Upon a light chuckle, the vampire strolls to her side and responds "well of course you're unable to get through. Can you not tell? A spell has been placed over this temple to stop outsiders from entering its doors. This particular spell can only be opened by a secret word. No amount of force will be able to break it otherwise."

Feeling deflated, Luke sighs with grief and looks up to the clouds. "Oh jeez... after all we did to get here, you're saying that we won't be able to go inside? The secret word could be anything."

"Yes, the secret word could be anything. However, I happen to know what it is" Umbra says. An air of suspense fills the air as Aurora and Luke stand back - yet again lost for words by the surprises of the vampire. Upon a small exhale, he utters the words "for love."

At that instant, the door swings open. Jumping with surprise, Luke and Aurora stand speechless while staring at their black-suited companion.

Eyes wide with disbelief, the golden-haired comrade asks "how in the world could you possibly know the word to break that spell?"

With a surprisingly mature and strong tone, the vampire replies "I have been here once before... but not as I am now. Come along and follow me."

Wasting no time he disappears into the temple, followed by the cautious female behind. Being the only one left outside, Luke stands with many questions - already overwhelmed by the experience so far. Under the quiet night, he prepares himself.

"It looks like this place is significant for many of us,

somehow. I would never have guessed that such a small temple would be so important, yet it is."

Suddenly, a familiar voice addresses the young boy from behind and says "please... I am begging you... don't go inside."

Turning around, Luke flinches at the sight of Diana the blue moon goddess. A desperate look can be seen on her face, like a mother worried for the safety of their child. The sight of her humbled demeanour surprises the boy, who finds it hard to respond. Slowly turning his back to her, Luke says "I am sorry but I need to join my friends."

"Wait..." the goddess says, in a tone that is weak and vague. The boy pauses to hear her out - glancing at her sparkling blue eyes. "Luke... I want you to know something. Everything I have ever done was for the continued safety of our world."

She vanishes into the sky, almost as quickly as she came - leaving the boy left to digest her words. Not to be deterred by the matter at hand, he puts it all to the back of his mind and enters the temple of Venus.

Once inside, the boy follows a dimly lit corridor - spurred on by a distant light ahead. Upon each weary step along the quiet and echoed route, a feeling of tragedy stirs within his head and heart, as though something was attempting to communicate with him.

"Why can't I shake this feeling? I can't explain it but... something terrible once happened here."

His feelings are heightened further, as he proceeds to run his hands along the ancient and dusty walls. As he glides each fingertip across the stone service, a rush of unexplainable memories floods his thoughts. The memories do not belong to him - nevertheless, the surge of images and foreign scenarios feel familiar somehow. "Are these the memories of my suit or the previous owner? I can't make sense of it" he whispers

- stumbling like a drunken individual. However, in this case, he is drunk on a forgotten time, filled with an abundance of sorrowful emotions.

"Hey boy... would you stop lagging? Hurry up and get your butt here!" Aurora shouts from up ahead where the bright light can be seen.

"Ok, I am coming..."

Struggling to his feet, Luke catches up with the pair. Entering the central hall, the boy glances around. The light that he had noticed is nothing more than the moonlight, shining through a glass ceiling above. The illumination hits every corner, as though the architect of the temple were a master of aesthetics. Catching his attention, the young hero notices broken pieces of what were wooden benches, covered with dust.

"What is this place and what happened here?"

Strolling to his side, Aurora also glances at the ruined floor and with a deep breath, she replies "your guess is as good as mine. I am led to believe that this was once used for a ceremony, which may have been abandoned and later ransacked by bandits."

As plausible as her theory seems, Luke cannot shake the feeling that perhaps another outcome had occurred. The room feels as though it were screaming at him - constantly depositing countless memories into his thoughts that overlap within seconds. The memories shown are of three warriors: a wizard, a demon, and a knight who sports a familiar blue armour. It isn't long before he falls to his knees again and lets out a painful shriek.

"Uh... Stop it!" He cries, pleading with the images to cease.

Kneeling to his side, the ally gasps with concern. "What is happening to you, Luke?"

"This place... it's trying to tell me something."

"What are you saying? Are you starting to lose your marbles?"

Strolling into view from a pulpit in front, the vampire Umbra comes into view and glances down at the pair with stern eyes

- getting their attention. The expression on his face surprises his friends, who watch as he addresses them.

"No, Luke is not losing his mind. The tragic memories of what was once a place of love is merely resonating with him. After all, the blue armour once journeyed here with the original wearer of course."

"Will you stop talking in riddles and start making sense!" Orders Aurora, who is in no mood for vague explanations. "Are you gonna tell us what is going on here or do I have to beat it out of you?"

With a small chuckle, the vampire looks up at the glass ceiling to the bold moon beyond, in all its glory. He stands quietly for a few moments, before replying "this place is called the temple of Venus, and it once belonged to one of the most beautiful goddesses in history: Aphrodite the goddess of love."

"Aphrodite?" Aurora asks, unfamiliar with the particular deity.

"Yes, Aphrodite was perhaps the most beautiful goddess in all of history. Gods and mortal men adored her, while goddesses and mortal females envied her. None could fault her benevolent beauty and love. Unfortunately, as fate would have it, love would become her downfall. You see, Aphrodite was at the centre of a new kind of love, a love that to this day remains unspoken."

Following every sentence from the black-suited ally's lips, Aurora and Luke stand transfixed. As his voice echoes around the quiet room, Umbra closes his eyes and continues the revelation.

"The Goddess Aphrodite had fallen in love with a mortal man. The man was not a noble, nor did he possess any heroic traits. He was but a simple commoner... nothing more and nothing less. Not even his very name was important enough for the world to remember. However, the world knew of their love. Unfortunately, such love had never been seen before."

"Are you truly saying that a goddess and mortal once fell in love? In that case, this must have occurred before the creation of the Apex Grail, correct?"

"That is correct. This all occurred one thousand years ago, at a time when men and gods lived together. However, this new kind of love was not accepted by many. It was deemed forbidden by almost fifty per cent of the gods. In addition, the one who led the charge against their love was Diana, goddess of the blue moon!"

Eyes wide with shock and disbelief, Luke steps forward with a gaping mouth. He waits for Umbra to laugh - hoping it was just a fleeting joke. However, the look in the vampire's eyes is unwavering.

"Diana? Why would she be against something as harmless as love?" Luke asks as the golden-haired ally crosses her arms as though having already sussed out the reason.

"Is it not obvious, boy? The goddess of the blue moon was jealous of Aphrodite's beauty. That would be the only explanation."

Shrugging his shoulders the vampire responds "I am afraid I do not know the official reason. The gods never disclosed their purpose for stopping the union. What I can tell you, was what happened to Aphrodite and her lover. They were killed. The most beautiful goddess in history, along with her mortal partner was killed by the orders of the goddess Diana... the very goddess you are working under."

Lost for words, Luke's heart feels as though it could fall from his chest. He looks down to the ground, mind racing with thoughts. "I don't believe it. Why would Diana do that? So does this mean that I have been working for an evil goddess or something? If so... she is no different than that awful wizard."

In contrast to Luke's bewilderment, Aurora's interest has finally been pricked by the accounts of the past. Caressing her chin like a detective who has pieced together a puzzle, she lets out a loud sigh and says "now it is all beginning to make sense. So, what you are saying is: That the divine war was caused by an objection to the union of a deity and her mortal lover. Those who were against such a love warred against the pair and killed them. After that, the victorious gods would decide to cut off the connection between man and god by creating the Apex Grail. The blue moon goddess sounds like a horrible lady if you ask me.

Overwhelmed, the hero falls to his knees. A series of thuds shake the ground, which to his surprise finds that it is by his fists - slamming against the floor without ceasing.

"She never told me this before. Why on earth would she do something so cruel?"

"Stop asking stupid questions" Aurora shouts to Luke, turning her gaze to Umbra. "What I would like to know is: how does this all relate to the wizard and his desire for the Apex Grail? Surely he must have been connected to the divine war somehow?"

With a firm head nod, Umbra replies "most likely... which brings me to the next part of the story. You see, although the gods warred, the one who dealt the killing blow to Aphrodite and her lover was not a god but the herald of Diana. His name was Solomon and he was the first Blue Lunar, the original wearer of the divine armour you now possess."

Upon hearing the peculiar name, Luke remembers its mention by the wizard during their second encounter. With each drop of information, it feels like a jigsaw puzzle is slowly coming together.

"So, Solomon was ordered to kill an innocent couple? How could he go through with that?"

"With a lot of doubt and reluctance, the same doubt you have been carrying all this time. I have watched you Luke, and your hesitant eyes each time the goddess meets with you. Solomon wrestled with his duty to defeat the goddess of love and he wasn't the only one. You see, Solomon had two comrades. The first was the demon prince Megethos, who after engaging with him in a duel, earned his respect and companionship. The second was an all powerful wizard named Felix, and the three were known as the mightiest warriors in the world. You wanna know the best part? After they had set out to accomplish their mission, the goddess Diana betrayed them and left the three for dead."

"Diana betrayed her herald? How? Umbra I don't understand!"

Breaking their conversation, a great force blows over the temple, which rocks the very pillars that sustain it. Within moments the temple collapses and buries the trio, as a legion of ghastly cackles rejoice into the night sky.

Chapter 14: The Prince of Darkness

Upon the mountain top, the temple of Venus has now crumbled, destroyed by the actions of a mysterious force that has buried the trio. Under a supernatural crimson sky, sounds of inhuman roars and cackles fill the night.

Slowly pulling themselves out from the rubble, the three glance at one another - dazed and confused with what is happening.

"Is everybody ok?" Aurora asks, brushing off stones and traces of debris.

"I am fine. I only wish I knew what caused the temple to give way" responds Luke - looking up at the nightmarish sky whilst hearing the eerie sounds of mysterious beasts. "What the hell is going on? Do you both see what I am seeing?"

"Never mind what is above. Look around you" Umbra Advises, as he holds his trusty briefcase tightly. To Luke and Aurora's surprise, they notice that Umbra is shaking - terrified by a dark presence. Taking his advice they glance from left to right and gasp at the sight of hundreds of beasts. Surrounding the three, the beings glare and laugh in a fashion that sends shivers down their spines.

"Are they... monsters?"

"No, those are not monsters. Those are something far worse. What we are seeing before us are... demons" replies Umbra - standing back to back with Aurora and Luke.

"Demons. Although I have come across a few creatures of the night in my time, I have never seen so many in one place. What are they doing here?"

"Allow me to explain" comes an unfamiliar voice from within the crowd of malevolent creatures. Emerging from the pack, a single man can be seen. Sporting a bright red tuxedo suit, he bears two horns upon his forehead. His face is pale like salt, which contrasts with his black eyes that resemble an endless abyss. The fellow demons bow at his sight and halt their cackles - as though he were their leader. "I the mightiest prince in all of hell have arrived."

His voice, although smooth and subtle belies a terrifying aura that grips the trio with fear. Around his feet, flowers and plants wither instantly, and above, flocks of birds fall and die - affected by his mere presence alone.

"Who... who is that?" Asks Luke - prodding Umbra for answers.

"That is the legendary demon prince: Megethos. Be on your guard!"

With a perked up glance, Aurora responds "Megethos? Wait... isn't he one of the comrades you mentioned who fought alongside Solomon and Felix during the divine war? What is he doing here?"

Upon a single step forward, the red foe yawns casually before replying "well isn't it obvious? I am here to kill you all. Not only have you been a pain for my friend Phantom, but you also dared to trespass the sacred temple of Venus. That is all the more reason I need."

Slowly unsheathing her white sword from its scabbard, Aurora responds boldly to the adversary "so, you are working with the wizard who has caused so much pain and sorrow? I assume you are after the Apex Grail then. What are you both trying to accomplish?"

With a small chuckle, Megethos proceeds to take hold of the pair of horns upon his forehead - pulling them out slowly. Before the trio's eyes, they notice that the horns are in fact hilts, each to a blade made of blackened bone. Holding a sword in each hand in a dual-wielding fashion, he declares to the three "come at me, fools. Make sure you give it your all!"

The crowd of demons go wild - cheering for their leader like he were a superstar. Their commotion rocks the very mountain, as Luke and his friends stand nervously.

Being the first to put on a courageous face amidst the bleak confrontation, Aurora whispers to the pair "I will take him on first. You two follow my lead!"

Wasting no time the woman runs to the demon prince while holding her shining sword in front. With each step closer, she senses his ferocious aura, which is so overwhelming it feels as though her spirit is being crushed. Nevertheless, she presses on and charges onward to the demonic adversary.

Leaping forward she performs a forward stab to the foe - however he evades the attack with a graceful spin. His movement is so masterful, that Aurora lets out a small gasp and says "Impossible..."

Before she has any time to react, Aurora is struck by the hilt of his blades - knocking her unconscious.

"Aurora!" Screams Luke - shocked by how quickly the world's strongest swordsman fell. Their plight seems to only excite the surrounding demons, who stomp their feet and chant as though spectators of a tournament.

Shaking his head, the demon prince looks down at the fallen warrior and gloats "your mistake was evident from the start. Had you unleashed your full power of the stigma, you may have stood a chance against me. Such a pity" he says before raising his swords to the sky to finish her off.

At that instant, a burst of light throws Megethos off guard, causing him to squint from the intensity. "What in the..."

Looking to the source of the light by his left side, he spots the blue hero - entering his transformation of knightly attire. "Leave her alone!" Luke screams, darting forward at blistering speeds with his claymore sword. "Wraaaaaaah!"

Their swords collide, resulting in a burst of light dispersing all around from the collision. Weapons pressed against the other, the blue hero displays eyes of hysteria, as his foe bears a nonchalant gaze.

"Why do you want the Apex Grail so badly? Is all this bloodshed worth it?"

"I need not explain myself to an impostor. You may possess the same suit as Solomon, but you will never be like him!"

Channelling his emotions into the sword, Luke rants "I don't want to be like anybody. I just want to be strong enough to protect this world!" Unleashing a beam of energy from his blade, the young hero blasts Megethos backwards.

The surrounding demons boo and jeer the young hero - displeased by the upper hand.

Un-phased by the projectile, the demon prince stands strong with a casual stare as the boy rants on.

"Umbra told us everything about what happened in the past. You and your friends were ordered to kill Aphrodite, before being betrayed. I won't pretend to know how it felt, but what you and Phantom are doing now won't bring anybody back!"

"Shut up you insolent mortal. You know nothing of our pain!"

Running to one another once more, the dark adversary and hero battle - striking sword against sword at intense speeds. As they clash continuously, the dark prince shouts to the young hero.

"We were betrayed by the moon goddess. We trusted her, especially Solomon the original Blue Lunar. She said that by killing the goddess of love, we would ensure everlasting peace.

However, after killing Aphrodite and then surviving the divine war, we found out the truth. Solomon and the rest of us were used and tossed aside like nothing. The moon goddess planned to deceive us all along!"

"There must have been some explanation for it. Why would Diana choose to deceive anybody?"

"That is just her nature, idiot boy. She preys on those purest of hearts to get what she wants. She is spurring you on with false promises when in reality you will never obtain them. What is it you desire? Friends, family, peace and harmony? The goddess knows the struggles of you mortals very well and uses those desires to her advantage. At least I as a demon do not hide the fact that I despise you mortals, unlike the gods who feign benevolence. That is why we will take the power of the gods for ourselves!"

With a well-timed strike, Megethos slashes Luke's breastplate - shattering his front armour completely. The boy spirals through the air before tumbling to the ground - devoid of strength.

"Great Scott... he is so powerful!"

Holding his pair of bone swords high, the red foe stands over the young hero and readies to deal a killing blow. However, at that moment, Umbra addresses the powerful demon prince.

"That is enough, Megethos. They are not your true targets. You and I both know that you came here for me, isn't that so?"

Flinching with surprise, the demon prince turns around and looks upon umbra, the only one standing. As their eyes meet, the crowd of demons become silent - sensing a kindred connection between the two. A profound silence covers the atmosphere, as the dual-wielding demon smiles.

"Umbra, it has been quite a while... one thousand years to be precise."

"Correct. For some time I wondered how long your slumber would last. The pain of losing Solomon must have impacted you greatly. However, it's ok because I am here now."

Lost for words, Luke watches the confrontation - mystified

as to how the two know of one another. "Have they met before?" Luke whispers, lying helpless on the ground.

Holding his arms out wide - Umbra begins strolling towards the red adversary, and with a great smile, he says "we don't need to fight anymore. Trust me... everything is going to be ok."

Baffled by his open arms, Megethos lowers his weapons and responds "what are you doing?"

Throwing his arms around the foe, Umbra hugs Megethos in an embrace that startles all the onlookers. The demon prince gasps with surprise - unable to comprehend Umbra's actions and the effect it is having on him. Like a ray of light piercing the darkness, Megethos' dreaded aura begins to wane.

"Everything will be ok. All this hatred and revenge... just let it all go... my dearest other self."

Slowly loosening the grip of his swords - Megethos looks up at the sky and embraces the hug from the black-suited boy.

Suddenly - as though being snapped back into the darkness, the demon prince grips his swords tightly and growls "no... I cannot allow this pain to go. It is all I have left!"

At that second, the dark adversary stabs Umbra through the chest with both blades, causing the surrounding crowd to cheer once again.

"Umbraaaa!" Luke cries, watching as his friend slumps to the ground. The crowd are ecstatic - praising their prince as he stands victorious like a world champion. Amidst the crimson sky and horrific creatures, the mountain top itself could be described as a piece of hell, with its king bathing in the suffering of his victims.

Sheathing his bone blades back into his forehead, Megethos raises his fists to the sky and cheers with his minions, as Luke watches helplessly.

"Is this the end for us?" The boy whispers to himself - powerless to fight against the dark swordsman.

At that moment the rowdy demons pause with surprise, looking up at the sky as though threatened by something from beyond the clouds. The demon prince stops also - displaying a bothered expression, like a child whose playtime has been disrupted.

"Who dares to disturb my victory!"

Following their line of sight, Luke lifts his head to the clouds - wondering what it is that has caught their attention. Before his eyes, the boy spots a golden star in the night, like a rod of benevolence. And as it descends to the mountain top, a great light envelops all that is upon it.

Chapter 15: The City of the Grail

As the night fades, the morning takes its place over the land once again - calling forth a blue sky, white clouds and bold sun.

Coming to - the young hero opens his eyes and finds himself on a soft ground, surrounded by pretty flowers and plants. A slightly uncomfortable heat brushes over him - pointing to a hot day. As the soothing sounds of chirping birds fill his ears, Luke ponders his predicament.

"Where in the world am I and how did I get here? The last thing I remember was being on the mountain with Umbra and Aurora. We were all hurt badly by that demon and then... oh god... am I dead? Is this the afterlife?"

At that moment an unfamiliar voice replies "no, this isn't the afterlife... thanks to me."

Upon a quick gasp, the boy sits up and turns to his right side - laying his eyes on the person who had just spoken to him.

The individual is a woman, sporting a long golden cloak and wearing a wide and pointed hat that covers most of her face, save for her gold-coloured lips. Arms crossed she leans against a small plinth, holding a warm smirk.

"We are in the royal palace gardens. Unfortunately, there weren't any more rooms available for you to recover your energy, so here was the best option."

As clear as her words are, the boy is no closer to understanding his whereabouts than before. The only thing he can be sure of is the intention of the stranger. An aura of warmth flows from her like a stream, which puts his mind at ease. Upon a deep breath, he attempts to assess his situation once more.

"I am so confused. Where am I exactly?"

Upon a small laugh, she replies "we are in the royal palace of Ergo: capital of Superbia. Just before the demon prince could finish you all off, I intervened and used my magic to transport you here."

"You used magic?"

"Yes of course. I am a witch after all. My name is Gold Star Gabriella - however, you may call me Gabi."

Hearing her introduction whilst marvelling at her attire, Luke stays in awe at the fascinating witch. Remembering his friends, the boy panics and asks "where are my friends? Where are Umbra and Aurora?"

Suddenly, a different voice calls to Luke from behind and grunts "where the hell are your manners, pip-squeak? Before spouting orders, you could at least say thank you to Gabi. You are in the presence of one of the most powerful witches in the realm. Know your place!"

Flinching with surprise, Luke turns around to find a second witch. Sitting upon a stone slab, she holds a cold and bullish glare at the boy. Unlike the previous witch, the volatile looking female sports a black cloak while wearing a pure black pointed hat.

"Oh, I am sorry... I didn't mean to offend anybody" the

timid boy asserts - like a school child in the presence of your neighbourhood bully. The intimidating witch simply huffs and looks away as though he were not worth her time. The stark contrast between the two witches throws Luke off guard.

Easing his worries - Gabriella says "that there is Black Star Bonnie. She can act a little tough sometimes, but I assure you that she means well. To answer your question about your friends; they are fine. Aurora has been awake for some time now and can be found somewhere within the palace walls. Umbra's wounds were far worse, so he is still resting, in the palace clocktower.

Confused by the information relating to Umbra, Luke whispers to himself "why would Umbra need healing? He is immortal."

Approaching the boy from his left side, a third witch introduces herself - sporting a white cloak and hat. "Um... my name is Silver Star Selene and I was the one who healed all your wounds with my magic. It is a pleasure to meet you."

The third witch blushes from under her great hat, which humours the young boy. Observing the personalities of all three witches together, Luke remains fascinated by them.

"Gabriella, Bonnie and Selene. It is a great pleasure to meet you all. I don't know what we would have done if you hadn't arrived to rescue us. If I may be so bold to ask: how did you know we were in trouble?"

"Worry not your sweet little mind. All you need to know is that we are fully aware of your mission and journey so far. Aurora told us everything. We know that Phantom and Megethos intend to steal the Apex Grail from this palace. Our sources tell us that a legion of monsters and demons are on their way here as we speak. As such, all of the strongest warriors in the land have gathered here to defend the Kingdom and stop them. Tomorrow we will hold a meeting to discuss our strategy, and we'd very much like you to be a part of it. Until then, get some more rest and perhaps explore the palace and city. My sisters and I shall depart now."

Wasting no time, the black-dressed witch claps her hands and states "thank heavens! I was beginning to lose my mind, being around the little pip-squeak. Can we please go someplace cooler? The heat is killing me!"

As she strolls off without so much as saying goodbye to the boy, Silver Star Selene bows in a shy fashion and says to Luke "uh... see you later", waving nervously before leaving the garden also.

Being the only witch left in the garden, Gabriella continues to stay gazing at the boy - admiring his every being. She holds an ever-present smile in contrast to his somewhat meek composure - amused by his innocent eyes.

Amidst a calming silence, the lead witch strolls towards Luke who remains on the ground. As she gets closer, keeping her gaze locked onto his eyes, Gabriella crouches - bringing her face inches apart from him. He blushes mildly - looking down in confusion and embarrassment.

"What... what are you doing?" He asks, displaying an uncomfortable look.

Slowly lifting her right hand to his face, the woman gently caresses his left cheek as though he were the most delicate creature in existence. As the warmth of her fingers stroke his skin, Luke flinches initially - not used to such a loving touch. The action is enough to bring him close to tears, for he had only seen such a gesture between families - something he had never been fortunate to have. As he continues to allow her touch to grace him, Gabriella speaks in a soft yet cryptic manner.

"You are even more beautiful than what my vision had shown me. The work of the gods is truly something to behold."

Upon a small bow, the witch departs, leaving the boy within the peaceful garden - pondering her words.

"Her vision?"

∞ ∞ ∞

The morning carries on, and the city folk of Ergo go about their daily lives. The city is vast and expansive - filled with tall buildings that are a sight to behold. The colour scheme of Ergo is that of yellow and gold - giving off a sense of richness to the city, especially under the bright rays of the glistening sun. Littered throughout the streets and squares, monuments and statues of legendary heroes, gods and goddesses are depicted. The inhabitants sport the latest and finest clothes - a testament to the popularity and fame of the country's capital city.

In the centre, the great palace of Ergo resides in all its glory. Multiple towers and quarters make up the great wonder, which is large enough to house thousands of people. The exterior of the palace is gold plated, which reflects all light - making it look like a beacon that can be seen from miles away. Inside the palace walls, every surface is made from the finest marble one can acquire, with not a trace of dust.

On one of the highest floors, upon a wide balcony, the golden-haired Aurora can be found. Standing close to its ledge, she overlooks the expansive city with a troubled expression.

"The people... they are worried. News must have reached about the wizard and his actions" she gossips to the wind - taking in the quietness of the humid day.

At that moment, a trio of footsteps can be heard coming from behind the female swordsman. As though already aware of the individuals, the warrior keeps her gaze over the city, and with a calm tone greets them.

"That was rather quick. How was the boy?"

Standing side by side, the three are revealed to be the witches: Gabriella, Bonnie and Selene. With her ever-present smile, the gold leader of the threesome approaches Aurora and childishly hugs her from behind. Chemistry of long-standing friendship can be felt between the two, as Gabriella responds "little Luke is such a cutie pie. He has the most adorable eyes I have ever seen!"

"That wasn't my question, Gold Star. Did he seem well?" Asks Aurora in a stern manner that excites Gabriella further.

"Relax my darling Aurora. You are far too uptight sometimes. As for the boy, he is well. We have left him alone to get his head together.

With an uninterested yawn, the black witch Bonnie crosses her arms in a moody manner before asserting "well if you ask me, I think the runt is nothing but trouble. What in the world convinced you to pair up with him and his demon friend?"

"If you must know, they saved my life. If it wasn't for them, I would be dead."

Holding her chest in a shy fashion, the white witch steps forward and says "I for one quite like Luke. Although, it is hard to imagine that he is the herald of the goddess Diana."

"I agree. The boy doesn't suit what your typical fearsome herald would look like. However, I assure you all that his strength is great."

"I sure hope it will be enough to defend our kingdom," says the gold witch - looking up at the sky with a concerned stare. "As you know, the Apex Grail is housed within this very palace, which means Phantom will no doubt make his way here. All our sources indicate that he most likely will appear any day now with his legion of monsters. Add on the fact that he is working with the demon lord Megethos, and you can only imagine how dire our situation is."

An air of helplessness and defeat overcomes the warrior, who recollects the night before during the confrontation with the prince of demons. She pauses - gritting her teeth before mumbling "how can we possibly stand against such power? It's already bad enough that we have the detestable wizard to fight against".

As her mind goes over their defeat yesterday, Aurora asks "say - how did you know where to find us yesterday? It surely wasn't a coincidence."

"Come now, darling Aurora. Have you already forgotten about my speciality? I possess the innate ability to foresee future events, giving me the chance to change the course of an outcome. I typically am given a vision, once a day."

"So that's how you came to the rescue. Once again, you prove why you are the greatest witch in the land. I sure hope that ability of yours will help us against the wizard and his minions."

"Don't worry. We have a few tricks in store for that ghastly wizard when he arrives. If he thinks that Ergo will fall like Spiritus, then he has another thing coming!"

At that moment, an additional pair of footsteps can be heard from behind, causing the four to turn around with intrigue. Standing before them, they notice a young boy roughly around twelve years of age, dressed in casual attire. Bearing long silver hair, he wears a left eye patch. Staring only at the gold haired woman, he produces a great smile as he greets her.

"Sister Aurora, there you are!"

"Yohan? Oh dear brother!" She gasps, overwhelmed at the sight of her younger sibling. The look upon her face brightens, even rivalling the sun as she opens her arms lovingly. Running into each other the brother and sister embrace one another.

"Sister, why didn't you tell me that you had arrived yesterday? I only knew of your arrival upon overhearing it from a few soldiers just now."

"Please forgive me, dear Yohan. I wasn't exactly in the best shape last night when I was brought here. However, I intended to surprise you later. My apologies."

Watching the brother and sister converse together, the three witches stand at a distance and whisper to one another.

"How sweet. Notice how our darling Aurora's attitude changed the moment she saw her precious little brother again? She truly cares deeply for him" says Gabriella - folding her arms like a wise old teacher.

Scoffing at her comment, the black witch responds "oh give me a break. What is so sweet about a pair of Stigma siblings?"

"There is no need to be like that" Selene expresses - looking over at the city and the inhabitants among it. "In any case, we need to make preparations for our meeting tomorrow. There's no telling when Phantom will strike, and Ergo will certainly be his next target."

The three stroll from the balcony, back into the palace - leaving the brother and sister.

∞∞∞

As afternoon arrives, the sun decides to hide behind a slew of grey clouds - offering a welcomed breeze over the land. Infrequent droplets of cool rain refresh the city folk after the beaming rays of the sun.

Within the palace gardens, the young hero can be found pressing his forehead against a brick wall - lost in thought and stress. He has been in the same position for some time, going over the revelations of yesterday.

"Aphrodite… Solomon…The divine war and The Apex Grail. All this tragedy is because of Diana. Had she simply left things alone, none of us would be in this mess to begin with. Oh god, what on earth am I doing?"

Thinking about the detestable wizard, Luke surprises himself upon coming to a shocking theory. "Wait… Umbra said that two of Solomon's friends were Megethos the demon prince and Felix the world's most powerful wizard at the time. What if Felix and Phantom share a connection somehow. Better yet, what if they are the same person?"

Interrupting his focus, a familiar voice calls to the hero. "I guess you now know the truth, little hero?"

Turning around, the grey-haired boy rests his eyes on the blue moon goddess who stands with a humble posture.

His fists clench almost instantly, as though threatened by the mere sight of her, along with his eyebrows that scrunch downward to form a face of unbridled resentment. The anger that exudes from him is so great, that it causes her to step back with surprise.

With a firm tone he replies to her "no, I am not letting you off the hook that easily. I want to hear it from your lips. Everything I was told about: The Divine War, Aphrodite, Solomon and his death... were you the one responsible?"

Standing opposite one another in silence, the goddess and mortal keep their eyes locked on the other - however, the roles have reversed. In contrast to previous days, when she was the one to give orders, now Luke is the questioner. Such a role reversal is to be expected, considering the revelation about her past, and as the boy awaits her response, Diana holds her head high and replies.

"Yes, it is all true. I ordered Solomon who was the original wearer of the suit you now carry, along with his friends Felix and Megethos to kill Aphrodite and her human lover. It was I who also had tasked them to wage war on the gods who supported the union, and it was I who had first thought of the Apex Grail."

Taken back by her swift and casual reply, Luke feels disgusted - hoping deep inside that she would provide a different response. "Why Diana? Why did you do it?"

"She... Aphrodite gave me no choice. She knew the risks that such a union would bring."

"So you decided to kill her? Who the hell does that and what did it have to do with you!"

"Fool, it had everything to do with me. It had everything to do with the world and still does" Diana shouts in defence of her past actions before sighing aloud.

"You see... amongst us gods, there is something that most of us fear. That is... the union of mortals and immortals. Nobody has ever seen what the offspring of a god and a human looks like and neither of us has dared to explore such a possibility, lest we create something that could jeopardise us all. I couldn't allow such a possibility to take place.

"So, you didn't even know what would happen and yet you still chose to kill Aphrodite and her lover? So it was all based on fear? What about your original herald Solomon? What excuse do you have for betraying him in whatever way you did?"

She gasps and pauses - holding her chest as though having struck the deepest nerve in her fibre. Clearing her throat as though holding back the urge to burst into tears, she struggles to keep a calm demeanour before saying "I have no excuse for what happened to Solomon. I betrayed him by not being honest about the armour he wore, from the start. I just didn't want him to hate me. In the same way, I don't want you to hate me too. Although, once you do finally discover the secret of the blessed armour, you will most likely detest me."

Eyes perked with shock and confusion, Luke stumbles forward before holding Diana's arms aggressively. "What the hell does that mean? What secret? What exactly happened to Solomon at the end that will happen to me? Come on Diana!"

"I am so sorry... I just can't do it right now..."

At that instant, she vanishes into thin air - leaving the overwhelmed boy yearning for answers. Like the many instances before, she has left him hanging yet again to discover the truth for himself. Words cannot explain the rage and frustration he feels inside, and like a volcano ready to erupt, he screams to the heavens "Dianaaaaaaaa!"

As his voice echoes into the wind, the helpless boy looks up at the heavens - tormented by the mystery of Diana's secret. "Why... why won't she tell me?"

At that moment, the door to the palace swings open, revealing the golden-haired Aurora along with her silver-haired brother Yohan. Stepping into the garden they find the weeping Luke - back turned to them.

"Hey boy, you ok?" She asks, in a typical stern yet considerate fashion. Her familiar voice soothes Luke's troubled heart, who upon slowly turning around, nods his head and produces a half-hearted smile.

"Hi, Aurora. It is good to see you are well."

"Well, I am not exactly one hundred per cent. That demon swordsman gave us a run for our money, that's for sure. To lift our spirits, I thought it would be a good idea to wander around the city and take our minds off things. Oh and this is my little brother, Yohan. You don't mind if he tags along, do you?"

Shifting his eyes to the younger sibling, Luke nods his head once again and replies "Sure thing. Nice to meet you, Yohan."

With a great smile, Yohan skips to the young hero - getting a closer look at his features. Inspecting his grey hair and divine imprint upon his forehead, Aurora's brother bows and says "you truly are the herald of Diana the moon goddess. Thank you for looking after my big sister. I am grateful!"

"You are welcome, but I would say that Aurora has been looking after us. Shall we get going?"

Together, the three depart the palace garden to wander through the vast city of Ergo. Like a trio of tourists, they visit each popular district, as the sun emerges through the grey clouds as though not to be overshadowed. They pass through the famous shopping district, known for its highly envied items in all of Sol. Compared to Luke's hometown of Heline, which only had a handful of stores, Ergo trumps it tenfold - with countless shops and outlets.

Visiting the historic quarter, they marvel at the many ancient statues that depict legendary heroes and weapons of the past. Although he is unfamiliar with the monuments, Luke cannot ignore the grandness and majesty that exude from each of them. He is humbled and inspired - wondering if he could ever be immortalised in such a fashion.

After a few hours, they stop by a small port area, filled with the most beautiful looking ships in the land. Sitting by the end of a pier, side by side the three overlook the blue waters and mountains in the distance.

"Incredible. Ergo is even more beautiful than I had ever imagined. It is like a utopia or something!" Comments Luke, feeling uplifted by the exploration. The smile on his face is like that of a child in a theme park - the perfect remedy for his low mood.

With a motherly smirk, Aurora responds "you shouldn't let this place get to your head. It is not all paradise, that's for sure. Although it has come a long way, this city still has a long way to go. Poverty is still a problem here, and many of us still face discrimination. Those like myself and Yohan are treated among the worst by regular citizens. Thank god the King of Ergo is unlike the rest. He saw us as an asset to the kingdom, rather than something to be shunned."

With his head held low, Aurora's younger brother adds "I am sure you are well aware, Luke. My sister and I are known as Stigma children, so normal people tend to dislike us. It isn't so bad now, but growing up was quite tough."

Luke resonates with their past - saying no more on the matter, for Yohan's words are enough to remind the boy of his struggles growing up. A kindred bond is felt between the three as they sit together - watching a pair of ships depart to sea. Keen to know more about the younger sibling, Luke enquires more.

"Yohan, are you a knight as well? You don't seem to be wearing any armour as Aurora does."

"Oh no, I am not a fighter at all. Unlike my sister, I have no talent in the realm of swordsmanship. However, I am a mighty good cook!"

Slapping his back, his older sister laughs and says "Yohan here can barely lift a sword. If he were out in the big bad world, he wouldn't last a second, haha. However, I kinda like it that way. The last thing I would want is for him to become a warrior... with all the pain and hurt it brings. All I want is for Yohan to live a normal life, full of happiness."

Luke nods his head in agreement, as the experienced fellow warrior, he has become. He knows all too well the weight it brings to fight for a cause. To his surprise, a feeling of envy overcomes the grey-haired hero, as he looks into Yohan's eyes that show no guilt. Unlike Luke and Aurora, who have acquired much blood on their hands, Yohan is free from such burdens.

Turning away from the pair, Luke gazes at his reflection in the water and asks "I wonder what people see when they look into my eyes? One of the good guys, or a murderer?" His mind is taken to the tragic city of Spiritus.

The golden-haired comrade doesn't answer - shrugging her shoulders as perplexed as he is. However, her lack of response belies a hidden opinion that she keeps to herself. In contrast, Yohan produces an innocent smile and replies to the hero.

"I don't know what others may think about you, but your eyes seem sincere. They are not pure and they're not tainted either. They simply seem real... if that makes any sense?"

"Real?"

"Yeah. You have the type of face that reveals everything on your mind."

Chiming in, Aurora adds "my thoughts exactly. Luke's eyes are like a clear ocean, revealing all beneath it."

Fascinated by their comments, Luke gasps pleasantly - welcoming their words. Feeling relieved, he takes in the fresh sea air in the knowledge that he still contains some humanity - despite how much has changed.

Clapping his hands together, Yohan states "I think that I should grab us all a bite to eat, don't you think? There's a delicious food stall nearby that you have to try. Give me a few moments while I go fetch us something. You two wait here."

Standing to his feet, the brother of Aurora skips down the pier, into the distance - leaving Luke and the female comrade alone.

"Your brother seems like a nice person. You and he are quite similar."

"Ha, now I know you are going crazy. Yohan and I couldn't be any more different. Thanks anyway though."

They hold their silence, attempting to delay the inevitable questions that have been plaguing their minds since yesterday's defeat. Putting on a courageous expression, the young hero is the first to speak.

"So... what do we do now? We are lucky to be alive, thanks to those witches. However, if Phantom and that demon decide to come here, what will we do?"

"It is not a question of if. They will most certainly come, that's for sure. After all, this is where the Apex Grail resides, have you forgotten? We have no choice but to fight... plain and simple."

Like an amateur that is overwhelmed by the challenges ahead, Luke sighs worryingly, in a way that can easily be read by the comrade. Testament to their level of friendship, she places her hand upon his knee and says "do not worry, boy. I will be with you, every step of the way. Just focus on doing what is right and staying alive."

"I wish I knew what that truly meant. I am not sure what the right thing is anymore. After all, this is all because of the goddess Diana. To be honest, I don't know if I believe any of what she says anymore. What am I fighting for? Who should I fight for?"

Laying flat, back against the ground - Aurora digests his plight as she looks up at the sun and its rays.

"Fight for yourself. You don't need to do what others tell you to do... that goes for the gods as well. You can do whatever you want, your way."

"My way?"

"Yeah dummy... your way. Do you wish to stop phantom from taking more lives?"

Pausing briefly as though it were a trick question, the boy replies slowly "well... yeah of course!"

"Then stop him, your way. Do you wish to bring peace to our land, so that those like your sister and my brother can achieve their dreams?"

Raising his tone bravely and courageously, the young hero shouts "most definitely. I want to protect my sister!"

"Then just do it. Lastly - do you want to live in a world where you can be who you want to be?"

Her final question strikes a chord with the young hero, who for a moment spaces out and enters a brief daydream. Within it he is sitting upon a field of flowers, with his sister Rose - filled with nothing but peace and bliss.

"Yes... yes, I do. So, I will live my life... my way."

"There is your answer."

At that moment, Yohan returns - bringing with him a handful of fresh sandwiches, stacked in his arms. "Hey, you two. I am back with some delicious food. These sandwiches are to die for!"

The sight of the boy holding the sandwiches, along with his excitement reminds Luke of another friend, who he had almost forgotten about.

Producing a look of worry, the young hero whispers to himself "I wonder how Umbra is doing?" As he recounts the scenes of yesterday night, feeling tearful.

Like the perceptive ally she is, Aurora senses his concerns - holding a watchful gaze for many moments before suggesting "I think we should head back now."

"What? But why sister?" Asks Yohan.

"I have to prepare for our meeting with the King tomorrow, and Luke needs to check on a good friend of ours, right Luke?"

With an appreciative gasp, the hero replies "yes that's right. I need to understand why umbra has not fully recovered yet."

"Then it's settled. I will go ahead and return to my palace quarters. You will find the idiot vampire within the clock tower, next to the palace. I will see you tomorrow morning, at the audience."

Picking herself up from the floor, the golden-haired comrade hurries into the distance, waving goodbye to her brother in the process. The younger sibling stands still - showing a look of deep thought as his sister disappears into the city.

Left with the brother, Luke senses an unexplainable feeling of sorrow from Yohan. Careful to approach, the boy takes a single step forward and asks "are you ok?"

He does not reply, in a manner that seems almost rude

- keeping his eyes focused on the palace and its golden brilliance. After a somewhat strange moment of silence, Yohan replies in a monotone and lifeless manner.

"Have you ever wished to see the light in someone so much, that you would become their very shadow?"

∞ ∞ ∞

The afternoon gives way - introducing a violet sunset that paints the sky, blessing all underneath it. As most of the city folk return to their homes, a restful atmosphere fills the city, along with sounds of moaning crows.

Within one of the palace's many rooms, the three witches reside. Seated by a desk of magic spell books, in front of a large window that welcomes the calming rays of the sun, Gold Star Gabriella flicks through each page - holding a frustrated expression.

By the darkest corner of the room, Black Star Bonnie can be seen leaning against the wall - holding a mystic ball which she peers into. Much like her sister, she holds an annoyed expression as though at a loss.

Laying upon a single kingsized bed, in the centre of the room - Silver Star Selene stares at the ceiling above, lost in thought. Humming a small melody, she tosses and turns, attempting to soothe their stress.

Closing the spellbook before her, Gabriella produces a deep sigh and says "it's no use. I have read each book over one hundred times, and there are no other ways to explain how the wizard was able to break free from his prison from mount Bember."

Sharing her plight, the black witch tosses her crystal ball to one side and adds "you got that right. I too am at a loss. Ever since the wizard of despair broke free from his prison, we have been trying to find out who or what had released him. The binding spell that the witches of old used against him was near invincible. Only the power of a god could break it and that shouldn't be possible because of the Apex Grail."

"This is quite troubling indeed, for if we are to capture the wizard again, we will need to know what caused him to break free in the first place. Otherwise, it is all pointless" Selene adds with a deflated sigh.

"Wait a moment. Is it not true that Megethos the demon prince is also running rampant? Perhaps he was the one who released Phantom?" Gabriella suggests - stroking her forehead like an investigator at a crime scene.

Shaking her head, Bonnie crosses her arms in disagreement and says "no, that theory is incorrect. I know for a fact that Megethos was still in his perpetual sleep when Phantom broke free. On the contrary, Megethos was the one awoken by Phantom."

"Jeez, this is so confusing! Ok, let me try and get this straight. Somebody freed Phantom from his one hundred year prison. After that, the wizard went on to awaken Megethos from his long sleep. If there is someone who has the power of the gods, strong enough to break Phantom's prison, then protecting the Grail will be impossible."

Gazing out the window with a worrisome look, Gabriella marvels at the glorious sunset - watching a flock of birds soar through the clouds. A drop of envy overcomes her, wishing the predicament could be as simple as a bird's flight. "The answer must be out there, somewhere. Perhaps we have overlooked a key piece of information..."

Suddenly - Gabriella lets out a great gasp as she is overcome with a divine force. The force is nothing new to the woman, as every day, the same mysterious sensation runs through her spirit, like a divine baptism from the heavens. This baptism is her speciality, which upon washing over her each day, a vision of a future event is received. As though lost in a trance, she begins to foresee the future, as her sisters stand on edge - awaiting her revelation.

The divine force leaves her - freeing Gabriella from the trance. However, as she comes to her senses, she buckles upon the table, face full of sweat. "Good heavens!"

"Gabriella, what did you see?" Shouts the black witch Bonnie, ready to race to her aid as Selene follows suit.

Gesturing for her sisters to stay put, Gabriella responds "do not be alarmed, I am fine. Unfortunately, I was unable to remember the vision. Such a pity."

Putting on an unconvincing smile, the witch dries her face with a nearby cloth before sitting back in her seat. Her quick and simple response does little to ease the minds of her fellow witches, who remain suspicious of her somewhat mellow demeanour.

"So, you weren't able to remember anything? That's a first. You usually can remember the visions you receive" utters Selene - attempting to prod further. A clear air of dishonesty is felt within the bedroom, and yet the gold witch continues to behave as nonchalant as ever. The silence in the air is such that one could hear a pin drop.

Keeping her eyes averted from the pair as though ashamed, the gold witch says "I remember nothing... nothing at all."

A further moment of quietness transpires before the black witch shrugs her shoulders and remarks "whatever. It probably wasn't important anyway. I am stepping out for some air. You coming Selene?"

Holding her chest with concern, the silver witch keeps her eyes upon their leader who remains back turned and cold. Eventually, Selene replies "yeah... I am coming with you. See you tomorrow, Gabi."

The pair exit the room, leaving the gold witch alone with her thoughts. With no company left to keep up false appearances, Gabriella breaks down into tears and weeps.

"Aurora... why is it always you?"

Chapter 16: Heart to Heart

N ighttime arrives, and heavy rain begins to fall over the land. The city folk outside run desperately for shelter, like scuttling ants to their nests. The absence of the moon and stars makes for a particularly lonely yet calming night.

Next to the palace, a tall old clocktower can be found. Compared to the gold-plated grandness of the palace, the clock tower is the complete opposite - like an undesirable sibling. Made from old and battered brickwork, the structure is far from pleasing to the eye. In addition, its clock face is dim and stained with dirt as though intentionally neglected.

Within it our hero ascends its mouldy steps - looking for someone in particular. Among the many concerns that plague his heart, the well-being of the friend remains his highest priority.

"This place is filthy. Did they have to keep him up here?" Luke wonders, covering his nose from the unbearable stench all around. As difficult as it is for him to press on, he continues traversing the stairs of the tower - growing even more anxious while getting closer.

Eventually, he reaches the top, coming to a single wooden door to the quarters where his friend resides. Unsure whether to knock or simply enter, the grey-haired hero decides to call out and say "Umbra… It's me, Luke. May I come in?"

There is no reply. The only sounds heard are the beating raindrops against the roof outside. "Perhaps he isn't there?" The boy asks himself - ears pressed against the door, listening for any movement on the other side.

At that moment, the familiar voice of his friend finally replies "come in…" with a surprisingly weak and sad tone. Wasting no time, Luke opens the door and steps inside.

"Umbra…" Luke utters while scanning the room before him. Akin to an unused attic, complete with all the dust and bugs that it brings, the room is cluttered with tools, rusted weapons and armour. In the far right corner, the boy spots his friend, laying on a small mattress. As though held in deep thought, Umbra stays still, looking up at the ceiling with a troubled gaze.

"Are you ok?" Luke asks, slowly treading towards him. An aura of sorrow exudes from the tuxedo sporting friend, who although realises Luke's company, refuses to look in his direction. "I was told that you needed some more time to recover."

"Yes. Unfortunately our enemy yesterday was the one and only demon prince. Not even I, with all the immortality I possess, am safe from his power. I am lucky to be alive. We all are."

Glancing at the hero for a quick second before looking to the ceiling, as though ashamed, Umbra stutters before uttering "I am sorry, Luke."

Perplexed by his words, the hero blinks with surprise and asks "what are you sorry for? You did nothing wrong."

Turning his back to the baffled friend, Umbra replies "what

happened yesterday was my fault. You see, the demon prince Megethos and I... we... we are connected. His very existence is because he and I used to... we were once..."

"It doesn't matter. You don't need to explain because as far as I am concerned, you did nothing wrong - whatever connection you have to that demon." Luke's blunt and supportive words shock Umbra, who gasps like one who has obtained forgiveness.

Looking at him with confusion he asks "are you serious? You don't care? But... I am not even a real vampire. I am something far worse."

"It makes no difference what you are. To me, you are and will always be my friend. Now move aside, will you?"

"Wait, what are you doing?"

To Umbra's astonishment, Luke climbs into the bed also - holding a sympathetic smile while scanning the old and cluttered room.

"You know, this room reminds me of my old place, back in the orphanage of my hometown. From time to time, I would share my room with other kids who were in the same situation. However, when they left to join new families of their own, I would often be left alone. I wouldn't want to wish that on anybody... especially you, my friend. I will keep you company until you're all better again."

Moved by his friend's desire to stay by his side, Umbra is lost for words as though unworthy of such a gesture. Closing his eyes, he turns away and utters words of gratitude.

"Thank you... Luke."

Meanwhile, many miles south of Superbia, in the country of Veritas, the sister of the young hero can be found in the same spot of the same bedroom of the protective mansion. Seated opposite the window, she watches the heavy rain as it assaults the glass and brickwork. A feeling of worry constricts her, not for her well-being but for the condition of her brother who she has not seen for some time.

"He hasn't returned yet. I wonder what's taking him so long?" Rose whispers to the shadows of the dark room - dimly lit by a nearby lamppost outside. Standing up she leans closer against the window, wishing that Luke would appear from around the corner. She has been wishing and expecting the same outcome, ever since he departed. Yet with each day and night, her hopes have slowly waned, like a follower who has lost their faith. "Oh, what's the use? He isn't gonna come back. I should have stopped him from leaving. I was such a fool!"

Throwing her head into her hands, she begins to cry - unable to control her sorrow and helplessness. Try as she might, the image of her brother refuses to leave her thoughts.

"I... I just want to know if he's ok."

Suddenly at that moment, a pebble hits the window from outside, startling the girl. She jumps with fright, almost falling off her chair while gasping with fear. Questioning her sanity, she asks herself why a random pebble would hit the window. It most certainly wouldn't be from a monster, and it is far too late for any person to be out at this time. The darkness of the room along with an eerie creak of the floorboards adds to her fear. Nevertheless, she puts on a brave face and stands up before opening the window.

"No way... I don't believe it!"

To her astonishment she sees Luke, standing by the lamppost outside. Pinching herself continuously, like a person held in disbelief she stays speechless. "You... you came back!"

The boy waves while holding a cheerful smile, perhaps far too cheery for one standing under heavy rain. Despite this, the sister puts all questions to one side before running out of the bedroom, eager to let him in. Bolting down the stairs like a girl gone mad, Rose hurries towards the main door, not caring about how her footsteps could wake the others who are fast asleep in their rooms. Like irritating obstacles, chairs, vases and tables are knocked from her path as she makes a beeline for the front entrance.

She reaches the front door and wastes no time opening it - forgetting to catch her breath in the process. Swinging the door fully open she anticipates the sight of her brother - however, who she sees is anything but her sibling.

"Who... who are you?" What happened to Luke... ?"

To her shock, she finds a grown man, covered from neck to toe with a purple cloak. Face painted black and white, he displays a devilish smile wearing a crown of thorns.

The fear in her heart is so great, that her chest could explode. Every fibre in her body is telling her to scream and run, but she is far too petrified to do either.

Looking into her helpless eyes, as though he were reading her very soul he places his finger over her lips and speaks with a dry and sinister tone.

"Do not be alarmed, Rose. You should be overjoyed, for I have come to take you to your precious brother. You will become the catalyst that will bring... ultimate despair.

Chapter 17: The Apex Grail

T he following day arrives, bringing with it a not so ambitious morning. A thick fog covers the country of Superbia, as a grey sky looms over the land. Drenched by the heavy rain of the previous night, the city of Ergo is wet with a strong scent of soil that fills the air.

Within the golden palace of Ergo, in a large meeting room dedicated to strategic purposes, plans are already underway. In the centre is a long marbled table, along with dozens of chairs on each side and one single golden chair by the head. The scheme of the room is a dark and passionate red, with portraits of roses that decorate the walls.

Sitting upon three of the chairs, the witches: Bonnie, Selene and Gabriella wait for the other attendees to arrive.

"Jeez, what's taking Aurora and her friends so long to get here? We don't have all day!" Bonnie fusses, slamming her hand to the table with frustration.

"Let us not be impatient, sister. After all, they have had quite a rough time. Besides, not even the king has arrived yet" Selene responds with her usual calm tone.

"I am sure that they will arrive any second now" Gabriella assures, holding a peculiar look - staring into space as though preoccupied with other thoughts.

No sooner after her words, the doors come swinging open, revealing the three heroes. The first to step inside is the golden-haired warrior Aurora, displaying a dominant stature.

"Apologies for our lateness. I had to go fetch the two numbskulls. They got lost trying to find this room" Aurora states in a nonchalant tone - quickly taking a seat opposite the three witches.

Second to walk in, the black-suited Umbra skips inside playfully - responding to the female warrior, "Well you could hardly blame us, Succubus. This palace seems to go on forever!"

Placing himself next to the warrior, he rests his feet upon the table like an entitled superior - watched by the three witches who are stunned by his bold nature.

The final comrade of the trio walks in, displaying a nervous look as he scans the room before him. "Sorry for being late. I promise that it won't happen again" says Luke, bowing continuously like a servant of the castle.

"Quit being so modest and just sit down, will you? We've already wasted enough time as it is!" Shouts Aurora, like the parent figure she is. Like a child slightly in fear of their strict parent, Luke hurries to the seat next to Umbra - watched by the witches who continue to observe their bickering antics.

"Hey, what's the big idea here? Do you mean to tell me that your king wasn't able to prepare at least one plate of food for us? I've seen better hospitality in hades!" Umbra complains, like a spoilt guest of a royal appointment.

"This isn't a celebration, idiot vampire. We are here to talk business, so the least you could do is not be disrespectful!" Aurora rants, swatting his legs off the table.

"Ouch! What was that for? You can't expect me to be respectful. After all, I am a demon, silly wench!"

Upon a foul look at one another, Aurora and Umbra sigh before slanting back on their chairs, watched by Luke who rolls his eyes with embarrassment. The communication between the three astounds the witches, who stay lost for words.

Taking a deep breath while putting on an optimistic smile, Gold Star Gabriella states "well at least we are all here. Now, all we need to do is wait for the King to arrive."

At that moment, much commotion and movement can be heard from outside the room, as though a multitude of people were delegating to one another. The sounds grow louder and nearer, as though a famous idol were about to arrive.

"Speak of the devil..." Aurora mutters - closing her eyes with her arms crossed - knowing exactly the reason for the commotion. No sooner after her comment, the door opens wide, revealing the King of Ergo and his band of advisors. Dressed in fur red attire, fitted with many diamonds and pearls throughout, the man steps inside showing off a golden crown that reflects all light. His stature is tall and large, with an overgrown stomach that is so big, that one could rest multiple palettes of food upon it. As grand as his clothes look, his demeanour betrays such importance, as he displays a warm and bubbly smile like a grown child.

"Whoa, it looks like everybody is early. Such enthusiasm!"

"We weren't early. You were just late as usual!" Aurora says sternly to the King, clearly not bedazzled by his royal status. For many, such a disrespectful way to address a King would spell a swift punishment - however, for the King of Ergo, her remarks are met with laughter.

"Haha, oh you haven't changed at all my darling Aurora. Come give your favourite King a big hug!"

"No, stay away and stop embarrassing me would you?"

Like a soft and loving father figure, the King skips to the golden-haired warrior and playfully pats her cheeks - annoying her even further.

"Awww, I see that cold and terrifying stare of yours hasn't waned in the slightest."

"Get off me, annoying King. Go bother somebody else!" She barks, clearly not the least bit amused by his embrace. As Luke watches their interaction, he stays shocked by the humour and warmth of the King. Among the many assumptions one would expect of royalty, a jolly and patient King would not be one of them.

"My my... so you must be the one everybody has been talking about!" Says the happy King, turning his gaze to the young hero. The boy's heart pauses, feeling overwhelmed and unable to react as the man locks eyes with him. "You must be Luke, right?"

"Uhh... um... yes your majesty!"

Leaning in closer, the King strokes Luke's grey hair while inspecting the letter D, imprinted on his forehead. The man stands speechless for many seconds, even forgetting to blink.

By the gods... that must be the mark of the goddess Diana. You truly are the great herald of the blue moon. It is a pleasure to meet you boy. I am King Leon.

"It is a pleasure to meet you too, your majesty!"

Interrupting the pair, the black-suited friend yawns aloud and cries "yadda yadda... when are we going to skip the formalities and get some breakfast?"

Caught off guard by his tone and manner, the King turns to the demon and asks "You must be the other comrade, Umbra correct? How was your stay in our famous clocktower?"

"Horrible! Everything was dirty, the walls needed a good paint job and to top it off, the bell kept ringing every hour. I didn't get an ounce of sleep. I would have rather slept outside!"

Laughing to the top of his lungs while slapping his stomach, King Leon turns to Aurora and says "ha, your friends are quite the interesting bunch. I am sure you all have had a great journey together so far. Now, let us get down to business shall we?"

The King takes a seat at the head of the table, and the

discussion of their situation involving the wizard and the Apex Grail begins.

"Right, I brought you all here to discuss everything we know of the recently released wizard. Firstly, have any of you managed to figure out who released the wretched wizard in the first place? He shouldn't have been able to break free by himself."

"Beats me. Perhaps the magic that contained him had an expiry date?" Aurora responds with a sigh - shrugging her shoulders as though refusing to burden herself with such a conundrum.

Unsatisfied with the only suggestion voiced, the King turns to the witch Gabriella and asks "Gabi, what do you think? I know that you have been hard at work trying to find out. Could you not find anything?"

A suspicious look appears on her face for but a second, so fast that most of the group does not detect it, save for Aurora who blinks with a subtle surprise.

"Uh... no your majesty. I couldn't find anything."

"That is quite a shame. How about your foresight magic? Were you able to foresee anything relating to that at least?"

Again, a small but barely noticeable look of nerves can be seen within her eyes, which as before are spotted by the master swordsman Aurora.

Hiding her face under her hat, Gabriella replies "no, I saw nothing at all."

"Very well. Moving on... The next topic is about the fiend's purpose. It is no mystery that he has been wanting to get his hands on the Apex Grail, ever since he first appeared one hundred years ago. Why would one wizard cause so much destruction for it? Granted, the Grail exists to separate the gods and us mortals, but how does such a thing benefit him?"

Raising his hand like a genius school child in a classroom, Umbra replies in a patronising manner "you humans are so dense, you know that? There are hundreds of ways a wizard like Phantom could benefit from it. For a start, he could use and manipulate the divine energy within the Apex Grail for himself. After all, the Grail was formed from the powers of almost every god and goddess. If you could harness that power for yourself, you would be no different from a god."

Impressed by his comments, the group nod their head in agreement with the tuxedo sporting comrade, satisfied by the theory. Looking down in thought as though lost in a daydream, Luke whispers to himself while trying to make sense of the wizard's past.

"Perhaps he wants the Apex Grail for revenge against Diana, if he is indeed connected to the tragedy of the past?"

Clearing his throat, the King claps his hands and says "finally, allow me to brief you on our current predicament and what I need you all to do. Our sources say that the wizard will arrive here at any moment. If that is true then this city is in grave danger. Fortunately, we have already evacuated the city folk to underground bunkers, where they will be safe. What I need from you all, as well as the soldiers of our kingdom is to protect the Apex Grail. My advisors and I have already decided on where you shall be stationed.

A moment of apprehension overcomes the six, as they wait to hear where they will be ordered to guard. An air of silence fills the room as the King is handed a sheet of paper - proceeding to read from it.

"Aurora and her two comrades will defend from outside the palace. I want Aurora to support our troops in the north quarter of the city. Umbra will support the southwest troops and Luke shall support the southeast unit. The finest warriors in Superbia will be by your side, so make sure to rely on your allies. The palace itself is protected by the strongest magic there is. As such, once all the doors and windows are closed, not even the wizard himself will be able to get inside. However, if he does manage to slip inside somehow, Gabriella, Selene and Bonnie will be waiting for him."

Interjecting in a somewhat perplexed manner, Umbra chuckles and asks "is that a wise idea? What are those three witches going to do against a foe such as Phantom, not to mention Megethos who will almost certainly be with him?"

Brushing off the boy's concerns, the King replies "worry not, for we have the power to subdue the wizard and the demon prince. The very same spell that bound Phantom one hundred years ago was taught to Gabriella, Bonnie and Selene. Once he is caught in that, there will be no way for him to break free!"

"Hmph, and yet he somehow managed to escape the spell in the first place. You humans have quite the bizarre logic. Very well, let's go with this plan of yours. It is not like we have any better ideas anyway."

Clapping his hands as though signalling for the meeting to close, King Leon puts on a jolly face and says "excellent! That concludes our meeting. Now, before we get you all into position, who would like to see the Apex Grail?"

Gasping with surprise by the King's request, Luke's eyes widen like a child ready to view a well-envied toy. Leaning forward, he takes a deep breath and replies "yes, yes please your majesty. It will be an honour!"

"I would like to see it too. It isn't every day that I get the chance to see a relic of the gods. Just promise me we'll eat something afterwards" Umbra adds - stomach growling more and more.

"Count me out. I have better things to do than lay eyes on troublesome things" says Aurora - proceeding to stand before turning her back to the group. "I will get ready to prepare. May the goddess of victory be us all."

Short moments pass and along a single corridor, Luke and Umbra are led by the King. Side by side the pair cannot contain their excitement - looking at each other after every few seconds.

By each side of the walls, a pair of heavily armoured guards can be seen, sporting gold-plated armour, each wielding a sword. As he glances in awe at the soldiers to his left and right, a feeling of loyalty and strength can be felt from them. Their stance is still and strong - bowing in unison by the presence of his majesty.

With each footstep, the young hero grows even more anxious as he imagines what the heavily sought after relic would look like.

"Not long now. The chamber to the grail is just up ahead" King Leon assures the two, as he walks with his hands behind his back like a wise guide.

The pair take a deep breath upon the king's words. Even Umbra, who happens to always have a question for everything is silent.

Eventually, they reach a single large, gold door, imprinted with images of men and deities. Standing opposite the door, the King pauses for a few seconds, as though admiring the sight before him. Reaching into this pocket he proceeds to take out a single key, before turning to the two.

"Here we go. Are you two ready to witness the work of the gods? What you are about to see, is something that most people will spend their lives imagining."

He inserts the key into the door and rotates it clockwise. As the sound of the door being unlocked is heard, Luke and Umbra inhale with anticipation and exhilaration. Watching as it slowly opens, the realisation of just how exclusive the opportunity before them, truly sets in.

"Well... go inside," says the King, gently pushing them into the chamber. As they stroll inside, the pair gasp with astonishment. The chamber is gigantic - enough to fit three stadiums in. The chamber is circular, made of old stone that reaches up to a curved ceiling. By the centre of the room, a great white light emanates from a barely recognisable item, which brightens the chamber like a bulb.

"Is... is that it?" Luke asks, looking to the King for

confirmation.

"Why don't you take a closer look and find out?" Replies King Leon, nodding warmly to the boy's apprehension.

Together, Luke and Umbra walk towards the centre of the light, watched by the King who stays by the entrance, allowing them to experience the moment uninterrupted.

As they slowly approach, they are overwhelmed by the energy and aura that flows from the divine relic. Amid the most wondrous creation and its intoxicating power, Luke feels unworthy of being in its presence. Even as he gazes in its direction, he feels ashamed as though human eyes were not meant to look upon it.

Finally, they reach the Apex Grail, sitting neatly upon a thin plinth. As they stand side by side, Luke and Umbra inspect the divine item. The Grail is golden - decorated with dozens of gemstones and engraved with an unfamiliar script.

"Those words... It's the language of the gods. How truly remarkable" Umbra whispers - stricken with shock and awe. "I have no idea what the words mean, but I am certain that they are necessary to maintaining its power."

To his surprise, Umbra notices the young hero weeping, eyes drenched in tears. "Why on earth are you crying, Luke?"

"I... I don't know why. I can't explain it but... I feel like the Apex Grail is breaking my heart."

Chiming in from afar, the King adds "that is the impact the Grail has on the human heart. Almost everybody who has laid eyes on it has been reduced to tears as if the divine item were stroking their soul. It's a mystery as to why such a feeling occurs, but I hope it proves just how valuable and important the Apex Grail is. We must not allow it to fall into the hands of Phantom."

Within one of the farthest quarters of the palace, in a small armoury room, the golden-haired warrior enters its doors. Closing the door behind her, she scans her surroundings - glazing over the many swords, shields and armour that hang neatly on the walls. She produces a relieved and long-awaited sigh.

"This place hasn't changed at all" she utters to the equipment - inhaling the smell of polished steel around her. Stopping her eyes dead ahead, she spots a particular piece of armour, held within a large glass container. "There you are... old friend," she says to it, slowly strolling towards the equipment.

The armour is dazzlingly white - complete with a polished breastplate, greaves, gauntlet, shoulder pads and helmet. By its side, a long sword can be found within a golden sheath. As the woman keeps her gaze fastened on the mysterious suit, a wave of nostalgia flows through her body, leaving her with a bittersweet sensation.

"I am sorry. I am going to need you to stay locked away, at least until a more worthy warrior appears... unlike me. I just came to say hi... that is all."

Suddenly, the door behind her opens wide, revealing her long time friend and witch: Gold Star Gabriella. As the pair lock eyes, Aurora displays a baffled expression.

"Gabi, what are you doing here?"

"I had a feeling I'd find you here. After all, this was where you would always reside, not to mention that your famous armour is kept here."

Strolling to her side the witch stares at the white armour as Aurora does the same. The two stay quiet - absorbing the peaceful silence of the room, lamenting moments of the past that have brought them together. Upon a light exhale, the witch speaks fondly about the armour before her.

"The legendary suit: Gospel. Its creation predated the Apex Grail and was used by only the most worthy of warriors. Only those who possess a Stigma can withstand the legendary suit.

If a normal person were to wear it, they would die almost instantly. Forged by a nameless yet generous god, as a gift to the kingdom of Ergo, it has been passed down through the ages. No blade can pierce its armour, and no form of magic can shatter its invincible metal. Aurora, you were its wearer until two years ago. Do you still refuse to reclaim it?"

Looking down with sadness, the female warrior clenches her fists as though conflicted. "I... I am not worthy of wearing Gospel, not after the amount of blood I had spilt within this very city, two years ago."

"You are referring to the failed coup that was instigated against King Leon, right? Seventy per cent of the soldiers took part in the plot, and they were almost successful - if it wasn't for you. I remember it like it was yesterday. You wore the legendary white suit and stopped them all. There was much blood spilt - however, if you hadn't acted, there would have been far more blood, innocent blood at that. Aurora, when are you going to stop blaming yourself for doing the right thing?"

Shrugging her shoulders, the warrior turns her back to the friend and prepares to retreat, unable to bear another second on the topic.

"I will leave now for the northern part of the city, where I will defend this palace and the Apex Grail."

"Wait... so you're truly not gonna use Gospel? What if you encounter Phantom out there? How do you expect to stand against him?"

"I don't need Gospel... I never did to begin with. I will fight as I am... my way."

Aurora exits the room and slams the door behind her, leaving the gold witch alone within the armoury. Breathing heavily with frustration, Gabriella catches her breath, hearing the faint sounds of the warrior's footsteps disappear into the distance. Turning around to face the white armour again, she whispers to it in an almost tearful tone.

"I guess I am unable to change our fate this time... for that I am sorry. You were once bestowed to us as a force for justice.

However, before the sun sets over this day, you will represent one of the greatest acts of betrayal.

Chapter 18: The Last Stand

O utside - the fog thickens as a moody howling from the wind whistles through the half-empty streets of the city, as though warning all of something terrible. With the civilians evacuated, the soldiers of Ergo and their allies get into position - preparing for the threat that is yet to present itself.

Mages, swordsmen and warriors of the highest class wait in anticipation. Some can be found crouching by alleyways, while others stand upon rooftops, armed with their weapon of choice. They are silent, as though experiencing a calm before the storm that could arrive at any moment. It is by no surprise that many soldiers are sweating and trembling, knowing that their lives are on the line against the world's most feared wizard. The fearful silence is so great that the sound of a chirping crow sends various troops into hysterics.

∞∞∞

By the north side of the city, standing upon a tall building, the golden-haired Aurora stands ready - sword already unsheathed, white coat blowing under a constant wind. Coming to understand the tactics of the wizard, she looks directly to the sky, waiting for his notorious portal to envelop the city.

"Come on... hurry up and show yourself already."

∞∞∞

By the southwest side of Ergo - the tuxedo sporting Umbra positions himself in the middle of a wide street. Holding his briefcase close to his chest, he mumbles to himself with concern.

"This fog... is not natural. An attack against us now would put us at a disadvantage. Yet again, the wizard is one step ahead."

∞∞∞

Strolling into the southeast side of the city, the blue hero enters an open square area of the shopping district - surrounded by abandoned stores and market stalls. Upon having already transformed into his knightly attire, he wanders around, clearly having lost his bearings.

"I hope I am in the right place? I can't see anybody around here. Damn, this isn't the time for me to get be getting lost."

"Hey, are you Blue Lunar?" Comes a nearby voice that catches the boy's attention. Looking to his left side, Luke spots a troop of soldiers through the fog - gesturing for him to come closer. As he approaches the group, they gasp and chatter with amazement as though having encountered a celebrity. "Oh wow, I never imagined that the famous Blue Lunar would be a part of our troop."

Taken back by their reactions to his appearance, Luke pauses with confusion before responding "how do you know about me?"

"Are you kidding? Everybody knows about you. Your name has spread far and wide as the one who has dared to challenge the wizard king of despair. Not just you, but Aurora and your vampire comrade too!"

Their faces beam with excitement and joy, as though in the presence of a living embodiment of hope. Their constant praise fills his ears and yet, each word of gratitude serves to only trouble the blue hero.

"I... I am not the warrior you think I am. After all, I have come no closer to stopping Phantom. People have still died" he says in a defeated manner - thinking of the fallen city of Spiritus and town of Fiory. His words cause the troop to stay their words of praise, as they keep their gaze upon him.

To Luke's surprise however, one of the soldiers approaches him before patting his shoulders. The soldier exudes unwavering confidence that many would consider being almost deluded, as he proclaims to the blue knight "you gave us hope. Thanks to you, others around the country have also fought against the monsters, even drawing the attention of neighbouring allies. Those allies are here today, to protect our Kingdom and the Apex Grail."

"Are you telling the truth?" Luke asks, stunned by the words of the random soldier. Never in a million years would the boy expect something inspiring to emerge from his regrettable actions. A single clap is heard, followed by another, and within seconds the whole troop cheer rejuvenation into themselves and Luke most of all. Their cheers are infectious, which spreads throughout the whole city - turning their fearful hearts into fearless spirits.

"I swear I will stop the wizard... once and for all!" Luke declares, looking up to the sky - hoping the wizard hears his words amidst the ongoing cries of courage. "Come on out, Phantom. My friends and I have a score to settle with you!"

Imitating his actions, the soldiers shout similar threats - raising their weapons while looking up towards the heavens. A spirit of unity and camaraderie flows through the ranks of soldiers, casting away their fear and doubt.

Suddenly, as though mocking the strength of their resolve, a sinister laugh fills the air for all to hear.

"Kwekekekeeee... Do you have a score to settle with me? How pitiful. It is me and my friends who have a score to settle... with all of you!"

Shawom - at that moment, the wizard's signature dark portal appears from the sky - stretching outward to cover the city of Ergo. As the portal blots out the light from above, the city becomes a dark and foggy battlefield. The cheers that could be heard only moments ago are no more, as the defenders of the Apex Grail brace themselves for what's to come.

"This is it. Get ready and give it everything. The wizard will be somewhere amongst his monsters. As soon as any of you spot him, let me know!" Orders Luke, holding a mighty and steadfast stance.

Within seconds thousands of monsters fall from the portal, descending to the city below. Cyclops, goblins and gargoyles along with countless other beings land on the ground before doing battle with the soldiers. The wind carries the screams of both monsters and men alike, as sounds of steel and broken bones follow amid the chaos.

"Sword!" Luke shouts, summoning his mighty blue blade to fall from the stars and attach itself to his hands. Wasting no time, he tears through hundreds of fiends - leaving a blurry afterimage as a testament to his speed. With just one swipe of his claymore, scores of beasts are obliterated. Finally becoming an adept user of the blessed armour, the hero can release short yet powerful bursts of light that is enough to harm the enemy yet leave his allies untouched. The fellow soldiers watch in amazement, lost in awe at his performance. However, as impressed as they are with him, the hero himself stays focused and anxious. "I won't allow it. I won't allow this city to suffer the same fate as the others!"

$$\infty \infty \infty$$

By the north side, the invincible swordsman Aurora dances through the dark and blood-soaked grounds, laying waste to every monster that opposes her. A master of the battlefield - each stab and strike is perfectly executed. As the blood and limbs of her foes fall around her, the woman shouts words of encouragement to her allies that fight by her side.

"Keep fighting and do not be dismayed by their numbers. We will survive this day and when we do, we shall cry tears of victory!"

$$\infty \infty \infty$$

By the southwest side of the city, the wise demon Umbra takes on scores of monsters - tossing dozens of knives from his suitcase in rapid succession. Standing on the spot with a calm and focused posture, he defeats groups of beasts without so much as breaking a sweat. While the supporting soldiers and allies race around desperately, fighting for their lives, the knife-wielding boy pays no attention to them and their cries. His thoughts are held on something else entirely, something that troubles him. Looking to the golden castle in the distance, he whispers to himself.

"This is all too predictable... too easy. Why hasn't the wizard shown himself yet?"

∞∞∞

Within the castle, inside the throne room, King Leon and his five trusty advisors can be found huddled together - hearing the battle from outside. A trio of long and vertical windows adorn the walls, allowing them to view the carnage of the city. However, the windows are stained with blood from both enemies and allies alike, leaving a dark and uneasy red tint to illuminate the throne room.

Although trembling with fear, the King does what he can to ease the worries of his advisors and says "fret not, men. Remember, this castle is protected and enchanted by formidable magic. As long as the entrances remain shut, not a single monster will get inside... that goes for the wizard too."

The battle intensifies, as larger monsters fall into the city. On the southeast side, the city is overrun by handfuls of cyclops. Trampling through the destruction they scoop each soldier within their hands and mercilessly devour them. Shards of armour shatter and fall about, as arms and legs are tossed through the air like bloody hailstones. The fighters of Ergo are overwhelmed - slowly being pushed back. However, amidst the impossible odds, one knight continues to press forward.

Like a blue bullet, Luke torpedoes through rows of fiends - leaving gaping holes through their chests as they fall to the ground like dominoes. As the fallen beasts crash to the ground, the earth trembles under their weight and the smoke scatters with fright over the war zone. Holding a brave and mighty posture, the blue hero breathes heavily and curses their existence.

"Keep coming, you damn monsters. I won't stop until I've cut every last one of you down!"

Suddenly, a familiar voice calls out to him from nearby and shouts "what on earth are you doing, boy? How stupid could you possibly be?"

Turning around, the hero is stunned to find the goddess Diana, standing with a grieved and angry expression.

"What do you want? I am busy!" Luke says, in no mood to converse with the deity of the moon.

"You are supposed to be protecting the Apex Grail. Not fooling around out here!"

"This isn't exactly what you'd call fooling around, Diana. Besides, the Apex Grail is safe. The palace is protected by magic that repels all who try to break in."

Shaking her head before sighing aloud, she slaps her forehead and responds "you are so utterly useless. Did you not stop to think that the wizard could have preempted such a basic strategy?"

∞∞∞

Within the palace throne room, as the King and his advisors continue to huddle together, a sinister laugh can be heard.

"Kwekekeeee... so here is where you've been hiding."

King Leon and his men freeze with terror at the voice - hoping that it was just a mild delusion.

A pair of footsteps can be heard from the far left corner of the room, and stepping out from its shadows the wizard king of despair reveals himself. Holding a sadistic smile, he chuckles as the King gasps with disbelief - sweating profusely as though coming face to face with fear itself.

"Dear gods... am I imagining things? Are you truly the one and only: Wizard king of despair?"

"My dear fellow, there is no use pleading to the gods. They abandoned us long ago. Now, I am gonna need you to be a good little king and die for me. I have been waiting an extremely long time to claim the Apex Grail, and I can't allow anybody to stand in my way, kwekekekeee!"

As the intruder raises his golden sceptre in front, King Leon and his advisors scream - tears running down their cheeks as the sounds of battle continue to sound off from outside.

"This can't be happening. Wait... how did you get inside in the first place? All the entrances were shut tight. How did you get through...?"

Midway through his sentence, King Leon and his men are torn to shreds by Phantom's invisible magic. As their blood stains the once pristine throne room, the wizard inhales the bloody smell as though it were an exotic freshener. Closing his eyes the man basks in a moment of bliss - turning around to exit the throne room. As he approaches the door, the wizard answers the fallen king's question.

"I was invited."

Chapter 19: Testimony

T he battle rages on throughout the city of Ergo, with signs of no letting up on either side. Suddenly, a great siren is heard from the palace, which causes all the soldiers to stand in shock and worry. The particular siren is one that the soldiers have been trained to understand, which sends shivers down their spines.

Shaking with disbelief, Aurora pauses as she looks to the golden house of the king and Apex Grail. A wave of heaviness overcomes her, as she utters the meaning of the siren.

"The palace has been infiltrated... but how?"

∞∞∞

Within the palace, a single wizard strolls down a long corridor. He takes his time, walking much slower than usual as if savouring the long-awaited moment. Like a fan who has been given exclusive access to a backstage event, he stays fascinated - admiring all that he sees while heading for his goal.

"I can sense it. The power of the Apex Grail is guiding me, like a moth to a flame. It won't be long now until I can make things right... for love... for love..."

Before the wizard's eyes, he finds a handful of royal knights, each brandishing a sword. However, irrespective of their weapons the guards are frozen with terror. Glancing over them as though they were but a minor nuisance, Phantom carries on walking at his slow yet enjoyable pace. Upon a mere sway of his sceptre, the guards are disposed of, dismembered into unrecognisable corpses as he skips over their remains - humming to himself "for love... for love... Kwekekeke."

He continues onwards, leaving a trail of blood in his wake after every encounter with the palaces' knights. He arrives at the large golden door of the chamber. Like an eager tourist of a museum, he inspects the designs of gods and men on its surface. As though offended by the depiction, his smile drops before expressing his distaste.

"Gods and men... together? How utterly pathetic" he hisses, raising his sceptre in front before stating "move!"

Within seconds the solid door is blasted apart - causing a great expel of smoke to sweep outward. Producing a small cough the intruder steps inside. As the smoke settles, he finds the one and only Apex Grail, sitting by the centre - producing its alluring and magnificent light.

"There it is... the great power the gods left behind!"

Eyes gaped open wide, Phantom stares at the sacred relic, unable to find the words to express his feelings. As if captivated in a state of euphoria, he drops his golden sceptre and proceeds to walk towards the Grail - barely stringing a complete sentence together.

"After all these years... my suffering... our suffering... will finally come to an end. One thousand years ago, you were created after my friends and I were betrayed... and we were expected to fade into the abyss. Now, we shall make the world remember us again. For love!"

With each footstep, his heart races further, like a sprinter nearing the finish line. The wizard has waited an eternity to gaze and grasp the relic of the gods. As it sits peacefully upon the plinth, shining its glorious rays of hypnotic light, Phantom sheds joyous tears.

At that moment, the wizard is surrounded by chains of light, like a trap that has been set in place specifically for him. As if caught in the centre of a tornado, the mystical chains spiral around - multiplying in number by the second.

"What in the world is this?"

Shom - before he has any time to react, the chains enclose the wizard and constrict him from neck to toe. As he lets out a short gasp while they tighten, Phantom hears the voice of a single female.

"I am sure you recognise those chains very well, Phantom. After all, this is the very same spell that had once imprisoned you, one hundred years ago!"

Appearing out from thin air, the great witch: Gold star Gabriella stands opposite the wizard, holding a small wand - eyes hidden under her large hat.

"Who are you? Give me your name, wretch!" The wizard growls, struggling to break free from the magic that binds him.

Chuckling in a taunting fashion, the woman replies "you do not deserve the liberty of knowing my name, let alone to gaze upon me. I figured that you'd find a way to sneak into our king's palace, so my sisters and I hid our presence and waited for you to let your guard down. Unfortunately for you, the ancient binding spell was passed down to me and my sisters."

"Curse you!"

Appearing on his left side, Black Star Bonnie also shows herself - holding a dim wand while also keeping her gaze hidden away from the wizard's notorious eyes.

There is no use struggling. No matter what you do, you'll

never be able to break free from those chains, pitiful wizard. Not only are they indestructible, but the formula for unlocking them also changes at a rate of zero point zero one seconds. Your shameless path of destruction is over!"

To the wizard's right side, Silver Star Selene appears, holding a white wand while supporting the words of her sisters. "Soon your powers will be neutralised and you will no longer be able to harm a single soul again. This is the end for you, Phantom."

"You swine!"

As the three witches surround the notorious wizard, he can do nothing but stand helplessly - trapped within the ancient chains.

The wizard hangs his head low for many moments as the witches continue to surround him. There is a long silence, and eventually, the dark wizard can be heard laughing.

"Kwekekeke... kweekeekeeee... I must commend your efforts."

Slightly bothered by Phantom's words, the three take a small step backward as he lifts his head to continue, with a loud and brazen tone.

"Between the three of you, you are quite formidable. However, if you think that I would allow myself to be imprisoned a second time, then you are a fool. Behold... witness my loyal servant!"

Shawoom - at that second, a white figure shoots into the chamber like a bolt of lightning. The mysterious individual weaves around the three sisters, so fast that they are unable to catch a clear sight - feeling a rush of wind as the unknown person zips past.

Somersaulting into the air like an acrobat before landing next to the chained wizard, the summoned individual stands proudly as the witches gasp at what they see before them.

"What...? That Armour..."

To their surprise they discover a mysterious white knight sporting the sacred armour: Gospel, the very armour that once belonged to Aurora. Identity hidden behind the shining helmet and battle gear, the un-named interloper proceeds to unsheathe an accompanying blade - watched by the trio who stands lost for words.

"What the hell is going on? Does Phantom have an accomplice? How were they able to break into the palace and steal the sacred armour, let alone wear it?" Bonnie asks - looking for answers from her sisters.

"This thief... he didn't simply break into the palace. He was already inside, to begin with. That was how the wizard was able to enter these walls. His accomplice was the one who invited him" Gabriella replies, sweating profusely as the wizard holds a cunning smile - delighting in their worries.

"Sister Gabriella, are you saying that there is a traitor in our kingdom?"

"Yes, that is exactly what I am saying. We underestimated the wizard. All this time, he had a servant who was sitting right under our noses."

Laughing to the top of his lungs, the wizard nods his head, confirming their theory and adds "such clever ladies. You see, even with my magic, it would be near impossible to force my way in. As such, I used a little help from a member of your kingdom. Now, let's see if you can figure out my next trick..."

Upon winking to his accomplice, the white knight performs a single swipe to the chains - shattering them in an instant. As the spell disperses into thin air, the witches gape with mouths wide open, watching as the wizard stands unbound.

"Impossible! How could they break the ancient spell: Lux Vinculum? Only a god has the power to do that!" Screams Bonnie, shuffling backwards in distress.

Testament to her insight, Gabriella responds "now it all makes sense. Although indeed, the ancient spell can only be broken by a god, there is one exception. Those who possess the Stigma, inheritors of the gods can break such chains. Not only is the thief a traitor but also a Stigma child!"

Shaking her head with refusal to accept her sister's words, Selene stutters "no... that can't be true. The only Stigma in Ergo who has access to the palace is Aurora, right?"

Interrupting the three, Phantom proceeds to pick up his golden sceptre and gloats "I hate to spoil your bickering, but I am afraid I must retrieve the Apex Grail now. You can debate all you like, in the afterlife. Kill them, my loyal servant!" The wizard orders the mysterious white knight. Wasting no time the silent accomplice leaps forth, blade in toe to do battle against the three witches.

With no other choice but to fight, Bonnie, Selene and Gabriella take on the unknown traitor, as the wizard strolls towards the Apex Grail, chuckling to himself.

Meanwhile, having entered the palace - Luke, Aurora and Umbra approach the doors of the throne room. As they slowly step inside, they gasp with horror at the dead bodies of the king and advisors.

Standing in the aftermath of the massacre, they cover their mouths as their worst fears come to fruition.

"It is as I feared. The wizard managed to sneak inside somehow" utters Umbra, biting his lips with frustration and pity for the fallen king.

Holding her chest with sorrow, the female swordsman whimpers "King Leon... I am sorry I wasn't there to protect you."

Placing his hand on her shoulder, the blue knight says "come on Aurora, we need to get going. Phantom is most likely headed for the Apex Grail..."

Breaking their moment of sadness, the sound of fighting and cries can be heard coming from afar, along with a sinister cackle. Growing alert, the three turn to the exit and panic.

"That commotion, it's coming from within the chamber room. Gabi and the others are in there!"

∞∞∞

Within the hall of the Apex Grail, the room becomes a scene of a desperate struggle. Using the full power of their magic, the three witches hurl bolts of fire, ice and lightning at the white knight who runs rings around them, effortlessly. As they battle against the mysterious foe, the dastardly wizard twirls on the spot - already holding the Apex Grail in his hands.

"Kill them, kill them all my loyal servant! Kwekekekekeeee!"

Pouncing from wall to wall, the knight treats the confrontation like it were a circus, evading the many hundreds of spells the witches cast. The chamber now resembles that of a lights show, complete with spectacular fireworks and sweeping smoke.

"It was you... it was you who freed the wizard, wasn't it! For what reason? Just who are you?" The black witch shouts, launching a great ball of fire from her wand.

Pouncing head onto the fiery projectile, the white knight cuts through the flames before charging onwards towards the black witch. Without mercy, the servant performs a quick and clean sword stroke, cutting the first of three witches down. As she falls to the ground the attacker summersaults through the air - letting out a cold chuckle.

"Bonnieeeeee!" Selene cries, taking on the white swordsman. With a great wave of her wand, she summons forth daggers of ice, which shower the foe from all directions. However, as the icy projectiles come at him, he evades every single dagger, cartwheeling through the room at blinding speeds, like an effortless game. He is so fast, that the silver witch loses sight of him. "Where... where did he go?"

A sword is pierced through her chest from behind. Crying a tearful scream of pain, she glances back with all the energy she has left, discovering the white knight has dealt a surprise attack. "Uhhh... I can't..."

Like her sister before her, she too falls to the ground, leaving her blood to stain the knight's sword. As the murderer turns to face the final witch Gabriella, a great silence hangs in the air. Holding his blade in front, the unknown enemy proceeds to step closer to the only remaining witch.

Upon each footstep, the sound of his steel boots against the ground sends an echoey chime that reverberates against the walls. As the knight gets closer, watched by the thrilled wizard from afar, Gold Star Gabriella holds a strong and fearless gaze.

Before the white attacker, she throws her wand to the ground - causing him to halt with confusion. As though giving her the benefit of explaining her action, the foe pauses to hear her last words in what will soon be her final moments.

Looking at him dead in the eye, she takes a deep breath and reveals "I saw you. Yesterday in my vision, I had already foreseen that you would come here today. I also know who you are, underneath that armour."

Lowering the sword before taking a mild step backwards, the enemy shows a glint of hesitancy, as the witch pleads with him.

"Why... why would you do this, after everything the kingdom has done for you and... her?"

Slowly raising the sword in front, the adversary decides to speak for the first time.

"I am the shadow that will make the sun shine even brighter!"

Chapter 20: The Unholy Reunion

R unning along the long corridor that leads to the chamber room, the three heroes race desperately to stop the schemes of the wizard. The corridor is bloody, containing the dead remains of countless guards who were defeated by the powerful sorcerer. The smell of rotten corpses is overwhelming for the blue knight in particular, who struggles to keep himself from passing out from the stench.

"Damn that wizard. How on earth did he get inside?"

"Boy, stop asking stupid questions, it doesn't matter now. Just focus on lobbing off his head when you see him!" Aurora shouts, leading the way while holding an ever worried expression. "I hope the others are ok?"

"I sure hope so too, succubus. However, I don't seem to hear any more commotion up ahead. I pray that they managed to subdue the wizard at the very least."

Not far off, they finally spot the entrance to the chamber -

golden doors blasted and ripped apart. They brace themselves, taking a deep breath as they draw closer. However, as they get nearer, they find a single body, hunched against the side of the wall. Almost instantly the female swordsman screams at the sight of the fallen individual.

"Gabriella? Gabriella noooooo!"

Covered in blood, the victim is revealed to be the gold witch Gabriella. Running to her side, Aurora kneels before holding her damaged body, watched by Umbra and Luke who stand speechless.

"Gabi... please... open your eyes, don't die on me" pleads Aurora, staring into her longtime friend's closed eyes. After a short moment of silence, the witch slowly opens her eyes, as if clinging to life, even if it is for one last moment.

Looking up at Aurora, she looks into her tearful eyes and says "my dear friend, is it truly you?"

"Yes, it's me, Aurora. Listen... you're going to be ok. Tell me where the bleeding is coming from..."

"No, it's too late for me, I am not gonna last very long. Bonnie and Selene have also been defeated. You... you need to stop the wizard. He's inside... he has the Apex Grail..."

Filled with heated emotions, the blue hero clenches his fists as though having reached the end of his tether. The sight of such suffering brings him to his boiling point, to which he arms his mighty sword and declares "I am going ahead. All of this murder has to end!"

Wasting no time he hurries inside to challenge the dark sorcerer. Following behind, his tuxedo sporting ally also races towards the chamber room and shouts "wait for me. I wish to beat the wizard to a pulp also!"

As the pair disappear into the resting place of the Apex Grail, Aurora stays within the corridor - disregarding the situation at hand while holding onto Gabriella. Like a delicate object that has been brutally damaged, Aurora gently places her hand on her friend's forehead. Her skin feels cold as her blood stains the white coat of the female swordsman.

"Aurora... please forgive me. I am... I am so sorry."

"Why are you apologising? None of this is your fault!"

"No, you don't understand. I could have stopped this all from occurring if I hadn't been so weak. The gods already forewarned me of the betrayal and bloodshed that would occur this day, and yet I chose to handle it my way... without getting you involved. How foolish of me, right?"

Shaking her head with confusion, Aurora tries her best to understand the words of the witch and rants "what are you saying? Betrayal? Are you telling me that you foresaw this day?"

"The wizard... he has a servant who has stolen your old suit Gospel, and is using it to aid the dark sorcerer. It was he who was the one who freed Phantom from the chains of the one hundred-year-old prison. The accomplice... he hails from this very kingdom, which was how the wizard was invited to set foot within these very walls."

"Yet, you foresaw that a traitor would surface and not only steal Gospel but cause such bloodshed, even upon yourself? Gabi... why didn't you tell me?"

Tears begin to roll down the witch's face, as a look of guilt and conflict overcomes her. Struggling to let her words out, she raises her right hand in an attempt to stroke her beloved friend's face before uttering "Aurora... I tried... I did. You see... the traitor of our kingdom... he... he is..."

At that moment she lets out her last breath - closing her eyes, leaving the golden-haired swordsman with a broken and sorrowful heart.

"Gabi... Gabrieeeeeellaaaaaaa!"

Within the room of the Apex Grail the blue knight and his loyal comrade stand opposite the wizard. Spaced far apart, the sorcerer stands at the farthest side of the chamber - holding the sacred relic as the pair hold a strong stance. As if anticipating their arrival, Phantom produces a devious smile while greeting the two.

"I am glad to see you made it, Mr imposter. I was beginning to grow tired of waiting. A trio of annoying witches did entertain me though. Their cries of suffering were a delight to hear."

Glancing to the left-hand side, Luke spots the fallen bodies of both Bonnie and Selene - discarded as though their lives were worthless. Covered by a feeling of guilt and frustration, the young hero closes his eyes and whispers "damn, if only I had gotten here sooner."

Catching the wizard's eye, the villain shifts his gaze to the black-suited Umbra. A look of mild confusion and suspicion overcomes the sorcerer, as though troubled by the sight of him. A tense silence hangs in the air before the wizard addresses Umbra.

"Have you and I met before?"

"Perhaps. However, if you hand over the Apex Grail, I just may tell you" says Umbra, holding a cunning smile in the presence of the dreaded foe.

Letting out a great cackle, the wizard keels over in hysterics like a humoured audience member of a stage show.

"Kwekekekeee... you are quite the comedian. Unfortunately, I'll have to decline your offer. You are most likely an imposter, like your pitiful friend there."

Challenging the wizard's cocky demeanour, Umbra laughs and replies in a perceptive manner "you are not the one to be calling anybody an imposter. After all, you are unable to be true to yourself... right Felix?"

As the last word echoes through the chamber - Luke is startled by the name used to address the dark wizard and whispers to himself "Felix? Wasn't that the best friend of Solomon the original Blue Lunar who was betrayed?"

Looking at the wizard, they notice a clear gaze of fury upon his face. Body shaking frantically, the sorcerer sees red -

triggered by the word addressed to him. As an unsettling aura flows from his body, the wizard glares with eyes of madness.

"How do you... how do you know that name? I stripped away that name long ago, along with all traces of my humanity!"

A great force of power rushes outward from the wizard, like a living expression of his anger. Finding themselves slowly pushed back, the pair struggle to resist the force - cape and attire bowling violently behind. Despite the overwhelming force that is coming against them, Umbra continues to trigger the wizard further - shouting bluntly and directly.

"Your humanity wasn't the only thing that was lost. Your best friend had died, along with the goddess of love: Aphrodite. Felix, why can't you understand... Solomon is gone. Nothing you do, even with the Apex Grail will bring him or Aphrodite back!"

"Silence! You know nothing of my ambition, fool. How about you stop blabbering and start begging for your life. Come forth, my loyal servant!" Says the wizard - looking upward to the ceiling.

Following his line of sight, Luke and Umbra gaze above and gasp at the sight of the pure white knight, descending to their position - sword armed and ready to strike.

"Out of the way!" Umbra shouts, pushing the blue knight from the path of the surprise strike. As Luke stumbles out of harm's way, his friend is struck instead by the attacker. Blood showers the grounds as Umbra screams with agony, followed by the sound of the chiming blade that pierces his chest.

"Umbraaaaaa!" Screams Luke - struggling to process the sight of the unknown adversary who is standing over the black-suited comrade.

"In a painful and raspy tone, Umbra replies" never mind me, idiot. I can't die... remember? However, I won't be able to help for a while. You are on your own for this one!"

Turning his gaze to the blue hero, the white knight raises his sword in front, like a declaration of a dual. The presence of the mysterious foe intimidates Luke who struggles to remain focused. As the pair hold their positions, the wizard can be heard cackling from the distance, like a presenter of a fighting ring.

"Kwekekeee... good work my loyal servant. Now, kill the imposter and don't hold back!"

By his order, the servant launches forth - swiping and stabbing at Blue Lunar with a series of lightning-quick strikes. Quickly pushed back, the young hero finds himself on the ropes, desperately blocking and dodging each attack by a hair's breadth.

"Just who is this person? They are so fast, I can barely keep up!"

The foe continues to pile on the pressure - landing a clean kick to Luke's chest, sending the hero spiralling across the room before crashing against the side of the wall. As smoke and debris shower the air, Luke utters "great Scott. This person is so strong and experienced compared to me. It feels like... like I am fighting against Aurora!"

Standing to his feet before assuming a strong stance, the blue hero says to himself "nevertheless... I can't give up now. I have come too far to throw in the towel. This fight is far from over!"

Resuming their duel, the blue and white knight collide - pouncing throughout the chamber room while clashing blades. Upon each collision, a burst of energy explodes between them, as the menacing sorcerer observes their performance - filled with pure bliss.

"Kwekekeeee... magnificent! The sight of a struggling hero, fighting with all his might is a sight to behold. I wonder if he'll unleash the power of his sword like last time? I would very much like to see this city obliterated like Spiritus was."

Amidst the battle, Luke once again finds himself being driven back, as the foe gains the upper hand. Dancing around the hero like a master of fighting, the nameless adversary spins, cartwheels and somersaults around every strike the blue knight throws at him.

"Why...? Why does this person remind me of Aurora? Is it

to do with the way they move or fight? Yes, it is. Those sword techniques… those all belong to Aurora, I am sure of it!"

Upon spacing out for a second, Luke lets his guard down, allowing for the white knight to kick the hero's blade out of his hands.

"Oh no!" The hero gasps, watching as his blade slides across the ground, just as the enemy leaps to perform an overhead strike upon him.

"Luke!" Umbra shouts, helpless to intervene - watching as the foe's sword falls closer to the helm of the unguarded knight. From the distance, the wizard stares with anticipation, watching the sword come closer as though in slow motion.

"Get him. Run your sword through his puny skull!"

With only inches away, an evasive manoeuvre would be impossible for the boy, who can only stand helplessly - closing his eyes.

Suddenly, however, the sound of a sword being struck reverberates throughout the room - echoing across the walls. As the ringing chimes away, the boy slowly opens his eyes, finding the enemy blade has been stopped by the sword of the golden-haired warrior.

"Aurora…"

To his relief, Luke finds his trusty comrade Aurora has leapt to his rescue, in the nick of time. Standing by his side, her shining blade halts the enemy's killing strike. As their swords remain pressed against the other, Aurora grunts to the young hero.

"Sorry for taking so long. I had to say goodbye to Gabriella."

Turning her gaze to the white knight, the woman displays an angered expression and says "as for you…" Kicking the foe with the heel of her boot. Tumbling across the ground before entering a crouched fighting stance, the white adversary watches as the battle maiden prepares to challenge him.

Flexing her shoulders, producing not an ounce of nerves, Aurora glances at Luke and says "stay out of this one. That foe is mine."

Ready to square off, Aurora and the enemy begin to circle one another - walking slowly while analysing the other's posture. With their blades drawn, they hold their silence as all eyes are focused on the pair.

"I must commend your boldness, whoever you are. Not only were you the one responsible for freeing the wizard, but you also allowed him within this castle to kill our King and obtain the Apex Grail. You also managed to kill three of the most powerful witches in our region, using my old armour: Gospel."

The enemy stays quiet, continuing to tread carefully while holding a firm stance that is without opening. In contrast, the female swordsman displays a slightly open stance, circling him as though in complete control.

"The legendary suit Gospel cannot be worn by most people. It was created to be used by Stigma individuals alone. That means you must be a Stigma also. It has been some time since I have come across another like myself. However, do not be mistaken. I have no intention of knowing your identity, I couldn't care less. My only intention... is to chop your head off!

Upon a speedy pounce forth, the female swordsman takes the first initiative - performing a forward lunge. However, the white knight dodges the stab before countering with a downward swipe. As though anticipating his movements like a true genius of fighting, Aurora evades his blade and using her boot she steps onto his weapon, pinning it to the ground.

"I have you!" She declares, performing an upward swipe to the face area, knocking the helmet off from the opponent's head. As the helmet spirals into the air, revealing the identity of the servant, Luke and Aurora freeze - lost for words at the true face of the wizard's servant.

Dropping her weapon in an instant, Aurora's heart sinks as she struggles to produce a single word from her trembling lips.

"No... Yohan!"

∞∞∞

The identity of the nameless knight and servant of Phantom the dark wizard is finally revealed. Wearing a black eye patch, and sporting long silver hair, the enemy is revealed to be Yohan, Aurora's younger brother. The one who freed Phantom, which in turn resulted in fear and death spreading through the land was none other than the sibling of the most famed swordsman in the world.

His face revealed, he holds a cold and deep stare as his sister stands confused - on the verge of tears.

"Yohan.. you were the one who did all of this? Why? For what reason?"

"I did all of this for you, my dear sister."

Taken back by the simple reply, she steps back - becoming even more baffled before responding "for me? How could all this murder and suffering possibly be for my sake?"

Clicking his fingers, the wizard interrupts the pair and says "that will be all for today. Now be a good little servant and go back into the shadows."

The dark sorcerer summons a portal from under Yohan's feet - causing him to descend into it. As he gladly retreats, the brother whispers to his sister "I will be waiting for you" before being swallowed into its darkness. The portal disappears, leaving Aurora heartbroken and hysterical. Picking up her blade, she turns to the grinning wizard at the far side and shouts loaded threats.

"What did you do to my brother? You must have used a spell to brainwash him into releasing you. Give him back now, otherwise, you'll wish you were never born!"

Running to her aid, Luke and Umbra draw their weapons also - eyes focused on the wizard who remains calm and jolly.

"Kwekekekeeee... I am afraid to disappoint you girl, but your brother has not been put under any spell of my doing. He came to me of his own accord. He asked for nothing in return, other than to be accepted into my scheme."

As the three stands huddled together - they console one

another while keeping their eyes glued to the powerful villain before them.

"Succubas, don't let his words get to you. You mustn't lose your focus."

"I am not losing my focus, idiot vampire!"

"Stop squabbling guys. We need to think of a way to get back the Apex Grail. We can't let him have his way."

Amused by the trio, the wizard proceeds to pace left and right, addressing them grandly - his voice echoing over the stone surfaces.

"Look at you. The three of you are bound by the most profound and unique friendship. The gods surely must have been amused - especially the goddess of the moon. However, as fascinating as you are, none of you can come close to the friendship that binds my friends and me. Our friendship is so strong, that not even death could tear us apart. Bow down before the presence of Megethos and the original Blue Lunar: Solomon!"

As though unveiling the final act, a dark portal materialises behind the wizard. Eyelids pinned open and mouths frozen like statues, the three stands in suspense awaiting what will emerge.

Before their eyes, the familiar demon prince Megethos steps into the open - sporting his bright red attire. His presence sends a shiver down their spines, as a reminder of their unforgettable encounter with him only recently. Standing side by side with the sorcerer, the pair exude an aura that is crippling.

The second and final figure emerges from the portal, revealing an old man. Clothes tattered and dirty, along with long and withered grey hair, he hobbles to the side of Phantom - using a sturdy walking stick to stand. As frail and innocent as the man looks, he causes Umbra to scream in disbelief "by the gods... are my eyes deceiving me? How could Solomon still be alive? He... he was supposed to be dead!"

The black-suited comrade slumps to his knees, dropping

his briefcase and knives in the process. The sound of his accessories hitting the ground communicates a type of surrender, one that troubles both Luke and Aurora who keep their swords steadfast.

"So that is Solomon? Does this mean that he has been alive all this time? I don't understand how that is possible", the blue knight whispers.

Glancing in front with small and squinted eyes, the man known as Solomon rests his gaze on the blue hero. Within the quiet suspense, he observes the blue armour with all its features. The breastplate, shoulder pads, gauntlets, sword, greaves, helmet and cape cause the man to let out a painful whimper, as though the mere sight of the armour has brought back deep and buried memories. The armour originally belonged to him, one thousand years ago under the service of the moon goddess. Looking at the legendary suit is the same as looking at one's own reflection.

"Do not cry, my lord. Now is the moment for joy and happiness, for I have finally obtained the Apex Grail!" Phantom says - holding the priceless item in front for Solomon to marvel at in all its glory and light. "Are you ready to receive the power of the gods, my lord?"

"Yes... do it now!"

Observing the exchange, Umbra rises to his feet as if understanding what is about to take place. "As I thought... he plans to manipulate the power of the Grail. Luke, Aurora - we need to stop them right now!"

Sensing the panic in Umbra's soul, Luke casts away his fears before sprinting straight towards the dark trio, along with his two comrades. As the heroes race desperately to prevent what is about to happen, they hear the words of Solomon proclaiming to the heavens "For love!"

Shakoom - before their eyes a great light sweeps outward from the Apex Grail, blasting the trio backwards in unison. The force of the light is like that of a tsunami, which washes away all in its path as a deafening sound envelopes the room. Unable to withstand the unbridled power that has been unleashed within the chamber, the very palace gives way and crumbles to the ground.

Tons of golden fragments pile on top of one another, as the trio are buried under the weight. Watching in horror, the army of soldiers around the city witnesses the fall of their county's most important building. The legendary house of Ergo, which housed the most wondrous item left by the gods, has fallen. As the sounds of the palace crumbling fill their ears, the soldiers cover their mouths, refusing to utter a single sound that would confirm what they see before them.

"Bursting out from the rubble, Luke gazes around, disoriented and dazed while standing amidst the destroyed palace of Ergo. "What... what the hell just happened? Umbra, Aurora... are you ok?"

"I see that Diana's suit is as durable as ever. Such a shame that it requires the soul of a mortal to sustain it" a familiar voice flows to him from above. Looking up to the clouds, the blue hero gasps with shock at the sight of Solomon, levitating in mid-air, bearing an altered appearance. In the place of his old and wrinkled skin is a plump and youthful body. Gone is his matted grey hair, which now dances over his shoulders, as if each strand possesses a personality. His once dirtied clothes are transformed into a robe that contains countless stars, as though a living universe dwelled within him. To top off his jaw-dropping countenance, a large halo floats behind his back - extending from the tip of his head to the bottom of his feet.

"What have you done with the Apex Grail?"

"Can you not tell? You are looking at it. I have become the Apex Grail, with all its tremendous power, left behind by those foolish gods."

The very same sensation of being brought to tears the first

time he laid eyes on the Grail, has once again surfaced as he stares upon the man of legend. "He's right. Somehow he managed to absorb the Apex Grail and become what he is now. What can I do then?"

The two look upon one another, sensing a similarity that cannot be put into words. The feeling is fleeting yet strong enough for the young hero to notice, and at that point, he asks "Solomon, why are you doing this? I understand how you must have felt, being betrayed by Diana, but how does harming innocent people today make you any better?"

Gazing down at the young hero, Solomon displays a look of pity for the boy, and with an unexplainable tone of sympathy, he replies "this whole world needs to start again, and I am the one who shall wipe the slate clean. I will no longer allow this world to be run by selfish gods and men. I will lead the world to true love, without mortals and deities... that is what she would have wanted."

"What are saying? Do you plan to destroy everybody in this world? Who would have wanted this?"

"I am done talking. Besides, your time is almost up. What happened to me, a thousand years ago will soon happen to you. Rest assured, the wretched moon goddess will get what's coming to her. I wish you well... on your way to the afterlife."

Joined by the sorcerer and demon prince, Solomon summons a portal to depart into. He enters first, followed by the red-suited Megethos. To Luke's surprise, the ever grinning wizard halts for a few seconds and turns around to address the blue knight one final time.

"I almost forgot. I have a gift for you, Mr imposter. Consider it a farewell present from me to you. Hopefully, this should teach you a lesson when involving yourself in matters that do not concern you. Ta ta..."

The wizard disappears into the portal - however, just before it closes, a single individual emerges before falling through the sky. The person is familiar to Luke, who can only watch as they fall closer to the ground. "Is that who I think it is?" The boy whispers, second-guessing himself as he makes out the appearance of a girl who has been close to his heart. "Rose? Oh my god... Rose!"

Questions race through his mind as to how his sister ended up in the clutches of Phantom, let alone given back in seemingly one piece. However, as she falls through the air, Rose looks far from conscious. Seen from a distance, one might be forgiven for thinking that it was a mannequin descending.

With all the constant thoughts, the young hero kicks himself for not thinking of the most important question. How will she survive such a fall? It is at that point Luke theorises the departed wizard's cruel idea for him. "He wants me to watch as Rose falls to her death!"

As though his distrain for the wizard is not enough, the shameless sorcerer has found yet another reason to be hated. Like a guilt-free troublemaker in a playground, Phantom is no different, whose tricks and unruly games are easily led back to him.

"I won't let you have your way", Luke shouts to the wind - hoping it carries his voice to wherever the wizard has fled to. "I won't let you do this to my sister!"

Finding all the courage in his soul, the boy enters a mild crouch, whispering to the greaves and gauntlets of his armour, "please help me catch her".

The city is silent, as every soldier stands unmovable, eyes glued to the falling body. The pressure is immense and overwhelming for the boy who only has mere seconds to act. Upon a great huff, he launches himself into the air in the direction of the descending and helpless girl. As his arms stay stretched outward, the boy prays, praying to every single god that he can think of to aid his trajectory. He knows that if he is off for but an inch, his sister will be lost. Somewhere deep inside, Luke rationalises that such an outcome of losing his one and only sister would be too cruel of the gods. After all, he has already witnessed far too much misfortune, since the day he could remember. Surely the gods will spare him another heartache.

"Gotcha!" He cheers, successfully catching Rose in mid-air before landing safely on the ground. The rubbled shards of the former palace scatter about as his firm greaves intrude upon the rubble. Kneeling low he holds his beloved sister - thanking the gods in his heart. "Rose, are you ok? Speak to me... open your eyes!"

As he holds her gentle and meek body, Luke finds that her eyes are closed tight. Initially fearing the worst, he allows his heart to build with heaviness. However, his mind reminds him of a universal truth that applies to most mammals. Her body is warm, which means that death has not claimed her. "It is me, your brother Luke. Please Rose, open your eyes and say something."

Holding his sister tight, the boy is reminded of his original desire. All he has ever wanted was a family, not the world or great status. The Apex Grail although lost, pales in comparison to the treasure that is within his hands.

To his joy, movement can be seen upon her face, followed by a mild grunt, like a child waking from a nap. Next to follow are her eyelids, which upon slowly opening a sound emerges from her lips which grace the boy's ears "Luke... Is that you?"

"Yes, it's me. It is me, your brother. Thank goodness you're alive."

A haughty grin appears upon the hero's face, not directed at the girl but at the wizard's scheme. For the first time since encountering the dreaded sorcerer, the boy has managed to stop at least one of his plans. Such a realisation gives Luke a sense of victory, as his heart jumps with relief. "How did you end up being captured by Phantom? You didn't go off looking for me, did you? Rose, I told you to stay in the Armley mansion where it's safe!"

"Please, believe me, I was in the mansion. However, he was the one who came to me. I don't know how he was aware that I knew you."

A frightening and unsettling feeling overcomes the boy as he hears her words. Although he cannot quite put his finger on it, something troubles him. How did the wizard know where to find Rose, let alone become aware of their recent brother and sisterhood. A small thunderclap sounds off in the distance, as though warning of something sinister - however, he throws his caution to the back of his mind and appreciates Rose's safety.

"Whatever that horrible wizard was planning, you are safe now."

"Thank you, my brother. This is the second time you have saved me, right? You are always there... when I need you" she says in a weak tone - conscious but exhausted.

Approaching the blue knight from behind, Umbra and Aurora limp to his side - upon finally emerging from the rubble. Clothes are torn and skin scarred all over upon being buried under the crumbled palace, they hold a defeated frown at the current situation.

"Damn it... we failed to protect the Apex Grail and those three villains have taken off!" Aurora grunts while turning her back to the soldiers and comrades, ashamed to look directly at any of them. A second thunderclap can be heard, this time slightly closer, befitting the failure she feels. "Yohan... I swear I will get you back."

Rain starts to fall, as a third sound of thunder cackles into the city. The raindrops are soothing to listen to, yet unbearable to take for they are cold, as though the god of the sky were punishing all who had failed to protect the divine relic.

"Hmmm... is that who I think it is?" Umbra asks, recognising the familiar girl in his friend's arms. Already knowing what the answer will be, the black-suited friend adds "how on earth did she get here?" He Displays a suspicious glare.

"It was Phantom. He abducted her from your old place and brought her here. He attempted to drop her from the sky, thinking I couldn't save her, but I did. Everything is ok now."

Contrasting Luke's relaxed smile, Umbra's glare only grows

more intense as he adopts the hat of an investigator, like many times before. "How did he know where to find her, and why her to begin with?"

"I don't know. He even knew her name and that she is my recent sister."

A panic overcomes Umbra, who emits an angered aura as though frustrated and offended by Luke's cluelessness. The young hero senses the aggression in Umbra's spirit, feeling somewhat frightened, like an amateur student on the receiving end of their teacher's temper.

"Listen to me Luke, did you look into the wizard's eyes at all? I told you once before... looking into his eyes will reveal everything about you!"

"No I..." stopping himself from finishing his sentence, Luke recollects the confrontation he and the wizard had in the castle of Spiritus. "I remember now. Back in Spiritus, he looked into my eyes. But it's ok because Rose is safe now!"

"Buffoon, why didn't you tell me this earlier?"

Breaking their heated exchange, Rose lets out a high pitched scream that is so loud, that every soldier jumps in surprise. Immediately after, her body starts to convulse uncontrollably as though she were possessed by a devil.

"Rose! Are you ok? What is happening to you?"

As the rain pours, a legion of dark clouds makes their presence known - intensifying the already unsettled moment.

"Uhhh... it hurts... something... something is inside of meeeee!"

"I don't understand what you're saying? For god sake, what is going on? Umbra do something!" Luke pleads - looking at his friend as though he were a doctor. Of course, he is far from a doctor, but Umbra has proven his knowledge of countless phenomena - including that of the dark arts. In contrast, the weary swordsman Aurora stands back, grasping the hilt of her sheathed sword as she senses something worrying from the girl.

As Umbra peers closer to the screaming sister of Luke, he

blinks twice and pauses - displaying a petrified body language that communicates more than words could ever show. Akin to the same feeling as when one has realised the most awful news, Umbra exudes similar energy, causing the comrades to hold their breath in anticipation.

"Oh no... you must put her down, now!"

"What? No way Umbra, I am not gonna leave her. She is my sister..."

Shawoom - before their eyes, a single tentacle emerges from the shoulder of the girl, which causes the trio to shriek collectively. The tentacle is large, green and scaly, which grows larger still as it extends upwards to the sky for all to see. Stopping just below the dark clouds, the end of the tentacle morphs into a face, resembling a dragon, complete with a snout, gaping jaw and piercing black eyes.

The surrounding soldiers scream with fear, as the dragon's head lets out a great roar that is so powerful, scores of houses are blown to pieces. Lost for words, Aurora and Luke stay speechless as Umbra displays a shocked gaze - uttering the name of the beast before them, in a small yet fearful tone.

"By the gods... it's Parasitus Draco!"

Chapter 21: The Beast

Lightning flashes as thunder tears into the rainy city. As though losing the king and Apex Grail weren't enough, a new threat appears before all who have eyes to see. Like an additional limb that no mortal would ever ask for, a ferocious creature is birthed from the shoulder of the helpless girl. A great dragon face towers over the city, connected to a tentacle that is bound to Rose.

"This can't be happening, this can't be happening..." the blue knight repeats over and over, like a deluded individual who is refusing to accept the sight before him. As he continues to hold onto his sister, regardless of the dragon that has grown from her, his friends can be heard ranting. However, whatever words of importance they say, seem to all fall on deaf ears. Even the screams of the beast as it roars over the city, seem to pass over the boy who has chosen to mentally shut down.

"You have some explaining to do, idiot vampire. What do you

know of that monster that has sewn itself to the girl?" Aurora says - sweating immensely while watching the dragon divert its eyes to the soldiers scattered around the city. "Hurry up and get talking!"

"That thing is Parasitus Draco, one of the most dreadful dragons to ever come into existence. It lives by attaching itself to a host - coming out to cause as much destruction as possible. What makes that dragon so hard to kill is that simply cutting it down will not end its life. Doing that will only make things worse. Damn that wizard. So this was how he planned to destroy the city of Ergo all along - using Luke's one and only sister!"

"So, Phantom put the dragon inside of that poor girl, brought her here and released it. How do we separate that monster from her?"

Without warning, a second tentacle bursts outward from the other shoulder, this time charging into the heroic trio. Aurora is knocked backwards into random houses with such force, they crumble over her. Umbra is sent tumbling in the opposite direction before crashing through heavy rubble. Lastly, upon being hit head-on, Luke is rammed through multiple buildings before finally slamming into the tall clock tower. A mighty explosion is heard as he hits the old structure and the clocktower itself sways before crashing down over the ground.

As the sound of destroyed buildings sweeps over the city, along with the desperate screams of soldiers, the second dragon head roars to the heavens, much louder than the first. The twin dragons dance through the air - watching the chaos and panic beneath them. All the while, the helpless girl who is bound to them watches in horror, unable to stop their actions.

"Please... stop this. Don't harm these people. Don't harm Luke!" She pleads, rising to her feet before reaching to the tentacles by her shoulders - attempting to pry herself away. Her attempts are futile, for not only are they now a piece of her limbs, but she also has no control over them. Like a pair of rebellious pets, the dragons ignore her cries, regardless of her being their host. To them, she is nothing more than a living home, one that allows them to live but not respect. As such, her cries are drowned out in the chaos.

Pulling himself out from the rubble, the blue knight stands in horror, observing the nightmarish scene in front of him. He blinks constantly, telling himself it is all just a dream. Perhaps everything that has occurred up until now has been one nightmare, which will soon end. Before he knows it, he will wake up and be back in the town orphanage of Heline, where he was extremely unhappy yet safe from such dreadful sights. "This can't be real. I must be dreaming."

He treads closer to the girl - watching as she struggles to break free from the dragons. With eyes of desperation, she cries to her brother, her voice barely being heard under the intensity of the roaring beasts. Although her sounds do not reach his ears, the fear in her eyes is louder than any scream one could produce. Overcome with helplessness, he looks to the ground, avoiding eye contact with her. "What can I do? No, I have to do something. I won't lose Rose!"

Armed with his sword, he proceeds to enter a fighting stance before looking up at the gloating dragons who peer menacingly over the city.

"Don't even think about it, Luke. Attempting to cut them down will only make the beasts more powerful!" Orders Umbra, appearing behind as though he were an expert advisor.

"Well, how am I supposed to help Rose then? What would you have me do?"

Suddenly at that moment, the first dragon begins its rampage - tearing through the city, leaving nothing but destruction in its wake. Houses, structures and even whole areas of Ergo are pounded to dust. The soldiers attempt to run for their lives, however, their efforts are in vain, for the second dragon has already chosen to make them its food - gobbling them up in droves, like a whale swallowing schools of fish.

"I am putting a stop to this... my way!" States Aurora, drawing her blade before sprinting to action, so fast her white coat falls from her.

"Don't do it, silly succubus!" Umbra shouts, however he is already too late. The headstrong comrade has already made up her mind, running towards the first dragon.

Leaping high, she performs a spinning summersault, becoming like a that of a golden wheel - racing to the dragon's exposed neck. Her mighty blade makes contact, and with all the strength and anger in her hands, she saws through the scaly skin of the beast - slicing its head clean off.

"She did it!" Luke cheers - watching as the severed dragon head rolls to the ground, motionless. Gallons of dark blood shower the area, as the swordsman holds a fierce stare. "That will teach you!"

Her action fills the boy with a sense of hope. However, just as a slither of confidence grows within him, the unthinkable occurs.

Before their very eyes, four new dragons erupt from Rose's shoulders before tearing through the city - causing more havoc than before. Chunks of rubble and broken structures fly through the air, under the stormy sky as Luke gasps with horror. By his side, the black-suited comrade sweats and says "I told you, cutting them down is futile. If one dragon is lost, four others will take its place out of vengeance. If another is defeated after that, eight more will emerge... then twelve... and so on."

The true peril of the situation sets in, as Luke digests the dragon's terrible nature and ability to self replicate. Such a beast would seem almost impossible to slay, and yet if the dragon cannot be killed, Rose will forever be its unwanted host.

"Seeing as you have all the answers, why don't you tell me how to stop them!"

A look of pity overcomes Umbra, who glances at Rose while replying in a slow yet concise manner. "There is only one way to stop the Parasitus Draco. You must kill... the host."

"What? Kill the host? You mean..." He pauses, refusing to

even utter what Umbra is suggesting. To even consider such a solution would be to entertain the idea of killing not only an innocent but Rose who was the first person to ever treat him with genuine kindness. As such, to say that the boy is not warmed to the idea would be an understatement. Looking to Umbra as though he were an enemy, Luke says "not a chance. I don't care if this whole city crumbles to dust, I am not going to do it!"

"Luke, there is no other way. Even if there was, the cure would most likely exist in a distant continent, yet to be discovered. We must end her suffering!"

"I am not gonna kill my sister!"

His voice is loud and painful - exuding a slightly broken tone that one makes when on the verge of tears. The black-suited friend takes a single step backwards, feeling guilty for even revealing the weakness of the dreaded dragon.

The city continues to pour not with rain, but anguish as the screams of fear reach the clouds that can be heard for many miles. The sound of constant thunder cackles without end, as though having a field day at the horrific sight of the city. Soldiers flee like chickens without heads, as the lone warrior Aurora takes on the many dragons at the same time. All the while, Luke and Umbra stand opposite Rose who continues to pray for a remedy.

To the pair's surprise, the girl shouts to them in clarity that cannot be mistaken.

"Kill me... set me free."

Flinching with disbelief, Luke pauses while slowly tilting his head in her direction. As he lays his eyes upon her, he finds that she is smiling - holding the same beaming smile that honoured him the very first time they had met. As one might conclude, the expression she portrays is but a facade that belies a sorrow that is without measure.

"Rose, what are you saying?"

"It's ok, it's the only way. You will just be saving me again, like when we first met. You do remember the night we met, right? Before you turned up, I was convinced that I wasn't gonna survive. Then you appeared, out of nowhere like some kind of angel. After you had told me that you were without a family, I wanted to hold you so tight. Then, after you had left I kept thinking of you... of my new brother. Luke, I know this wasn't how things were meant to end, but it doesn't have to be a tragedy. Once I am gone, I will be with you, to watch as you beat the living daylights out of that wizard. You can do it, you can save everybody... including me."

"Rose I..."

With his hands held firmly onto his blade, the hero closes his eyes and channels his emotions into the moon sword. The day he and his sister had met, the short time they had spent together and their tearful farewell flashes before his eyes as he supplies every memory into the divine blue sword. Responding almost instantly, the blade glows bright, the brightest it has ever shone - lighting the darkness of the stormy weather. Like a candle in the dark, it draws the attention of the many dragon heads that have achieved more than enough destruction to last a lifetime. Gazing down at the radiant knight, the dragons' hiss - threatened by the aura that flows outward.

Taking a deep breath, Luke raises the glowing sword upwards - preparing to unleash the power of the blue moon sword. Holding himself back, he forces his eyes open to see the figure of the most special person he had the privilege of knowing, for the last time. Their eyes meet, and as she stands with arms open wide as though accepting her fate, the young hero swings his sword downward and screams "I will never forget you, my sister!"

A great beam of light is unleashed from his sword that races to the girl and the dragons alike. As it gets closer, the sheer force of the great light wipes away her tears as she responds "farewell my brother. I love you..."

The girl along with the dreaded dragons is engulfed by the rod of light - obliterated in seconds. Like a gigantic wave, the beam races through and out of the city, extending far beyond the distance for all to see. The surviving soldiers stop and stare at the mesmerising wonder that has saved them all, cutting through the darkness like a beacon of light. As the beam hits a distant mountain, a mighty explosion ensues and erupts, as though sounding off like a mighty bell of victory.

Chapter 22: Deeper than Despair

A shy sunset approaches the land, giving off an orange tint from the escaping light through the heavy clouds. Although the city has finally been saved, it is by no means a proud achievement, as the once-prosperous kingdom is now reduced to ruins. A collective sense of loss is shared amongst every inhabitant of Ergo. The civilians, who had been safely hidden underground have resurfaced - weeping on the shoulders of their neighbours like a mass mourning.

On the city's outskirts, two individuals sit side by side, embracing one another's company as though bringing a sense of comfort to the other. The pair are Aurora and Umbra, two allies that have rarely seen eye to eye. For the first time, they bring their defences down and become vulnerable. They have sat in silence for the longest time, reminiscing the events of the day, wishing they could have acted differently.

Looking down at her own bruised and bloodied hands, like

a reminder of her failed efforts, one image and revelation refuses to escape her thoughts.

"Gabriella... she knew... she knew what was going to happen. She foresaw what my brother was plotting, even the fact that she would die by his hands, and yet she still chose to keep it to herself... to protect my feelings. Gabi... you must have felt so alone, knowing everything but being unable to tell me... being unable to change your fate." Planting her face into her cold and scarred hands, Aurora cries without pause, barely catching her breath as though in the middle of a panic attack. "Brother... why did you do it?"

Compared with all the other moments of grief in her life, losing her King, friends and sibling all in one day sets a new bar. She is encompassed in pain. Everything from what she sees, thinks about, hears and smells, is pain.

Suddenly, she feels a gentle touch on her shoulder. The touch is warm and soft, a welcomed contrast to the rough and cold interactions with the enemies faced earlier. With an equally considerate tone, Umbra says "I do not doubt that your friends fought valiantly to protect this kingdom. They will forever be in your heart."

"They already are in my heart, you don't need to tell me that. However, for them to be at peace, I must find Yohan. I need to know why he chose to align himself with that wizard."

"Well, that is a first. You are rarely interested in answers. Be that as it may, we must locate the ones who stole the Apex Grail, for I too have a score to settle. We need to find them as soon as possible, for there is no telling what their next move will be. Shall we go fetch Luke now and make our way?"

Looking over to their left side, over an obstacle course of debris and half-broken houses, the pair see their young leader of the trio - sitting alone against a wall, without his armour.

"Give him a little more time" replies Aurora.

∞ ∞ ∞

Sitting in silence, slanted against an old wall, the young hero stares up at the sun. However - his eyes are trapped in the past, seeing nothing but events of the many things that have been lost. His body is still, so still that one would be forgiven for believing he was simply a fatal casualty of war, and yet as he stays slanted, Luke can only whisper to himself.

"I have lost everything... I failed. Everybody is gone. The King... dead. The witches... dead. The Apex Grail... gone. Rose..." he forces his mouth shut, to deny himself the pain of recollecting her final moments. However, whereas his lips stay disciplined, his mind does not, and like a mocking jester, it proceeds to show him his sister's last moments. Clutching his head he pleads with his thoughts to take pity on him and cries "stop it, just stop. I don't want to see it anymore!"

A sympathetic wind howl blows over him - whose sound offers the boy's mind a distraction. Focusing on the soothing howl he feels a micro sense of respite.

At that moment, a single individual strolls from behind the boy before stopping just in front of his view - obstructing the sun. As he looks upon the person, Luke stays motionless, letting out an exhausted greeting as though beyond sore of her sight.

"Hello, Diana. Have you come to scold me again, like you always do?"

The goddess of the blue moon stands opposite her herald, holding a sympathetic frown. There is silence between the pair, as the howling of the wind leaves, like an opening act ready to make way for the final highlight.

"No Luke, I haven't come here to tell you off. I merely came here, to say goodbye."

His eyebrows rise just enough to express his mild curiosity about her words. Although the thought of never seeing the goddess' face again brings him much joy, something about her words troubles him. "Boy, I think it is time that I told you the truth."

His eyebrows retract into their previous position, as he braces himself for the deity's words.

"To become a herald of a god, one must give up something... a forfeit if you will. This could be anything from vision, hearing, voice, body parts, or even characteristics. However, to be a herald of the blue moon, one must give up their life. You see, the armour you carry feeds on your life force. Each time you fought and used its powers, a piece of your life force drained. That was the reason why your hair turned grey. Eventually, the suit will take your life completely, and you will die."

Mouth wide with shock, the boy digests the words of her revelation. To her surprise, he lets out a mild laugh, as though humoured by the true nature of the blue armour. After such a long thread of misfortune, one can only laugh at their life. Perhaps the gods created him out of boredom, to bring comedy into their lives he wonders. His laughter however comes from a place of defeat, for he can no longer spare additional pain and sorrow for another tragedy. He is calm and collected, portraying a sensibility that scares the goddess.

"I should have known that there would be a catch to all this, right? Was there a reason why you didn't tell me this before when we first met?"

"If I had told you back then, you wouldn't have accepted my request. Even if you had, the suit would not have fully functioned. You see, the armour is as powerful as the wearer's hopes and dreams. I had to make you, an orphan with no family believe a normal life would be possible. That hope you carried was what allowed you to overcome the challenges you faced. Unfortunately, even with your level of hope, you still couldn't succeed."

Her voice is soft and clear, too clear to be considered sympathetic. The look in her eyes is one of conflict, as though she is struggling to maintain a collected demeanour in the presence of the boy who has continued to find failure at every turn.

"You tricked me. All along, you knew that I would never be able to live like everybody else. Now I understand how you betrayed Solomon, your previous herald. Like me, you made him into your hero, knowing full well the forfeit the armour carried. That is why his friend Felix, later known as Phantom sought revenge. He and his friends must all hate you and this world to the very core, and I don't blame them one bit."

She turns away, guilt struck by the boy whose response is direct and blunt. In a bizarre turn, she looks at him as though seeking approval and asks "what about you then? Do you hate me too?"

"No... I don't hate you", he replies with a sincerity that confuses her even more. If their exchange were a battle, then the goddess would surely be the losing opponent, dazed and disoriented by an unreadable foe. Coming away from the wall, he leans forward and continues "if it weren't for you, I would have stayed dead. To be able to live off borrowed time is still something I guess. Speaking of which, how long do I have anyway?"

She is floored, bested by a boy who not only has accepted his eventual demise but is without hatred for the very person who was responsible. A coldness is felt upon her cheek, which upon further notice she finds is a tear from her own azure eyes.

"You have about six hours left, maybe less."

"Ok. That is fine by me. After all, there isn't much left here for me anyway. The world will be better off without a kid with no family."

"Luke I... I know that you probably don't believe a word from me right now, but I truly wanted you to be happy. Even though it was short, I hope you were able to find some comfort in this world..."

Suddenly - breaking their conversation the ground erupts, causing the earth to shake and shudder. An earthquake rocks the very land, so great it feels as though two giants were tussling with the world. Large sections of land split apart, like scars and open wounds, as mountains that have long stood the test of time crumble in an instant. The scene resembles that of what many would consider Armageddon. Completing the doomsday-like moment, the clouds suddenly scatter like scuttling insects, giving way to something threatening.

Before the eyes of the world, the blue moon emerges through the clouds, like a bully wanting to make his presence known. However, the celestial body seems different. It is large, larger than it has ever been, or so it seems. The sight causes Luke to jump to his feet, standing to attention like a soldier, as the goddess speaks in a truly fearful manner.

"My moon... it's falling!"

"What? But why?" Asks her herald, looking at her as though she were the one responsible. Of course, based on her current track record, the boy can not be sure, and like an accuser, his eyes express an already assumed judgment. "Diana, has this got something to do with you, again?"

"No, this time I had no idea. I am just as clueless as you are!" She replies, like a defendant pleading their innocence. Her words do little to sway the boy's current mindset, as the sounds of the crumbling mountains continue to fill their ears. A strong wind tears through the land, pushed by the force of the falling moon. "Who is doing this? Who could possess such power?"

At that moment, a great bang is heard from the distance, briefly taking away the attention from the descending moon above. As though the day of surprises has refused to go quietly, a large and great structure can be seen emerging from the ground. Not only does it rise to the surface, but it also defies the laws of nature - levitating high into the air before stopping below the stars, just enough to be seen by almost every inhabitant of the world.

It is a castle, large and wide. Spanning a width that could almost rival a small island. The mysterious castle consists of semi-transparent crystals that magnify the blue light of the falling moon. Like an unashamed and brazen foe who is not afraid to confess their actions, the mysterious structure greets the world and all its terrified inhabitants.

"It's a floating fortress!" Shouts the goddess, turning her gaze to the boy one last time. Her failed look at being considerate falls and resumes to a stone-cold glare, the look the boy feels suits her best. With a less than heartfelt tone, she says "farewell, I will take over from here", disappearing into the sky.

Left alone, he continues to look up at the twin phenomena that hang in the air. A sense of urgency overcomes him, the same kind that had spurred him on through his journey. However, remembering the reality of his fate, the boy takes a deep breath and comes to his senses. "Why am I getting ahead of myself? It's not as though I'll be able to stop anything anyway. I'll probably be dead, just before that thing hits the ground."

As the earthquakes cease he sits down, back into the same position he assumed before - kept company by the old brittle wall. Shifting his eyes to the ground, Luke ignores the threats of the descending sphere and mysterious castle - instead choosing to await his demise in peace.

"Time to go, Luke. The enemy has made its move and even dared to show themselves" the voice of the golden-haired comrade calls to him - approaching his relaxed frame from behind. Her tone is full of resolve, which humours the young hero who has already admitted defeat. Slowly rotating his head in a fashion that is devoid of haste, he exudes an almost mocking gaze to her stern demeanour. Glancing at the tuxedo-wearing comrade beside her, Luke looks at him deeply, as though communicating with his eyes the revelation of the blue armour. Already familiar with the false ignorance he portrays to the world, Luke ascertains that umbra has been well aware of the fatal forfeit the suit carries, all along.

A sorrowful look is seen upon Umbra, as he notices a never seen gaze within the young hero. It is a look of truth, the same kind one makes when finally figuring out a harsh reality. Such eyes could conclude to Umbra that Luke has been told of his eventual and unavoidable death.

"Haha.. you two can go on without me. I will stay behind" the grey-haired hero responds, in a manner that is concerning to the pair.

His response is stark, causing Aurora's mind to go blank with shock and pause. It is only due to another earthquake that she is reminded of their predicament. Taking a step forward, she barks "excuse me? Did you not hear me the first time, boy? We must go and stop those fiends, and why is that so funny?"

"I am laughing because it's already too late... for me anyway."

"What are you babbling about? Stop acting weird and pull yourself together!"

Chiming in like a spokesman for the bizarrely behaving Luke, Umbra proceeds to speak in a slow and heartfelt tone. "Luke is right, his time is almost up. The consequences of becoming the herald of Diana means that his life will soon come to an end. The armour requires his life force, which is why his fate is sealed. In many ways, his life came to an end the moment he made the contract."

The woman stands lost for words, bearing a wide stare in contrast to the pair's half-shut eyes of acceptance. Like a third wheel that is out of place, her reaction is a contrast to her comrades, which almost makes her feel like the odd one out.

"So that's it then? You are just going to stay here while the world comes to an end?"

"Well... yeah. There isn't much I can do now, is there?" Luke replies, leaving the woman with the rhetorical question.

Overwhelmed, Umbra turns his back to the pair for no reason other than to hide his helplessness. Although he knew from the very beginning that the outcome would be this way, the reality is still too much to bear. As the moon continues to loom above the world, the demon wishes that such a moment were but a fleeting daydream - created in his mind by a horrendous imagination. Of course, he knows that such a predicament is impossible to be denied, no matter how hard he tries.

To his surprise, Umbra hears a loud smack, the kind that can only be produced by a parent when disciplining their child. The sound echoes, causing him to spin around to understand what had caused it. To his shock, he sees the young hero, hand placed over his right cheek. Looking through the gaps of his fingers, redness can be identified - giving away the clue that something firm must have struck his skin. Shifting his gaze, Umbra finds the female swordsman standing opposite Luke with her left-hand open - a telling pose one would make after inflicting a stern slap.

The young hero is frozen - staring up at the comrade with gaping eyes, not understanding why she decided to lay hands on him. He is afraid, yet not afraid enough to run, for an even greater urge overcomes him, wanting answers. The look in Aurora's painful eyes seems to already provide him with the answers to his questions, and it isn't long before the weight of her words homes in for the kill.

"Are you kidding me? Are you of all people, truly telling me that you've given up? In that case, why the hell did you save my life when I wanted to die back in that forest? What was it all for then, to give me false hope?"

"No, I... I did want you to live, that's why I saved you. But what can I do now?"

Ignoring his excuses, she reaches to his collar before yanking him upward, so high his feet leave the ground. As a domestic altercation ensues, it is almost as though the descending moon and mysterious floating castle in the distance are an afterthought. For those who have come to know the famed swordsman well, the wrath of her temper could tear the very sky.

"The only reason why I was able to keep going was because of you. You gave me the courage to face my demons and keep moving forward. You said that the three of us would be together, and now you're just gonna go back on your word? Coward!"

"You can insult me all you want, but it still doesn't change the fact that there is nothing left for me. I have no family, no sister and no future... nothing!"

It is the first time the boy has ever talked back to the woman, which surprises her and the watchful Umbra close by. His bold words could be considered courageous by many, like a subtle classmate who has found the strength to stand up to their bully. Perhaps within a classroom, his response would earn him a clap and cheer, even new respect. However, in the presence of Aurora, all the boy earns is a gaze of fire. Right-hand curling into a ball, she wastes no time launching a fist that strikes him with such force, he is smashed through the very wall that had kept him company.

"Succubus, I think that's enough", umbra says - watching as the smoke from the debris covers the young hero like a blanket. "You don't want to kill him before he is scheduled to die."

"Stay out of this, idiot vampire!" She mumbles - waiting patiently for the smoke to clear. As though also afraid of her, the debris of rocks scuttles off from Luke's injured body, not to stand in the angered woman's way. A tensely quiet moment shrouds the area, as only the sound of heavy breathing can be heard. She looks down at the boy's frame, sprawled out on his back, eyes continuously fixated on her. The young hero looks pitiful to her, like a once-respected king who has stained his title. "So, if you have nothing, then what am I? Am I nothing to you? Answer me... Luke!"

"Of course, you're something to me... both you and Umbra have been my rock. But what can I do? Diana says that I will die in a matter of hours!"

A drop of mocking humour exudes from Aurora, as she replies "Diana says this, Diana says that... Diana, Diana. Who cares about Diana and what she has to say? Stop allowing other people to dictate your life!"

Pointing to the floating castle above, Aurora continues "in case you have forgotten, Solomon, her original herald was supposed to have suffered the same fate, and yet he still lives on. That must tell you there is a way to stay alive!"

Her words are remarkable to both Luke and Umbra alike. Her tongue is like that of a volt, powering up the lightbulbs of their brains, causing them to question what they were told.

"You do have a point there," Umbra says in a low yet intrigued manner, just enough for her to catch his agreeing comment. Remaining flat on the ground, Luke utters not a single word - eyes coming to life as a renewed perspective enters his thoughts.

"Luke, if you are going to die, let it be on your terms. If your death is truly unavoidable, at least welcome it after you have made something of yourself... after you have stopped the world from being wiped out!"

Her words are like rays of the sun, piercing through the dark clouds of doubt that had covered him. He sits upward in response, mouth wide with a renewed purpose for living, however short his life may be. An image of his sister Rose flashes into his thoughts, enforcing a determination that stirs a fire within his soul. Rising to his feet, the boy looks up at the treacherous filled sky and states "I won't allow things to end here... not for me or anybody else for that matter. Death can claim my soul all it wants after I have finished what I started. Until then, I am gonna live!"

Raising his index finger to his forehead, the grey-haired hero readies to transform, perhaps for the last time. He hesitates for a fraction of a second, saying the briefest of prayers before striking the divine letter that has inscribed itself to his forehead since the very night he became a herald. He transforms within a burst of light, summoning his mighty blue armour to attention. As the divine suit attaches itself to him, Luke shows a mighty glare at the crystal fortress in the clouds. "I am gonna give it another shot... one last time!"

Embracing him from behind, both Aurora and Umbra wrap

their arms around him, and in a collective phrase they whisper "we all will… one final time!"

Their words fill the hero with love and support that cannot be quantified. It is familiar and reminds him of how he had felt when he became a brother to Rose.

"Well, now that we've cleared that up, how do you suggest we get to that great castle up there? Any ideas?" Umbra asks, presenting yet another question for the trio to figure out.

Luke's eyes gravitate to the female ally, as though expecting her to offer a solution. She rolls her eyes in response before placing her hands on her hips and replies "don't look at me, I can't help with that. After all, my steed abandoned me, remember?"

With a look of disappointment, the three can only stand helplessly, bound to the ground with no way of reaching the menacing castle above. For all their joint bravado and resolution, they find themselves at a simple yet complex stumbling block. As the moon continues to slowly get closer, the trio can only hope for a miracle.

With the sun fully set, the night sky blankets the land beneath it, teasing the inhabitants with an array of countless stars that are so beautiful, that one could marvel upon them forever. It is a fitting sight for a world that may soon come to an end.

Suddenly, a twinkling can be seen zipping through the sky - catching the attention of many onlookers, especially the three heroes. They know that it is not a shooting star, due to the conflicting directions it makes. In addition, the strange sight doesn't seem threatening. The sound of a horse shouts from the travelling light, which instantly alarms Aurora, who steps forward to call out its name.

"By the gods... Starlight?"

Descending to their position, the radiant unicorn Starlight returns. As its great wings stretch outward for all to see, Luke and his friends marvel at the wondrous steed that has arrived in their darkest hours. The sound of its flapping wings is music to their ears - providing the trio with their only route to the floating castle.

As traces of its white feathers fall over the three, Luke catches a piece within his hand - picking up a smile as he says "this is it... our only chance."

To his right side, the witty Umbra sneezes as a feather lands upon his nose - causing him to moan "well, better late than never. It is only the end of the world after all."

Next to the demon, the steed's original rider Aurora stands like a mother who has just been reunited with a long lost child. A flurry of feathers brushes past her face - drying the tears that are unable to stop. "Welcome back, my loyal friend. I promise you, this time I will make you proud."

Chapter 23: The Castle of Truth

T he world is on the brink of destruction. Incredible power has forced the descent of the blue moon - causing it to plunge towards the world. Due to the disruptive lunar waves of the falling wonder, a multitude of catastrophes reacts across the globe. The oceans lash out uncontrollably, as though having lost their calm - assaulting countries with their tides and even submerging smaller lands. The earth screams with insanity, rocking back and forth as though having lost its temper.

A sense of doom is felt amongst the people of the world, who stand helplessly - praying to the gods for salvation. Is this a test of faith or a just punishment? These two questions stay in the minds of almost every mortal alike, for with every praying individual, another can be seen cursing the world - scolding their fellow man for not believing in the gods enough.

As fear and chaos fill the land, the floating castle that has hung in the air for some time watches the events unfold. Dwelling above the clouds, its presence is sinister and mysterious, like an omen.

Within the drifting castle, by one of its large open balconies, a single man can be found. Perhaps to be more accurate, a former man, for the individual has ascended the realms of mortality. Draped in a robe of stars and accompanied by a great halo, he looks up at the descending moon with pleasure. Like a father who imagines the future of their child, the smiling man turn god bears the same hope for the celestial body. However, his ambition for the moon is not one that others would find welcoming.

With his right hand stretched forth, he constantly emits a force that pulls the blue wonder further towards the earth, like a magnet. "Finally, I will be able to seek my revenge. We are so close!"

At that moment, a familiar presence enters the balcony. He pauses and gasps, for It has been over one thousand years since being greeted by the presence. However, regardless of how long the passage of time has transpired, he remembers it like it were yesterday. Fond memories and nostalgia overcome him, whisking the man to a time when he served as a herald to the service of a goddess. Turning around, he gazes at that very same goddess who appears in all her blue glory. She stands both strong and overwhelmed, looking at the very first Blue Lunar.

"It has been quite some time, hasn't it... Diana?"

"Solomon..."

The greatest goddess and her greatest herald stand opposite one another, coming face to face. Their eyes are locked onto the other, as though trying to anticipate the other's thoughts. A well of emotions stirs between them that is so great one could drown under it.

"I knew you would come, eventually. What a shame that it has taken all this time and hard work to gaze upon your beauty once again."

"Solomon, I had no idea that you were still alive. How is that possible?"

"How is that possible you say?" Replies the man, exuding a vengeful aura. "I stand before you today because the hatred in my heart allowed me to surpass even death. I simply couldn't allow you to have your way, while my friends and I faded into the darkness."

His reply is difficult to accept, let alone fathom. For as amazing as the human mind is, one cannot simply overcome death. The goddess senses another reason at play for how he has been able to stay alive - however, she reminds herself of a far more urgent matter as her moon can be seen taking up half the sky above. She senses the power of the Apex Grail from within the man, as he shines with the same majestic light that brings most mortals to tears.

"So this is your decision? You have absorbed the Apex Grail and are using its power to send my moon crashing down. Do you realise what will happen once the moon hits this world? There will be nothing left! Why are you doing this, Solomon?"

"Why did you desert me?" He hits back, in a small yet painful tone. As small as his tone sounds, it leaves a heavy print upon the goddess' heart, like a burden that has never ceased. She holds her silence, leaving only the wind to take the place of her words. Her quietness is all the answer he needs, and he whispers "as I thought. Even after all these years, you still are unable to be honest with me. Are you afraid that I will hate you even more or are you simply ashamed of the forfeit the divine armour brings? You surely are not that ashamed, as from what I could see you had already selected a successor. You always seem to choose the most naive ones. To answer your original question, I am doing this because this world is one huge lie, and it needs to start over. Only then will she find peace."

As his last few words reach her ears, the goddess flinches - eyes wide with shock A wave of guilt overcomes the goddess, feeling sympathy for the man before her. "My dear Solomon... are you doing this for Aphrodite's sake? Have you gone mad? The beloved goddess of love never would have wanted this!"

"That is rather humorous, coming from you, the one who ordered her execution. You are in no position to tell me what Aphrodite would have wanted, Diana. Just sit back and watch the end of the world take place. How ironic that the very power you have used to manipulate others for the safety of this world, will now be used to destroy it most astoundingly. Once your moon lands, its unbridled power will explode - wiping out all life in this world. Whether I survive or not makes no difference at all."

"No, I won't allow it. I will stop you, right here and right now!" She shouts - placing her hands together to conjure a great ball of intense energy. The balcony shines bright by the power within her hands, and as she holds the ball of light, Solomon stands unthreatened. She throws the light directly at him - causing a gigantic blast of energy that engulfs the entire balcony.

The force of her attack is so great, that the castle itself sways and shakes - a testament to her power as one of the greatest goddesses. A semi satisfying sound of matter being vaporised whispers to her ears, as the energy blast slowly settles. "I did it... I stopped him" she says within her herself, hoping that her burst of energy was enough to subdue her former herald. She feels confident, for never has a single being survived a direct hit from her great power, not once since the creation of the world. Even so, the thought of having to use her power against someone so dear to her brings the goddess deep sorrow.

The smoke begins to settle, allowing for her to soon see the remains of Solomon. Preparing herself, she braces for the sight of a defeated man - perhaps sprawled out on the floor with the Apex Grail next to him. However, as the smoke clears, what she finds is a man who has remained untouched and unharmed.

"Was that all you had?" He asks in an already disinterested manner, like a giant pitying a child who has dared to raise her fists. The blue moon goddess gasps with disbelief, for her powerful attack seemed to prove futile. Some might argue that her projectile failed to touch him at all, judging by the lack of change to his attire. Not a single inch of his robe has been disrupted, failing to even rival the wind's ability to at least flutter his clothing. "I am sure you don't need me to tell you why your efforts are meaningless, do you?"

She stays silent, becoming like that of a student as Solomon departs a knowledge that she should have been well aware of. "Diana, I am the Apex Grail now. How many times do you need to understand that? As such, its powers of negation belong to me. Its purpose of severing the interaction between man and god still stands, and I am still very much a mortal of sorts, but with the powers of a god. That is why your power is ineffective against me. That goes for all the other gods too." The man turns his back to the woman - leaving her to stare helplessly at his radiant halo as its light humbles the goddess. "Of course, even if you could destroy me, you would ultimately destroy the Apex Grail, reuniting man and god once again... something you have worked so hard to keep separate.

The sound of gritting teeth can be heard, and for a moment the goddess wonders where it is coming from. Surprised, she finds it is nobody else but herself, reacting to an overwhelming tide of helplessness. A puzzle has been presented to her, one that she cannot solve, for not only is she helpless to stop the powerful foe, but even if she could harm him, the Apex Grail would shatter - unifying the link between man and god.

"What can I do?" She asks herself, like a mortal seeking guidance from above when all seems lost. Watching the moon continue to fall, she follows suit and falls also, legs giving way before dropping to her knees.

"You can do nothing... you will do nothing."

With no rebuttal, she stays on the grounds of the balcony - hearing the distant sounds of earthquakes and sweeping tides, as if the world were screaming in desperation to be saved.

To her surprise, she hears the faint sound of a steed crying out. The sound is vague, which for a moment causes her to question her sanity. It is only upon hearing it again that Diana says to herself "a horse? No... a unicorn" jumping to her feet before racing to the balcony ledge. She looks down at the dim clouds amidst the dark sky and instantly freezes with dismay. Like a shooting star through the darkness, she sees a single white unicorn, carrying three individuals. The first two are of no concern to her - however, the sight of the third, that being her current herald sends Diana into a state of panic and confusion. "That idiot!"

Luke, Aurora and Umbra can be seen galloping upon the flying steed Starlight. Their appearance stirs hope within the goddess, who is unable to comprehend their motives. Surely they are not thinking of challenging Solomon? She wonders for Luke especially, who by now would only have a short time to live.

Approaching the balcony ledge also, Solomon looks down at the trio as they ascend towards him and the floating castle. He pauses as though having seen a ghost, as clearly in all his newfound power and glory, such bravery would not be expected. A glint fills his eyes, one that ignites the man's soul. Unable to understand why, the more he stares at the blue hero, the more he is reminded of something from long ago. He chuckles with irony, upon realising who the young hero reminds him of.

"He... he is just like me."

Turning around - Solomon looks to the opposite side of the balcony and finds the dark wizard standing readily. As though he had been there the whole time, Phantom holds a sly smile as he awaits his orders.

"There are three annoying pests on their way. Please give them a warm welcome."

"As you wish, my lord... Kwekekee!" Phantom laughs before disappearing into a portal, leaving Solomon alone with the goddess of the blue moon.

"Hmph, I bet you're enjoying every last moment, right Diana...?" He says, or at least he wishes to say, for as he shifts his gaze to where the woman was only a moment ago, he finds that Diana has disappeared - taken off without a goodbye. The man smiles, reminiscing about her particular habit. "I guess some things never change."

Soaring through the dark of night, upwards towards the gigantic floating castle, the trio race against time as the blue moon continues to plummet. With everything stacked against them, the heroes refuse to back down - challenging their fate under the stars.

"My goodness, succubus... does this steed of yours have to ride so violently? At this rate, I will fall off!"

"We don't have the luxury of time so quit your moaning, idiot vampire. Another word out of you and I'll throw you off!"

"Come on you two... can't you get along for just this once? After all, we are facing the end of the world."

"Quiet, boy. Nobody asked you!"

As usual, the three find room to bicker, even in the darkest of hours. For many, such insistent quarrelling is proof of an unorganised team spirit. However, for the trio, their constant fighting serves as a way to cope with their trials and tribulations. As the wind brushes past their faces, a collective sense of strength stirs within each of them, as though the very elements were on their side. Although they are too high up to hear, they know that the inhabitants of the world are cheering for them. At the very least they hope so.

"We are getting closer. I expect there will be some resistance from here on out!" Says Aurora, sitting by the front of the steed. Suddenly, the castle makes its move, no sooner after she had spoken.

From beyond the stars above, a dozen or so balls of red lights make their way toward the heroes. Upon closer exception, the three find that the balls are in fact meteorites, summoned and commanded to obstruct their way. The sight is jaw-dropping, as though a violent god were spitting flames of anger toward them.

"Watch out. The wizard has conjured rocks of flame to destroy us!" Umbra barks, covering his eyes like a fearful adolescent in the presence of a frightening show. The heat from the meteorites can be felt way before entering the world's atmosphere, which causes Luke to take a deep breath. His inhale is one of fear, watching as the projectiles grow larger as they approach.

To their surprise, the golden-haired warrior produces a minor chuckle, before shouting "this is nothing for the likes of Starlight and me!" Challenging the balls of flame. Effortlessly the unicorn dodges and evades each meteorite - zipping out from harm's way at astonishing speeds. Not a single meteor makes contact with the pure white steed, which continues its ascent higher and higher - carrying the trio towards their destination.

"Whoa..." the blue hero gasps - bathed in awe at the speed and instinct of Aurora's unicorn. A sense of experience flows from the steed, as though it were used to such adversity and more. As helpful as the horses of Luke's hometown were, a mere dog bark or magical phenomenon was enough to send them darting miles away. In contrast, Starlight is a creature of bravery, exuding a presence as though welcoming such opposition. If the unicorn were a person, it would be a daring warrior, perhaps the strongest in the land. It would be Aurora -

which explains why the two are the same.

"Impressive. I guess your little pony has some uses after all, succubus. If we survive this night, I'd love to cook it into a stew."

"Don't even think about it, silly demon. Starlight will never be on your menu!"

"Pay attention, Aurora and Umbra. We are not out of the woods just yet" Luke warns - gesturing for the pair to focus in front. Right before them, a fleet of Gargoyles can be seen emerging from the castle, before diving towards the three upon the winged steed. Their numbers are great - being around three hundred in number at least. The sky screams with the sounds of the winged monsters, sending a chill up the three heroes' spines, resulting in pools of sweat dripping from them.

As before, Umbra covers his eyes as Luke braces himself, attempting to remain calm. However, Aurora smiles as though already achieved victory, in the face of the many foes before them. Patting her white steed on the head, she says "do it now, Starlight!" Commanding the unicorn to take the offensive. Before their eyes, the horn of the unicorn begins to pulsate before releasing a great flash of light, brighter than the sun itself. Within seconds the Gargoyles fall from the sky - releasing a scream, but this time the scream is not one to be feared. The light has blinded them, causing the monsters to cry out helplessly.

Beholden with the wonder of Aurora and her loyal unicorn, a sense of admiration overcomes Luke, who can only stare in awe. Alone, Aurora is an extremely amazing individual, who lives up to her name as Aurora the invincible. However, combined with Starlight, the pair make for a duo that not even the gods could pull asunder.

To their relief, they finally reach the castle - drifting just above it. Seen up close, they find the structure is not one complete building, but multiple buildings, consisting of many towers and columns, connected by intertwining bridges that seem to go on for eternity. The steed decreases the rate of its flapping wings - gliding through the air as the heroic trio observes the mysterious castle before them. Every surface consists of alluring crystals that magnify and reflect the moon and stars - giving off a blue glow that captures their hearts. For a moment, they wonder if they have indeed reached the home of the ones who stole the Apex Grail and caused so much pain. The sight of the castle is truly a work of divinity.

"So beautiful", Luke says - quickly feeling a sense of guilt, for surely one should not praise the work of the enemy, especially an enemy that is intent on destroying the world. He is forgiven, for the look in his friends' eyes displays the same capture.

A great and peaceful silence hangs in the air, one that is so comforting, that he wishes that it could last forever. However, a simple glimpse above reminds him of the world's impending demise.

"This place is huge. Where do you think we should land?" The hero asks.

Pointing to the largest structure in front, Aurora gestures to a large and wide palace. It is gigantic and difficult to miss - big enough to fit five Ergo castles in. As well as being grand, it is topped off with a domelike roof, the only one of its kind amongst the vast buildings around. "That there must be where our enemies are hiding," she says, commanding her white steed to descend nearby. The Unicorn lands on a single crystal bridge, which leads directly to the entrance of the great palace.

After each of them climbs off the unicorn and places their feet on the ground, the three look to a pair of sealed doors, by the entrance. They are surprised, as they do not seem to come against any further resistance. Not even a threatening aura can be felt around them, which in turn worries the heroes. If this truly is a place that houses the dark wizard and more, one would expect to at least taste death on the tip of their tongue.

Turning to face her loyal pet, Aurora bows before Starlight and says "thank you for your help. Please wait here for our return. I promise you that we will all come back alive."

The unicorn responds with a satisfied nod as if holding the

swordsman to her word. Resuming her direction to the palace in front, Aurora, Umbra and Luke stare at its great sealed doors, taking a deep breath - appreciating the privilege of breathing air itself.

"Don't take this the wrong way, but you really shouldn't make promises you can't keep, succubus. Judging by the rate of the moon's descent, we have less than two hours to prevent absolute disaster. Our chances of success are less than one per cent, haha!"

"I don't intend to break any promises, dumb vampire" Aurora responds, leading the way as usual, before adding with surety "besides... you may not believe in miracles, seeing as you're nothing but an annoying demon, but I sure do. The odds that are against us now will only make for a sweeter victory. Even if nobody remembers our deeds this night and our names are lost in the pages of history, we will succeed. Now, let's get going."

At that moment, a hand is placed on her shoulder, as if signalling for her to halt for just a second. Surprised, she looks to her side and finds the one who has stopped her is Luke - displaying courageous body language. "Let me lead the way," he says, like a boy who has decided to become a man or a child who has found the courage to walk in the dark. His request isn't taken seriously at first, as she resists the urge to burst into laughter. Not due to any lack of strength, but because of his shy and innocent nature. During their journey, the role of him taking a slightly subdued stance between the three of them seemed like his rightful place. Now, he is breaking free from such a position, and as felt by the firm grip upon her shoulder, the boy is in no mood to accept a refusal.

A cold wind rushes past the three, causing their attires to flutter as though nature is pushing for her response. "As you wish, boy."

With a righteous head nod, the boy steps forward and proceeds to lead the way - followed closely by his most loyal friends: Umbra and Aurora. They reach the doors of the palace, stopping by the closed doors before each taking a deep breath.

Well, this is it. Are you ready?" Asks Luke, peering to his comrades from the corner of his eyes. They respond with a joint nod that is somewhere between bravery and caution. Their feelings are well understood to the young hero, for on the other side of the doors may lie their worst challenge to date. To their surprise, the entrance vibrates and shakes, as though reacting to their presence. Like a gift box popping open, the doors swing forth on their own.

"It would seem our enemies our inviting us inside. That is rather kind of them" says Umbra, with a tone that couldn't be more patronising. His comment lightens the mood for Luke and Aurora, who display a grateful smile toward him. No matter how dire and bleak their situations have been, Umbra has always seemed to make way for the most unimportant words, as though the experience were one huge game. Nevertheless, his dark humour serves as dew of calm - helping them to stay focused and relaxed.

With Blue Lunar in front, they enter the open doors of the palace and step inside. Once within, the doors slam shut behind them - causing the trio to jump with fright. The sounds of their unsheathed weapons sing collectively across the walls, as the heroes arm themselves - each entering a strong fighting pose.

"Keep your guard up, everybody. Don't drop your focus for a second!" Luke proclaims - holding his moon sword so tight, it could shatter. Scanning their surroundings, they observe the interior of the palace - finding themselves at the start of a long and wide crystal hallway, which emits a hypnotic glow of varying colours. The hallway looks to have no end - extending forth in what seems to be many meters. To their surprise, they find the palace bears no scent in the very least, as though it were not even real. Of course, it is real enough to dwell in, but not enough to be considered of this reality. It is almost as though it were spruced up by the thoughts of a powerful god.

The inside is as fascinating as the exterior, however, the

black-suited comrade comments in a somewhat disturbed manner and whispers "this place is filled with intense magic and energy. It is almost hard to breathe. Can you not sense it too?"

"Well, I can't say I feel anything, to be honest... which is kind of weird. However, It does feel as though this place lacks something. What do you think, Aurora?"

Raising her white sword in front, as though signalling for the pair to follow her line of sight, the woman replies "how about you two numbskulls stop thinking and start striking at the enemies right in front of us?" For a moment the two boys blink with confusion, failing to see a single enemy before them. Has the golden-haired beauty finally lost her sanity or is it the work of the palace calling forth mirages to baffle the trio? Thankfully, both assumptions turn out to be untrue, for within seconds they notice a gang of creatures, materialising into being as gargoyles. However, the beasts are unlike any other seen before, for they are made from the same material as the palace: Crystal. Standing like proud figurines, the crystallised monsters face Luke and his friends, akin to a kind of security force and defence mechanism of the palace.

Remembering Umbra's witty comment only moments prior, Luke resists the urge to laugh at such a standoff, for it was only a few minutes ago that the doors greeted them with open arms. "The wizard and Solomon must be somewhere at the end of the hallway, which is why they are trying to stop us. At least we know we're on the right track!"

"Indeed. In that case, let us keep moving forward and litter this cursed palace with the fallen bodies of our foes!"

Charging forth, the three take on the crystallised beasts, and within the large pathway, fighting ensues. Like a trio of shameless intruders, Umbra, Aurora and Luke smash their way through the many foes before them. Crystal shards fly about and hit the walls, upon each beast's defeat as the heroes press onwards - side by side.

Although they are too preoccupied to express it, the friends sense a feeling between them. They are in ultimate sync with one another, making up for the other's blind spots and weaknesses. What Aurora lacks in long-range, is made up for by Umbra, whose lack of armour is compensated for by Luke. Their natural battle instincts are almost symbiotic, as though possessing a shared mindset. At this point, words would only impede their teamwork. After all, they have shared many experiences. Something as carnal as words would do them no favours.

"We are unstoppable," the young hero says within himself - taken back by how in tune he and his greatest friends are with one another. He realises, as do the others that this is the first time that they have fought together in one single space. As such, his heart is elated, filled with a joy that has never been experienced before. Even if the moon were to come crashing down at this moment, he would feel content knowing that he and his loyal comrades are fighting to their fullest, together.

As wave upon wave of foes come against the uninvited heroes, the three display not an ounce of fear or doubt - relying on each other to strive onwards. And onwards they go, like javelins who have been shot forth by a champion. They cover hundreds of meters within moments, and like a battering ram, they crush the crystal monsters, much like how one would crush toys. If the lord of the castle is watching, he must surely be raging with humiliation.

They soon reach the end of the hallway, coming to a single door. The opposing monsters cease - disappearing into the walls and ceiling of the hallway, which slightly baffles the three. However, the sight of the door overrides their concerns, for they are yet again a step closer.

With no foe left, the silence returns, save for the harsh breathing of the trio who catch their breath. As they shift their eyes from one to the other, an ever-present grin stains their faces. To an onlooker, one might assume that they have gone mad - lost their minds in the frenzy of battle. However, to the three, the reason is all too simple: Hope. "We can win. We might be able to succeed this time", says Luke - looking at his reflection from a crystal wall.

"I admit, we sure do make quite a formidable bunch, fighting together" Umbra adds, strolling to the door before placing his hand against it. "However, don't be too confident. The foes we defeated so easily were there to test us or better yet to stall our progress. Things will get much harder from here on out, I assure you."

∞∞∞

The three push open the door and waste no time stepping inside. However, once inside they find themselves in a place that could hardly be classed as inside. The first thing they feel is a warm breeze, followed by the sounds of running water. Before their eyes they notice they are under a yellow sky, accompanied by twin suns: one gold and one silver. By their feet, they discover that they are upon a long stone bridge that extends almost half a mile in front, which leads to a glowing door. The bridge itself is supported by pillars that stretch down to a shallow stream that encompasses the bizarre land they are in.

"Are we… are we still within the palace?"

"Yes, no doubt about it. However, what you are witnessing is the result of magic. This castle can create locations that are beyond our wildest dreams" Umbra replies - looking down with reflective eyes, as though reminiscing on a particular individual. "Good old Felix always did want to create the ultimate castle. I guess he finally managed to pull it off."

"Did you say something, idiot vampire?"

"Huh? No… I was just thinking out loud as all.

Pressing onward, they walk together along the bridge, amidst the bizarre and surreal location. The setting is quiet and still, almost as though they were in a living painting. However, an overwhelming sadness enshrouds the atmosphere, as though they were experiencing the emotions of its creator.

"I wonder where all the monsters have gone? I expected a few thousand of them, at least" says Luke - somewhat suspicious by the absence of enemies.

Like an old fashioned man of superstition, Umbra places his hand over the hero's mouthguard and says "be quiet, buffoon. You will give the wizard ideas with words like that. Goodness, gracious, must I school you on everything?"

Lagging a pace or two behind, Aurora giggles to herself - ears following the exchange between the boy and vampire. Staring upon their backs, she remembers the first time she had met the pair. Never in a million years would the most famous swordsman in the land imagine teaming up with such a duo. After all, the two are lazy, naive, frustrating and unpredictable. Nevertheless, for all their shortcomings, they have succeeded in capturing her heart, giving her a reason to live.

"Luke and Umbra... thank you" she attempts to say, with words of gratitude ready to launch from her lips and catapult through the air. However, an intrusive sound of a blade being drawn drowns out her voice - causing the three to stop with fright. The blade sounds familiar to the woman especially, as it chimes from behind through to her front. "I guess gratitudes will have to wait, for now" she whispers - slowly turning around to face the lone enemy who has unsheathed their blade.

As the pair turn around also, they gasp at the sight of Yohan, Aurora's younger brother, sporting the legendary white armour: Gospel. Seen without his helmet, with his left eyepatch and shining silver hair, he stands with the tip of his sword directed solely at his sister. A monotone and unreadable face is portrayed to the golden-haired swordsman, as a tense standoff begins. There is not a sound from any of them, as the shallow stream below hums with fear - amid a great confrontation.

"You finally came, as I knew you would," Yohan says, in a tone that could never be mistaken for anybody else. His voice is cheery, innocent and light. However, as angelic as his natural pitch is, he is aligned with the dark, which tugs at his sister's heart like an unbearable anchor.

"Yohan, I finally found you."

A single step forward is taken by Umbra and Luke, ready to support their golden-haired comrade. Judging by the way they fought just a moment ago, the blue hero is convinced that the three of them against one opponent will be an easy accomplishment. Perhaps they could convince him to join their side and save the world also? A well of possibility flows from his spirit, and like a flame, it can be felt by the others. However, his flame is not reciprocated.

Turning around, Aurora says to Luke "I am afraid this is where we say our goodbyes, for now. I need to do this alone. Go on... I will catch up with you when I am done here."

"What? We are splitting up? I thought we were gonna fight together?" He says, showing his age as but a simple youngster who is unable to make sense of her actions.

His eyes rattle with confusion, so much so they could escape his face, as Aurora replies "we still are fighting together, but apart. Now get moving and don't make me repeat myself." Swinging her blade, she cuts into the bridge - separating herself and her two teammates.

As fragments of stone collapse between them, Luke shouts desperately "Aurora!"

Snatching his arm before pulling him away, Umbra advises "it's no use, Luke. She has already made up her mind, so let her settle things here. We must carry on!"

Reluctantly, Luke and Umbra press onwards, running towards the exit door without turning their backs for a moment. Not due to a lack of caring, but instead due to the bitter sight of departure.

As the boys disappear into the distance, Aurora shifts her gaze back to the opponent in front of her.

"Brother, now it is just you and me. Just so you know, you have a lot of explaining to do."

"I beg to differ, sister. You see, I did this simply for one thing and one thing only... for love!"

Chapter 24: Light and Dark

The Apex Grail is the most sacred item in all of existence. Created at the peak of a catastrophic war between the gods, the grail was put in place to ensure their future quarrels and affairs do not impact the mortal world. Forged using the collective powers of the gods themselves, its sole purpose has always been to negate direct interaction between god and man.

Unfortunately, the circumstances around its creation have always left a bitter feeling in the hearts of some. Some such as Phantom, Solomon and Megethos, were tasked with slaying a goddess whose crime was purely due to falling in love with a human. Upon completing their mission, the three were betrayed by the blue moon goddess, who had gifted the leader of the group with the Blue Lunar armour. In actuality, his armour had been eating away at his life force all along, and it wasn't long until the armour took his life. His two friends fell into deep despair and disappeared from the world for hundreds of years.

Throughout recent events, Solomon had seemingly returned, along with the two comrades that were by his side in the days of old. However, today their goal is to end all life - using the blue moon itself. Upon absorbing the power of the Apex Grail, Solomon ascended to become a god of the mortal world - possessing the divine power of the Apex Grail. The gods cannot touch him, for the rule of the Apex Grail still stands and yet no mortal can reach him, due to dwelling in a floating castle named: The castle of truth.

All is not lost, for within the darkness, three lights dare to challenge not only the world's fate but their own.

Progressing through the castle, Luke and Umbra carry onwards - pushing through each door that they come across. However, choosing to stay behind, Aurora faces off with her brother in what is far from a pleasant meeting.

Standing opposite one another, upon the stone bridge, the siblings of the Stigma hold their silence for many seconds, until the older sister addresses the brother.

"Yohan, you were the one who released Phantom from his prison, which in turn caused an untold amount of bloodshed. Why did you do it?"

With a cheerful and pure demeanour, as though the bleak situation were an afterthought, the brother smiles and says "I did it, for you."

Although his words are pure and simple, they are not understood in the slightest by Aurora. One could argue that speaking a completely different language would be more helpful to her, as all his current words serve to do is infuriate her. To associate the release of such a monster with Aurora's wishes is akin to bearing her responsible, which angers her to no end.

As though on autopilot, her body takes over. Drawing her blade to eye level in her fiercest battle-ready pose. To put it more accurately, her rage takes over, and like a siren warning of a strike beforehand, she screams "you did it for me? What the hell are you saying, Yohan? I never asked for this!" Launching forth like a blazing arrow.

The two collide and their swords clash against the other - resulting in a spectacular clanging sound that sweeps through the air, so great it disrupts the waters below. Within seconds the two are blasted backwards - repelled by the released force of their opposing strength and aura. The wind screams with terror as though caught in a godly confrontation. The bridge that once stood firmly gives way due to the impact - causing a scene of disaster as chunks explode and fall through the air.

Like a duo of masterful acrobats, Aurora and Yohan somersault to the shallow stream below, landing gracefully on the ground without so much as leaving a ripple as their feet penetrates the waters. Standing opposite one another, eyes locked in a tense stare, the two size the other up, as the bridge around them crumbles to the ground.

"Sister, do you remember when we were young? It was quite a difficult time for us, wouldn't you agree? Before we were picked up and brought into the kingdom of Ergo, you and I lived on the streets of various places, upon being abandoned by our parents. Nobody wanted us around, and it wasn't long before we were often chased away, simply for being a Stigma. The nights were often cold, so cold that I would often wish for death, and when the morning came, I would again wish for death due to hunger. Regardless of how unfair our lives were, I quickly understood it. However, there was one thing that I could never understand, and that was… your smile."

His words, although cryptic seems to intrigue his sister, which moves her to the point of briefly subsiding her anger. As though putting a lid on a boiling pot, she suppresses her rage - allowing the sounds of the flowing waters to aid her focus. "My smile? What do you mean?"

"I first noticed the smile, one day while I was being pushed around by a gang of bullies. They roughed me up badly, and no matter how hard I pleaded for them to stop, they didn't. Fortunately, you arrived just in the nick of time and inflicted twice as much pain to them. It was at that moment I saw it. It only lasted for a few seconds, but as you stood over them, I saw a smile that I had never seen before from you. It was a look of utter freedom and bliss!"

Zipping around the golden-haired swordsman like a human whirlwind, Yohan continues to converse with his sister as she stands in the centre, following his explanation. "That smile... it haunted me for years on end, for no matter what I or anybody did, you never showed it again. That was, until two years."

"Two years ago? Wait, are you referring to the coup?"

Leaping directly to her, the pair clash swords once more - releasing a great shockwave that shakes the very battleground. The sea scatters, pushed backwards by their collision, causing the waters to blast upwards as though attempting to touch the sky for safety.

As the waters rain back down like tiny droplets, the siblings run side by side - swords pressed against the other.

"Precisely, sister. On that fateful evening, you alone raised your sword against the majority of your brothers in arms, all to protect the King. Sporting the white suit that I now carry, you laid waste to all of them, unleashing the full might of your Stigma. It was said that you became like that of a phoenix, however, I beg to differ. To me, you became a demon, a glorious demon who upon standing victorious, revealed the same liberated smile that I spotted years prior. At that moment, at that second, I finally figured it out. For you, fighting against impossible odds brings you the most exquisite joy!"

Upon yet another collision, an even greater shockwave erupts forth, splitting parts of the ground in two, followed by a mighty earthquake. Although the opponents are human, right now it feels as though two giants were in a grave dual. The force propels them apart, and they tumble along the now ravenous stream.

Terrible exhaustion makes itself known throughout the body of the swordsman. For a second she wonders why her body seems so fragile, seeing as no clean strikes were inflicted upon her. However, she quickly realises the reason and whispers "it's the suit: Gospel. I have forgotten how powerful it is. It's taking almost all my energy just to keep up with him", eyes closed as though attempting to shut the pain away.

As Aurora lay on the ground of the shallow waters, she feels a cold pinch against the centre of her neck. Her initial thoughts assume it to be a single drop of water, splashed upon her from the battle. However, this sensation is longer lasting and solid, as though an ice cube were placed on her neck. Opening her eyes, she discovers it to be the tip of the enemy blade - pressed firmly against her skin. Looking upwards she finds the white knight adversary, standing over her as the light of the twin suns above magnifies his armour, to an almost blinding sight.

"I am right, aren't I? Tell me I am lying" Yohan says, like an opposing lawyer in a courtroom. As the ground settles and the waters relax, the two stay silent as the brother allows his sister to deny his claim. Not a single word comes from her mouth to her defence, which confirms that which he already knew. "I am right, you were smiling on that day. You had no idea that all this time, I was observing you... carefully learning your fighting style through mere sight alone. Would you like to know something else, my dear sister? The one who instigated the coup against the King of Ergo was me!"

Her heart stops upon hearing the stunning revelation and confession from her brother. She is still, eyes refusing to blink as though placed under a spell of petrification. The images of that fateful day erupt to the surface, as the words of the one who instigated it all along, can be heard saying "I was the one who was responsible for starting the coup. From the sidelines, I had spread false rumours amongst the soldiers, gradually placing blame on the King. I did that, knowing what would eventually happen… knowing that you would slaughter them all for rising up against our king who took us in as children."

"You… you are lying…"

"I am not lying, sister. And I would do it all again, at a drop of a hat. You see, when I saw that liberated smile and freedom in your eyes that day, I truly realised my purpose in this world. I was created to be the darkness to help you shine bright."

At that second, a barrage of blows is inflicted on the silver-haired boy. The speed at which they have come is so fast, that he barely can react. Although he sees multiple fists against his face, it feels like dozens more, and upon a great strike, he is knocked backwards for many paces. Upon rolling into a crouched position, he shakes from mild disorientation. Before his eyes he sees Aurora, standing tall and mighty, exuding a wave of anger that is almost frightening. With her blade held in front, she readies to resume their duel.

Such fire in her spirit would most likely cause most men to beg for forgiveness. However, her feelings seem to have the opposite result on her brother, as an untamed grin is born upon his face instead. "Are you unhappy with me, sister? Why? Everything I have done was for you alone."

"Yohan, because of fabrication, you made me kill my comrades, people I fought side by side with. Do you have any idea the amount of pain you have caused?"

"Indeed, I am well aware of my actions, and I couldn't care less about the pain it brought, for joy without pain is meaningless. Don't you see? For us Stigmas, our whole history is struggle!"

They battle - colliding continuously as they race through the land, leaving a trail of devastation upon each released shockwave. Craters form upon every step as waves of water are blasted in every direction. Like a deadly dance of death, the siblings tear past one another - barely being seen by the naked eye. Such a battle is not meant for the eyes of mere mortals, for doing so would almost certainly be futile. Like a pair of gold and silver lights, they charge back and forth at one another, mirroring the other's action in perfect unison.

"So, do you mean to tell me that you released Phantom, stole Gospel and killed Gabriella, all for a smile? You are insane!"

"Absolutely. I knew that if I released and aligned myself with the wizard of despair, he would unleash a wrath that would be almost impossible to overcome. Like I said before, your freedom is achieved by succeeding against such odds. You may deny it all you want, but you know that deep inside, this was what you have been craving all along, and it is my destiny to grant it!"

She fights on, fighting against who she thought was her brother, for the one that she battles against, is a stranger. Her brother would never plot something so heinous. Yohan would never align himself with the worst wizard to ever grace the world, and Yohan would never cause so much pain. And yet, even as she tells herself that the one before her is an impostor, deep within her heart she knows that she is only fooling herself.

"Idiot, do you truly believe that this is your destiny?"

"Not just my destiny, but our destiny. This path of ours was unavoidable, sister. Even Gabriella realised this, before meeting her end. She tried her very best to stop our fated confrontation and woefully failed. Open your eyes, this night was preordained!"

To her shock and surprise, she watches as her brother reaches for his eyepatch. As though the world had entered a slow-motion, she stares in disbelief, knowing what such an action would cause. Mind taken to many days ago, back in the town of Fiory, her thoughts play the events of what transpired upon removing her eye patch. As if rewatching the events of a tragic play, she remembers the power that was unleashed - the true power of the Stigma.

"Yohan, don't do it..." she cries, praying that her words can reach him, for once he removes his eyepatch, there is no going back. Such power from him would ultimately force her hand, leaving only one victor. "... the second you remove that, I will have no other choice but to fight at full strength!"

"Precisely. If you want to live, then you must come at me with everything you have, using the same power that slaughtered your soldiers. Sister, let us put on the greatest show, so that the gods may even be humbled!"

Without hesitation, the silver-haired opponent throws off his eyepatch, and as the piece of material falls towards the water, so do his sister's hopes. She had hoped to convince him to return home, either with kindness or aggression. In the worst-case scenario, she had expected to beat her brother to an inch of his life, just enough to be taken back to the land below. However, as she watches his eyepatch swimming along the stream before slipping into a crevasse, her heart sinks.

A burst of light is released from the white adversary, causing Aurora to cover her eyes. Her coat and hair flutter backwards violently, as though caught amid a great gale. "Yohan... Yohaaaaan!" She screams desperately, lowering her arms and allowing a clear view of her opponent. Standing like an angel, her brotherly rival can be seen bearing two silver wings of light that emanate streams of countless energy. Feet neatly clasped together, he displays a graceful posture, holding his sword in the gentlest of fashion, as his glowing eye shines bright.

"So beautiful" Aurora lets slip, captivated by his angelic appearance. Like a living embodiment from books of old, Yohan resembles what many would describe as an angel. For the first time, she is put in the same shoes like the ones who have marvelled upon her. "So this is what it looks like... to gaze at the full power of a Stigma," she says within her heart.

At that moment her winged foe enters a mild crouch, like a sprinter who is ready to blast off across a sports pitch. Wasting no time, Aurora removes her eyepatch, unleashing her true power also. Two golden wings of light sit upon her shoulders, releasing a contrasting stream of golden energy that opposes her brother. The warring aura from both swordsmen is so great the ground trembles, before literally splitting into two great halves.

Within seconds the two soar into the sky and do battle - colliding into one another as they soar higher and higher. Watched by the twin suns overhead, the fierce battle seems more like a divine dance, as siblings zip to and fro, equally matched.

For Aurora, to witness such skill and power from her younger brother, who never had expressed nor displayed any fighting capability is mesmerising to her. Each technique and manoeuvre he is performing had come from her alone. She realises that all this time, every night fought, whether minor to great and epic battles was silently adopted by her brother. "Amazing" she wishes to say, applauding her young sibling, for he has become one of the most powerful swordsmen she has ever faced.

For Yohan, to witness the power that has given his sister the title Aurora the invincible astounds him. Against all odds and overwhelming power, she still stands. As they strike continuously, faster than the wind itself, he whispers "even with the added strength of Gospel, I am still unable to land a clean strike. Your power is unimaginable, sister."

Enveloped by their aura, they each take the form of a radiant bird amongst the heavens - singing a heavenly melody as they charge into one another for the last strike. A great crash ensues, resulting in a blinding force of light that is so great, that the majority of the ground crumbles. Not a single stone is left unturned, as what was once a scenic location, fit for a painting is now a wasteland.

A short time passes and the battle ends, bringing peace to the terrain once more. However, the sight of the ruined area of broken bridges, scarred earth and disrupted waters cannot hide the chaotic confrontation that had taken place. A slow wind returns, finding the coast clear to blow freely. It stops by two siblings, who are found by a piece of earth that had managed to avoid the destruction.

Laying defeated on the ground, the white knight can be seen held in the arms of his older sister. Eyelids half-closed and breath as small as a sleeping baby, the younger brother shows all the signs of one who will pass. With their wings and radiant auras dispelled, the close siblings look at each other with a deep gaze.

"I knew... I knew that I could never stand a chance against you, sister. Even so, I had to do it. I had to be the one who could make you smile and shine within this dark and awful world" he says, slowly raising his hands to her cheeks. Her face feels warm yet wet, due to tears. Nevertheless, the sister displays a smile that fills him with nostalgia. "Ahh... there it is... that smile. Only when you have beaten all odds, does such a smile presents itself, right sister?"

Her smile is evident and cannot be hidden. However, as she places her hands against his bloodied forehead, Aurora replies "you are mistaken, my brother. This smile of mine has never been because I enjoyed fighting difficult opponents. It was born through the satisfaction of protecting you."

"Protecting... me?"

"Yes. Back when we were young when I saved you from those idiots who tried to hurt you, I smiled because I was able to protect you. Then, during the coup two years ago, I smiled because I was able to keep you from harm. Now, do you understand?"

A confused look appears in his eyes, as he struggles and says "I had no idea. I didn't realise that it was because of me. I messed up, right sis? Tell me something, why are you smiling now then?"

She holds her silence, looking down at the brother with a teary gaze. "I am smiling because I have saved you from yourself because you have made me so proud and because there is another person in my life who also means the world to me now" she wants to say. However, such a reply would not capture the feelings within her heart at this moment, especially as she watches Yohan's eyes slip lower and lower. Instead, she settles on a short farewell and utters "you fought magnificently."

His eyes shut completely and his heart retires, exuding a peaceful and content sleep as his soul departs - leaving Aurora alone as the victor.

"Keep up the pace, Luke!" Shouts Umbra - voice echoing along the walls of a new quarter of the palace. The two can be found ascending a large spiral stairwell, made of pure glass. As the constant sounds of each advancing step reverberate off the solid surfaces, an ominous and foreboding feeling shrouds the atmosphere. A choral humming of a devious wind mocks the pair, along with a cold breeze that can be seen as a semi-white mist. Nevertheless, the two press on, not to be deterred. However, for the tuxedo sporting comrade, he notices something far more troubling.

As though weighed down by a ball and chain, Luke's progress has become slower. Not just slower, but more difficult, as harsh breathing can be heard from behind Umbra who is already many steps ahead. It is the first time that Luke has known fatigue while wearing the Blue Lunar suit, which should not be possible. As he attempts to understand why, he calls out to his friend "slow down, Umbra. I just need to catch my breath."

"Catch your breath? This isn't the time to be taking naps..."

At that moment the blue knight tumbles and falls. As the sound of his collapse reaches the ears of his friend, Umbra freezes with shock before turning back. Before his eyes, he finds the young hero laying on a row of steps, in a position like that of a lifeless puppet. "Luke!"

Hurrying to his aid, even buckling over himself due to panic, Umbra kneels to his friend. As he observes his limp body and closed eyes, Umbra fears the worst as the surrounding sound from the low wind hums like a farewell prayer. "No, not now... not when we are so close!" Umbra pleads, witnessing the inescapable forfeit of the divine armour at work. Teeth crushed together with frustration, a feeling of guilt overcomes him as he whispers "damn, I thought we would have made it in time, seeing as only an hour or so has passed. It's too soon, too soon for you to leave us now!"

Suddenly to his relief, the blue knight lets out an acute cough, causing Umbra to jump with surprise.

"Uh... what happened just now? Did I just blackout for a moment?" Asks Luke, confused as to how he has wound up slouched against the stairs. "Are you ok, Umbra? You look concerned. Is something the matter?" Dumbfounded by Umbra's worried gaze.

To the young hero's surprise, the black-suited friend wraps his arms around him - embracing Luke in a firm hold. The action is so spontaneous, that the blue knight stays with eyes wide with shock, wondering what has come over the comrade. A feeling of sadness emanates from Umbra.

"Promise me something, Luke. Don't die yet. I don't care how you do it... just don't leave me, please."

His words are deep, as though plucked from the farthest reaches of one's heart. It isn't often that the smiling demon speaks with such desperation, which strikes the blue knight even more. Luke finally realises why his friend is acting so strangely. "I am slowly dying, which is why I've become so exhausted. This armour, it's claiming my life" Luke says to his own heart, overcome with peculiar guilt. As though responsible for the hurt he senses within Umbra, he reciprocates the hug and says "I am sorry for scaring you. I promise I am not gonna die... not here."

A short and moist sniff is heard from Umbra, the kind one makes when tears have roamed freely down a person's cheeks. Luke's heart pauses with surprise, because of a realisation that has only just now come to him. Oblivious all this time, Luke realises that the friend has never once cried along their journey. Even the strong-hearted Aurora, has shed tears - however, none has ever been seen on the demon's face.

Unfastening his hands, Umbra stands to his feet, revealing a smiling and chirpy expression, with not a single tear seen. Perplexed by the dry-eyed friend, Luke questions his sanity, for he was certain that Umbra had been sobbing. Was it just his imagination or yet again one of Umbra's tricks? If it were the latter, Luke understands that it is not a foul trick in the slightest, for as he looks into the grinning friend's eyes, he discerns a type of poker face. A deep sadness belies his smile, one that Luke finally notices. "I wonder just how long he's been feeling like this?" The hero says within himself, annoyed for not noticing sooner.

"Well, shall we continue?" Asks Umbra - reaching out his right hand to the blue hero who is still sitting on the steps. His voice is as bubbly and positive as it has always been. However, as confident as he sounds, Luke is far from convinced by it. Regardless, he plays along.

"Yeah, let's keep going, my friend."

Together they finally reach the top of the stairs, coming to a single door. The door is dark and black - giving off a terrifying aura. The dark aura coming from it is so great, that one wouldn't be surprised if they wound up cursed by merely touching it. A unified exhale is produced by the two friends, who proceed to push the door open and enter.

Upon stepping inside, they find themselves in another otherworldly location - however, unlike the scenic landscape where they left Aurora, this is a complete contrast. A putrid smell of rotten flesh attacks their noses, followed by sounds of sinister mourning and laughter. Finding themselves within a throne room of sorts, Luke and Umbra notice the very floor, walls and ceiling are of unique material. Consisting of red, followed by blue lines throughout, the surfaces resemble living flesh, as though they were standing inside of a beating heart.

"Is this hell?" Luke asks, in a terrified tone - scanning the large and wide room. By the distant sides of the throne room, he spots an untold amount of horrific creatures, each kneeling as though having welcomed royalty. "Those are demons. But why are they bowing at us?"

A small but noticeable slap is felt against his shoulder pad. It is his comrade Umbra, gesturing for him to pay attention to something evident. Following Umbra's line of sight, he looks directly in front and finds a familiar individual, sitting upon a large and dark throne. Sporting a red tuxedo suit, bearing two horns upon the front of his forehead, the demon prince Megethos is seen with a dark and threatening smirk.

"Greetings again, Umbra. I see that you just can't help being a thorn in my side."

"Indeed, and I am sure you know why I have come here? It is time to end this madness."

The exchange between Umbra and the demon prince astounds Luke, much like the first time he observed their volley of words. Again, a sense of kindred spirits is felt between the two, which mystifies him even more. A serious stare can be found upon Umbra, as though recollecting their previous encounter that saw the trio badly injured.

Drawing his greatsword, Luke stands in front in a protective manner and whispers "don't worry my friend. We are not gonna lose, like the last time. You and I are in this together!"

To the young hero's surprise, Umbra places his hand upon the blade before easing it downwards - gesturing for him to withhold his sword. As though anticipating the knight's confused response, the black-suited friend smiles and says "could you let me handle this, alone? You will only get in my way if you stay here."

"Are you serious? Have you forgotten what happened to you, the last time you faced him?"

"I know, but things will be different this time... trust me. I have a confession to make. You see, my reason for tagging along with you on your journey wasn't because of Phantom. I exist for the sole purpose of making peace with Megethos."

The knight stays lost, lost in a daydream as the explanation of his friend goes through one ear and out the other. Although he doesn't understand the finer specifics of Umbra's words, he understands that he will continue alone. An uncomfortable feeling overcomes the boy, like one whose support network is slowly being taken away. "First Aurora and now Umbra" he thinks to himself.

"Don't worry, crybaby. I promise that I will catch up with you. Just do me a favour and don't die... not to Phantom, Solomon or your armour. Now, get going. You are our only hope" Umbra says as his eyes grow moist as though holding back a torrent of tears.

With reluctance, Luke slowly turns his back and runs towards the only other exit nearby - shouting to Umbra as he goes "you had better not die on me also, or I'll never forgive you!"

As the hero disappears into the distance, advancing into the palace further, the black-suited Umbra continues to hold his smile. As though unable to fully hold back the tears, a single drop manages to sneak through and roll down his cheek.

Turning his head back to the mighty foe in front, his smile evolves into a cold stare, and he chuckles to Megethos "now that I have gotten rid of that weakling, I don't need to worry about my friends getting caught in our crossfire." Tossing his black briefcase to the floor, Umbra deliberately lets his guard down, much like their previous confrontation on the mountain of Venus. However, unlike then, a powerful aura exudes from him as he gloats in a sinister manner "you have been trying to eliminate me for some time, and I know exactly why. You are afraid of me because I represent something that you fear the most... yourself!"

Chapter 25: Two Sides, One Coin

Within the throne room, two individuals stand opposite one another, squaring off like fighters of a great tournament. As a score of demons observes the confrontation, like a crowd of spectators, a tense silence hangs in the air. Coming away from the seated throne, the first fighter holds a firm and tense glare, hands inserted into the pockets of his red attire.

Standing opposite, the opponent in black mirrors his stance, bearing the same face. He too displays a strong stare, which suddenly gives way to a look of warmth as he addresses the dark prince.

"You are me... and I am you. Just as the moon is bound to our world, you and I are bound together. That much cannot be denied."

"You are nothing but a shadow" Megethos responds, in a tone that is filled with pure hatred. An aura of resentment flows from the demon prince, causing the surrounding minions to huddle backwards against the walls, as a surge of malevolence chokes their chests.

Amid the threatening energy that has engulfed the space they are in, Umbra maintains his warm gaze and says "so, you truly do hate me that much. It is ironic, to think that you and I were once the same. Do you remember the day everything changed? The day we separated?"

The demon prince emits a grieved sigh, the type one makes when overwhelmed with a situation. As his hands curl into miniature boulders, it is clear that Megethos doesn't want Umbra to continue. However, the black-suited boy proceeds to recount their shared testimony.

"It all started one thousand years ago, on that fateful night, the night that will forever be etched into our souls. You, Felix and Solomon, were tasked with killing the goddess Aphrodite and her lover. Upon succeeding, the divine armour that was bestowed on Solomon claimed his life. Shortly after he had died, Felix disappeared and you fell into deep despair - entering a long sleep. However, something else took place during your sleep of anguish. You had cast off a piece of yourself, the side that knew: reason, logic, trust, humour and respect. You had split yourself into two, with the noble side becoming me - leaving yourself with nothing but anger and hatred. We are two sides of the same coin."

"That is enough... anomaly."

"At first I had no recollection of anything, and for hundreds of years, I wandered the world, searching for a reason for my existence. Over time, I found that the humans would associate me with the vampire class of demons, so I embraced it. However, as the years passed, your memories flowed to mine, and I started to remember just who I used to be and what had occurred. Although you were still asleep, I could feel your emotions, your pain. I tried my very best to find you, but I had no idea where you were. It was only when I encountered Luke, that I knew that I would bump into you eventually."

Through with listening, the demon prince reaches to the pair of horns upon his forehead - proceeding to unsheathe them like a pair of blades. Wielding the two swords of black bone, he lets out a shout that shakes the very palace, "I don't need you. Because of you I was weak and allowed myself to suffer unimaginable despair!"

His words are not only directed at Umbra, but at everything Umbra represents. Umbra is the living embodiment of all the noble qualities that once were a part of Megethos.

"Very well, my other-self. If you truly think that you can stop me as you are, then go right ahead. Give it your best shot."

Needing no further encouragement, the red adversary leaps forth at lightning speed - so fast the onlookers lose sight of him. Even the air itself fails to follow in time, delaying longer than it should before rushing forward, causing a mighty gust of wind to sweep outward. "Die!" Megethos shouts - performing a cross slash with his twin swords. A deafening screech tears throughout the room, as the cursed blades cut into the air itself. As the swords come only inches away from Umbra, the boy miraculously disappears within seconds, causing the weapons to strike the ground instead. The floor explodes, erupting into a red mist that covers the area. "Where... where did you go?"

As the smoke dissipates, the black-suited boy is nowhere to be found. The speed of his escape was so great, that one would assume that he simply vanished into thin air. Standing alone within the centre of the room, a feeling of humiliation overcomes Megethos, as his minions bare a baffled stare - mouths wide with suspense.

"Up here, my friend" comes the chirpy voice of Umbra.

Looking directly upward, the dark swordsman gasps at the sight of the grinning boy, standing upside down on the ceiling above. Arms folded comfortably, Umbra exudes a playful aura, toying with the demon prince like he were but a simpleton. The surrounding demons also gasp with astonishment, displaying impressed twinkles in their eyes, moved by his seemingly effortless manoeuvre. "Goodness gracious, you are mighty slow. Wanna give it another try?"

"Do not mock me, foolish shadow!" Megethos screams, releasing a ray of dark energy from his eyes. As the blast races upwards, Umbra vanishes yet again, causing the beam to hit the ceiling - causing a mighty explosion that sees chunks of roof crashing to the floor. "Curses... I missed again!" He rants, watching as a specific hole in the ceiling reveals the bold moon amidst the masses of glistening stars. As his eyes lay upon the celestial sphere, a surge of fond memories stir within his heart - causing him to drop his weapons as though lost in a daydream.

"What is the matter? You look like you've seen a ghost" Umbra says, appearing this time upon the throne itself, arms and legs crossed like a calculating warrior. As though reading the thoughts of the red adversary, Umbra utters "when you and Solomon first met one thousand years ago, you were enemies. However, upon a duel, he earned your respect, and it was then that he became your best friend, right? You are still hurting over the fact that you allowed him, your greatest friend and rival to die back then."

Shaking with denial, Megethos hardens his heart once more and replies "you are wrong, I am not reminiscing at all. Besides, Solomon is with me once more, along with Felix!"

"And yet, you are still unable to forgive yourself, which is why you reject me. Listen to me... you will never be as strong as you once was if you continue to deny yourself!"

A tense standoff fills the room, watched by the moon above. Casting a spotlight over the demon prince, he stands still - head held low as the surrounding demons await his next move. "Hehehe... you are right. I am not the same, and neither are my friends. Our friendship was first united by optimism. Now, we are united by despair. However, this is who I am now, and I won't stop until my anger pounds this world to dust. Umbra, mere words are meaningless. Show me with your strength why I should embrace you once more!"

Picking up his twin blades, a fire of anger reignites from

the demon prince - releasing a burst of energy that is so catastrophic, that it obliterates the entire legion of his minions. Arms held protectively in front like a shield, Umbra covers his face from the intensity - clothes slowly burning away as they flutter violently. "I guess I have no choice then. I will stop you, right now" he proclaims, raising his hand in front before shouting to the four walls "bloody sword!"

By his command, a sword of pure blood materialises in Umbra's hands - releasing an aura of its own that counters Megetho's outpour of energy. "What in the..." his eyes are beholden with shock as he stares at the crimson sword, and while he expresses his wonder, the black-suited opponent is already in motion to strike. Within seconds Umbra zips forward like a dart and performs a flawless strike - cutting through the red foe's chest before stopping, side by side, like a sprinter at the end of a finish line.

The power of the bloody sword is so great, that the whole roof of the throne room crumbles to pieces - exposing the pair to the open sky above.

Inflicted with the deadly strike, Megethos stays in a standing position - continuously looking upward at the moon. Within the moon's gaze, he recollects the events of a dual, one thousand years ago, which led him to his very first friend.

"You fight well, for a human being. What was your name again? Solomon? I am Megethos."

As he recollects his most treasured memory, he falls backwards to the ground. "I am sorry... I am so sorry."

Kneeling by his side, Umbra places his hand upon the dark prince's chest, and with a warm and loving manner he says "everything is going to be ok, trust me."

Warmth is felt upon the red adversary's cheeks, which to his surprise discovers they are tears. Accompanying his tears, the words from his heart leaps out as though having thoughts of their own. "I... I couldn't save him, I couldn't save Solomon my best friend. How could I, Megethos the demon prince of hell allow something like that to happen to him? I didn't mean to cause this. I just didn't want to deal with all the pain!"

"And so you decided to get rid of all those feelings. I know, you were just trying to cope, but it's ok now because you can forgive yourself. Those feelings have been trying to come back to you... and here I am. Are you ready to come home?"

The red-suited prince hesitates for a moment - taking a breath of reluctance and fear. Upon a brave nod, he answers "Yes, I am ready... my other self" extending his hand forth. Umbra does the same, and as their palms meet, a warm light envelops the pair - reuniting their souls once more.

Chapter 26: The Fool and the Fiend

T he sound of steel greaves chimes against many glass
steps of a long flight of stairs, which seem to know no
end. Their echoes reverberate against the crystal walls, like a
hypnotic bell befitting the start of a melodic mantra. A lone
knight has been ascending the stairs for some time, ever since
he departed from his two comrades.

"I must... keep going..." he says to himself, in a voice that
is filled with heavy exhaustion. Each footstep feels as if it
were weighed down by the largest beast known to man, as
his chest produces a pain akin to a thousand needles within
his heart. Breath becoming strained, the blue knight thinks it
best to keep his words short, even to himself, for what he is
experiencing is the slow destruction of his spirit. Posture like
that of an old man, he uses his claymore sword as a walking
stick - neglecting its proper use. Vision slowly dipping in and
out of focus, the boy constantly slaps his forehead, hoping it

will recalibrate his eyesight.

A robed individual enters his line of sight, appearing a few steps in front. At first, he assumes it is a mirage - brought on by his extreme fatigue. However, a familiar voice is produced from the image in front, and says "what on earth are you doing here, boy? What are you trying to do?"

As Luke lifts his head, just enough to gaze upon the face, he finds the goddess Diana, holding a desperate frown as she gazes at him. For a goddess, her eyes are as lost as the most confused mortal, which humours the struggling hero - briefly taking away the pain throughout his body. "Well, isn't it obvious? My friends and I have come here to stop the moon from falling."

"Like hell you are. Just look at yourself, you can barely stand without almost falling yourself. Don't you see? You have almost reached your limit. You should have found a resting place to depart quietly, instead of coming here. Haven't you already suffered enough!" Her voice echoes against the attentive walls, which passes her plead to the ceiling and beyond.

With an unmovable stance, her herald portrays a nonchalant half grin and responds "it's ok, I can handle it. I have had my fair share of suffering, after all. This here is nothing."

A smack is heard, which again is passed around by the walls and ceiling, like nosey neighbours eavesdropping on an altercation. The reflections of the glass stairs reveal a struck boy, slapped by the goddess who at this moment would be mistaken for a stern mother. As her azure eyes grow wider, she follows through and says "don't do it. I am begging you... don't. I already feel bad enough for involving you in all this..."

At that moment, a warmth surrounds Diana, causing her to gasp with shock and dismay, as the knight embraces her. The young boy wraps his arms around the woman, becoming like a blanket. Tears of stardust fall from her alluring eyes, as Luke whispers into her ears. "Thank you, Diana. If it weren't for you, I wouldn't have made it this far. If it weren't for you, I would have died... along with the rest of my people back in Heline. Because of the borrowed time you gave me, I was able to make the most amazing friends, even a sister too. So please, let me continue as your herald until my time is spent."

"But... the wizard and Solomon are too powerful for you. Even if you were to succeed, Solomon has become the Apex Grail now. If you destroy it, then everything I have worked so hard for would have been all for nothing. Aphrodite's death would be in vain!"

Taking a deep breath, the boy strolls past the woman and continues up the stairs - footsteps emitting the resonating chime against the glass. As he hobbles onwards, leaving her in a frozen daze, Luke departs to her "see you around, Diana."

Before long, the blue hero reaches the top of the stairs, coming to a single door that is already opened. He wastes no time stepping inside.

Upon entry, he finds himself in a wide and marbled room, held together by multiple pillars throughout. A row of large rectangular windows adorns each wall, allowing the light of the moon to shine inside - giving off a blue-tinted colour upon every surface of the room. From the ceiling, dozens of large white curtains extend downwards to touch the ground - swayed by a cold draft. Other than the knight, not a single person can be seen in the quiet and eerie space. However, a familiar and unsettling presence is evident, which the boy detects almost instantly.

"Come on out, Phantom!" Luke says in a bold and mighty tone, as he stands in a wary posture - hunched over on his sword for support. For a short moment, a silence hangs in the cold air - refusing to deliver anything back, until the words of the dark sorcerer arrives ominously.

"I am surprised you came, Luke. It is clear that you still haven't learned your lesson, even after the many gifts I have given you. Kwekekekeeee."

"Gifts you say? All the things you did to me, my friends and Rose were not gifts. They were despicable. I was told that at one point in time, you were a nice and kind wizard named Felix. I don't understand what changed in you, but I must stop you before the moon falls to this world!"

At that moment, a silhouette of the wizard appears upon one of the swaying curtains, like an apparition. Although the boy cannot read the facial expression from the shadowy outline, he guesses that the sorcerer is smiling mockingly. "Kwekekekeee... what could you possibly stop in your shape right now. By the looks of things, you will have more trouble against a grain of dust, than anything else." The silhouette disappears before reappearing upon another curtain and continues "I have seen the same deteriorated state once before, and I know that very shortly you will die. As such, I need not do anything at all, for your death is assured. Seeing as you've already lost, how about I tell you a little story... my story."

Vanishing from the curtain, the silhouette shifts to the marbled ground - appearing under Luke's feet, as if taking the place of the boy's shadow. Fear grips the boy's heart, as though caught in the middle of dark trickery. However, he closes his eyes and relies on his ears to hear the words of the man known as Phantom.

"One thousand years ago, when gods and men coexisted, there lived a boy named Felix. Like you, he was an orphan - without a family of his own. His parents were slaughtered by bandits, during a raid upon his home village. The only survivors were himself and one other boy, who went by the name of Solomon."

"I see... you and Solomon were childhood friends" Luke confirms, as his mind paints the scene of the sorcerer's origins, upon every telling that echoes through the moonlit room.

"Yes... Solomon and I wandered through a treacherous world. Back then, the world was far more dangerous than ever, for not only did mankind war with one another but so did the gods. We were only children, looking for a place that we could call home. We survived countless predicaments together, thanks to our talents. I was born a gifted wizard from birth, and I possessed the greatest understanding of magic ever seen. Even at such a young age, I could best other sorcerers twice my age." The shadowy silhouette morphs - becoming that of a young boy as he continues "Solomon on the other hand, was talented in combat. Throughout the years, great warriors would seek him out, just to test his skills and it wasn't long before we had a name for ourselves. I was known as Felix the Wizard Of Hope, and Solomon was called the Miracle Swordsman."

"So then, what changed?"

A whisper is heard, not from the shadow in front but much closer, which replies "the goddess, my boy. The goddess changed everything."

As though standing behind him the whole time, the wizard appears inches from the hero - so close his breath strokes the hairs upon his neck. Overcome with panic, Luke flinches before turning around - producing a strong stance with shoulders high like a hedgehog threatened. However, like a menacing ghost Phantom has already disappeared - leaving the boy to question his senses. As his eyes dart around uncontrollably - the voice of the excited wizard can be heard reiterating "the goddess... the wretched goddess Diana ruined everything. Curse the very day that our paths crossed!"

The surrounding windows smash into pieces without warning, caused by the wizard of despair. The sound is rough and jarring, as though enforcing the agony that can be heard from the wizard's voice. And as the shards of glass scuttle inside, Phantom says "Solomon and I were already a capable duo, who grew to rely on ourselves - even though what we had always longed for, was a place to belong. The blue moon goddess knew our plight well and offered a deal. She said, if Solomon were to become her herald, then in the future we will have families of our own and live a life of peace and harmony. Solomon agreed, and at that moment he became Blue Lunar Solomon."

The sound of many footsteps makes themselves known,

causing Luke to glance left and right for their source. Again, as if caught in a foul trick to deliberately disorient him, the wizard utters from a dark corner of the room "he was given a task to slay a goddess for committing an unforgivable act - although Diana neglected to explain the crime itself. Being the fools that we were, Solomon and I ventured on our mission, him now stronger than ever before. Throughout our travels our status grew, even attracting the demon prince Megethos, who upon witnessing Solomon's swordsmanship, became a friend and also joined us."

Privy to the final tragedy of the tale, Luke utters "that's when the three of you arrived at the temple of Venus, where Aphrodite was dwelling with her mortal lover."

"It wasn't only a place of dwelling, but a place of union. When we arrived, the pair were halfway through making their wedding vows. We killed Aphrodite, along with her lover and then, once the gods found out, chaos ensued. That was the start of the Divine war, which saw almost every god fighting for or against love. The whole world was nearly close to crumbling under the godly battle. When the war was over, Diana was deemed the winner, along with her allied gods. As for Solomon and I, we were told that our original deal was all a lie. Diana confessed that she had to make Solomon believe in something, for the armour to work at its best. In truth, the suit was draining his life, and before we all knew it, he died."

A shower of deep sympathy falls over the blue knight, for not only can he picture the revelation, but he also relates the story to his own. Even without knowing the man named Solomon, he senses a connection, one that binds their tragic fates as heralds of the moon goddess.

"Can you envision it, boy? Solomon and I... fought so hard to do what Diana wanted - killed the kindest goddess in the world, even fought against mighty gods of the Divine War, just to be cast aside. Our loyalty meant nothing to her."

"Tell me something. If Solomon had died back then, why is he alive now?"

Appearing directly in front of Luke, Phantom reveals himself - holding his golden sceptre in front. A deep breath is produced by the boy, who recounts the many times he had encountered the murderous man, during his journey. However - unlike the previous times, not an ounce of fear can be felt. Not even anger or hatred for causing the death of the boy's sister. Instead, a feeling of humanity dances between the pair, as though they were somehow the same. Nevertheless, the young hero braces for the wizard's slow reply.

"Solomon lives now, because of my sacrifice. You see, when Solomon died, Megethos disappeared back into the underworld - leaving me all alone. I was determined to get my friends back and make the goddess pay. So, before the Apex Grail was due to be created, I sought out a forbidden deity and became their herald" the sorcerer says before removing the crown of thorns upon his head. As the crown hits the floor, before being carried out the shattered windows by a strong breeze, the sorcerer's forehead is revealed, displaying a glowing symbol of a dragon."

"What...? You are a herald too? To which god?"

"That is not important, boy. What is important was what they offered in exchange for my loyalty. Solomon could be brought back, providing I became the forbidden deity's servant. However, as with every god and goddess, they require a forfeit. In my case, the forfeit was my sanity and compassion."

The hero pauses - slowly digesting the words of the wizard. As though within a delayed response, Luke eventually blinks and breathes sharply, overcome with a sense of sadness upon reflection. "You... you willingly gave away your sanity and compassion, to save your friend."

"Yes, I did so without a second's thought. One might say that it is a fate worse than death. However, it was the only way to bring him back. That is true friendship! After Solomon was resurrected, he and I lived below ground and plotted our revenge for countless years. We were able to extend our lives through all those years, due to a forbidden spell that slowed down the ageing process. Once I had finally awoken Megethos, the three of us decided to make not only the goddess but the whole world pay for its past deeds. This world is sick, and it must be wiped clean! Kwekeee!"

As the boy watches the man's insane laughter and gaze, he feels nothing but pity. Standing before him is a man who paid the ultimate sacrifice, for friendship. "He chose madness, all for the sake of his friends," Luke says to his heart, wondering how the wizard's life would have turned out, had he never suffered such a tragedy. Most likely, he would have continued as a great and kind wizard. An air of misjudgement is realised, which although not enough to excuse his recent actions, paints a deeper conundrum.

"Should this world be wiped out? After all, it has made home to so much suffering. Is it such a bad idea to have it all end? That way nobody wins, right?" Luke finds no objections to his questions.

At that moment, his thoughts stop, along with his beating heart. The armour has come to collect. Wham - he falls flat on his stomach, as the suit slowly disappears from his body. He wants to move, stand and fight. However, on second thought, he realises that he would not know who to fight or what he is fighting for. Eyelids slowly draping over his vision like alluring blankets, he reluctantly embraces his defeat.

"Such a pity. None of this would have occurred if neither of us had encountered the goddess of the moon. Worry not, for the rest of the world will soon be following you to the afterlife. For love" the wizard sighs - turning his back to the fallen boy. As his cloak flutters amidst the intruding wind, he touches his face - finding a long-forgotten substance upon his cheeks. To his surprise, he notices tears, which surprises him as he whispers "am I indeed crying? Why on earth would I do that? Am I crying for the boy?"

Dropping his sceptre before grasping his head, the sorcerer

struggles as an internal conflict begins to take place. A long-forgotten desire for hope rekindles its light within him, wrestling against his current desire for despair. Glancing at the boy who remains still, save for a few twitches of his eyes, the sorcerer rants "why... why do I wish for you to live? I am Phantom Wizard of Despair, am I not? No, I am Felix Wizard of Hope." As though an inner voice was breaking free from somewhere deep within his soul, Phantom shouts to the hero "get up, boy... this fight isn't over. You didn't come all the way here just to die!"

The boy flinches mildly, as the wizard's tormented words of encouragement hits his ears. He is surprised yet still too exhausted to move an inch. However, he uses all his might to lift his eyes - looking to his opponent for support.

"You have been through far worse to let it all end here, boy. Nobody in your hometown wanted or liked you, save for the lady named Jill who I killed. You have been through the worst types of pain - watching innocent people die. Don't let it end here, Luke. Don't let what I and my friends have become, rule this day!"

"I... I want to live..." Luke states with a waning voice - slowly moving his index finger towards his forehead. The action, although simple in the past now feels like he is moving a mountain, and as the wizard can be heard screaming words of motivation in the background, Luke says to the blue moon "I won't allow myself to die here, not yet. You can try all you want to claim my life, but I promise you that I will fulfil my duty as a herald... my way!"

Suddenly, a burst of light flows from out of the boy - filling the room with a bright and wondrous light. Engulfed in its radiance, the wizard produces a relieved smile, a smile he long had cast away and says "you did it... you overcame the armour!"

As the light vanishes, the smiling sorcerer casts his eyes on the boy, once again sporting the divine amour of the moon, with the sword in hand. His posture is strong and confident, the opposite of his weakened stance earlier. A sense of pride fills the atmosphere, not from the boy but the wizard, like a mentor, pleased with a student. With arms stretched apart, the man formally known as Felix calls to the blue hero and says "do it… save me from this unyielding despair."

As quickly as his request came, it is granted. Like a bolt of lightning, the hero zips to the wizard in an instant before landing a clean stab through his chest. The speed at which he struck is so fast, that the man gasps and freezes - not fully realising what had happened until he hears the light droplets of his blood against the solid floor.

"You are finally free now, and you don't need to hurt anybody else, ever again" Luke whispers to Phantom, in a tone reminiscent of one comrade assisting the other.

As his words touch the wizard's heart, a look of immense gratitude fills his eyes as he responds warmly, "thank you… Blue Lunar Luke" slumping to the ground before letting out his last breath. All that can be heard is the constant wind, which hums like a sad prayer - blowing the hero's cape, gracefully through the air.

"Thank you… Felix Wizard of Hope."

Chapter 27: We will never fight alone

O utside upon the palace balcony, an ascended man stands at its farthest side, leaning over its ledge. The sky is populated with many wonders on such an eventful night. Like a legion of fireflies, the stars glow amidst the darkness. Flocks of every winged creature soar through the clouds, like actors in the middle of a dramatic scene. However, only one wonder catches the eye of the man. Bright, bold and blue, it fills the sky with both awe and terror.

∞∞∞

"Don't be shy. Come closer and kiss the world" Solomon says to the blue moon, gesturing for it to fall further, like a parent encouraging their child. Unable to resist, the moon continues its descent - causing the world to tremble further by its incoming presence. A satisfaction and relief sparkle within the man's eyes, being the only individual in the world who is delighted by its approach. "It won't be long now, till everything is crushed to dust. Then the world can start over."

The sound of a steel boot reaches his ears, breaking the man from his blissful moment, as though waking from a daydream. The sound comes from behind, by the entrance of the balcony. As the sound of armour brings back nostalgic memories for Solomon, he keeps his head still - only lowering it a few inches, expressing deep thoughts.

"So... Phantom too has failed. You are quite the hero" the man says, slowly turning around to face his successor. As Solomon's bright halo shines over the blue knight like a flowing stream, he adds "and it would seem that my former suit has not claimed you. Could it be that you have overcome the forfeit? I wonder for how long?"

His words fail to touch the boy's thoughts, for the only thing on Luke's mind is stopping him and the rapid descent of the moon. As the distant sounds of earthquakes and screams sound off in the distance, the hero says "I am begging you... stop this at once!"

"Stop? You want me to stop? It is too late to stop now, and why should I? Thanks to those selfish gods, my friends and I were never the same again. When I had first died, Megethos could not bear the heartache and became half of what he used to be, while Felix lost his sanity to rescue me from the afterlife. This world owes us all, for what it put us through."

With his sword held tightly by his side, Luke responds in a tone that is far braver than expected. "I don't deny that. This world can be a horrible place. However, you cannot deny that it has granted some truly great things too - your friends being one of them. To just get rid of everything would be unfair to all the precious memories you had, right?"

Tilting his head with intrigue, Solomon displays a pleasant gaze as though having just realised something spectacular about the boy. Like an irony that has presented itself at the last moment. "Now it all makes sense, as to why you are so intent on stopping me. You are grateful to this world. As such, you believe it is worth fighting for, much like how I used to think. However, I am different now. For me, this world is beyond redemption. It has shown me far too much hatred, selfishness and pain... which is why I must erase all of it. You are just like the younger me: foolish and naive."

As ironic as the boy is to the man, a similar irony overcomes Luke just the same. Standing before the young hero is a future self, one that had believed in the world but lost all faith. Could the same faithlessness occur within Luke too, he wonders? "I won't think like you... I'll never become what you are!" The boy shouts - activating the power of his sword. Lifting it high above, the blue knight channels every emotion he has within him, into the blade - causing it to shine bright in the presence of the godly foe.

"That light... so beautiful. I had almost forgotten about the legendary attack of the moon sword that is amplified by the human spirit. Do you think you can destroy me, with your naive emotions alone? Your young and inexperienced willpower pales in comparison to my pain of a thousand years!" Solomon shouts, raising his right hand to the heavens. By his command, he summons a golden sword, decorated with many jewels and unreadable words, the same found upon the Apex Grail. As Luke gasps with assumption, the man takes the words out of his mouth and declares "behold, the Apex Sword. All of the power within me is now channelled into this blade. Come... show me the strength of your spirit!"

"Yaaaaah!" Luke screams - releasing the legendary beam of light from the blue moon sword. The wind blows violently out of harm's way, as the powerful blast races to Solomon who stands unthreatened.

"You fool!" He shouts in response, unleashing an opposing light of his own. The two projectiles collide - resulting in a mighty force that shatters chunks of the surrounding balcony apart. The opposing beams of light remain conflicted, like bulls that have locked horns in a deadly duel. The light from the wrestling energies shines bright, being seen from almost every corner of the world. Although the gods cannot be seen by human eyes, they too are captivated by the confrontation - on the edge of their seats like eager spectators.

Refusing to be overpowered, Blue Lunar summons every ounce of emotion in his spirit and rants "this world has given me far more than I could ever hope for. Although I have always been an orphan, not knowing about my parents, I was loved by Jill the owner of the orphanage. Then there was Diana, who offered me a chance to be someone in this world and I did. I fought against many monsters and even made a sister along the way. All those things are what this world has given me, and I don't want to lose them!" Luke's energy ray grows stronger - slowly but surely pushing Solomon's light backwards. Tears emerge from the boy's eyes, testifying to his passion in the face of the adversary.

"You insolent fool. None of those are things to hold onto. You have already lost them. Your home town and everybody in it no longer exists. Your beloved sister died at your hands. Even you are nothing but a walking zombie, for you already had died once before. You have nothing!" Solomon hits back with his truth - pushing against the boy's energy. The force from the Apex sword quickly overwhelms the hero, who within seconds is brought to his knees as the enemy projectile charges closer towards him.

"I... I am not..."

Barely able to speak, the boy struggles - feeling as though the weight of the world were against him. His emotions are seemingly not enough, a drop of doubt enters his mind - weakening the power of his sword further. All he can do is stay in a feeble defensive stance - praying for a miracle to aid him.

Suddenly, a familiar voice sweeps onto the balcony, one that surprises the man and boy. "Nothing, you say? I hate to break it to you, but Luke has lost nothing!"

To Luke's surprise, a hand extends from behind his back -

reaching towards the sword he holds. Upon watching as their fingers proceed to grasp the blade hilt, the boy turns to his side and gasps at the sight of the golden-haired comrade. If words could be expressed by her arrival, they would still not come close to describing Luke's exhilaration. Like a lost piece of himself that has been reunited, the hero blinks twice and says "Aurora... you came."

"Of course. I promised you that we will fight together" she utters with a bright smile, like a golden angel in a desperate time of need. Clutching the hilt of the blade with Luke, she whispers in the gentlest of fashions and says "here, take my feelings. Use them and put a stop to this madness."

Remarkably, the power of the moon sword heightens - releasing a wave of energy that is golden. Not only is the blade harnessing the power of Luke, but Aurora too, which flows into the weapon like an amplifier. With their hands wrapped around the handle, the boy lets out a mild squeal, overcome with a sensation that is new to him. Acting as a type of conduit, the sword connects their hearts, allowing Luke to sense the depths of her spirit, as though they were one and the same.

With Aurora's added strength, the projectile begins to push against Solomon's divine energy - yet not enough to bring him to his knees. Like a great king insulted by the works of lowly commoners, the man glares with rage and shouts "who the hell do you think you are!"

"I am the greatest swordsman in the whole world, and I won't allow my title to be erased by the likes of you!" Shouts Aurora - matching his rage with a fierce glare that is enough to tear down the sky.

Not a single inch of the palace is still. The floors screams to the walls, who panic to the roof, which cries to the heavens for relief as the impact of the conflicting energies shakes the floating structure to the core.

A small yet troubling gloat leaps from the man, followed by a snout-like laugh. "You are even more foolish than the herald.

You should know as well as anybody, that a Stigma could never hope to achieve true status. Just like as it was in the days of old, Stigmas are either feared or envied - such is the stupidity of humanity. Your glory is but a speck of dust in the grand scheme of history, for when you die, the people will soon forget all about your exploits!"

As if knowing of her deepest weaknesses, Solomon's words stab at her spirit, greater than any physical blade. Her resolve fluctuates, as seeds of negativity drop within her mind - sprouting into daydreams of possible future scenarios of being endlessly detested.

Joining the pair upon the balcony, a black figure comes to their side and says to the adversary "love, friendship, hatred... these are attributes that make this world both horrible and wonderful. Just like darkness cannot exist without the light, the experience known as life cannot be without its ups and downs."

Reaching out before also grasping the blade hilt, Umbra reunites with the two. As Luke stares into the eyes of the loyal friend, he finds that his appearance has altered somewhat. Upon his forehead, two horns protrude outward, the same horns seen upon the demon prince Megethos.

"You sure took your time... idiot vampire!" Aurora scolds with a smile, in a relieved tone, pleased to see the black-suited comrade. He laughs and winks, equally as satisfied to see them both.

"Give me a break, succubus. Besides, we have more important things to worry about, right Luke?" He says - eyes locked to the blue knight who stays lost for words and frozen like a statue.

It is only when he senses the transfer of Umbra's feelings also, which pour into the blade, that Luke snaps out of his brief bedazzlement. The combined energies of all three heroes increase the energy blast - pushing further against Solomon's energy. Brought to his knees, the man now finds himself struggling to withstand the spirit of all three.

"Megethos... you too? You of all people, who witnessed our

betrayal and agony should understand why the world must come to an end!"

"Old friend, believe me, I do. However, our time ended long ago, for better or for worse. We need to trust the next generation of truth seekers, and allow them to carve this world into a better future!"

The combined projectile of the three is gargantuan, almost swallowing Solomon within its blinding light. Yet, using every ounce and fibre within his soul, he resists it just enough to let out a desperate cry to the blue hero. "Boy... herald of Diana... you must not stop me. If you kill me now, then the Apex Grail will also be destroyed, and the gods will return - bringing with it newfound wars and suffering. Is that what you truly want?"

The man's question is great - like an impenetrable wall that is unavoidable. The boy halts once again, as the adversary's words seep within him. Is stopping him now truly the right thing to do? If the Apex Grail were shattered, who knows what levels of suffering could appear in the future? To allow the world to be destroyed now would eliminate such possibilities. As though lost in a fog of thoughts with no exit, Luke struggles within himself.

"I... is this truly the right thing to do? What if I make the world worse in the long run? I am so confused!"

At that instant, warmth is felt upon Luke's back. It is a single hand, both small and gentle, which fills him with such bewilderment, that he almost drops his sword altogether. The touch is familiar, so familiar that words or even a gaze are not needed. As fond memories of their very first encounter floods his heart, like a fresh tide that wipes away the darkness - Luke's conviction begins to resurface. A whisper flows into his ears that cannot be heard by Umbra and Aurora, as though meant only for his attention.

"Keep going, my brother."

The voice of the girl who showed him unconditional love fills him with a hope that is unwavering as the brightest star above. "Thank you… my sister" he replies - tears streaming down his cheeks as he grips the blade tight. Challenging Solomon's predication, the boy shouts to the moon and stars "no matter what challenges come our way, we will overcome them!"

The surge of light obliterates Solomon, before racing forth across the sky. A divine rode of magnificent wonder, the energy soars through the clouds - travelling across the many countries of the world like a global symbol of peace. Earthquakes cease and tides retreat, as though the wandering light were an elixir to the wounds of the world. The creatures of the air stop in awe, as do the beasts of land - looking up at the wonder. The trembling trees that had been screaming during the dreaded night breathe a sigh of calm, followed by the wind that resumes its gentle breath. Like a stubborn child that has been caught misbehaving, the falling moon stops before slowly creeping back to its abode amongst the stars.

Upon the now quiet balcony, the three heroes stand tall. In between his two comrades, Luke stands in dismay at their accomplishment, as his suit begins to disappear from his body. "We did it. We did it!" He smiles - praying that it is not a dream.

Before they can rest easy, a great rumbling sound is heard once more, this time much closer to the three. Before they know it, the castle of truth begins to crumble - falling at the same time. "The castle, it's falling apart!"

As the crystal walls and bridges cry as they shatter, along with the glass stairs that shriek loudly, the hero panics - watching as telling cracks appear upon the balcony grounds. "Oh no… we're not gonna make it!"

"Yes, we are!" Aurora responds confidently - snatching the boy's arm like he were a rag doll, proceeding to sprint towards the far end of the balcony. Barely giving him time to maintain his balance, Luke's feet drag across the floor - having no choice but to follow her lead. The boy spots a daring look within her eyes, once that is all too familiar to him. It is the kind of bold gaze that dares to defy destiny itself. And as the boy stays in awe of her, he smiles with a feeling of comfort - trusting whatever idea she has.

"What on earth do you think you're planning, damn succubus?" Rants the black-suited Umbra - lagging reluctantly, as more fragments of the castle give way.

"Will you quit your moaning for once, vampire? I know what I am doing, so just keep up will you?"

"Keep up? Have you gone insane? There is nothing at the end of the balcony!"

"I know that. We are not stopping there, moron. We are going past it!"

"Past it? Do you mean that we're gonna make a jump for it?" Luke interrupts - equally as shocked as Umbra. For a fragment of a second, they disbelieve their assumptions. However, reminded of Aurora's track record of solutions in the past, they quickly realise that the most reckless way is most likely Aurora's way. Before they know it, the three leap from the crumbling structure - holding each other's arms as they plummet.

The wind rushes against them, as sounds of croaking hawks glide by. As Luke and Umbra stay terrified - Aurora holds her brave gaze before whistling to the wind. The wind passes her sound through the air, eventually stopping at the ears of a pure white unicorn, which gallops to their aid.

Scooped upon the back of the winged horse - the trio breathe a sigh of relief, clutching onto the steed like it were their very life. Deep breaths of adrenaline are exchanged between the three, as they watch the castle hit the ground below - never to be seen again. A great expulsion of smoke and debris sweeps outward from the crumbled lair, overwhelming their noses. As they continue to look down at the failed ambition of the late adversaries, a moment of reflection and sadness overcome each of them. Although they have succeeded in saving the world from the falling moon, their victory is not without heartache. For to ensure the safety of the world, they had to confront and face those who were connected to each of them.

The legion of stars begins to disappear beyond the clouds of the night sky, as the blue moon hides its presence - casting a dark and sorrowful shadow over the land. A silence hangs over the world, a lamenting silence. "If only things had been different," the three of them say within their hearts - unknowingly plagued by the same regret.

Suddenly, a different kind of light appears within the night sky, which catches the attention of all in the world. Consisting of countless lights, one would be forgiven for thinking that they were twinkling stars. However, upon just a second's glance, one finds that the countless lights are of varying shapes and sizes. Some bear the images of men, while others of women. Some sport glorious wings while others without - sporting attire that no man could ever design.

Their numbers increase as they float into the atmosphere, akin to snowflakes of a winter's night. However, this night is golden and one of a kind - a phenomenon for the history books to remember for all eternity. "Those are... the gods" Luke utters - grateful for his very eyes to witness the benevolence of the deities. Adding to the beauty, the rays of the sun creep through the clouds, as though not to be left out. As the beginnings of a sunrise light up the land, the young hero is reminded of a similar sunrise, the day he had saved his sister. "It is... so beautiful."

"It is. The gods have returned. I must say, I am quite pleased to see them once again" says Umbra.

"That must be because the Apex Grail is no more. I admit I don't know what to expect from now on. What will the future hold, now that they have returned? Whatever happens, we will be there to see it, our way. Right, Luke?" Aurora says, glancing at the grey-haired hero. "Luke?" She says again, finding his eyes closed and body still. "Hey, you're not sleeping are you?" She asks, in a tone that is no longer carefree. A worry is felt within her voice, as her eyes widen with shock - looking to the black-suited comrade for answers.

His lowered head already says more than enough, and as a

lone breeze glides over the trio - fluttering their hair and attire, Umbra says "his time has finally come. Not even he could fully escape the forfeit."

The steed descends - carrying the three comrades back to the land below. As they drift towards the city of Ergo, a round of applause reaches their ears. Looking down, they notice countless hands, clapping upon a triumphant return. Not a drop of sadness can be seen on their faces - displaying eyes of renewed hope and joy. Cries of happiness from the south are drowned out by the cheers from the north. And as prayers can be heard from the east, a collective song of praise sounds off from the west. A united sense of togetherness runs throughout all that is witnessing the glorious moment. However, Umbra and Aurora are far from happy.

The body of the hero is placed on the ground by the pair, ever so gently, like a jewel that is being offered to the spirit of the earth. The surrounding celebrations cease, as the rest of the city folk look upon the hero who saved the world. As the gods above remain clung to the sky, basking in their heavenly light - the people of Ergo below hang their heads, wrapped in sadness.

"I will never forget you" Aurora whispers - standing amongst a vast crowd with the departed blue hero in its centre. All are silent - paying their respects to the soul of Blue Lunar Luke.

"Step aside, mortals" comes a grand voice, like a bolt of thunder. The tone is great, enough to rival the largest earthquake. Jumping with fright the crowd disperses - parting into two sides, revealing the owner of the thunderous voice in between. Hair long and beautiful, a single woman stands before them. Bearing azure eyes, she gazes directly in front - emanating a presence that is beyond comprehension for the crowd. As though entranced by her presence, the crowd are mere moments away from bowing at her feet - humbled by her very sight. They are humbled by the presence of the moon goddess. "I have come for my herald."

For the first time in one thousand years, Diana reveals herself to mortal men and women once more. In her elegant gown that sways effortlessly through the wind, she takes slow and petit steps forward - hearing small and beholden whispers around her. Like a living miracle, each step she takes causes a spot of earth to bloom into a bed of roses. The whispers evolve into gasps, as they watch nature stretch out and adore the goddess. Nevertheless, their praise serves to only annoy her, as she continues to make her way towards her target in front.

A glance is made to the fallen hero's two comrades, Aurora and Umbra. "Thank you" she wishes to say to them - however, she stays her words and seals her lips instead. Judging by their defensive eyes, uttering a word to the pair would prove meaningless and would only cause more sadness.

Stopping by the boy, she falls to her knees and stares at his still body. "You brave child. Although the cards dealt to you in life were unfortunate, you kept going. Even as those close to you were taken away, you still managed to find the courage to succeed. Of all the heralds that I have ever known, you are by far the greatest, and I am proud to have been your master." Shifting her eyes to her signature engraving upon his forehead, the goddess says "I will be taking this back now. It is only right that you leave this world as a free spirit... not a herald of a cruel and pitiful goddess like me."

Chapter 28: For Love

Within a dark space, a single soul floats, like a creature within the deepest depths of the ocean. The soul is a boy, who had endured far more challenges than he could count. The darkness is familiar to him, as though revisiting a brief destination in the past. As for how long he has been drifting, let alone how long he will be within the dark is unknown to him. Not a single sound or movement takes place within the mysterious space, and yet he is overcome with relief, like a restful soldier who has returned from a great battle.

"This place again. I wonder what happens now? Do I just stay here for all eternity? Well, I am ok with that. Everyone else is safe... that is most important" he utters, voice echoing into the abyss. As accepting as his words make out, his voice belies a longing within his heart - a longing that can be seen all over his face. "But what about me? Why can't I be amongst the rest?

Why am I left to wander in this darkness, after everything I had done? I... I want to go back to my friends!"

An image of a single man intrudes itself into the boy's mind, reminding him of a similar injustice that had caused great resentment. Upon a brief pause, he whispers "this must have been exactly how Solomon felt too. All those years, put aside in similar darkness. So, am I no different from him then? Will I end up just like Solomon and curse the world also? I... I don't know what to do or think. Somebody, please help me!"

At that moment the blackness disappears - morphing into pure white space. As he covers his eyes from the sudden transformation, the boy hears a song. It is the most beautiful song he has ever heard, which keeps him mesmerised and lost in awe. His soul feels purified by the melody, and it isn't long before he forgets the previous worries he had dwelled on, moments ago. Grateful to the mysterious serenade, he puts his hands together as though in prayer - praying that the composer of the song will not cease.

The melody fades like a warm ray of the sun, giving way to the chilly wind. As such, the boy becomes disappointed - holding his head low once more. However - regaining his attention, an unfamiliar voice speaks forth "what are you doing in the afterlife, again? This isn't where you should be, young one."

"Who said that? Is that you, Diana?" He replies. However, no sooner after his response - his logic shames him for such a misjudged assumption. The voice that has reached him is gentle and soft, like thin petals against his ears. In contrast, the tone of the moon goddess is often stern, like icicles against one's cheeks.

Two hands reach forth from behind and caress the boy. Left hand upon his chin, with the right over his forehead. The touch is invigorating, as a sense of unyielding and endless love flows through his soul. There is no other place or moment he would rather be right now, and for the first time in his life, Luke finally achieves something that he has always longed for:

a place to belong.

The gentle fingertips tap the signature mark upon his head, as the soothing voice utters "yet again, Diana's power has claimed another innocent. Don't take it personally. She means well. At the same time, I can't allow you to stay here, for there is much work for you still to do. Behold... the forfeit of the moon will no longer have power over you. Go back to where you belong, Luke."

Curiosity getting the better of him, the boy spins around - hoping to get a clear sight of the holy being. However, as quick as his surprise turn was, he is too late. The mysterious figure has disappeared - leaving him alone within the white space, left with the lingering aura they left behind. With only the leftover presence to interrogate, the boy closes his eyes and whispers "love... was she the goddess of..."

Luke's eyes open once more. However, to his surprise, he is no longer within the empty white space. A warm breeze from an early morning sky can be felt over his face, and as his vision stabilises, he sees the blue moon goddess kneeling beside him, surrounded by a crowd. Her face is shocked with disbelief - remaining still before saying "you... how?"

The boy remains on the ground - taking in a well-appreciated inhale before breathing outward with gratitude. A yellow sky arrives under the brilliant morning, where the abundance of gods and goddesses can be seen drifting just under the sun. The sound of a nearby rooster crowing in the air affirms the reality that he is living once more. The herald of Diana has been given yet another chance at living, this time by a goddess of love.

Sitting upward he glances around, through the perplexed faces of the goddess and crowd before stopping at his two most treasured comrades. Their faces are identical to the rest, like statues. Luke smiles and chuckles at their confusion, before declaring to the heavens "I am home."

The afternoon approaches, bringing with it a sunny blue sky. The returned gods have dispersed from the clouds - off to various abodes, away from the sight of mortals. Already, mankind has begun recording the events of their re-appearance - naming the day: The Great Return.

By one of the exits of Ergo, three friends can be found in conversation. With a sad gaze, the grey-haired boy stands opposite the smiling Umbra. By the gates, Aurora leans against its doors with a far from pleasing demeanour. Both Luke and Aurora's reactions are a result of Umbra's sudden news of departure, like a spanner that has been thrown in the works of their long built friendship.

"Do you have to go?" The young hero says, like a child whose sibling is being taken from him. A short pause of silence that seems like it could last for eternity is present, followed by the rustling leaves from a nearby tree.

Hands inserted in his pockets, the black-suited comrade takes a deep breath, inhaling the fresh scent of grass - pleased to witness another day. "I am afraid so, my friend. I am needed elsewhere. After all, I am the demon prince. I can't waste my time with you mortals forever, haha."

"Well then, take us with you? We are a team, after all, right?"

"Yes, we are. However, from now on we will work together from afar. You and misery guts over there need to help the people rebuild and get their lives together. You also need to be present for the many changes that will soon come. Seeing as the gods have returned, a new order will almost certainly govern this world. You will have your hands full."

Slowly turning his back to the pair, Umbra looks up at the sky as a gust of wind sweeps past - fluttering his black attire. Another moment of silence hangs between the three, as he says "Luke, you truly are special... you know that right? Although you remain the herald of Diana, you no longer bear the forfeit the armour carries. I do not doubt that you will grow into one of the finest heralds in history."

Touched by the words of encouragement, Luke stays lost for words - mind already carried away by what the future may bring for the young hero. Pulling him down from his whimsical daydream, Umbra adds "promise me that you won't become like Solomon. Whatever happens from here on out, don't lose faith in this world. Keep striving to make it a place worth saving, because if you don't, you will become just like him."

Raising his hand high, Umbra waves a farewell and shouts to the golden-haired warrior by the gates "see you around, succubus. Take care of little Luke while I am gone, will you?"

"Good riddance, annoying vampire. If I ever see you again it will be too soon!" She replies sternly with a fierce gaze that belies a saddened heart. Seeing through her exterior, the demon prince produces another wave goodbye, before strolling into the distance.

Looking down at his hands, the very same hands that saw joy, sadness, life and death, a feeling of undeniable purpose shines within Luke. "Well, I had better get to work then," he says, turning around before strolling back into the demolished city with Aurora.

The city folk of Ergo begin their rebuild of the capital city, aided by the blue hero and his golden comrade. The many towns and cities that were impacted by the rampage of the wizard of despair also follow suit. Men and women from various classes and creeds alike, come together to repair a battered but not broken world - watched by the gods above. A joyous and vibrant atmosphere is felt in the air, as the rays of the sun shine down gloriously over the land.

"I no longer wish for acceptance or for a family to call my own, for I have finally achieved those things. Thank you, my friends... and Rose."

∞ ∞ ∞

Above the clouds, beyond the endless sea of stars, the blue moon hangs peacefully once more. Sitting upon it, a single goddess oversees the world with her bright blue eyes. Soaking in the solemn silence of space, she displays sweet happiness, upon experiencing a miracle along with the rest of the world.

"Everything will be ok... I am sure of it" she whispers to the stars - filled with satisfaction that cannot be shaken.

At that moment, a familiar presence greets her, one that has not been felt since the beginning of time itself. It is a deep love, a love that is without judgment, which causes her to gasp with surprise. The presence of another goddess appears directly next to her, emanating a fond aura. Diana catches a brief glimpse of the fellow deity, whose robes and skin are semi-transparent, as though she were an apparition or illusion.

Almost instinctively, Diana realises who the goddess beside her is, and with a warm tone, she says "so I guess it is true what they say; love is forever. I take it that you were the one who removed Luke's forfeit, correct?" The fellow goddess does not answer - allowing Diana to answer her own question. "I'll take your silence as a yes, then. Once again, you prove why you are so loved by all. I must admit, I have always been somewhat jealous of you. Even so, you never held that against me, even after everything I had put you through" she says - opening her eyes once more, unloading a flurry of tears in the process. "Even after I had you killed along with your lover, you are still able to show nothing but love!"

Turning to face her directly, the goddess of the moon attempts to throw her arms around the once loved goddess. However, as soon as she does, the apparition disappears like a fleeting visitor whose time has run dry. Left alone upon the blue moon, Diana dries her eyes and whispers "thank you...

Aphrodite."

The End

Epilogue

Somewhere within a small dark room, neither high nor low, a congregation takes place. An absence of light and warmth is prevalent, filling the space with a sense of dread that could choke the life of any mortal within. By the centre a large round table sits, revealing the world as though it were a portal. By the head of the table, a dark female figure sits - back straight and well postured as though she were royalty. Body webbed with black silk, her face is covered by a silver marionette mask that bears a dragon symbol on its forehead. Shadowy figures can be seen behind the woman, gazing passionately at her as though she were their master.

With a seductive and smooth tone, she says "interesting.

My herald the wizard of despair has finally fallen. No matter, for he had played his part perfectly. It is almost time for the main event."

By her command, the mysterious table reveals an image of the blue moon, whose sight almost takes her breath away. Although her eyes cannot be seen behind the darkness of the room and mask, the shadowy figures sense an aura of excitement from her. Leaning forward she utters a series of chilling words.

"Hear now the words of the original one: from before time itself the kin were the overseers of life, giving birth to the gods, to which mankind become their lesser image. Upon being forged by the King of the Moon, the four grimoires incased our leader in a prison of azure. Waiting patiently for the pages to reunite, we wait and writhe with anguish, until the appointed hour."

The woman proceeds to take off her mask - revealing a left eye that is blacker than the night sky, and a right eye that is bluer than the purest sea. The table reveals another image - this time of the blue moon goddess, unaware of the watchful eyes of the mysterious lady.

"The resurrection of the ancient dragons draws near, and there's nothing you can do to stop it... Sister."

To be continued...

Acknowledgement

To my younger self... thank you.

Extras/Lore:

The Blue Moon:

The mighty wonder that orbits the world. Its owner is Diana the moon goddess, who uses its power to bestow chosen mortals with the title of Blue Lunar.

Once a herald, a mortal can utilise the unlimited power of the divine blue moon - calling forth invincible armour and a sword.

However, the power of the blue moon bears a great forfeit, for each time its power is used, the owner's life force is slowly sapped away. Such a fate befell a man named Solomon the very first Blue Lunar, who eventually perished as a result.

The Apex Grail:

A divine grail created by the victorious gods. It negates direct communication between gods and humans. If you were to ask a god the reason for its creation, he would say that it was for the protection of mankind. In truth, the grail was created as a way to forbid a potential union between deity and mortal - for what the gods fear the most is a new type of love, and the result it could bring.

Aphrodite:

The most beautiful goddess who ever lived. Her lover was but a simple man. The pair were about to get married to solidify their love. However, the herald of the moon goddess Diana halted the marriage and slew the pair.

Sitis Monstrum:

An evil fountain that can only be summoned by an expert sorcerer of the dark arts. It lures its prey with its beauty and fresh water. However, once a human drinks it, they eventually become a servant of the fountain.

Its origins date back to ancient times and were created to aid Kings who strived to discipline their unruly citizens. However, the spell was eventually deemed forbidden, as oftentimes Kings themselves would fall victim to the cursed fountain. As such, whole kingdoms would often be enslaved.

The legendary Grimoires:

4 legendary Grimoires. Assembled by the father of Diana the moon goddess, the mysterious grimoires are said to be encyclopaedias of all the known magic, miracles and demon arts ever known:

Grimoire of Obscurum

Grimoire of Light

Grimoire of Neutrality

Grimoire of Heaven

Stigma Children:

Revered and yet reviled. To be a Stigma child is to be a person on the fringes of society. Roughly making up ten per cent of the human population, it is said that one in a hundred mortals end up being born a Stigma child. Possessing a radiant eye with the symbol of the Valkyrie, the eye must be covered to suppress the power of the Stigma. If ever uncovered, the full power of the Stigma will be unleashed - rivalling the power of the gods. For girls, their hair is cursed to always be golden, while boys possess silver hair.

Contrary to various assumptions about their creation, the Stigma Children are descendants of the Valkyrie.

Mercies of the nameless God

It is said that a nameless god took pity on the persecution of the Stigma children across the world. As such, the unknown deity sent down three divine suits of armour to the world of mortals: Gospel, Testament and Faith.

Once worn by a Stigma child, their speed, skill and strength are amplified one hundredfold - even bringing the gods to their knees.

Unfortunately, the three suits were not created for normal mortals to wear. For if a normal person were to foolishly equip themselves with such armour, they would suffer an agonising and painful death.

Parasitus Draco

A dragon parasite that has existed since the dawn of time itself, when dragons were the only beings in existence. It has survived to this very day - outlasting the golden age of the ancient dragons.

The Parasitus Draco can be found in cursed waters, amidst woods where no man dare tread. Taking even a sip of the parasite-infested waters spells death and destruction, for you and those around you.

Within seconds of digesting the parasite, the unlucky host becomes a home for the dragon who wastes no time emerging from his or her shoulder, to wreak havoc. Not a single soul can get close and help the host, lest they be devoured by the menacing dragon that has sewn itself to the victim. Even if you were to sever the head of the dragon, your glory would only be for a short moment, for within seconds four more heads will emerge from the host to avenge the slain dragon. The more you kill, the more copies it will make. The only way to fully stop the Parasitus Draco is to kill the victim.

According to legend, there was once a mortal who was able to tame the dragon parasite that had sewn itself to his body. The host was able to control the dragon and have it obey his will. However, the technique used to discipline the dragon was never shared by the mortal, who vanished into the pages of history.

Lux vinculum:

An ancient spell of binding. Used to constrict fiends such as the ever powerful Phantom. It can only be broken by the power of a god or Stigma child.

Once upon a time, a pair of curious sorcerers set out on a quest to seek all knowledge. Their journey led them to a particular realm of the gods that housed the most powerful spells in existence. The wizards wondered why such spells were kept hidden from the eyes of mortals. The first man decided to take only one spell, that being the Lux Vinculum before returning to the world of men. However, the second wizard was in awe at the legion of spells and decided to stay behind - hoping to learn the vast secrets of the universe.

Years passed, and the two sorcerers encountered one another. The first who had obtained only the one spell had become an esteemed wizard. The second however, had gone insane - having spent many years digesting sacred spells that were too great for the human mind.

Felix: Wizard of Hope

One of the greatest Wizards of all time. Felix was a natural-born prodigy, who could master almost any type of spell within moments. His most historic victory occurred when he bested an evil sorcerer at the time named: Shabaz the wretched one. At the time, the land was gripped by the powerful sorcerer's magic. However, in an epic showdown, Felix ultimately defeated him and gave the land hope - hence the title: Felix Wizard of Hope.

Unfortunately, due to losing his best friend, Felix discard his name and title and forged a pact with a nameless deity who offered to resurrect his fallen friend in exchange for his sanity and compassion. The once noble wizard would emerge as Phantom: Wizard of despair to seek out the Apex Grail. Unfortunately, his first attempt was unsuccessful and he was sealed away within Mount Bemba - unable to break free due to the Lux Vinculum spell.

Phantom would later break free from the spell and mountain, thanks to Yohan: Aurora's younger brother, who released the dark sorcerer for his personal agenda.

Luke

Blue Lunar & The Apex Grail

R.L.Baxter

Umbra

R.L.Baxter

Aurora

R.L.Baxter

Starlight

Blue Lunar & The Apex Grail

R.L.Baxter

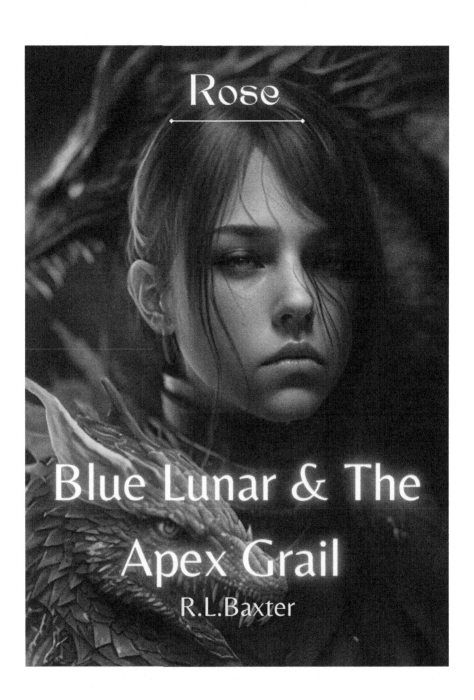

Rose

Blue Lunar & The Apex Grail

R.L.Baxter

Gold Star Gabriella

Blue Lunar & The Apex Grail

P.L. Baxter

Black Star Bonnie

Blue Lunar & The Apex Grail

R.L.Baxter

Silver Star Selene

Blue Lunar & The Apex Grail

R.L.Baxter

Megethos

Blue Lunar & The Apex Grail

R.L.Baxter

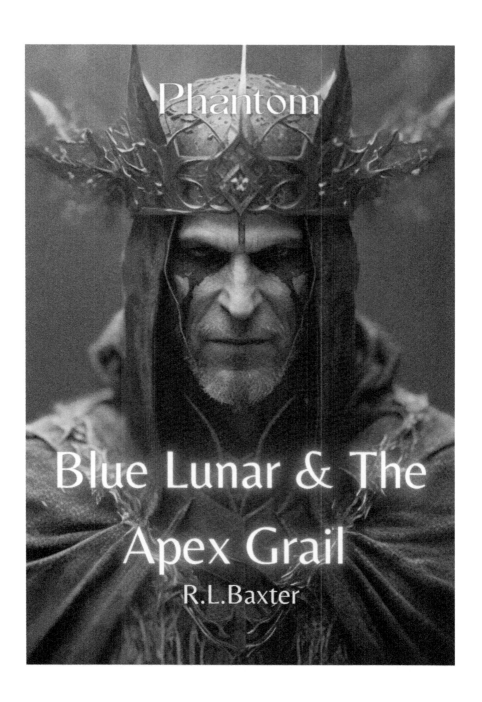

Phantom

Blue Lunar & The Apex Grail

R.L.Baxter

Solomon

Blue Lunar & The Apex Grail

R.L.Baxter

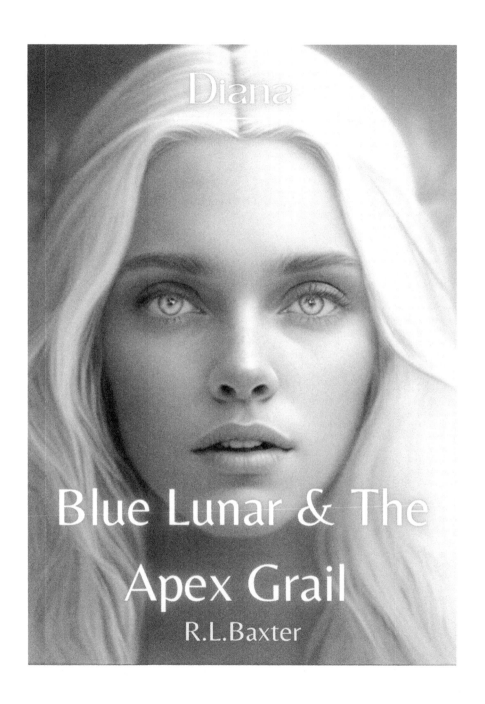

Diana

Blue Lunar & The Apex Grail

R.L.Baxter

Blue Lunar And the Apex Grail

About The Author

Ricky Lee Baxter

Ricky Baxter is a London born, fantasy author of novels and short novellas. He is an avid blogger, giving advice and thoughts to fellow creators from all walks of life. Starting out as a composer since graduating with a Ba(Hons) in music and multimedia, Ricky worked for many independent short film directors, gaining notable IMDB credits. Since then, he has embraced his earlier passion for writing fictional stories.

Books By This Author

Gideon And The Crimson Samurai

Gideon Joust is your average twelve-year-old boy, with all the growing insecurities one would expect, following the mysterious disappearance of his father. On one fateful day, the boy's world is turned upside down – leading to a chance encounter with a brash child warrior: Kibishi the Crimson Samurai.

Gideon And The Crimson Samurai 2

Gideon Joust is your average twelve-year-old boy, with all the growing insecurities one would expect, following the mysterious disappearance of his father. However thanks to Kibishi the Crimson Samurai, Gideon was finally able to discover the true events surrounding his disappearance – bringing to light a sinister plan that seems all but unavoidable. Fierce foes and old friends return, in a confrontation that will decide the fate of the future. Winner takes all.

To Save Santa

Santa has disappeared! During Christmas Eve, Lilly and her brother Alfred discover that our big and jolly giver of gifts has gone missing. A mean bunch of adults have taken him for themselves. However, with the help of the brave Elf Poplo, they may have a chance of saving him in time for Christmas! Food fights, ridiculous pursuits and even a meeting with the queen await in this family-friendly British tale.

What are you waiting for? Let's get cracking!

Mother Gaia

Of all the species that have evolved, mankind has exceeded the most. From the discovery of fire to the Internet and advanced machinery. Unfortunately the hearts of men have changed for the worse, due to greed, corruption and manipulative warfare. As such the wrath of the earth has been stirred and its creator Mother Gaia takes it upon herself, to end humanity.

Lilly And The Diamond Warrior

The world has been pushed to the brink of collapse, by nature itself. The natural world has wiped out millions of people, leaving only a few left on the planet. A mysterious boy from the stars is sent to save mankind and encounters a lost girl named Lilly. Together, they will face the wrath of the angered planet, to save everybody from extinction.

The Seventh Blessing

Within the world of Popla, the gods rule over mankind. Thanks to their order, mankind lives safe from the dangers of the world's monsters and demon beasts. However, even with their protection, there are some who have chosen to rebel against their benevolent masters.

Having lost his sister to a mysterious sickness called the Seventh Blessing, rumoured to have been created by the gods themselves, A young man named Luna will attempt to rescue her soul from death. Armed with a living blade, he will oppose the order of the gods - going as far as to request the aid of a legendary demon named Ten.

Within this epic fantasy adventure, the trio will explore a world together, where divinity and mortality are intertwined. However, at the end of their journey, will the true secret of the Seventh Blessing tear them apart?

Moonlight Requiem

Summoned by the wishes of a mad emperor, three young abominations enter a world plagued by tragedy and conflict. Following the commands of their bitter master, to kill the world's most powerful wizard king, the three will discover a vicious cycle of revenge and despair. Will they continue to be a part of this tragic cycle, or will they find the strength to carve forth a brighter path?

Queen

Sonia wakes to find herself in Heaven - world of no suffering and pain. However she soon finds a valuable and important piece of herself missing, despite living in eternal paradise. A longing to be close to someone special is felt deep inside her soul – causing her to question the world around her. Aided by a mysterious angel, Sonia will defy the kingdom of heaven, in an attempt to reclaim her missing past.

The Worst Death

Responsibility is not for some – especially when it comes to a somewhat laid back teenager, with thoughts of sleeping usually on his mind. Being an underachiever is all he's ever known – however when a loved one loses their life due to his irresponsibility, the naive teenager decides to put things right by making a deal… with death.

A Sinless Horizon

In a world bound by conflict, orchestrated by two world powers that have fought for centuries – one teenager's somewhat peaceful life has been destroyed, along with everything he once knew. Saved by an ancient alien species, before given their mightiest suit to achieve his revenge, the boy will become the world's greatest threat. In order to dismantle the constant cycle of war, Aldara will go up against the armies of the world – in a search to find a Sinless Horizon.

The Blue Witch

Growing up in the city of London, a young lady has reached her limit living in the hustle and bustle of the UK's capital.

Living with a shameless mother, adulterer father and working at a dead end job, Ophelia has just about given up on life in The Big Smoke. That is, until she is transported to the magical world of Pecopia - a land where she is tasked with overthrowing an evil witch queen.

However, unlike most girls who learn a valuable lesson of love and hope by the end of their journey - Ophelia's only thought is one of revenge.

Printed in Great Britain
by Amazon

25651917R00223